BACK TO
THE VARA

BY
JOHN KERRY

BACK TO THE VARA

First published in Britain by EATEOM Publishing Ltd
Copyright © John Kerry 2018 (a)

ISBN 13: 978-0-9572389-2-3

Cover illustration: Maxime Desmettre.
Titling and Design: The Designers Republic.
Editing services: Tanya Natalie.

Printed in Great Britain by Lightning Source UK Ltd.
Printed in the US by Lightning Source US Ltd.
Printed in Australia by Lightning Source AU Ltd.

www.eateom.com

For my girls

–ONE–
Before Sammy

Behnam didn't have to wait long for his young partner to catch up.

Hami emerged from the shadows, his skin purple under the magenta smog that hung over the city. He strode purposefully up the centre of the street, passing through the ephemeral wisps of the smog that floated at ground level, his head up, and dark hair and black cloak flowing behind him. He had the beginnings of a smile, but one damaged by pain and loss.

The men he'd been questioning would be dead.

In hindsight, Behnam should've interrogated the men himself. He stepped out of the doorway, into Hami's path. "Should you be walking up the centre of the street so brazenly?" he asked.

"Who's going to see me?"

Behnam had hoped he'd been wrong about the men. He tried to suppress the disappointment, but it must've shown.

"They'd have given us away," Hami said, his smile gone now.

"Not if you'd tied them."

"It's safer this way."

"You'd be a master by now if you could suppress that vicious streak of yours."

"If I'd developed a vicious streak sooner, your sister might still be alive."

Behnam withdrew. The memory of that night hit him with almost physical force. It came from nowhere. The blood, the crying. The surprised look on his sister's face as she breathed her last. The pain he experienced now was as raw as the night it happened. As it would be for Hami. They'd both suffered the loss of Jamileh, but Hami had perhaps taken it harder.

Behnam decided then that he was going to tell Hami the full story. The boy had a right to know the events that led up to Jamileh's death. "You couldn't have prevented it, you know. It wasn't your fault—"

"It's not a good time."

"There's never a good time, but we need to talk about it."

"After the mission," Hami said. He softened. "Please."

Reluctantly, Behnam held his tongue. He should've kept going, relieved Hami of his burden, but instead he allowed himself to be silenced again.

Hami was right. A lengthy debate and probable argument in the old capital would be irresponsible. They needed to keep their wits about them. There were other patrols of Order members roving throughout the city and Hami couldn't kill them all. They'd already left a substantial trail of bodies through the district that had once housed the rich and powerful.

Behnam had never known this place. Few living had. The entire city had been vacated generations ago when the smog came, and only members of the Order and a few wasters remained.

He led the way off the street and into an oval courtyard surrounded by grand marble arches and pillars. At the far end stood a large circular building with a shallow dome. It was a beautiful piece of architecture with a grand doorway, carved lintels and window frames. Behnam felt almost ashamed that he didn't know the name of it. He closed his eyes and accessed the magi network, scanned for Aratta maps, articles and building plans.

"What are we waiting for?" Hami asked.

Behnam opened his eyes. "This building used to be the royal opera house. We're standing in the courtyard where the sultan and his family held social events." Silence. "There's a staircase inside the doorway that will take us to the roof."

Hami gazed up through the open courtyard at the magenta clouds churning above them. They were lower here than he was used to, fine wisps floating just above the rooftops. Hami had been born in the outskirts of Aratta, but this would be the closest he'd ever been to the centre. He'd changed a lot since then. Since the wounded street urchin he'd been when Behnam found him.

"Those men didn't deserve to live," Hami said after a time. "It's better for the realm that I've killed them."

Behnam said nothing. There was no talking to Hami when he was dwelling on Jamileh. Behnam had never appreciated how badly the boy had fallen for her until she'd been killed. It had changed him. Something inside him had broken. Behnam wanted more than ever to speak to Hami then, explain how he knew it wasn't his fault, but he suppressed the urge. On the way home he'd explain the truth. But not now, not while their lives were in the balance.

They crouched behind a fallen pillar. The smog was already making Behnam woozy. Half a day more and the hallucinations would begin. They'd need to be out long before that if they wished to survive.

"Did you learn anything before you killed them?" Behnam asked.

"They gave away the location of a base up in the Atrabiliar mountains."

"A base?"

"On the northern slopes of Dev's Peak."

"That's thousands of stadia from here. Why there?"

"They didn't know. We'll need to question someone higher up for that information."

Behnam wondered how Hami had extracted what little information he had. Then realised that perhaps he didn't want to know. He led the way across the courtyard at a crouched run and in through the opera house doorway.

"The staircase is just in here," he said. "We should have a decent view from the top."

They climbed the stairs in the dark. At the top, they emerged onto a curved balcony that circled the building.

Ahead loomed the sultan's palace. Little more than a silhouette in the smog, but at six storeys high it dominated the skyline. Thick purple smoke still billowed from a ragged fissure in the vast dome and clouds hung thick about it.

"I've never seen it this close before," Hami said.

"An impressive building," Behnam agreed. "But thankfully, not somewhere we need to visit tonight."

They walked further around the balcony and stopped.

A black tower, gnarled and crooked, had grown from the earth in the centre of the piazza ahead of them, twisting its way skyward and reaching up into the smog above. At its base, a line of men and women funnelled into the entrance carrying stone blocks. Spikey grey crabmen stood either side of the slaves, twitching in the strange manner of their kind, chattering and poking people with their sword arms.

There were human slavers too, interspersed among the crabmen. Most were dressed in furs and many were scribbling notes on parchment.

"Should we fall in with the slaves?" Hami asked. "Follow them into the tower?"

"We'd have to lose our lightning staffs if we wanted to blend in," Behnam said. "It would be risky."

"I can't see how else we'll get in."

"We don't necessarily need to. Let's take a closer look. See what we can find out from outside. We'll have to leave soon, as it is. Before we contract smog sickness."

They left the opera house and made their way towards the tower. It was an easy landmark to locate, given its height, but one that wouldn't be easy to get close to. The area around the piazza had been cleared of buildings. Those closest to the tower had been reduced to their floorplans with only a few low sections of wall remaining among the heaps of rubble.

"Do you think anyone at the top can see us?" Hami asked as he looked up at the tower.

"I doubt it," Behnam said. "It's dark down here in the shadows. And even if someone does spot us, we'll be long gone by the time they can get a message to ground level."

They crawled through the foundations of one of the derelict houses that skirted the piazza. The building had been mostly destroyed, aside from the exterior wall, which at its highest point was around waist-high. Hami and Behnam arranged themselves either side of the gap that had once been the front door and sat down with their backs against the wall to catch their breath. The house they occupied was in a row parallel to the line of slaves entering the tower. They would have to crawl through adjacent houses to get closer to the entrance.

Behnam was about to get up when the atmosphere changed. An increase in air pressure accompanied by an almost metallic tang he could feel in his teeth. A wave of panic washed over him. He turned to Hami. The young magus's eyes were wide, his chest pumping. He'd make himself sick if he didn't calm his breathing and stop inhaling smog. This was bad. And could only mean one thing. *Ramaask.*

Some of the slaves were experiencing the atmospheric change, too. A few had stopped walking and were clutching their heads. Others were shaking or crying.

Behnam nodded to Hami and they both dropped off the magi network. They wouldn't be able to communicate for a while. Inconvenient, but nothing compared to the risk of Ramaask sensing them.

Moving slowly, Behnam turned to peer through the doorway.

Ramaask emerged from the darkness across the square. The Nightmare, some called him. Others knew him simply as the Lurker at the Gate. Impressive titles for an impressive creature. A giant dressed in thick, black plate and trailing a cloak that floated impossibly on a non-existent breeze. His face was obscured by a visor and on his helmet, three serrated ridges ran from front to back. One at the top like a fin and one on each side.

The air around him distorted and rippled as he strode across the piazza.

Following him was an equally tall figure, but this one was thin. It was cloaked all in black, its hooded head hanging limp at its chest. It kept pace with Ramaask, gliding across the square without any outward appearance of motion, as if it were floating.

The temperature was going up as the two monsters approached. The slaves parted and backed away. All of them, bar an older man that collapsed to the ground. He tried to raise himself but didn't make it up. He spasmed as the thin figure drew close, then went limp as steam began to rise from his body.

Hami pointed to his ear. Behnam concentrated his mind, amplifying sound around them.

The two monsters were talking. Behnam hadn't realised, due to Ramaask's face being obscured by his visor, and the thin figure's by his hood. Hami had known, though. In many ways, Hami's powers were exceeding his own. How fast the apprentice was becoming the master.

"Instinct," Ramaask's deep but strained voice rasped. "I can feel a change in the air. She's coming. And I want to know: why now?"

"Does it matter?" the thin figure asked in a metallic monotone. "You already know what she'll do."

"I want to know everything else. We have the opportunity to interrogate her, and if need be ..."

They fell silent as a man emerged from the shadows of the column. A trail of smoke and glowing embers followed him across the piazza, billowing out from under his black cloak as if his body were smouldering beneath his clothes. The skin on his head was charred black, cracked with glowing orange fissures, and his eyes burned yellow.

"I must return to the mountains," the burned man said when he reached them. He stood to attention before Ramaask, dwarfed by the giant creature. "I'm needed there."

"No," Ramaask replied. "You did well setting up the installation, but the General can manage the final preparations by himself."

Hami looked to Behnam and mouthed, "The General?"

"I no longer trust him," the burned man said.

"He's been loyal to me for over a century," Ramaask replied.

"He means to use the portal for himself."

What portal were they talking about? And how was it that the magi were just learning of it now?

"You should destroy it," the thin figure said. "You know what will happen if it remains."

"Enough," Ramaask said. "We can still change the outcome. And you," he said to the burned man. "You are to remain here and oversee my tower."

"But master, you don't understand …"

Ramaask moved closer so that he was looking down on the man. "It is *you* who do not understand. I don't ask twice. I thought you'd have learned that by now."

"You are right, as always, my lord." The man bowed low. He shuffled backwards before turning and walking swiftly away across the piazza.

Ramaask watched him go. "We need to find the girl."

Who was this girl they were referring to? Behnam had learned more on this mission than he'd ever hoped to, yet he could tell there was more. He had a responsibility now to stay and find out what that was.

"I've sensed roughly where she'll appear," the thin figure said. "I will retrieve her while you head to the snow base."

"I'm not leaving the city until the portal is ready. You know I won't leave Aratta exposed unless necessary."

"The portal is your gateway to the Mother World. You no longer need to guard the gate in the palace."

Portal to the Mother World? The shock in Hami's eyes mirrored Behnam's reaction. Ramaask couldn't have built a portal to the Mother World. It wasn't possible.

"You would like that, wouldn't you, brother?" Ramaask said. "But I'm not leaving Aratta until I have the girl in my possession."

"You're making a mistake. Your best hope of survival is to head to the snow base now."

"Do you think me so fragile?" Ramaask spoke quietly but with a threatening undertone. "I have armies of crabmen at my disposal, men excavating in the Cataclysm. I have the portal and my tower of silence nearing completion. I can't be stopped. I will escape this realm."

"I meant no offence," the thin figure said. "Some things are said to be fate and cannot be averted. The visitor arriving to bring your downfall. Our master to follow."

"Our master?" Ramaask said. "Your loyalty is to me now. I brought you here, rescued you from the darkness."

"Rescued me to exist in this half form. Neither extinct nor truly existing."

"Would you rather go back?"

"No!" the thin figure backed away. "I am grateful, truly, brother."

Ramaask walked towards him, closing the gap. "Your existence in this half form, on multiple planes, is to our advantage. You see things that others can't. If I give you your body now, you'll lose the abilities that make you useful to me. Abilities that will allow you to find the girl before the magi do. Assuming you wish to help me."

"As always." The thin figure bowed. "And perhaps with this gesture, I will prove my loyalty and you will restore me to my rightful form."

"I will stop the girl myself if I have to."

"That won't be necessary. I will bring her to you."

12

"Only when that is done will I go to the mountains to oversee the final preparations for the portal."

"As you wish," said the thin figure. "I believe the girl will be arriving soon. There is already a density of energy building in the Fungi Forest. I will seek her there."

"Go then. Seek her out, and bring her to me."

The thin figure bowed again and floated away.

Behnam nodded to Hami and pointed after the thin figure.

Hami's expression turned stricken. He mouthed 'you' and pointed back at Behnam.

Behnam fixed him with a stare until the young magus got up and crept away. Hami would be devastated about leaving Behnam alone in such close proximity to Ramaask, but it made sense to send the boy after the thin figure. He was younger, fitter and would stand a better chance of keeping up. And as an added benefit, it would get him out of the smog. Behnam would remain a while longer to see if there was anything else worth learning, then he'd catch up with Hami in the forest.

Ramaask walked to the tower and entered the doorway. Behnam gave him a moment longer, then crept through the foundations, working his way through the demolished houses and towards the foot of the tower.

After a painstakingly slow crawl through the rubble, Behnam reached the remains of the house opposite the tower entrance. There were no walls, but a pile of sandbags were stacked in the area that the front room had once occupied. It would give him some concealment, but it wasn't ideal. The building one row back was better. It was still intact and the balcony on the second floor would give him a vantage point to look down on the tower entrance. He crept into the shadows behind the sandbags, paused, and was about to move on when the atmosphere changed.

Ramaask had exited the tower behind him. Behnam shrank further down behind the sandbags. He should've kept his distance, but he hadn't, and now he'd trapped himself.

What now? Hami wouldn't have travelled far yet. Both of them together might have a chance at holding the demon back long enough to escape. Alone, Behnam was a dead man. But if he connected to the network, Ramaask would sense the transmission and might even kill him before Hami returned. There was no other option but to keep telepathic silence.

Behnam's heart pounded with an intensity he was sure Ramaask could hear. He was sweating, breathing hard and inhaling poisonous smog. It was making him light-headed, yet there was nothing he could do but wait and hope Ramaask moved on. His body trembled and an all-consuming desire to run took over.

"Lord VorMask," a shaky voice said. "We've been making excellent progress. We've gained two more storeys since—"

"Wait," Ramaask said.

"I'm sorry, my lord," said the man. "I—"

"Silence!" Then Ramaask quietened. "I smell something."

Behnam closed his eyes and held his breath. He heard Ramaask inhale deeply. Then nothing. Time seemed to stretch out for an eternity as Behnam waited behind the sandbags, heart palpitating and lungs bursting.

Finally, Ramaask spoke. "I smell ... magus."

–TWO–

The Hunter and the Hunted

The thin figure floated wraith-like along the darkened street ahead, as if no physical presence existed beneath its cloak. Yet something was there, some skeletal form beneath the fabric. Hami had never seen its like before. The creature had most likely been brought to Perseopia by Ramaask from the same dark place he came from. Brother, Ramaask had called it, yet the creature was nothing like him physically. Perhaps a brother in the same way the magi were to each other.

Hami ran through the shadows along the side of the street. He'd have more chance keeping up with the thin figure if he could get to his greenbuck, Fozmot, but the animal was tied up in a barn near where he'd entered the city. The detour would mean losing this wraith and if that happened he'd never find it again. He'd have to remain on foot and hope he didn't tire.

The smog was already in his chest, weakening him, making his limbs heavy. He'd spent too long in Aratta already and now he was accelerating the effects of the poison by raising his heart rate. But it couldn't be helped. He had to find out where this creature was going and who it was after. Ramaask had said it was a girl. Would she be like the last one that arrived in Perseopia? Like the one Grand Master Onora Bruche discovered before he was killed? If Hami escaped the city without suffering smog poisoning, perhaps he'd find out.

He wondered how Behnam was getting on. This was the first time he'd left his partner in danger since Jamileh's death and he didn't like it.

Hami always made sure he carried out the riskier tasks, but on this occasion he'd conceded to his master. Behnam had overruled him and he'd been right to, Hami was the faster of the two. He'd be more capable of keeping up with this wraith. And it was just one time. Behnam would be okay and when they met up again they'd talk like he'd wanted to. Hami would apologise. He'd open up about Jamileh's death and beg for forgiveness. Not only for being responsible, but for all the times he hadn't had the courage to speak up about it.

Behnam held a special place in Hami's heart. He'd been the one that came for Hami when he'd first registered on the magi network. The one who'd rescued him from his life of loneliness.

Hami had spent most of his early years living in a squat on the outskirts of Aratta. At eight, he became the provider for the small community he grew up in. He hunted, rats mostly, while his mother and friends ventured into the city to inhale smog and get high. He was a natural hunter and would always return with enough food for everyone. In hindsight, he'd been exhibiting magi abilities well before he'd registered on the network.

It had been a deprived existence, but doing a job that none of the others could gave him a certain satisfaction. It made him feel important to be relied upon. To be needed by people.

One night his mother and friends didn't come back. And then it was just him. He didn't go into the city to look for her. She'd never shown any affection towards him and he'd seen first-hand how the smog had changed her. He was more upset that he had no one to hunt for than caring what had happened to any of them. His mother had implied that one of the men in the group had been his father, but if she knew which one, it was never made clear.

He moved on alone, walking north and finding a deserted village to live in.

He was hunting big game when Behnam found him and took him away to the magi garrison. There he was fed, clothed and taught to use his powers. It had been difficult adjusting to his new

16

life. A rebellious streak and anti-social behaviour got him into trouble often, and the brotherhood told Behnam to halt his training. But Behnam had seen his potential. He took him on as a student when no one else would. He taught him to read, to write, and spent countless evenings tutoring him in the magi arts. And he'd done it all without asking for anything in return. Behnam was only fifteen years older but he was what Hami imagined a real father would be like.

Then Hami had seduced Behnam's sister and led the crabmen to her home.

He drew a sleeve over his eyes to wipe away the tears that blurred his vision but he only succeeded in making them sore by rubbing in smog from his saturated clothes.

This area of the city was like the one he'd grown up in all those years ago. Pre-Behnam. Pre-everything that had been good in his life. Now he was back and similarly his life had little purpose. Only tracking and hunting.

Hami followed the wraith up a long arcade. Giant forest mushrooms had grown up in the middle of a square at the end. A small orchard of them illuminating an island of dirt, hemmed in by cobbled streets. It seemed strange to see them here in the old capital, but the warm yellow glow provided welcome respite from the churning smog that stained everything else purple.

The wraith passed through the mushrooms, swirling the glowing spores that hung in the air, and disappeared.

Hami ran towards the square, paused, then skirted left around the outside, keeping out of the light as he worked his way to the far side.

The creature had gone.

Hami slipped further into the shadows of a nearby house and waited. Some of the smaller mushrooms were burnt with shrivelled edges, and their light had been extinguished, yet there was no sign of the creature in amongst them.

He looked away from the mushrooms until his eyes adjusted to the gloom. He was sickening, his breath becoming ragged.

The creature hadn't carried on up the street, which meant it hadn't gone all the way through the mushrooms. The area was still warm so surely it must be close.

Had it known it was being followed? Perhaps it had run into the mushrooms, then taken a left or right down an adjoining street. Perhaps it was still here waiting to see who had followed.

Hami had been careful. He'd kept to the shadows. No one could have seen him. Could they? The longer he waited, the more distance the creature might be putting between them.

Hami couldn't risk being seen, though. Even if it meant losing the wraith. If he was spotted, Ramaask would be notified and Behnam would be compromised. There might've been a time when he'd have taken that risk. But not now. Not with Behnam.

He peered through the darkness at the houses surrounding the square. No doors in the doorways, no frames or shutters in the windows. Nothing wooden remaining. All either stolen by scavengers or decimated by ambrosia beetles.

Then he saw it. A silhouette at one of the windows. If he'd taken the right-hand path around the square, he'd have walked right past the creature and it would have seen him. It'd suspected it had been followed so had waited. Suspected or known? Why would it think anyone had followed? It hadn't long left the city centre.

Then Hami realised why.

His forehead ran slick with sweat. Bile rose in his stomach. An alarm had been sent. And he could think of only one thing that would trigger an alarm. Behnam had been spotted.

Hami clutched his stomach and vomited. It came out black and acrid, burning his throat as it launched out of his mouth. He bent double, holding his middle. He would have to get out of Aratta soon before the hallucinations began.

He looked back to the window. The wraith had gone. Hami ran to the house, up the steps and in through the doorway. He had to catch it now and find out what had happened to Behnam.

The house was empty.

He ran through to the back, leaping through a window and landing in the alley behind. Nothing up or down the path. He picked the direction that led out of the city, the direction that closest matched the one they'd been heading in, and ran.

He didn't know how long he could keep running at a sprint, but as far as he knew the creature hadn't seen him yet, so if he kept his pace going he might catch it when it stopped. In the meantime, he'd have to pray that Behnam would be okay and that he'd re-join the network soon.

———

Behnam pressed his back up against the sandbags.

"Come out, magus," Ramaask called.

He sounded more amused than angry. Did he know where Behnam hid? Behnam didn't want to risk standing up to find out.

Over to his left was a pile of rubble high enough for someone to be crouching behind. He concentrated on a stone at the back, tipping it over so it rolled down over the other stones and made the required distraction. He peered over the top of the sacks to see if everyone's attention had been drawn.

The plan had partially worked. Nearly everyone had been distracted. But not Ramaask. He stood by the tower entrance facing the pile where Behnam hid.

Dread seeped into every extremity. There was no point continuing to hide. It was all over. He'd never see Hami again. Never have the chance to apologise and give him peace.

His body rebelled against him. Limbs numb. Palms sweating. Head dizzy.

He got to his feet and turned to face Ramaask.

The air around the demon was dark. His arms were crossed over his armoured chest and even though he hadn't raised his visor, he was clearly watching Behnam.

The men around him drew their weapons and the crabmen chattered as they spread out to the sides.

Ramaask raised a hand and they stopped.

"Leave him to me," he said. "Everyone, back to work."

The men backed away, but kept their weapons raised. The crabmen scattered spiderlike, back to the shadows.

An uncomfortable silence settled between them before Ramaask spoke. "And which magus do I have the pleasure of meeting today?" he asked.

"Behnam Baktash," Behnam said, his voice cracking.

"Master Behnam Baktash?" Ramaask took several steps towards him. "Didn't I expressly forbid anyone from returning to this city? I know that was 146 years ago, but the magi are reputed to possess a reasonably long collective memory. I would've assumed you'd remembered."

"It must have slipped our minds," Behnam said. "I'll be on my way."

Ramaask laughed a terrible, choking, death rattle of a laugh. "Now that you're here, you're welcome to stay."

Ramaask wasn't going to keep talking forever. Behnam needed to do something quick. He recalled the intact building behind him with the balcony on the second floor. It had an open arch leading inside. That was his way out.

Behnam whipped his staff round and fired at the sandbags in front of him. The explosion sent the bags in all directions and launched him up and backwards into a backward somersault.

Behnam landed on the second-floor balcony.

Ramaask ripped through the bags that came at him. He paused, tipped his head back and laughed. "Let the chase begin!"

That was Behnam's cue to leave.

He flew into the house, through the empty rooms and onto a balcony at the front of the property. There was a square below and a dense neighbourhood of houses on the other side. If he could make it across to them, he might have a chance of escape.

He dodged to the side, leaping onto the balcony of an adjacent house as Ramaask came crashing through the wall behind him, destroying the building in his wake and dropping into the square below. He turned towards Behnam as the whole structure folded in on itself, expelling clouds of dust and debris.

Ramaask launched himself at Behnam again.

Behnam dropped to the floor of the balcony and rolled to the side as Ramaask ploughed through the wall above his head.

The building collapsed around Behnam. He managed a last-ditch effort to guide himself clear of the falling masonry, yet still landed badly.

Back on his feet, he ran, half-sprinting, half-limping across the square towards the road opposite. If he could get to his greenbuck, he might be able to outrun Ramaask to the Fungi Forest and lose him.

A huge chunk of masonry sailed past, narrowly missing him and kicking up stone chips as it bounced across the cobbled square.

Behnam reached the road and ducked down the first alley to the right as a second block demolished the corner of the building he'd passed. He heard Ramaask land in the square behind him with a thump.

Behnam turned down a second passage as thunderous feet echoed in the alley he'd just left.

He fired a lightning bolt from his staff at a town house as he passed, allowing the wall to collapse into the passage behind him. He ducked into a property on the right, through the open doorway and into an ancient living area. He went up a staircase, then leapt through an open window on the second floor into the window of the house opposite.

He kept going, running downstairs, out of the back door, sprinting along another street and down another alley. Finally, he jumped a wall and entered a house through the back door.

Behnam stopped and ducked to the side, flattening his back up against the wall between the doorway and window.

Silence. The only sound the beating of his heart. Adrenaline was making the desire to keep running unbearable, but he couldn't let this panic force him into making a wrong move. Any error could be fatal.

Behnam took in his surroundings while he caught his breath. The room had been a simple kitchen with ceramic wash basin and tiled floor. Wooden cupboards, surfaces and tables that may have once furnished the place had long since decayed. It was dark but for the dim purple light of the smog outside. The hallway lay ahead, a black void leading into the heart of the house.

Behnam edged to the window. The walled back garden was bare, the plot hemmed in by houses on either side.

No movement.

He needed to get his bearings, figure out where the greenbucks were. But perhaps he should lie low until Ramaask moved on. Find a cellar and bed down.

Behnam peered outside one last time, then crept towards the hall.

The kitchen darkened behind him.

Behnam spun around, lighting up his staff as two shovel-sized hands clamped his head on either side and lifted him from the floor. Ramaask had his visor up and he brought their heads together. His black, skeletal face shimmered purple in the staff light and his sharp black teeth parted. It was the last thing Behnam saw as Ramaask's thumbs closed over his eyes.

He fired his staff into Ramaask's chest, unleashing everything he had. But the hands held firm and the thumbs pressed in, forcing their way into his skull.

Behnam screamed as his eyes burst and his world went black.

–THREE–
The Bully Bully

Street lights intermittently flushed the interior of the car orange through the sun roof as they navigated the streets of Sheffield.

Sammy stared out of the passenger window trying to seem interested in the grey, plastic-clad housing blocks that huddled together by the side of the ring road. If she didn't make eye contact with her mum, perhaps the woman would leave her alone. A child's game. Look away and no one can see you. But she'd been treated like a child, and now she felt like acting like one.

"Do you have anything to say for yourself?" It was the first time her mum had spoken since leaving the head's office.

"Not really."

"You're turning into a bully like your father?" She'd only said it to get a reaction, but Sammy couldn't let the comment go unchallenged.

"I'm nothing like him." She made eye contact. "Don't *ever* compare me to him."

"You've been suspended for beating up kids in the year below you. I'd say that sounds a lot like him."

"Five big *college* lads in the year below me," she said, staring back out of the window. "Five *seventeen*-year-old boys versus me. By myself. I'd hardly call them kids. And they were attempting to bully me. Not the other way around." She tried to sound like the conversation was boring her. "Although, if you saw what they looked like after I'd finished with them, I suppose you could call that bullying."

"That's not funny." Her mother let out a long, shuddering exhalation.

Sammy wondered how long she'd been crying for and whether some of it was for effect.

"One of those boys is in hospital with a broken arm because of you," her mother said. "If he presses charges you'll wind up with a criminal record. You know you're old enough to get one, right?"

"He tripped off the curb when I came at him. He landed badly. I didn't even touch him."

Her mum's mascara had run and she looked like a sad, pouty panda. Sammy went back to staring out of the window. Her stomach was tying itself in knots. She hadn't meant to make her mum cry, but she resented being made to feel like it was always her fault. It had been five against one. How could she be to blame? It was because she'd taken Reece's spot on the football team. Because she was a girl. It was as simple as that. The only South Yorkshire team in the league with a female striker. They should be proud, they were pioneers. But was her college celebrating equality? Were they, heck. She was their best player. She'd even saved them from relegation last season. Why couldn't the less talented players cheer her on from the subs bench and be happy to be a small part of her victories?

"I don't understand what happened to you, Sammy." Her mum just wouldn't let it go. "This is the third time I've been in the head's office this term. Do you want to get expelled from Manor Rise too? You used to be such a sweet girl ..."

"... before I came back from Perseopia."

"I thought we'd stopped talking about that place."

"You hoped we'd stopped talking about it."

"Why do you think these boys pick on you, when you're completely disconnected from reality?"

So this is what it was really about. "How am I disconnected from reality, *mother*? Is it because of the *fantasy world* I travelled to? Because you know you're the only person I told about that, the one person I hoped would believe me. I haven't told anyone else." Sammy sighed. "Trust me, I know how crazy it sounds."

"You're distracted all the time. Vacant. You never engage with anyone."

"The fight started because I humiliated Reece and Connor at football. Nothing to do with me being vacant. Anyway, I'm part of a team. Isn't that engaging with people?"

The remainder of the journey home was a silent one. They parked on the road outside their stunted terrace house, then her mum left her on the pavement as she walked away up the alley between their house and the neighbour's.

Sammy stayed where she was, psyching herself up for the argument that would continue inside.

One of the street lights flickered overhead. She gazed up past it at the dark sky and the three stars visible through the city's light pollution. She liked the night. Liked the lack of people and noise. The air seemed fresher somehow, full of excitement and opportunity.

She could walk away. Give her mum some breathing space. Come back later when she'd calmed down. But that wasn't going to happen this time. Better to go in and get the rest of the argument over with.

"Mum—" she said as she closed the kitchen door behind her.

"The time for talking is over. I'll leave your dinner outside your bedroom door."

This was new. She didn't even sound angry. Was she resigned to the fact her only child was a delinquent? A lost cause, maybe? Sammy wasn't about to let that lie. "The time for talking never started. Every time I try, you shut me out."

"How can I listen when you tell me stories of secret worlds filled with crabmen?"

Sammy was done. She walked away, climbed the stairs to her bedroom and closed the door. She dropped her rucksack by the bed, planted her face as deep into her pillow as she could, and screamed. When she ran low on oxygen, she lifted her head, took a breath, then shoved her face back into the pillow and screamed again.

She got up and, clutching the pillow to her chest, walked to the dresser to look at herself in the mirror. A raging she-beast with messy hair and a red face glared back from the other side of the frame. She looked a state. Her mum had turned her into this crazed person that stood before her.

Always the same argument. Her mother was the lost cause. Not her. She'd at least tried to talk it out.

"I'm not staying here," she said to herself. She punched the pillow back at the bed and got her mobile out. She scrolled through her contacts, tapped on a number and put the phone to her ear.

"Hiya," came the tinny reply.

"I need a goalie. Meet me outside my house in twenty minutes."

"I need to revise for my General Studies A-Level."

"Do you really need to revise for that?"

"My mum said—"

"You're eighteen, Wayne, technically an adult. Why don't you grow a pair? And when you've done that, be over here in twenty minutes." And she hung up.

Sammy sat down at her dresser. She occasionally wondered if Perseopia had ever happened, whether it was a figment of her imagination that she'd created to escape her mundane reality. Yet, bizarrely, her time in Perseopia was the only part of her life that had ever felt real. It was her current existence that seemed like someone else's. An infinite grey corridor of closed doors. A linear first person shooter. No alternative paths, no side quests and no opportunities. College, home, argument, bed, college, football, fight, headmaster's office, home, argument, bed.

Sammy concentrated on a pencil resting on her desk. Imagined all the molecules connected throughout the wooden structure, willing it to move. It wobbled, tilted, and the hexagonal prism tipped over onto its next flat side, then the next, and the one after. Soon the pencil was rolling along the table.

Sammy stopped it with the palm of her hand.

If she'd never been to Perseopia, then how was that possible? Unless it was all in her mind like her mother had tried to convince her, and which, during her darkest moments, she had almost believed. She'd tried to show her mum the pencil trick a couple of times, but the woman never paid attention. Whenever the 'fantasy land' was brought up, her mum stiffened and switched off.

Sammy had found it difficult to readjust to life back in Sheffield despite spending less than a week in Perseopia. There she'd been important. Enough to be pursued by both the magi and the Order. Then she'd been dumped back into the real world where she had no purpose and no one wanted her. No one except her mother, and that was only until Jerry came along. They'd lost their closeness soon after.

She should've stayed in Perseopia. Ramaask had gone into the Cataclysm, the magi would've defeated the crabmen soon after, the slaves would've been freed and eventually order would've been restored to the realm. Sammy might even have become a magus by now if she'd remained.

She stared into the mirror. The psycho stared back. She should at least make an effort for Wayne, seeing as he was coming over for her to kick footballs at. Not that he was her boyfriend, but that didn't stop him trying to fill the vacancy. She should at least throw him a bone every once in a while and make herself look presentable. Surely he wouldn't put up with being her on-call goalie forever. Although it had worked for a surprisingly long time.

Sammy got up from the desk, swapped her jeans for leggings, put on a black t-shirt and red scarf combo that she figured looked as close to cool as she'd ever manage, and scraped her blond mop back into a ponytail. She needed something else. Make-up was too good for Wayne. Even accessories were a stretch, but what the hell? She'd do it this one time. Her mum would have something she could pilfer.

On the carpet outside her bedroom door sat a cheese-spread sandwich on a paper plate.

A poor approximation of a Mariah Carey arpeggio warbled up the stairs from the sitting room, letting Sammy know that her mother had settled in to watch a TV talent show. Sammy stepped over the sandwich, crept along the landing to her mum's bedroom and went straight to the dresser. New items would be stashed there.

Her mother spent more than she could afford each month on clothes and, because she always dressed younger than she should, there was usually something worth borrowing. Sammy rummaged through the drawers to see if there was anything new or interesting. Surprisingly, there wasn't.

Sammy moved on to the jewellery boxes stacked on top of the dresser. Her mother rarely wore jewellery yet she'd still managed to accrue three boxes worth. Some were bound to be presents from Jerry, worn once then discarded and left to tarnish in their mother of pearl inlaid coffins.

Sammy never wore jewellery. She didn't really see the point. It wasn't as if it had a purpose other than to draw attention to you. Perhaps tonight she'd find something that would persuade her otherwise.

As a kid she'd spent hours rummaging around in these boxes, dressing up in all the sparkly necklaces and rings, then at some point in her formative years she'd lost interest. From that point onwards it had been comics, books and video games.

She lifted down the boxes, arranged them in a crescent on the floor, sat in the middle, then emptied each one in turn into separate piles.

There was a selection of rings, some plain, some jewelled. There were necklaces in silver, gold, and plastic. And then there were the hoop earrings. Millions of them, and all virtually identical. Sammy smiled when she recognised a plastic tiara with the silver paint flaking off. It had been her favourite thing in the world when she'd been five. She thought her dad had binned it years ago when she'd failed to eat the macaroni and cheese he'd microwaved for her. Her mum must've rescued it from the rubbish.

Guilt pierced Sammy's heart like an adamantium claw through the ribcage. She couldn't carry on being angry with her mum. She'd go downstairs and apologise. Her mum was in the wrong, but she'd hold her tongue and fix the relationship. Standard. She began packing the jewellery away, but as she dropped a bundle of knotted necklaces into one of the boxes, a delicate gold chain caught her eye. The only golden item in the box that hadn't tarnished.

Sammy took hold and pulled at it. The chain snagged, but a second tug released a golden locket into her lap.

Sammy tilted the locket in the light. There was a burning sun engraved on the front, and on the back an inscription in the unusual looping script of Avestan; a language that she'd never been taught, but one that she'd magically known how to translate and read since her visit to Perseopia.

"A wish can be as good as a map."

Sammy shakily picked up her mobile and redialled the last called number.

"Hiya," came the tinny reply again. "I'm nearly at your house …"

"Turn around, Wayne," Sammy said. "I'm not coming out tonight."

And she hung up.

–FOUR–
Evidence

Her mother was by the fridge, wringing the last dregs of rosé out of a three litre box into a mug.

"I don't want to fight any more," she said over her shoulder when Sammy entered the kitchen. "You don't need to be in college for the next few days. Let's talk tomorrow when we've calmed down." When Sammy didn't reply, she put down the wine and turned to face her.

Sammy remained in the doorway and held out her arm with the locket dangling from her fist.

"Where did you get that?"

"The last two years I've doubted myself. Sometimes wondering if I'd imagined the whole thing. And this entire time you've kept this from me?"

Her mother's face was hard. "The locket was around your neck that day I found you under my bed. I rescued it when I dragged you back to your bedroom."

Sammy tried her best to keep her voice calm and measured, but she couldn't keep it from cracking. "Why didn't you give it back to me when I woke up the next morning?"

"Because you'd stolen it." The hard lines of her mother's face were dissolving. Her lip trembled and tears were running down her cheeks. "Like you stole that bracelet."

"Stolen?" The accusation lodged in Sammy's throat.

"When you told me that story about a land full of giant mushrooms and dinosaurs, I knew something was wrong. I tried to take the jewellery to school to see if any of the teachers or parents claimed them." She closed her eyes. "I didn't take them to the police station because I didn't want you to get into trouble."

Sammy had heard enough. She turned away and went upstairs. When she reached her bedroom she closed the door behind her and approached the bed, readying herself for the scream that didn't come.

An eerie calm settled over her. She put the locket over her head, picked up her football and ran back downstairs.

Her mother was in the same place she'd left her.

"Where are you going?"

Sammy didn't answer, she carried on through the kitchen and slammed the front door as she left.

————

The common at the bottom of the road was dark, lit faintly by the lights in the council blocks that loomed at the far end. Dark was fine. Being alone at night didn't scare Sammy like it might other young women.

She kicked the football wide of the goal. As it lifted off the ground, she concentrated on it, imagining the molecules making up the leather and stitching. She willed it back towards the goal, spinning it, pulling it round in an arc. The ball pinged off the post and into the back of the net.

Ever since she'd returned from Perseopia, she'd been able to do that. Plenty of guys in the team could curl a ball. None of them could curl it like she could. Not even close. The least bitter guys called her banana feet. The ones who'd lost places to her on the team? She'd once overheard them call her 'soccer slut', as if being good at football somehow made her promiscuous. She imagined they said worse behind her back.

Perseopia had changed her. She was able to shift small objects if she concentrated hard enough. She couldn't do much with heavy or stationary objects. The forces of gravity and friction were generally too strong for her new powers, but airborne objects she had some sway over.

She knew things, too. Could feel without seeing. Not a lot, just the merest suggestion of someone's feelings. But it was enough. She could tell when someone was approaching. Had a vague sense of their intentions before they opened their mouths. Which meant she was never afraid of going out alone after dark. And why she never lost a fight. Punches were telegraphed well before the attacker clenched their fist, and when they swung, it was as if they were moving through treacle.

How powerful would she be by now if she'd stayed in Perseopia to be trained by Hami? He'd used her as bait to draw out the evil Ramaask. Which was not cool. But ultimately the plan had worked, she'd survived, and the realm had been saved. She didn't like it, but could see why it had been a price worth paying.

But her powers weren't focused. She needed tuition, to talk with someone who knew what was happening to her. If she'd remained in Perseopia with Hami guiding her, she could've been on her way to becoming a master magus. Instead she'd returned home to Sheffield. She'd come back to be with her mum, only to have her possessions taken away, and to be labelled a thief.

And then there was Jerry. When he came into their lives, the relationship Sammy had enjoyed with her mother had drifted even further apart. In some ways that was a blessing. Sammy was left to her own devices and that meant she could do what she wanted. But what was there to do? There was nowhere to go and she had no prospects for the future.

She was smart, and when her teachers weren't shouting at her she produced some decent work, but her grades had taken a hit by getting expelled from and changing school several times. She might not even get into University on her current trajectory. Not that she could afford to go even if that avenue presented itself to her. Jerry had offered to loan her the fees, but she wasn't taking that chump's money. She should find herself a part time job, but then she'd be stuck with her mum and Jerry until she could afford to leave. Which was never.

The future was looking bleak.

———

Her mum wasn't around when she got home. She'd be at Jerry's. An angry note on the kitchen table confirmed as much. Sammy balled it in her fist and threw it over her shoulder, guiding it into the bin with her mind.

The microwave clock displayed 23:45.

Sammy went to the cellar door and opened it. She shivered as she descended into the dark. Despite being summer, it was always cold and damp down there.

At the bottom of the stairs, she flicked on the light and used its dim glow to pick her way through soggy cardboard boxes to a pile of her dad's old possessions in the far corner. A chipboard TV stand, a cricket bat, an old suitcase that contained the family photos he'd been in, and behind them, a mouldy golf bag with a single club inserted the wrong way, handle up. Sammy took the grip and pulled it out.

The Midnight Emerald bracelet dangled from the head.

Sammy had stashed it in the golf bag to be protected by the repellent force of her father's possessions and the eight-legged guardians that dwelled in the webs adorning the ceiling.

She'd once found it in her mother's handbag and had decided to take it back. In hindsight, she realised it had probably been in there from one of the times her mum had tried taking it to school. If she'd rummaged deeper she might've found the locket too. Why hadn't her mum come to her first? To talk to her before assuming the worst? Sammy often had lapses in judgement, but she wasn't a thief. How had their relationship come to that?

Sammy held the golden bracelet up to the single bare light bulb.

The bottle-top sized emerald—if in fact it ever had been an emerald—was dull and brown, and had been since she'd returned from Perseopia. Looping around the gem's fixing was a stanza written in the Avestan script. The same script used on the locket dangling at her throat. Esther had translated the words for her pre-Perseopia. Now she was able to read it herself.

"Raise your hands to the skies
"on the tone of midnight,
"and you will travel to the land
"of endless twilight."

The *hands,* which she'd figured out referred to the clock hands either side of the gemstone fitting, were stiff and unresponsive.

Sammy polished the gemstone on her t-shirt and peered into it.

The emerald lit up for a split second, pulsing with green light, then returned to the dull brown that had become its natural state. Sammy never flinched. The emerald had done the same thing on numerous other occasions in the last several months. She didn't know when it had started happening. Only that it had.

She'd been down in the cellar many times since, to look at the bracelet and to remember Perseopia, Mehrak, and Louis. And more recently, Hami ... wondering if he'd saved the day. Or if he'd been arrested for treason. She would often daydream about the realm returning to life, the skies clearing, people celebrating. There was no doubt in her mind that she should've stayed.

Esther, 'The Chosen One', had never returned for the bracelet. Sammy had gone to the market every Saturday for weeks afterwards, wandered the streets of Sheffield, even waited outside the gates of her old school. Yet the woman never returned. Unlocking the portal to save Perseopia clearly wasn't as important as she'd made it out to be. Unless she'd sensed that Sammy had already used the bracelet and it no longer worked. Maybe she knew, somehow, that the realm had been saved and she could chill out. In the end, the reason didn't matter. Esther had vanished, along with any chance of Sammy ever returning to Perseopia.

It had been difficult to put the adventure behind her. She'd stopped visiting the bracelet down in the cellar and was on her way to assimilating back into an ordinary existence. Until around four months ago. She'd been in the cellar looking for a tennis ball and noticed a flash of green light coming from the golf bag.

The bracelet had been out several times since then.

Sammy had tried raising the dial's hands at midnight but they wouldn't budge. The emerald never pulsed green exactly on the stroke of midnight. Only ever a little while beforehand or sometime after. Never dead on.

Sammy switched off the cellar light and climbed the stairs back up to the kitchen. She sat at the table, placed the bracelet in front of her, and slumped over it, hands on her cheeks and elbows planted either side.

She couldn't manipulate the emerald with her mental abilities. There wasn't anything inside it to manipulate.

Sammy's phone buzzed. She fished it out of her waistband, saw the message was from Wayne, so placed her phone face down on the table.

She stretched and got up. She filled the kettle at the sink, put it back on its base and flicked it on. The time on the microwave flashed to 23:58. Almost midnight. Sammy sat back down at the kitchen table.

How many times had she been down to the cellar to fetch out the bracelet? Too many. And always after an argument with her mother. She wasn't sure why she kept trying to work the mechanism. Frustration with the status quo, she assumed. Only today she wasn't frustrated, today she was calm. Nothing would change unless she took charge of her own destiny. She'd had enough of life with mum and Jerry. And her dad. What a joke that man was. She couldn't believe how long it had taken her to see him for the bullying and abusive human waste he truly was.

Sammy absentmindedly clicked open and shut the locket at her throat. She wasn't sure that going back to Perseopia was the change she needed, but something compelled her to keep trying. Two years ago her reason had been Mehrak. She'd had a pretty big crush on him then, even though he'd been married. Silly. Nothing could've happened between them. She'd still like to see him again though, hang out in Golden Egg Cottage. Really though, it was the powers she'd developed that drew her back to Perseopia and the bracelet. She needed to find out who she was. What she was. Only the magi could answer that for her. And she had nothing left in Sheffield to stick around for.

The kettle began hissing as the water warmed up. Sammy leaned in close to the emerald on the bracelet. She concentrated her mind on the gem, imagining the atoms inside moving. Imagining swaying grass.

Nothing.

She sat back. It wasn't going to happen, but she continued to watch the gem.

Then it flashed.

In that millisecond, Sammy saw a blade of grass inside the gem. And that was all she needed. She latched on to it, her mental feelers grabbing hold, keeping the blade inside the emerald going. The light remained and now it was getting brighter. More blades of grass appeared and she latched on to them too, swaying them faster.

Sammy leaned in further, placing her thumbs under the dial hands. They budged up a little, but not enough. They wouldn't move any more. Why? What time was it? Had she missed midnight? She didn't want to look away and lose sight of the grass.

The blades were moving relatively slowly. They'd moved faster last time she'd been in this situation. She gritted her teeth and pushed harder. She imagined the atoms in the grass thrown side to side. Rushing back and forth, getting faster, the light brightening.

The clock hands shifted up a little more.

The kettle began boiling, bubbling urgently behind her.

Sammy gritted her teeth, concentrating hard, swaying the blades ever faster. The light was dazzling, almost too bright to look into.

She pushed harder still. The clock hands loosened. Her head was hurting, but she wasn't about to stop.

The gem was humming. Burning ever brighter.

Sammy gave the clock hands one final push.

Both dial hands snapped to the top and green light engulfed the kitchen.

–FIVE–
Familiar Surroundings

Sammy was back.

She hadn't opened her eyes yet, but she knew, could feel it.

She extended her arms out to the sides and ran her fingers through the soil. She inhaled the fusty aroma of mushrooms and her nerves pulsed with the electric atmosphere of Perseopia.

She opened her eyes.

The large green mushroom canopies that had populated her dreams since the day she'd left hung above her, scattering their glowing spores in a lazy cascade of glitter.

Everything was familiar, real. Much more real than where she'd come from. Sheffield was a cardboard cut-out. A movie set that when you looked too closely, would give away the scaffolding behind a painted façade.

It had been two years since she'd been here, but it was like she'd never left. Smells and sights seemed richer, the world brighter and more alive. Perseopia was taking hold of her again. Energy being channelled into her.

She realised then that the realm had never left her, had always been there in the deepest recesses of her soul, drawing her back. Her mum telling her it never existed only made her resolve to come back stronger. She was going to find Hami and have him explain what had happened to her; what Perseopia had done to her.

Sammy got up off the ground. Turned 360 degrees on the spot.

Finding Hami might take a while.

She clicked open and shut the locket at her throat. The Fungi Forest was enormous. She remembered that from the last time she'd been here. It had taken days to cross and that was on the back of a dinosaur. How would she find anyone? Or even know which direction to walk in?

The first flurry of panic settled over her. She'd returned only to become lost, as she had been before. Mehrak had told her no one travelled the Fungi Forest alone, and that she was lucky he and Louis had found her.

There were giant tigers lurking here. Crabmen too, with their dead eyes and mechanical movements, ready to crush her skull and hack the rest of her to pieces.

A flock of white birds erupted from the bushes. Sammy dived to the ground in a trembling cower as they wheeled above her, then dispersed back into the vegetation.

The forest was still when she regained her feet. She'd been so desperate to return, she hadn't considered the consequences of being back. There hadn't been time. It had taken all her effort to keep the grass inside the emerald moving. If she'd stopped concentrating to consider what she was doing, the gem might've gone dull and she'd have missed her only opportunity to return.

Sammy closed her eyes and tried to relax. She felt the forest around her, the animals, the mushrooms, the brown creepers and small yellow bushes. And something else. Danger.

She opened her eyes. There was something approaching. An animal, but she couldn't tell what kind.

Movement through the haze of mushroom spores. A four-legged silhouette, like a dog but misshapen. It was keeping to the shadows, circling.

Sammy scanned the floor for a weapon. A fist-sized rock at her feet was the closest object available. It would have to do. She snatched it up and raised it as the animal prowled closer, slowly decreasing the distance between them.

It moved into the light of a mushroom and revealed itself to be some kind of half-pig, half-dog creature. Hyena-shaped with a hunch, thick forearms, and an elongated snout with tusks like a boar. Sammy concentrated on the beast. She could feel conflicting emotions, reticence to approach, while also readying an attack.

She sensed the move just before it came, yet a scream still escaped her as it lunged. She dodged to the side and backed away. The creature barked in a strained, guttural manner.

Sammy threw the rock. The beast caught it in its jaws and crunched it up.

She'd allowed it to get too close. It was dictating the flow of the fight. She didn't let that happen at college, she shouldn't let it happen here.

The pig-dog growled and chomped its maw. It feigned a lunge. Sammy squeaked and stumbled backwards.

If she calmed down, she'd be able to deal with it the same way she dealt with bullies. The barrier of the Mother World had been shed. She was absorbing Perseopia's energy, charging herself up. She could take this beast down.

She reached out her mental feelers to the animal but couldn't picture the molecules in its hide, couldn't latch on to anything. The only thing she could feel was a vague sense of its emotional state. Hunger and fear, and the hunger was overpowering its desire to flee.

She was ready for the second attack when it came. She read the creature's intention to charge and sidestepped as it lumbered past and kept going, the inertia of its bulk carrying it on and away.

That bought her some time. Not much, but enough to find a rugby-ball-sized rock. She heaved it up to her waist, cleared her mind, concentrated on its molecular structure and imagined it getting lighter. The effect was instant. And profound.

Sammy raised the rock over her head.

The pig-dog pawed at the ground and their eyes met, jarring Sammy back into the moment.

Then it charged.

Sammy brought the rock down, accelerating it at the animal's head with her mind, guiding it towards the point between its eyes.

The beast yelped as its skull collapsed inwards. It hit the ground hard, shuddered, and fell still.

A moment passed before Sammy fully absorbed what she'd done. And then it took her a longer moment to get over it. The murder of a living creature, albeit one that had been trying to kill her. She'd killed a crabman on her previous visit, but this was somehow different. This had been closer, more intimate. A living, breathing red-blooded mammal rather than a robotic alien with slimy, blue bodily fluids.

The pig-dog's head was a mess, and too disgusting to look at directly. Sammy peered side on with squinted eyes as metallic green and yellow beetles emerged from the dirt around it. They crawled across the ruined skull and began feeding on the goo inside. Sammy gagged, then turned away and began walking.

The last time she'd been in Perseopia, she'd stopped a crabman's arm from chopping her head off. She hadn't been able to do anything remotely close to that with the pig-dog, and that was worrying. Perhaps her powers didn't work on normal animals. Or was she losing them? That would be especially problematic, now that she found herself back in the Fungi Forest with potentially worse creatures to contend with. And the pig-dog fight had been stressful enough.

The dizziness came out of nowhere. Her stomach turned and she staggered to a mushroom where she sat and rested her head between her knees. The trauma of fighting the pig-dog had affected her more than she'd realised.

Sammy waited until her head stopped spinning and her hands stopped shaking. She couldn't stay where she was in the hope someone found her. She'd got herself into this mess. She'd get herself out of it.

She got up and walked.

Sammy pushed through a curtain of creepers on the way out of the clearing, zigzagged through a pack of closely packed mushrooms, wandered down a short slope and skirted several yellow bushes.

She was beginning to feel better already. Perhaps all she'd needed was a brisk stroll to burn off some nervous energy.

Then she stepped into another clearing, and stopped. The sight that greeted her made her light-headed and panicky all over again.

A depression in the earth and human footprints leading away. Small, bare footprints similar in size to hers. It was irrational, but it brought to mind Samara, the freaky girl from The Ring. Another human being out in the forest should be a welcome thing. Shouldn't it? Sammy couldn't convince herself of it. A person that stalked the forest alone in bare feet was creepy whichever way you looked at it.

She wasn't going to follow the footprints. They probably belonged to a feral forest child waiting to shoot her with poison darts, scalp her and make clothes of her skin.

Sammy took a different path, moving purposefully and quietly.

————

Long after the threat of being dragged down a well by a dark-haired demon girl had abated, Sammy found a clearing large enough that she could see the sky for the first time.

The churning magenta clouds were as mesmerising as she remembered. She watched for a while, swept away by their beauty.

Why hadn't the clouds dispersed since Ramaask had gone? She wasn't expecting clear blue skies, but it was as if nothing had happened since she'd been gone. Maybe defeating Ramaask hadn't been the environmental fix that Hami had hoped it would be.

Then an unrelated thought occurred to her. How had Louis known what direction to travel in? There were no stars in the sky and nothing that distinguished one part of the forest from any other. How did he navigate? She was pretty sure he hadn't made the journey across the Fungi Forest before. And while he and Mehrak had been travelling, they'd made several deviations. Once when the crabmen chased them and again when they detoured to meet Hami. Come to think of it, how did Hami even know which way he was going? He'd been travelling alone when they met. Louis might've used some kind of smell. What did Hami use? Some secret magi ability? A compass? Sammy's phone was still on the kitchen table back in Sheffield. There'd be no reception or GPS in Perseopia, but the compass might've still worked. Maybe.

Which direction was she supposed to head in? She could end up walking in circles. Mehrak had spent weeks, maybe even months, travelling across Perseopia, and he was travelling on Louis's back. She might never find her way out of the forest.

Sammy stopped herself. She was getting worked up. She took a deep breath and tried to think calming thoughts. More exercise was what she needed. Exercise would reduce stress. She set off again through the forest.

She walked for hours, long enough to burn off all her nervous energy. And the terrain didn't change once in that time.

Sammy shuffled to a halt. She couldn't go any further. There may be crabmen, pig-dogs or any number of other threats lurking in the mushrooms, but she'd take her chances. Her carcass wasn't travelling any further today.

She drew a large arrow in the dirt to remind herself which direction to continue walking in when she woke, then shuffled over to a shallow ditch surrounded by yellowing bushes and a low mushroom. She climbed through the bushes and rolled under the mushroom.

Sammy doubted anything could see her where she hid. Getting found would depend on how good her hunter's other senses were. But right then, she didn't have the energy to care. She lay back and closed her eyes.

Annoyingly, the underside of the mushroom was bright enough to show through her eyelids. Sammy ran a hand through the gills in an attempt to extinguish the light, but instead covered herself in glowing spores that made her face itch.

She slumped back. A stone was pressing into the small of her back, adding to her overall discomfort, but she couldn't find the strength to move so let the weight of fatigue drag her into unconsciousness.

–SIX–
WITH GREAT POWER COMES GREAT RESPONSIBILITY

Sammy stood on the stone bridge that spanned the Cataclysm. On one side, the dark plain stretched out to the strip of glowing Fungi Forest mushrooms in the distance, on the other loomed the mountain where the fire temple sat.

The skies above were black and the chasm below was white, the light of which shimmered across the marble walls of the temple and lit up the golden dome like a flaming rosebud.

She approached the edge of the bridge.

I'm coming for you, my princess of darkness.

The words came from the fire below, calling to her. She recoiled from the light. Too bright to look into.

More than anything, she wanted to return to the dark.

Sammy stirred. She flinched at the headache she was just beginning to acknowledge. Then squinted. It was brighter than it should be. It couldn't be morning already.

Something was tickling her face. She tried to bat it away but couldn't connect with anything. "Leave me alone," she murmured. "I want to sleep."

She tried to push the thing away but it kept coming back, tickling. It was Pussy Riot, her friend Brigit's cat. They'd been out, they'd drunk too much and now that mangy mog was climbing over her face, tickling her with its belly fur. It was like the animal could sense when she was at her most hungover and punished her for it.

Sammy needed pain killers and water.

She hadn't been out, though.

Sammy sat up, stuffing her head into the underside of the mushroom she'd been sleeping under and covering herself in more luminous spores. She sneezed, slumped back onto the painful stone she'd been sleeping on, then rolled to the side. She remained where she was, face down in the dirt. She considered going back to sleep, but her mouth was dry and her stomach was chewing a hole in itself.

Sammy slowly dragged herself from under the mushroom and, with excruciating lethargy, heaved herself up out of the yellow bushes. The first time she came to Perseopia, she awoke to the soft, voluminous bedding of Golden Egg Cottage, not crawling out of a shallow ditch covered in itchy mushroom dust.

Mehrak had even left her a bowl of mushroom soup to wake up to. She still remembered how good it had been. Or rather, thought she remembered. Nothing seemed clear to her right then.

Sammy stretched, then slouched. She had no energy to do anything. Time to dig deep and find some hidden reserves. This was an opportunity to prove she could fend for herself. Finding food and water was the first order of the day. Mehrak had cooked mushrooms as part of every meal and they were clearly in abundance. She'd start with that.

Sammy set her sights on a small one, kicked it over and picked it up.

She took a bite. The mushroom ruptured in her mouth, gushing with bitter tasting slime. She spat it out.

Perhaps you were supposed to cook it first. That made sorting a campfire the new first objective on the agenda. Or maybe second. Before that, she needed water to wash the taste away. She was thirsty. The heat wasn't helping. She hadn't remembered it being this warm in the forest before. Aside from when the tall figure in black had appeared.

Sammy dropped the mushroom. She located the arrow she'd drawn in the dirt and moved swiftly in the prescribed direction.

After a while, she slowed up.

The temperature wasn't going up. She was just jumpy. Bizarrely, the hit of panic induced adrenaline had eased her headache somewhat. She still needed to find food and water, but at least she was feeling better. Someone once told her that you could live for days without food, but not water. That gave her no choice but to keep going until she found a river or body of water.

A flock of white sparrows with thin beaks flew past in perfect formation. They wheeled around her like a miniature cloud, then blew away through the brown creepers.

She realised then that she'd not been sending out mental feelers to scan the area for threats. Perseopia was continually lulling her into a false sense of security on account of how fantastical the environment was. It was doing it again now, making her forget the dangers lurking just around the corner. Her absentmindedness was probably linked to her lack of hydration and general fatigue, but regardless of the cause, the result would be the same if she let a threat sneak up on her. She'd have to remember to be more careful going forward.

The scan came back clear. Nothing big, no pig-dogs certainly. She sensed a family of small mammals burrowing nearby, but nothing else.

The forest may be dangerous, but her Perseopia-charged superpowers were far greater now than they'd been back home.

She picked up a fist-sized stone and launched it into the air. As it flew upward, she imagined it in great detail, willing it to the side. The stone veered sharply from its upward trajectory and she lost it.

The direction change had been immediate. Sammy laughed. She shouldn't be surprised, given how easy it had been to lift the rock that she'd killed the pig-dog with, but the force she'd been able to summon just then had been immense.

She searched the ground for another stone. She spotted one poking out of the dirt and went to pick it up. Then stopped. She should hone her skills in case she needed to use them again.

Sammy concentrated on the stone. It wobbled, but stayed where it was. She relaxed and held out her arm. With her hand above the stone, she latched onto it with her mind and pulled.

The stone burst from the soil, clipping her hand and continuing up into the sky.

Sammy yelped. She squeezed her hand between her thighs, took it out and blew on it. She hadn't expected the stone to move so quickly. Her palm was in pain. Like, proper pain. She could've broken her hand if the stone had hit her full on. She stepped back a pace in case the stone landed on her head on the way back, but she needn't have worried. She sensed it returning and latched onto it as it fell. The stone slowed until it floated down to head height and stopped. She was actually doing this. Suspending the entire weight of the stone in the air with her powers. *Sweet.*

She'd possessed her manipulative powers for over two years back in Sheffield. She'd progressed them as much as she was able. But this? This was way beyond what she'd been capable of. She rubbed the pain out of her palm, then held it out.

She flew the stone a quick loop around her head. Spun it on its axis and then lowered it into her hand.

She looked around for other stones. She spotted four and in a second all four had freed themselves from the earth and were sailing around her like mini satellites. She tossed the first stone from her hand to join the others floating in the air.

This was so awesome.

She sent the stones flying at a large tree-sized mushroom. They thudded into the trunk like bullets, embedding themselves in the rubbery flesh.

These were genuine superhero powers. Forget rolling a pencil across a table.

Sammy made gun shapes with her hands using her index and middle fingers as barrels. She raised more stones from the dirt and brought them over to hang around her wrists like floating bracelet beads. She aimed her right 'hand' gun at a large mushroom and fired a stone from her floating bracelet. She spun on her heel and fired a second from her left. She performed a flawless commando roll, then leapt up. Three shots with her right and two with her left. Sammy blew on the tips of her fingers and pretended to holster them. Man, did she have some awesome skills! No pig-dogs would stand a chance against her. She almost felt sorry for them, but not entirely.

She continued to fire off stones in all directions as she walked through the forest, replenishing her floating bracelets with other stones as she went. Occasionally she'd spot a baby mushroom with a wide hood that she'd use as a target. Sometimes she'd pattern the mushroom trunks by embedding the stones at high velocity. On one trunk she recreated her initials in stones. It looked like it had been written by a toddler but that didn't matter. She'd get better.

From a distance, Sammy spotted another pig-dog. It saw her too, however, a volley of stone projectiles had it running away, squealing.

She probably should've shot the animal for her supper. Her stomach constricted then. She'd been having such a good time exercising her superhuman abilities that she'd almost forgotten the needs of her mortal body.

Movement in the bushes ahead. She aimed both arms and let rip, emptying both bracelet clips into the plants.

A feeble squeak followed. Then silence.

That didn't sound good. Sammy squirmed uneasily. She approached the bush, tip-toeing closer until she could peer through the leaves.

A small furry body lay prone on the ground. A rabbit with long, almost kangaroo-like legs. Its fur was matted with blood and its ribcage pumped rapidly.

Black, round eyes stared up at Sammy as the animal shivered in a small pool of its own blood.

It flinched when she extended a hand towards it, so she withdrew.

"I'm sorry," she whispered. She was normally so good at remaining impassive in her day-to-day life, yet tears were already rolling down her cheeks. "I didn't mean to …"

The rabbit squeaked and twitched. Sammy moved to scoop the poor creature up in her arms, but it saw her coming and began frantically crawling away on its front paws, dragging its limp hind legs behind it.

Its back was broken. There was no chance of survival in the Fungi Forest if you couldn't outrun predators. Its life was essentially over because Sammy thought she was cool with her new powers.

She couldn't keep it together. She dropped to her knees and wept. How could she have done such a thing to a defenceless little creature? A pig-dog when it attacked was fair game, but an innocent little rabbit that posed no threat and had never hurt anyone?

She'd have to put it out of its misery. That was the only humane thing she could do for it now. With tears blurring her vision, Sammy scavenged around for a large rock.

She found one, floated it into the air over the rabbit and took several steps backwards. She'd send the rock flying at its head, then turn away at the last minute so she didn't have to watch it die.

She held the rock in mid-air while she psyched herself up. She was a coward. She didn't even possess the courage to watch.

No. Not like this. She was going to do it properly. She took a deep breath, plucked the rock out of the air and crouched by the rabbit. Dragging a sleeve across her eyes, she positioned herself over the wretched little creature. She watched its breathing get more ragged, then slow. She raised the rock.

Come on. Just do it!

The rabbit stopped trembling, its breathing slowed further, then stopped.

Sammy waited, then tossed the rock aside. Saved from having to do something unpleasant. She'd been too cowardly to put the poor animal out of its misery and had let it live its last moments in agony.

Sammy often felt that she lived outside the lives of everyone else. Others were mostly unaffected by her presence. Being unimportant had become her safety blanket. Something she'd initially hated, but over time had come to embrace. She enjoyed her anonymity, preferred not to make impressions in other's lives, because then no one would have expectations of her. But she hadn't remained on the outside this time. She'd inserted herself into this rabbit's life and she'd killed it by her actions.

She picked up the still-warm animal, carried it to an area devoid of mushrooms and shrubs and laid it down. She scraped out a hole in the earth with her hands, put the rabbit at the bottom, refilled it and placed a ring of stones around the burial mound.

Then she got up and walked away.

–SEVEN–
THE WHISPER

Crying had majorly diminished her water reserves. Sammy rubbed her puffy eyelids and kneaded the headache lingering in her temples. She was so thirsty, hungry and drained she could barely go on, so she shuffled to a stop.

She didn't care what happened to her any more. She was a cold-blooded murderer and deserved whatever fate had in store. She slumped to the ground and rolled over onto her back.

When had dirt become so exquisitely soft? It was like the memory foam mattress Jerry had in his spare room. What a bizarre recollection to have as she lay in a forest of mushrooms, dying of dehydration.

Her eyes were already closing as she reached out her mental feelers to scan for potential threats. The sweep came back clear as she drifted off, half-hallucinating, half-dreaming.

Sammy was playing football. Playing hard, running, getting thirsty. She grabbed a water bottle at the sideline and drank heavily. Finishing the bottle, she grabbed another but her thirst wasn't being quenched.

A few of the guys were beginning to jeer at her, telling her she didn't belong on the team. She thought nothing of it, but then they were chasing her from the pitch.

They cornered her outside the library block. Instinctively, she raised stones from the driveway and let them fly. The bullets cut through the boys, tearing them to shreds, making them dance like marionettes.

When their bodies hit the floor, the realisation of what she'd done sank in. What should she do? Should she run? The boys were writhing around on the floor in pools of their own blood, looking up at her in shock, pleading with their eyes. Dragging themselves away with paralysed back legs.

Then she was behind bars.

Her mother was outside the cell with Jerry. "I always knew you'd end up like this," she said. "I tried to be there for you but you shut me out. You're a thug. Just like your father."

"Mum. Please!" Sammy pushed her face into the space between two of the bars. "Help me!"

"You're past helping, Sam. You're a murderer. I want nothing to do with you. Come, Jerry. Let's go."

Sammy pulled the bars apart, bending them out of her way. She ran after her mother finding herself back in the Fungi Forest. Lost.

She wheeled around. "Come back!" she called. But her mother had gone.

She started running, charging between the mushrooms, tearing creepers out of her way. The thirst was unbearable. She tripped and fell, rolled over on the ground.

Then a voice came to her, whispering, echoing through the forest.

"Seek out the path, cross the river of light,
"Descend through the depths and when you alight,
"Take a trip through the gate, where the mountain will fall,
"And that's when the realm becomes darkest of all."

Sammy woke with a jolt as the rhyme came to an end. For a moment, she thought she could still hear an echo of it being whispered. Like it hadn't totally been part of her dream. She was so weak and exhausted she could well be hallucinating, but she couldn't get over the feeling that the rhyme was still present, echoing in her head.

Pain was also in her head. Not so much echoing, but jack-hammering on the inside of her skull.

Why had she come back? She was hopelessly lost and dying of thirst. She would've cried if it were possible to wring any more liquid out of her barren tear ducts. How could she not have considered the consequences? She'd signed her own death sentence to spite her mum, who probably wouldn't be that bothered anyway.

That wasn't fair. Of course she'd be bothered. After she'd calmed down.

Sammy staggered to her feet and dusted herself down. Her head was all over the place but she had powers, so she was safe ... relatively. She hadn't tested them on crabmen, but she'd killed one the last time she'd been here and she'd only been sixteen. Her powers had come on loads since then. If she put some effort in, she might even be able to use them to create fire and cook something.

Sammy rolled her head on her shoulders and massaged the base of her neck.

Food and water. The obtaining of which was becoming increasingly pressing. She wasn't about to kill any more animals, but she could cook up some mushrooms. She picked a few, small, juicy-looking specimens and piled them on the floor. Now for something flammable to light. Sammy trawled the surrounding area until she found a dead bush and pulled it from the ground. She dragged it over to the mushrooms, sat cross-legged and began snapping pieces off and piling them up. When the bush had been dismantled, she placed one of the larger sticks in front of her and rotated a second stick back and forth on top of it to create a divot. Divot achieved, she latched onto the vertical stick with her mind and let go with her hands. The stick remained upright. Then she made it spin. Fast. In moments, the stick began whirring, producing a whistling noise. Smoke trailed up from the point of contact. Then it caught.

Sammy kept it going until the entire stick was aflame, then she sent it onto the pile and the whole lot went up. Easy.

She picked up a baby mushroom, skewered it on another stick, then held it over the fire. When it had browned sufficiently and the gills had stopped glowing, she blew on it and took a bite. Hot, and still squidgy, but much nicer than the uncooked one she'd tried earlier. It was quite juicy, too. Juicy enough that by the time she'd finished, it had taken the edge off her headache.

She would need to find proper water, but at least she might survive another day.

–EIGHT–
The Capital

Baxter stared out of the window as he waited. The roofs, the buildings, everything outside city hall tainted purple by the smog roiling above them. He hated purple. The only parts of the city not purple were the main thoroughfares and parliament square below him, lit up brilliant white by gas lampposts that banished purple to the alleyways between buildings. Citizens of the capital milled about, heading to and from work. In this part of the city, most of them would be civil servants, carrying out their daily duties, blissfully unaware of the crabman armies amassing hundreds of stadia to the west and cutting off trade routes to the other big cities. All they saw were food and produce price hikes and unscrupulous politicians wringing their purses for more tax. If that was the extent of their worries then perhaps they were better off living in ignorance as they were. Still, it would be nice for some appreciation or even recognition that the government was protecting the population from troubles going on elsewhere in Perseopia.

Footsteps behind him.

Grand Master Zubin Aegis came lumbering along the corridor. He was a large, hunched man with broad shoulders and big hands. It was said he'd developed his stooped gait by listening rather than talking. The half-closed eyes that peered out from under his black hood made him look dopey and half asleep, but Baxter knew that much went on behind those eyes. The few times he'd seen the man speak, he'd cut down those with opposing views in moments. He could shatter preconceived notions, convince people of his opinions, and they'd leave his company with their prior beliefs in tatters. People said he could defeat any who came before him with words, and from Baxter's limited experience, he was inclined to believe it.

Clutching his notes, Baxter turned from the window and fell into step with the grand master as he walked.

Aegis lifted the hood of his cloak back to reveal a scant thatch of unkempt white hair that had spread down the sides of his head and joined the thin beard that clung to his chin. "I'm on my way to an appointment," he said.

"I'll be quick then," Baxter replied.

The grand master gave no indication of whether communication would be forthcoming or not, as they passed between the clean white columns lining the corridor in silence.

"Has there been any news from Aratta?" Baxter prompted.

"There has." Aegis volunteered nothing more. He wasn't going to make this easy.

Baxter lowered his voice. "Excellent. What do we know?"

"I told the Prime Minister I'd give him a full update as soon as he can take time out of his busy schedule to see me. However, there is still much for the brotherhood to contemplate. Following me around won't get you answers any quicker."

"I understand, Grand Master, but crabman numbers are accelerating, Perseopia is changing. The minister is worried about developments in the old capital. He's worried about the black column."

"The black column? How interesting." Aegis smiled a moment before becoming serious. "I've travelled from the magi garrison to New Ecbatana to be here in person, Mr Baxter. The Prime Minister will know everything I know when he dignifies me with a meeting."

"Is there nothing I can take back to him in the meantime?"

The Grand Master paused. "He shows an interest in the black column. That's … a start. Tell him the Order are continuing to increase its height and we strongly believe they're recreating their own version of the citadel, the Naziarabad Monument at Ameretat.

A black column that will eventually extend up past the smog and that, I imagine, they hope to turn into a gateway to the Mother World."

"Why wouldn't they use the already existing monument?"

"The citadel is occupied, not to mention heavily guarded. They could rush it, fight their way inside and hope to make it to the summit, but they don't have a key. Or rather an object that will allow them to leave Perseopia. Better to build their own column closer to home while the search for the right object continues. Portals have been opened before with varying levels of success. We all know what happened last time an Order member opened a portal."

"The Lurker at the Gate. Lord VorMask."

"Lord VorMask, indeed." The Grand Master paused. "I'll fill you in on the rest of the details when we meet later."

"I have a few more questions," Baxter said. He unravelled the parchment in his hands.

Aegis held up his hand. "Your minister doesn't have time for me so he'll have to be patient until he does."

"Where's Hami?"

"Why is that important?"

"He's seen this black column. He survived the journey into Aratta and returned with information."

"He's in the process of making a delivery to Honton Keep."

"What about the column, though? Is there no one we can send back to find out more?" Baxter checked his notes. "Couldn't … Victa Wild make the delivery to Honton Keep while Hami returns to Aratta?"

"Excuse me?"

"I spoke to Master Gobi earlier today, apparently Victa is in the Fungi Forest. Not far from Honton Keep or the location Hami last communicated from."

The Grand Master remained impassive. "I assign tasks to the magi, Baxter. Neither you nor the minister do. Victa has been given his duties. Hami has been given his."

"I'm sorry, Grand Master. It's only a question that the minister will ask."

"I've given Victa instructions to get out of the Fungi Forest as soon as he's able. The boy can handle himself, to a degree, but he's still young and inexperienced and I don't want to pressure him with duties over his capabilities."

"Isn't Hami around the same age?"

"Hami has extraordinary power and can handle virtually anything we throw at him."

"He's also reckless. If he hadn't redeemed himself recently, I'd question you using him for much more than delivery duties."

The Grand Master didn't reply.

"But results are results and he got them when no one else did." Baxter paused. He wasn't getting anywhere. "What was this lower order magus, Victa, doing in the Fungi Forest anyway?" he asked.

Aegis frowned.

"Just so I can tell the minister."

"He was originally heading to Honton Keep to become the Regent's point of communication for the magi, but the forest is teeming with crabmen. Far more than it had been previously. It became too dangerous for him to carry on further. But then something came up. Someone in the forest joining the magi network close to where Victa was passing. We're sending him to pick them up."

"Couldn't Hami have picked up the recruit? Surely a new magus recruit is more important than a delivery?"

"A potential magus recruit is more important than your average delivery. But not this one. Besides, Hami is almost at the Keep. I'll get him to relay information in Victa's absence. Victa, on the other hand, is on a greenbuck gazelle and is best positioned to safely escort the recruit out of the forest and to the magi garrison."

Baxter shrugged. "I thought you'd have more for me than that."

"There is a great deal more. You can't comprehend the significance of the delivery Hami is making. And what is at stake if he's not successful." The Grand Master stopped. He acted as if he'd said too much and pinched his lips. Yet he was far too intelligent to have made such a mistake. This undoubtedly was Aegis's ploy, teasing at information to fast-track an appointment with the minister. Baxter was close to learning something major and the fact that the Grand Master had let so much slip already meant there was a lot more to uncover.

"What is Hami delivering?" Baxter had no expectation of being answered, but he had to ask.

"'*Who* is Hami delivering?' is the question you should be asking. But I'm afraid that the minister will have to wait for me to tell him in person. I've already said too much." And with that, Aegis turned and walked away.

–NINE–
An Unlikely Reunion

Sammy stumbled on through the Fungi Forest. Her stomach, although full, was cramping, and her dehydration headache had returned even bigger and over-the-top as the big budget sequel.

It was unlikely she'd meet anyone out here in the middle of nowhere. And her chances of running into Mehrak again were especially slim. That was if he'd survived the earthquakes at the Temple of Paths.

She was being overly negative. He would've survived. Hami would've rescued him. But the fire temple had been two years ago, they could be anywhere by now. Mehrak was probably thousands of miles away, back on the trail of that book he'd been looking for. He might even have found his wife. She snorted a joyless laugh. Imagine if she'd braved the Fungi Forest, fought pig-dogs, become a bunny murderer, eaten slimy mushrooms and travelled thousands of miles across Perseopia, to find Mehrak settled back at home with his wife. She tried to purge that depressing thought from her head. She'd deal with that scenario if it materialised. Dwelling on it wouldn't help her get out of her current predicament.

On the bright side, she could always join the magi. Get trained up. Have battles, save people. Hijinks like that. That would be a pretty awesome life. But not if it meant living it alone. What she wanted more than anything was to be back in Golden Egg Cottage, travelling across Perseopia with Mehrak. She'd dreamed of little else since she'd left and sometimes wondered if it was Mehrak that had drawn her back or the life she could be living in the caravan on Louis's back.

She sighed. Her brain was a mess. She still hadn't found water. She'd been back, what? A day? Day and a half? Two? She hadn't seen anyone, and the scenery hadn't changed. With no compass and no stars to guide her, she could be walking in circles. All because she'd argued with her mother. And now it was getting warmer. She sat down and held her head in her hands.

It was getting hotter still and her eyelids were sticking to her eyeballs. She rubbed at them, massaging her tear ducts for the remotest chance they'd excrete more liquid. She'd scared herself once already, imagining that the forest was getting warmer. She was probably doing it again.

Or not.

A shadow slid out from amongst the mushrooms. It registered in her peripheral vision and she stumbled backwards, falling over her mushroom.

The creature that had given her nightmares frequently since she'd last been to the realm approached from the undergrowth. The tall, thin figure, human-shaped, head limp at its chest with narrow shoulders and shrouded in black cloth.

It stopped short.

"You … again?" the creature said in its metallic, monotonous voice. It sounded genuinely surprised to see her. "You're different. Taller."

Sammy remained on her back. She had to get up, run, but her body was drained. She should try to defend herself with stones, except she couldn't concentrate on anything but the thin figure above her.

"You actually make it," it said. "But where have you come from? And should I use this opportunity to kill you?"

The world around Sammy ground to a halt as her heart stalled. Her brain seized up and she found herself incapable of action.

"No," the creature said after a pause. "You still need to fulfil your destiny."

Sammy's heart resumed beating, albeit in an uneven stuttering fashion, and she managed to catch her breath.

"There's a river not far away. In that direction." The creature held out a long-sleeved arm indicating the way. "Be quick. It would be a waste for you to die while there's still much to be done.' Then it slid backwards, blending into the shadows, and vanished.

Sammy remained on the floor, staring after the creature long after the temperature had resumed normal Fungi Forest levels. What were the chances of running into that same creature again upon returning to Perseopia? It had tried to kill her last time. Now it was letting her go? And what did it mean about fulfilling her destiny?

There was a chance it was sending her into a trap. But there'd been ample opportunity to attack her while she'd been floundering and it hadn't. If there was any possibility of there being a river in the direction it had pointed, Sammy should take it. She had nothing to lose at this point. Trap or not, she'd die if she went much longer without water.

Sammy struggled to her feet and set off at a slow, shambling pace.

She still didn't trust the thin figure, so made sure to stop and scan the area every so often with her super senses. But each time she did, the scan came back clear, and so each time she carried on a little further.

Eventually she found the river.

Sammy stopped behind a curtain of creepers just off the riverbank and waited. There was no one around. Certainly no one waiting for her.

The water was black and fast flowing. It would be treacherous to cross, so an attack from the far bank was unlikely. Yet an attack could come from beneath the surface. She recalled the black creature that had gone for Mehrak when he'd fetched water from the lake.

She waited, briefly, but her thirst was getting the better of her. She'd have to chance it. Sammy legged it out onto the riverbank and stopped halfway to the water.

Something disappeared under the surface by the opposite shore. She'd only seen it from the corner of her eye and couldn't tell exactly what it was, but it hadn't seemed big. Probably a rodent of some sort. She wasn't going to risk it, though. If she used her brain—and her powers—she could bring the water to her.

Sammy concentrated on the water molecules on the surface, but couldn't latch onto them. The flow of the river was too fast. No sooner had she visualised the molecules in her mind's eye than she'd lost them again.

Sod it. She'd make a run for it. As long as she was quick, she'd be fine. She ran back to the forest edge, kicked over a small mushroom, scrapped out the glowing gills to create a makeshift bowl, and ran to the water's edge.

Water exploded from the river and a wide, red mouth closed just short of her face. Sammy screamed, losing the mushroom as she scrambled away from the water. She sprinted back to the relative safety of the forest where she chanced a return glance.

A large, black, salamander-like creature with a yellow belly ungainly dragged itself back into the water.

Sammy waited and watched the water while she caught her breath.

She'd felt bad killing the rabbit. It had been an innocent. But this creature had made the first move. Murder had left a shadow over her heart, a blackened ulcer that was still raw and tormented her when she thought about it, and ordinarily it would've been her preference to spare other living creatures, but she'd die if she didn't get water soon. She'd make an exception for this oversized and inconsiderate newt.

In moments, she'd hoovered up two bracelet clips worth of stones and begun rotating them around her wrists.

She fired several shots into the area of water the newt had returned to.

Nothing.

Playing hardball eh, slimy? Sammy sent one of the stones over to the water's edge and dipped it in. Still nothing. She wiggled it side to side, gently.

The newt salamander thing launched as Sammy accelerated all her remaining stones into it.

The creature was dead before it hit the bank with a wet slop. Its head and chest hung in tatters. One moment it had been in the prime of its life, attacking its prey, the next, oblivion.

Sammy turned away from the disgusting mess. It was sickening to look at, but not enough that she was going to miss getting a drink.

She grabbed another small mushroom, hollowed out the gills and made sure she walked upriver of the splattered newt. No way was she drinking amphibian slime and blood-flavoured water. She legged it to the river's edge, scooped up some icy water and ran back to the forest. She sat on a mushroom and drank, giving herself a head freeze and stomach cramps in the process, but she didn't care. Water had never tasted so good.

The magenta clouds dimmed over the period it took for Sammy to make multiple trips to the river. It turned out that Mehrak had been right about the sky. It did get marginally darker at night. She once again wished he was there with her and not wherever else he was.

On a positive note, she'd survived another day. She could cook mushrooms, and even though they were disgusting, she hadn't poisoned herself yet. She'd also defended herself against Perseopian wildlife twice. And found water. Actually, she hadn't found water. The tall thin figure had shown her where to go. There was something disconcerting about that. What had changed since the last time she'd been here and that same creature had chased her across Perseopia? Was it because she'd been partially responsible for Ramaask's defeat? Maybe she'd released the thin figure from a life of servitude. Or perhaps it'd sensed her powers and was too scared to fight. Unlikely. She didn't believe any of those scenarios and a niggling doubt remained. What did it mean when it had told her there was still much to do? And that she had to fulfil her destiny?

The shadow over Sammy's heart was spreading. Three deaths on her conscience so far. A hat trick. Four if you included the crabman she'd killed last time. Perhaps that was the reason she hadn't been attacked by that evil creature. It could sense the evil in her too. She'd become a kindred spirit and it'd let her live to continue spreading death.

Sammy snorted mirthlessly. Now she was being ridiculous.

She needed to make it to a big town or city. There were other more dangerous inhabitants lurking in the Fungi Forest to worry about. With luck, she'd survive another day without having to meet or kill any of them.

–TEN–

Other More Dangerous Inhabitants Lurking in the Fungi Forest

The fire had diminished, reduced to embers by the time Sammy woke. She rolled over and mentally scanned the vicinity. Nothing. One more night survived. Bonus.

She breathed a sigh of relief, dragged herself to her feet, stretched, then slumped. She was still groggy, but her headache had gone. Life was better after food, water and sleep. She could do with brushing her teeth, but if that was the extent of her problems then she was doing pretty alright. Sammy snapped a twig from a nearby bush and rubbed the torn, fibrous end over her teeth to remove the plaque that had built up overnight.

Dental hygiene taken care of, Sammy sent a stone over to the river and splashed it around to lure out any potential newt monsters. Nothing took the bait, which was something else to be positive about. She carried her scooped-out mushroom to the water, filled it and drank.

When she'd finished, she tossed the mushroom, washed her face and neck, and left her temporary campsite to follow the river. Rivers usually led somewhere, and as she'd almost died of thirst it was probably a good idea to remain close to a water supply.

She was beginning to feel better, physically. Her sleep grogginess was dissipating and even though she hadn't eaten yet today, yesterday's mushroom had given her energy levels a much-needed boost.

She followed the riverbank for the remainder of the morning encountering nothing more ominous than a pack of naked hedgehogs with Stegosaurus plates on their backs.

At what Sammy guessed was around lunchtime, she stopped to get a fire going for some roast mushroom action. Fire sorted, she went foraging for the least disgusting fungus she could find.

She was rooting around under a dense cascade of creepers when she heard a distant chatter.

She stopped.

Sammy wasn't entirely sure whether she'd imagined it or not. She hoped she had. The fire was crackling somewhat. Perhaps it'd been that. Please let it be that. The alternative would be too scary to comprehend. She took a few paces further into the forest, away from the fire. And held her breath.

Silence. But for the insects humming under the canopies. Sammy cleared her head and waited.

A chatter. Louder this time. The chatter that crickets make, but deeper. Her legs wobbled and she leant on a mushroom to support herself. She hadn't heard that sound in over two years, yet she knew instinctively what it was. Crabmen.

Sammy dropped the mushroom and ran. Her nerves sang, adrenaline levels surged. She may not have eaten yet, but the sound of approaching crabmen was enough to fuel her legs.

The chattering was getting louder. They were heading in her direction.

Sammy powered on. Dodging mushrooms, jumping over bushes and sweeping creepers out of her face. She couldn't make out where she was going and might lose the river, but she had to get away.

She burst into a clearing, slammed into a large animal, screamed and stumbled backwards onto her bottom.

The animal startled, braying and rising up on its hind legs, bucking off a rider, who fell squawking to the ground. Then it bolted.

Sammy sprung back to her feet, ready to go, but paused.

The animal had stopped a little way off, hiding behind a dense thicket of bushes. A large, olive green antelope of some kind.

The rider got up from the floor and dusted himself down. He looked young, not much older than Sammy. He had long black hair, a pale complexion, and wore a stiff leather breast plate with a black cloak over the top.

"Are you okay?" he asked distractedly as he scanned the ground.

Spotting what he was looking for, he walked over to a long white stick and picked it up. Not a stick, but a staff with a black ball wedged into a split in the end. A staff like Hami's.

He was a magus! And that meant she was saved. Sammy's emotions threatened to overwhelm her. She felt like crying, but instead a laugh escaped before she could stop herself.

The young guy looked at her, then towards his green antelope that peered back at him from behind a mushroom.

Sammy realised then that she hadn't answered his question. Hadn't even spoken yet. "There are crabmen chasing me," she said.

"I heard them. We'll be fine if we can get Dohsie back. She can outrun them." He scampered after the animal as it moved further away.

Sammy walked after him. "It didn't sound like there were that many. You could probably take them."

"I doubt it," the magus replied. "Dohsie?" he cooed, walking quickly to catch up. "We need to get on my greenbuck and get out of here. I've not fought crabmen before."

"You're a magus though, aren't you?"

"I am, but even magi don't take on crabmen if they can help it. Dohsie!" he called, more urgently this time. "Here, girl."

"Hami fought loads of crabmen."

"Principal Hootan? I'm sure he did. My powers are a fraction of his. You aren't trained yet and I bet we aren't much different in ability." The magus stopped. "When it comes to crabmen, I've always been taught that when you hear them, you move quickly in the opposite direction."

"How do you know I need training?"

"That's why I'm here. To collect you. We felt you appear on the network. You heard the enrolment whisper, right? *Seek out the path, cross the river of light, descend through the depths* ... and all that?"

"You know about my dream?"

"It wasn't a dream. All new magi recruits hear it. It's how you can tell you've been chosen by the Great Ahura Mazda to serve the realm. So they say. The magi felt you connect and as I was closest at the time, I came to make contact and take you to the garrison for training."

Training? This was fantastic! Then a thought occurred to her. "Will Hami be at the garrison?"

"No. He's currently out in the field. How do you know him, anyway?"

Sammy was about to reply when the crabmen stopped chattering.

The magus froze. "They know we're here!" He grabbed Sammy's hand and dragged her to the green antelope. The animal started back.

"Dohsie!" the man urged in a strangled whisper. The antelope tilted its head, looking at him quizzically, but stayed.

The magus grabbed the reins before it could bolt again and pulled its head to the floor, forcing it to its knees.

He leapt onto the greenbuck's back and held his hand out to Sammy. "Let's go."

Sammy took the hand and climbed on. The man dug his heels in and the animal found its feet.

"Hold on tight!" he said as the sound of vegetation rustling grew louder. "Yar!" he shouted, and the greenbuck launched itself into the air, whipping Sammy's head back.

The animal landed squarely on top of a mushroom, then with a second jump leapt to a higher one. The third leap launched them above canopy level and they landed atop a large tree-sized mushroom.

Spiky flashes of grey tore through the undergrowth below.

The crabmen had reached them.

The magus kicked the greenbuck onward and it bounced gazelle-like from canopy to canopy.

With each leap, Sammy's stomach lurched as she experienced momentary weightlessness, before they hit the next mushroom with a jerk and rebounded back into the air again.

"They won't be able to keep up for long!" the magus shouted over the rushing air.

Then a mushroom ahead tilted. The greenbuck skittered on the sloped surface, just gaining enough momentum to leap on.

"They're ahead of us!" Sammy screamed. "They're cutting the mushrooms!"

The magus yanked the reins and they veered off at a tangent. The greenbuck leapt successfully to the next mushroom, but the one after dropped as they landed.

One moment they were flying through the air, the next they were falling.

Sammy hit the fallen mushroom canopy, bouncing off at an angle and landing on another mushroom, before rolling off the side and hitting the forest floor.

The fall knocked the wind from her. She tried to suck in air but her lungs wouldn't open.

She raised her head as a crabman seized the greenbuck by its throat, holding it in place with a large claw.

The crabman was as terrifying as Sammy remembered. A human-shaped head and torso, jagged spider legs from the waist down and a spiky shell on its back. Charcoal grey all over with pale pink joints. The right arm was long and serrated like a sword, its left like a construction crane's hook. The creature twitched like a house fly as its stalk eyes fixed on Sammy.

The greenbuck's eyes were wide, white all the way around its irises. It made a strangled bleating and tried to buck, but the crabman held firm.

Then the claw closed and the greenbuck's head came off like a rose bud snipped from the stem. Its lifeless body dropped to the ground and blood pumped from the stump of its neck.

Time seemed to slow as panic shorted Sammy's central nervous system. She was unable to move. She tried to lock on to the crabman's mindset. Sense what it was planning, but she couldn't. It was like no other living creature she'd encountered. No intention, no desire and no empathy, as if it were soulless, just a biological machine. That's what made them such formidable enemies. And why most magi couldn't fight them.

The crabman jerked towards her. And its head exploded.

Blue goop splattered the surrounding area and the crabman's body dropped to the floor revealing the magus stood behind it, the orb of his staff glowing white.

"Climb the mushrooms!" he shouted. "Get to the top of a large one, lie down and hope they don't find you. You can't outrun them."

Sammy ran. She leapt onto a small mushroom, then another, using each one as a stepping stone to take her higher. She zigzagged back and forth to pick out a path of mushroom stepping-stones that would lead to the forest ceiling. The higher she went, the wider the mushrooms became and the wider the distance between each one.

The chattering increased as Sammy neared the top.

She slowed up to check after the magus while she caught her breath. There were four crabmen circling him at a distance. One broke off from the others and rushed him.

"Keep going!" he yelled, as he blasted the crabman in the chest.

It screamed and fell as another leapt over, swinging its sword arm down at him. He caught it on his staff and batted it away.

The remaining two crabmen weren't attacking. Their heads jerked upwards in unison to look at Sammy.

Sammy turned. And ran.

She took a running jump to reach a larger, higher mushroom. Her foot landed close to the edge and she slipped. She landed on her stomach, just managing to hang on by digging her fingers into the fleshy surface of the hood, while her legs dangled over the edge.

The crabmen were coming, scaling the mushrooms, closing in. She heaved herself up, gained her feet and made a run for the next mushroom. She made the leap easily this time, but as she landed a crabman scuttled onto the mushroom she'd planned to jump to next. She doubled back as the second crabman crested the mushroom that had been behind her, closing off her escape route.

She was blocked on either side with no weapons. Why hadn't she stayed on the ground where there were plenty of stone bullets? Now she was trapped.

The first crabman leapt at her. Instinct took over and Sammy held out her arm, guiding all her energy at the crabman's shell breastplate. In her mind's eye, she saw it not as a mixture of compounds and tissues like the pig-dog had been, but as a solid structure of repeating molecules, like stone. She concentrated on that structure, slowing its velocity.

The crabman didn't make the jump and dropped down the gap to the forest floor.

The second crabman landed behind her and thrust its sword arm as she turned. Sammy locked on, slowing it, but not quick enough.

The tip entered her abdomen.

There was no pain at first. Instead, she experienced a detached curiosity like she was looking down at someone else's body. She watched the blood blossoming from the point of entry, felt the wetness of it soaking into her t-shirt.

The sword arm twitched, trying to force itself deeper, and she felt the first spasm of pain. She was going into shock. Her body was threatening to give out and already she could feel Perseopia drifting away.

Sammy held the sword arm steady with her mind, but she was losing it. She had to get back to the forest floor, collect some stone ammo. It was her only chance of beating these things. Her only chance of survival.

Digging deep and with tremendous effort, she staggered back, sliding off the spike and fell backwards. She landed on a canopy below, collapsing the mushroom, simultaneously breaking her fall and tilting her onto the mushroom below that. The impact brought her round, jolting her back into the moment. Her brain was scrambled but she found her feet and hopped down the last several mushrooms to the forest floor. Her lungs were screaming, she was bleeding, but she was still alive. She'd stopped the crabmen from killing her and now she had a readily available supply of ammo.

She was powerful. She could win this.

Stones flew to her wrists as she ran towards the flash of the magus's staff light. He might not be able to take on the crabmen, but she could.

Sammy rounded a dense clump of mushrooms to find the magus struggling against one of the crabmen. She let rip with a barrage of bullets. Several ricocheted off the creature's carapace but a few tore into the softer abdomen below the breast plate.

The beast slumped to the floor.

The magus turned to face her, laughed nervously. "How did you do that?"

Sammy didn't have time to answer.

The fallen crabman shifted, lashed out with its sword arm, swinging it through the magus's shins, severing his feet from his legs. He cried out as he flopped down, spraying blood from the stumps.

The horror shocked Sammy into inaction. She stared at the magus's ruined legs, the shortened ends where his feet had once been, dark red flesh and circular bone exposed. His blood emptying into the dirt, staining the soil.

The wounded crabman watched her from the floor. She was too far away to reach. It was waiting in the hope she strayed close enough to kill too, and that tipped her over the edge.

She loosed her remaining stones into the dying crabman's head, tearing it to pieces.

As its body flopped over and fell still, Sammy found herself surrounded on either side by the last two crabmen. The two that had chased her to the forest canopy.

They stood there twitching in their mechanical manner, mandibles chattering. Blood dripped from the sword arm of the one that had stabbed her.

She'd make them pay. Sammy plucked a stone from the ground and sent it hurtling at her attacker. The monster caught it in a heavy claw and crushed it.

The magus whimpered at her feet. He grasped for his staff, failed, then slumped and fell still.

Sammy had lit Hami's staff the last time she'd been in the realm. She could do it again.

The staff flew to her hand. She caught it as the first crabman lunged. The black orb appeared in her mind's eye, she saw the particles floating inside, accelerated them, and the forest lit up with burning white light.

Build power … aim … *release!*

The beam hit the crabman that had stabbed her, blasting it backwards through the forest, sending it through bushes and creepers, and leaving a trail of devastation behind it.

The other crabman went for her. She raised the staff as its sword arm came down. The blow knocked her to her knees and she nearly lost the staff. The crabman had a significant strength advantage, but she had abilities it didn't. By simultaneously slowing the crabman's limbs and accelerating her staff's movements, she batted away the creature's attacks and soon began to dominate the fight. A powerful jab to the crabman's stomach sent it sprawling backwards, giving her time to level the orb, power it up and explode the beast's head.

Now for the last one. The one that had dared to stab her. Sammy charged through the undergrowth following the trail of torn bushes and scored trunks. The crabman came limping towards her. Its chest black and smoking, dragging its sword arm, broken and useless.

Sammy powered up the staff and obliterated the offending arm. It spiralled away into the mushrooms.

"No more stabby stabby for you." She spoke the words quietly through gritted teeth, sounding strangely maniacal. She laughed. She couldn't believe a moment ago she was about to let this pathetic creature kill her.

The crabman made no move to attack so she took off its other arm with a second blast. The heavy claw hit the ground and slowly opened and closed where it lay, twitching and moving independently from its body. The crabman remained upright, displaying no visible signs of discomfort. It was then Sammy's mind cleared and she realised how she'd been torturing the animal to get a reaction. Her behaviour was disgusting. Regardless of what the crabman had done, treating a living creature this way was sick.

Sammy fired a searing column of lightning through the crabman's chest, splattering herself and the surrounding forest with blue bodily fluids.

She spat out the filthy gloop that had found its way into her mouth.

She'd glimpsed a darker side to herself. A primitive, savage trait that had revealed itself before receding back into her subconscious. How quickly she'd gone from killing small mammals to giant crabmen. At least she'd put this creature out of its misery, which was more than she'd done for the rabbit. Sammy's strength gave out then and she collapsed to the floor. Her hands shook and she dropped the staff. She closed her eyes and concentrated on not puking.

The young magus. She'd left him by himself. She snatched up the staff and ran back to where he lay.

Sammy double-checked all the crabmen were dead before attending to the guy. She'd seen enough movies where baddies had found the energy for one last attack. She wasn't ready to lose her own legs, too.

The magus was bleeding heavily. It looked like he'd attempted a tourniquet on one of his legs but had passed out before finishing. Sammy pulled the leather straps from his sandals while trying not to look too closely at his severed feet. She tied the laces around his stumps, staunching the blood, but his skin was already white. He'd lost a lot of blood.

She shook him. "Wake up!"

The magus grimaced and his eyes flickered.

"Can you hear me?"

He croaked a word that Sammy took to be yes.

"What do I do with you? Where do I take you?"

The guy groaned in response.

Then she remembered. "Connect to the magi network!" she yelled at him. "Contact the other magi and call them here."

"Can't …" he mumbled. "Can't concentrate. Can't …"

"What do I do with you?" Sammy screamed.

"Marzban. That way." He indicated with the barest movement of a finger. "Follow … river. All the way … Get help …" And he went limp.

If he didn't get medical aid soon, he'd bleed to death. She tried to focus her mind on moving him. She could move a rock, a crabman, but she already knew she wouldn't be able to shift a human. She gave it a go anyway. She concentrated but couldn't picture any molecules past the skin layer. What else could she try? She could wedge something solid underneath him and move the object, but she couldn't see anything large enough and time was running out. It made more sense for her to get help and bring them here rather than to slow herself down by dragging him with her. And he wasn't the only one that needed medical attention. Her t-shirt and the top of her leggings were soaked with her own blood. If she didn't make it to safety, then the magus had no hope.

Sammy pulled several weedy-looking bushes out of the ground and piled them up around him in an effort to conceal him from other threats. He didn't seem particularly well hidden after she'd finished, but it would have to do.

She took one last look at the guy. He was still breathing, barely, sucking in ragged breaths and shivering. She didn't even know his name. Blood was on her hands yet again. She'd killed the rabbit, and if her first instinct hadn't been to run, then this poor guy wouldn't have lost his legs. She was responsible for his life now. If something happened to him, it was because she'd failed.

She collected the staff and ran in the direction he'd pointed, and in what she hoped was the direction of someone that could help.

–ELEVEN–
HELP

The river had been easy to find. The Marzban, not so much.

Sammy walked miles and found no one. She tried her best to keep going, but as the excitement of the crabman skirmish dwindled, her adrenaline levels plummeted and fatigue threatened to crush her. The fast jog that her rescue mission had started off at quickly deteriorated into little more than a forward shuffling motion. Her leggings and t-shirt were now soaked with blood and her head was woozy.

Guilt overwhelmed her each time she rested, an occurrence that was becoming more frequent as her body edged closer to shut down and her legs seized up, making it a struggle each time she had to drag them on again.

Sammy slowed and dropped to the floor. She hunched over on knees and elbows and closed her eyes. They were only closed a moment, yet she felt herself jerk awake. She couldn't allow herself to sleep. Think of the magus. She leant on the staff and used every sliver of willpower she could muster to hoist herself back to her feet and start working her legs. The guy's life was in her hands, she couldn't let him die.

She shuffled on along the riverbank. The sky was darkening, she was bleeding profusely, but she kept moving. Time drifted by. It felt like days were elapsing. On and on she went, until finally an orange glow in the distance. The faintest glimmer of a different coloured light up ahead through the mushrooms, like the sun's first rays of a new dawn.

The light spurred her on. Then she tripped. Sammy pitched forward and for a moment everything slipped out of focus and she thought she'd pass out, yet she dug deep and staggered on to the next bend in the river.

The forest opened up into a clearing.

The river continued straight through the centre, passing a small two-storey stone tower and a barn next to it. The orange glow was coming from a downstairs window.

In the semi-darkness of the clearing, she could just make out the shapes of two enormous woolly rhino, tossing their heads and grunting. Karkadann, the beasts ridden by the Marzban guard. She'd made it.

"Hey!" she called out, then collapsed.

She rolled over and stared up at the undulating purple clouds above. She heard a door unbolt, far off voices. She tried to get up again but couldn't. Her body was spent.

The Marzban wouldn't find her in the dark. She needed to get their attention. She closed her eyes and raised the magus's staff, picturing the black orb in her head. The black particles were floating around inside. She watched them distractedly.

Concentrate. The particles moved quicker. She concentrated harder and they got faster still. Flying around inside the sphere, colliding and sparking. A flash of light. Then nothing, as she lost it and her mind drifted off.

She dreamt of nothing. Spiralling blackness and running footsteps.

Then light dazzled her.

"Are you okay?" someone asked.

Sammy opened her eyes to locate the speaker. It was dark and she could only make out a silhouette. A man in a turban. She closed her eyes again.

"Is she a magus?"

"It's a girl," a different guy said. "You don't get girl magi."

"There's a magus in the forest," Sammy mumbled, as she remembered her priorities. She tried to sit up but the pain in her stomach spiked. "We were attacked. You've got to save him. He's dying ..."

"Do you think she means Victa?" one said.

"Where is he?" said the other.

"Back up the river." Sammy did her best to point. "A long way along."

"I'll take a karkadann. We'll sniff him out."

"There were crabmen," Sammy said, then she passed out.

–TWELVE–
The Outpost

Sammy opened her eyes. The candlelit room she found herself in was a simple space with purely functional architecture. A circular ceiling hung above, to the sides whitewashed walls were adorned with children's drawings, crudely illustrated and tacked haphazardly to any available free space. They were the sort of drawings she'd have done for her mother at age five or six.

She tried to sit up. A flare of pain in her abdomen ended the attempt and she fell back against the pillow. She vaguely recalled being carried upstairs and placed in a bed, but that was about all she remembered.

Sammy searched out her injury under the covers with her fingers and found the wound had been dressed.

Where was everyone? She couldn't see any doors or stairs from her reclined position, but to the left was a row of neatly made beds.

Two down was the magus. And he was breathing. Thank god they'd found him. Sammy allowed her muscles to relax. She'd found help and saved his life. She'd done something right, at least. Then she recalled leaving him to the crabmen while she made her escape up the mushroom hoods and her positive mood dwindled. If she hadn't left him to fend for himself, he'd still have legs. In fact, if she hadn't returned to Perseopia at all, he wouldn't have been out in the forest looking for her. All consequences of activating the Midnight Emerald Dial again and returning. A chain reaction of events she'd set in motion because she'd been feeling unwanted and unfulfilled at home.

Now she'd returned and had powers, people would expect things of her. Magi had responsibilities. She might not be allowed to kick back and travel Perseopia with Mehrak. Would she have to get involved? Could they make her?

Sammy went to get up again and earned herself another stab of pain.

She lay back and watched the magus sleep, his chest slowly rising and falling under the sheets. He'd have to be on some pretty serious painkillers to sleep as peacefully as he was doing.

The mounds further down the bed, where his feet should've been poking up under the covers, were conspicuously absent. The poor guy would never walk again. Her fault. She stared up at the ceiling above. What would the life of a magus without legs look like? Would he still be useful? Or would he get dismissed from duty and become homeless?

In a way, he'd put himself in danger coming to collect her. She'd never asked him to. He was also the one that had told her to leave him and climb away up the mushrooms. Technically, his injuries weren't really her fault.

She lay there trying to rationalise what she'd done and what she probably should've done, but the dull ache in her abdomen was making it difficult to focus.

She was hungry. She hadn't eaten in at least twenty-four hours, maybe more. She was going to get up.

Sammy tossed the covers off the bed and half-rolled, half-slid her legs to the floor so she wouldn't have to sit up.

When she stood, the blood drained from her head and the resulting surge of dizziness almost sent her back to bed. She staggered to the windowsill and clung on, resting her forehead against the cool glass. Her body was a wreck. The muscles in her legs were trashed, and she'd gained an abundance of aches and bruises from the previous day.

She wiped the condensation away from where she'd steamed up the window. The glittering perimeter of mushroom forest stood distant from the barren clearing surrounding the tower. Everything else was dark and tinged purple.

A large black mass moved below the window. One of the karkadann. That meant at least one of the Marzban was still here.

She left the window and approached the bed with the magus in it.

He didn't stir when she put a hand to his brow. She tapped his forehead. No reaction. He was completely out of it. At least he was breathing peacefully. How long would that last? Soon he'd wake and remember he had no feet.

She was still watching him when the sweet, fatty aroma of frying animal found her. She inhaled deeply and her stomach rumbled. The pull of food was strong. The magus wasn't going anywhere, she'd check back on him once she'd eaten.

Sammy tucked the covers in around his neck and left him to sleep.

She found the Marzban downstairs in the kitchen. Both were wearing the purple uniforms and pink turbans she remembered as being their standard issue attire. The blue cloaks that completed their outfits hung on pegs by the front door, and on the floor their boots were lined up against the wall. One of them had his back to her, cooking at the stove, the second was at the kitchen table cupping a steaming mug in his hands. He looked up as Sammy reached the bottom of the stairs.

"You want grated roan shrub on yours?" asked the guy at the stove.

The one at the table cleared his throat to get the other's attention.

"Hi," Sammy said.

The Marzban at the table got up. He looked to be early thirties, had dark eyes, and possessed a neat black beard. "How are you feeling?"

"Better. Thank you," Sammy said.

"I'm Ramin. Our cook here is Calven."

Calven was younger, uncommonly good looking and could've easily been a model where Sammy came from. He had broad shoulders, a clean-shaven face, neat eyebrows, a square jaw and beautiful cheek bones. He smiled at her as he wiped his hands on the apron he wore over his uniform.

Sammy held up her hand in greeting and attempted a smile. "I'm Sammy," she said.

Ramin scooted around the table and pulled out a chair for her. "Sit. You'll pull your stitches. You shouldn't be up and walking yet."

"Thanks." Sammy grimaced as she eased herself down onto the chair. "You know, for saving me. And the magus."

"Victa?" Calven said. "It's horrific what happened to that poor boy."

"You knew him?"

"A little. He spent some time here with us before he went into the forest to find a new magus that had appeared on their network. I'm guessing that was you? And those dead crabmen were your doing?"

Sammy stared down at her lap.

"A female magus," Calven said. He shook his head. "When was the last time Perseopia had one of those? What were you doing in the forest, anyway?"

"I'm not sure. It was irresponsible of me …"

Ramin went to a chest by the sink and slid out a drawer. "You saved his life, you know?"

"Did I? If he hadn't come to find me, he'd still have legs."

Ramin gathered some cutlery and closed the drawer. "You couldn't have known that would happen." He began setting the table.

Calven returned to his cooking. The room fell silent, but for the sizzling of fatty meat.

"Do you think he'll survive?" Sammy asked after a time.

Ramin shrugged. "He's lost a lot of blood. But he's doing okay, considering. We've cleaned and bandaged him up, and he's on some pretty serious pain killers. All we can do now is wait. He's been unconscious since we got him back here."

"He woke briefly when I found him," Calven said.

"Really?" Sammy looked up. "Did he say anything?"

"He asked if you were alright. And said we had to take you to Honton Keep to Principal Hami Hootan."

"Hami?" That meant he'd survived the crabman battle outside the fire temple. "He's at Honton Keep?" Then it stood to reason that Mehrak was probably okay too, because Hami surely would've rescued him from the underground maze.

Ramin sat down opposite. "I presume Victa's original orders were to transport you safely to the magi garrison for training. I suppose now it'll have to be Hami taking you there."

Sammy experienced a flurry of nerves. She leant forward and rested her forehead on the table.

"Easy," Calven said, coming over and putting a hand on her shoulder. "You need to get your strength back. I'll have your breakfast ready soon. You'll feel better once you've eaten."

"I'm fine," Sammy said. "I'm just relieved you found me and you'll be taking me to Hami."

"You know him?"

How much should she tell these guys? "Sort of," she said. "I mean, we've met before."

"Was it him that taught you how to kill crabmen?" Calven asked.

"Calven!" Ramin said.

"What?" Calven held up his hands in mock offence. "I'm only asking. There were five of them. Five! I couldn't have taken on that many without a karkadann."

"How will I get to Honton Keep?" Sammy asked.

"We'll take you," Ramin said. "It's changeover day. We're heading there this afternoon."

"Time off," Calven said, rubbing his hands together.

"Some other Marzban are swapping places with you?" Sammy asked. "To guard this tower?"

"Not the tower." Ramin took a long draught from his mug. "The trade route into Honton Keep. It passes by here, crosses the river heading north. We protect the food shipments against crabmen and bandits. Our thirty day attachment is finally over and now it's the turn of three other guards to come down and take our place."

"But there are only two of you."

"Our third man left us a few days ago," Ramin said. "He found a boy in the forest and decided to leave his post early to take him to the Keep."

"A boy?"

"Yeah. With yellow hair like yours. Bizarre. I've never seen anyone with hair like it, then two of you arrive within days of each other. You haven't lost a brother, have you?"

Sammy shook her head. "No."

"Anyway, Borzin took him to the Keep—"

"Borzin?" Sammy recognised the name, but couldn't place it.

"Young guy. Only joined the Marzban this year."

Sammy remembered. The young guard that had been burnt to death by the tall thin figure. How could she forget? She'd been unsuccessfully suppressing memories of it since the day it'd happened. The screams, the burning flesh.

"You've gone awfully pale," Ramin said. "Perhaps you should lie down again. We can bring the food up to you."

"The guy that found the boy was called Borzin?" Sammy asked. "Like the guard that got burnt to death a couple of years ago?"

Calven turned from the stove and the two men looked at each other quizzically.

"You must be thinking of someone else," Ramin said at last. "Borzin only signed up this year."

It couldn't be the same guy, then. The Borzin she'd known had been young but he'd died over two years ago. Well before this other Borzin had started. Yet even hearing the name again set off an eerie feeling of not being in control. Of knowing there were dark creatures out there plotting and killing. Armies of crabmen searching for her.

Sammy was beginning to sweat. She needed to lie down. She made her excuses, shuffled back upstairs and climbed into bed.

–THIRTEEN–
Reliving the Past

Sammy wandered aimlessly along the riverbank by the tower. She felt loads better after having eaten. Ramin had washed her clothes too, and it was surprising how good clean cloth felt against her skin. A little stiff after being dried over the stove, but she couldn't exactly fault them for not having conditioner.

Occasionally, her stomach injury would catch her with piercing discomfort, but it didn't happen often, and was only when she was being careless or twisting at the waist. If she was sensible, she could more or less walk without it hurting much.

Victa had shown no sign of waking. He was still out when she'd last checked on him so she'd relieved him of his lightning staff. And now that she was alone, she had the perfect opportunity to practise using it.

When she'd walked sufficiently far from the tower and was convinced that no one was looking, she fired a shot into the river.

The explosion was incredible. Vaporised water filled the air and droplets rained down on her.

Sammy massaged her ringing ears. The Marzban must have heard that. She thought she saw a silhouette at the downstairs window, but no one came running.

She brushed the water off her shoulders before it soaked through the fabric and wiped her face with an arm.

She'd roamed quite a way from the tower. From where she stood, the squat building was little more than a marshmallow with windows. Calven and Ramin clearly trusted her not to run off. Because she could quite easily escape if she wanted to. Maybe they figured she wouldn't bother. They weren't keeping her prisoner. She could come and go as she pleased. And it wasn't like they had to worry about her safety. She had defeated a group of crabmen. Although, not all of them. Technically, Victa had managed to kill two himself. But she could've taken out all five, given the chance. Calven the hottie had been impressed with her prowess. Sammy spun the staff around her wrist, fumbled the catch and dropped it. She checked that no one was watching from the tower before gingerly bent down to pick it up.

At the edge of the forest, the sparkling golden spores of the giant mushrooms fell by her feet. She held out her palm to catch some, closed her eyes and felt the connection to everything. The connection she'd never felt to anything at home.

She really could walk away. No one was looking. She had Victa's lightning staff, clean clothes. Perseopia was her oyster.

She didn't know where she was going, though. And the thought of spending more time alone in the Fungi Forest brought beads of cold sweat to her forehead. As far as she could see, her choices were to leave now and track down Mehrak herself, or stay and get delivered to Hami.

Hami had been a jerk. But becoming a magus, the *only* female magus, would be awesome.

Living with Mehrak in Golden Egg Cottage would be pretty fantastic too. Travelling all over Perseopia with Louis, no responsibilities, and every day an adventure.

Distant hoof beats interrupted Sammy from her ruminations.

Three karkadann emerged from the forest not far from the outpost. They lumbered up to the building where their Marzban climbed off, tied up the animals and entered the tower.

Calven and Ramin's replacements from the Keep. They might have news from Hami. She'd see what they had to say for themselves and that might help her make a decision.

"Here she is," Calven said as she entered the room. "Guys, this is Sammy."

The three new Marzban were already at the table with drinks in their hands. Two women, one guy. They smiled and dipped their heads as Sammy entered the room. The women introduced themselves as Golnessa, a huge lady with hands like wicket keeper's gloves, and Moneer, a lean and severe-looking woman. The guy was Yaghoub. He looked kind of weedy, and if he were in a one-on-one fight with anyone else in the room, Sammy was pretty sure he'd get his ass handed to him.

Golnessa pulled out a chair for her with one of her giant hands, and Ramin slid a steaming mug of brown slop to her as she sat down. It slopped over the rim and onto the table, sending Sammy a whiff of chocolate.

Perseopian hot chocolate was one delicacy Sammy remembered from her previous trip to the realm. There had been maggots floating in it last time. She left the mug where it sat.

Ramin went back to the billycan on the stove to fetch a mug for himself. "Did any of you guys see Principal Hootan before you left?" he asked over his shoulder.

"Moneer did, didn't you?" Golnessa replied. Her voice was higher and girlier than Sammy would have expected from such a large woman.

"From a distance." Moneer's mouth barely moved when she spoke. "General Grotta took him around camp and introduced him to some of the guys. Even First Chief came out of his tent to meet him."

Ramin joined them at the table. "You'll probably get to meet him tomorrow, Calven. When you take Sammy to the Keep."

"I doubt it," Yaghoub said. "He's leaving tomorrow."

"Leaving?" Sammy asked. It was the first time she'd spoken and everyone turned in her direction. "Where's he going?"

Yaghoub leant in close, a conspiratorial smile on his lips. "No one knows. He's been talking with the Regent and has arranged a Marzban escort somewhere. A destination that he hasn't told anyone about."

A Marzban escort from Honton Keep? Sammy took a deep breath and steadied herself on the edge of the table. Something wasn't right here. A guard called Borzin, and a Marzban escort like the last time she'd been in Perseopia. She experienced a weird déjà-vu-like sensation that elevated her heartrate making her feel flustered and panicky.

"Why hasn't he told anyone?" Ramin asked.

"I don't know," Yaghoub said. "We left soon after we heard about it."

"Did you see Borzin?" Calven asked.

"No. I heard he'd come back, though. Leaving his outpost duties early." He shook his head and tutted.

"I heard he even got to meet Principal Hootan and his friends," Golnessa said, her eyes alight with excitement.

"Friends?" Sammy croaked, her mouth suddenly dry.

"Well, I don't know about friends. Travellers that he'd joined up with. They arrived together in a caravan on the back of a giant gastrosaur."

Panic locked Sammy to the table. She held on, forcing herself to breathe.

"What did the travellers look like?" she asked, her heart racing now.

"Just a man and a young girl. She had blond hair like yours," Moneer said, turning in her seat to face Sammy. "In fact, you look very much like her. Don't you think, Golnessa?"

Sammy's heart was accelerating towards a state of arrest and too much blood was forcing its way into her head.

"I don't know," Golnessa said. "I didn't get a good look."

"Yes, very similar," Moneer said, squinting at her. "She was a little younger maybe, but you could almost be sisters."

Sammy leapt up from her chair, knocking it over and pulling her stitches. She bolted for the door, threw it open, but collapsed against the frame. She clung on, struggling to make sense of everything. It couldn't be her with Mehrak. It had been two years!

Calven came and put a hand to her elbow. "Are you feeling alright?"

Sammy didn't reply. She stayed in the doorway, inhaling cool air from outside, trying to absorb energy from the forest. Her mental fog was clearing. The situation made no sense, but if she could get to Hami there was a chance he'd have answers.

She pushed herself back upright. Her bandage must've come away, as small patches of fresh blood spotted her top inside the stain rings of the washed, but not quite removed, blood patches. She allowed Calven to walk her back to the table, but shrugged him off when they got close.

She faced Yaghoub. "You said Hami is leaving Honton Keep tomorrow?"

The weedy-looking Marzban put down his mug and looked her in the eye. "I did," he said.

Sammy turned back to Calven. "Can we get to Honton Keep before then?"

"That depends when he's leaving. If we set off immediately, we might make it to the Keep by late morning tomorrow. But that would be travelling at one heck of a pace. It's more likely we'll arrive after lunch."

Sammy went to the sink to get some water. She pumped the handle until there was a steady stream, then she splashed some of it on her face.

No one said anything for a while. Sammy could feel their eyes on her. They probably thought she was crackers.

Eventually, Moneer spoke. "I still can't believe Borzin got away from outpost duties and met Principal Hootan," she said. "He's always in the right place at the right time, isn't he? I heard he and Leiss are babysitting those travellers. It's because of the girl. Everyone's saying she's special."

Sammy's heart stopped. She clung to the sink, fearful that her legs would give way and she'd fall if she let go. Moneer had all but confirmed her worst suspicions. There was no doubt in her mind that she'd returned to Perseopia at the same time as before. There were two of her here. Right now. She stared at the water swirling down the plughole and tried to work out how this had happened. She pumped the handle again and watched the water drain away. She couldn't rationalise the situation. But then, she supposed that wasn't important right now. What was important was what she did with the information.

The day they'd set off from Honton Keep with the Marzban escort, they'd left early. First thing in the morning. She remembered now. The market had been empty. Even the market traders hadn't set up for the day. She'd been tired, had hardly slept the night before … because it was the night after Borzin had been killed. Crippling grief racked her body. Tears filled her eyes.

Sammy pumped the handle again, blinked away the tears and stared into the draining water. She splashed her face so no one could see she was crying. What would they be thinking of her? Watching her pumping water and repeatedly washing her face.

Sammy took a deep breath and shakily took a place back at the table. Then she realised; if they were leaving the Keep tomorrow, then today was the day Borzin died. He might even be burning to death in front of her other self right now.

"Are you okay?" Ramin asked.

Sammy looked up. Wiped the tears from her cheeks. She'd never forget the events of that day. The nightmare carved into her mind's eye. Borzin's lidless eyes, bare ping pong balls with pupils, white and staring. The bloody and charred skin. And the smell. That was the worst part. The smell of burning meat had almost turned her veggie. She suppressed her gag as the fried animal she'd eaten for breakfast threatened to launch itself up and out of her throat.

"I'm sorry," she said. "I still don't feel so good."

What now? She couldn't tell them Hami was with her other self and that she'd travelled back in time. The whole situation was insane. Where was there to go from here? She needed more information.

"Has there been a crabman attack on the Keep?" she asked. "Like a huge invasion?"

Golnessa frowned at her. "When? Recently?"

Sammy thought about it. Borzin and Leiss had been protecting them the day Borzin died because Hami had been worried about her after the crabman invasion the night before. "I don't know. When did you set off from the Keep?"

"Yesterday."

"After you'd seen Hami and those travellers arrive?"

"Yeah, they arrived early that morning. We left after lunchtime. We hadn't gone far when Moneer caught us up so she could swap places with Eva. Eva was being recalled to the Keep to join the escort mission Hami had arranged with the Regent."

"Lucky me," Moneer said. "I get to spend thirty days away from my family."

So they'd missed the crabman attack. They'd seen her previous self arrive with Hami and Mehrak, then they'd left the Keep and the attack had happened that night. Today, her other self would've been to see Mehrak's friend and his angry wife, and Borzin would ... Sammy suppressed the thought. The important thing to remember was that if she left for Honton Keep now, she'd arrive tomorrow, after Hami and her other self had already gone. Which meant there was no point in going to Honton Keep.

Sammy rubbed her temples. The Marzban didn't know where the escort was going, but she did. The fire temple in the lava. If they set off for the temple now, they might get there in time to meet up with Hami and Mehrak. Her previous self would be there. That would be weird, but this was her best opportunity to catch up with everyone.

"Hami won't be at Honton Keep," she said. "We need to go to the temple. The one that's on a mountain in a ravine full of lava."

"What?" Calven asked.

"The temple on a mountain in the big flaming ravine."

"The Fifth Azaran?"

"Yes! That's it! That's the name of it."

"Why would we want to go there?"

"It's where the Marzban escort is taking Hami and the other girl."

"How could you possibly know that?" Yaghoub asked.

He was right. How did she know that? "Victa told me," she said, trying to sound convincing. "Before the crabmen attacked us."

"Really?" Calven asked. "Victa only just met you. And you didn't even know his name when we brought you here. Yaghoub here doesn't even know where they're going and he normally knows everything."

Yaghoub raised his eyebrows and shrugged in what Sammy guessed was a show of 'It's true, I know everything'.

"Are you calling me a liar?" Sammy said, mustering all her dignity. "You said Victa told you to take me to Hami. He told me that's where Hami was going before he passed out. We didn't have time for pleasantries. That's why I know it was on a mountain in the lava. I just forgot the name."

"You said he told you before the crabmen attacked."

"I think he repeated it after to make sure I went to the right place." Sammy managed a sob to make herself sound convincing. Which wasn't difficult, considering she was still dwelling on Borzin's death. "Everything happened so quickly. The crabmen. Victa's legs. It was traumatic, okay?"

Calven flushed. "I'm sorry. I didn't mean to imply ..."

Ramin came and put his arm around Sammy. "It's okay. We just want to be sure. You're positive that's where we need to go? The Fifth Azaran?"

Sammy rubbed the tears away with her forearm and looked Ramin in the eye. "I'm completely sure."

–FOURTEEN–
MOVING ON

The boy had been in Honton Keep two days already and was beginning to find his way around. He didn't like it though. The black alleyways, the refuse and stagnant air. He missed the mushroom forest with its fantastical animals and giant sparkling mushrooms. It was a magical place, and he desperately wanted to return. He wished he hadn't allowed Borzin to take him to the Keep, but apparently the forest was unsafe.

From the shadows he watched the man in the turban lead the yellow-haired girl away. After they'd gone, he slipped out of his hiding place between two stone-walled gardens. He opened his palm and a flame sprung to life in his hand. He concentrated and the fire grew to a golden, peach-sized ball.

The girl was the only other person he'd seen with yellow hair like his. And there was something about her. She was different from everyone else. Like he was. The man had called her Sammy.

He closed his hand, extinguishing the flame. Did she come from the same place he did? And had this land changed her like it had him? Could she make fire in her hands too?

A wave of heat consumed and wrapped itself around him.

"You're getting good at that," the cold metallic voice said. "I knew I was right to teach you."

The tall thin figure emerged from the darkness just outside the reach of the cul-de-sac's single lamppost.

"Who was that girl?" the boy asked.

"Someone you should steer clear of."

The boy said nothing, he stared after the girl, towards the entrance of the alley where he'd seen her go.

"I must leave you again," the thin figure said. "Keep practising your abilities, but reveal them to no one."

"Am I to remain here?"

"For the time being, yes. But I will return soon. Then you can come with me."

"What about my friend, Borzin? The man that found me. He said he'll adopt me as his own and I can live here with his family."

"He's gone." The thin person paused. "That girl with the yellow hair; she killed him. You'll have to find new lodgings and food from now on."

———

Sammy tentatively approached the karkadann while Calven and Ramin fetched the cart from the shed. It was about time she got over her apprehension towards the monster rhinos. They were pretty scary, what with their pointed canines and their ludicrous size, which consistently surprised Sammy every time she came into close proximity with them.

She held out her hand and patted the coarse hair on the animal's cheek while the two Marzban pulled the cart up behind it.

"Are you sure it wouldn't be more sensible to take you to Honton Keep?" Calven asked her as he began hitching the cart to the karkadann's harness. "The road to the Keep has Marzban outposts every hundred stadia. It's much safer. The trail to the Fifth Azaran isn't patrolled and is rarely used. I'm sure Hami would prefer you to be safe. He could collect you from the Keep on his way back from the fire temple."

"He might not be going back to the Keep," Sammy said as she stepped away from the karkadann. "Victa told you to take me to Hami. And the fire temple is where he's going to be. Victa also said there might be a purpose for me to fulfil there." Another lie, but

Calven seemed to be wavering. And then the icing on top of the cake. "I have magi abilities, after all. They need me."

"But I should be spending my time off with my brother and his niece," Calven said.

Ramin chuckled. "You can't stand in the way of the magi."

"Thanks for your input, Ramin." Calven stepped back from the cart to inspect the harness. "Shame *you* can't take her."

"A damn shame," Ramin said. "Regrettably, I have to report back to my unit. And you're the one with six days leave."

"Six days that I'll lose travelling to the Fifth Azaran and back. And, by the way, you don't sound particularly regretful."

"You'll be helping the magi," Sammy said. "You'll get your days back. Hami will square it with your boss. Trust me."

Calven shrugged but didn't reply.

Moneer and Golnessa brought Victa out on a stretcher. They carried him over to the back of the cart and carefully slid him in.

"You'll have to take it easy," Golnessa said. "He isn't strapped down. We'll pack your provisions around him, but take it slow and remember to keep him drugged up on Opiroot leaf. There's a small bushel in this satchel." She placed it at the top of the cart near Victa's head.

"But not too slow, because we're in a rush," Sammy said.

"And why is that?" Calven asked.

"Because … Hami might not stay at the temple long. He might be on his way somewhere else after."

Calven raised his eyebrows like he wasn't convinced. "If they need you for a special magi purpose, I'm sure they'll wait."

"And if they don't, you'll be taking me and Victa back to the Keep. And you'll have wasted all six days of your holiday because Hami won't be able to sort your time off with your boss."

Calven rolled his eyes. "Grab the tents, Ramin," he said. "Let's get this over with."

–FIFTEEN–
The Event

Perseopia's First Minister to the high council didn't appreciate being kept waiting.

Baxter watched him pace from the safety of his high-backed armchair while he clutched a handful of papyrus sheets and a quill to his chest like a shield. The minister walked up and down the council chambers, dragging his gown back and forth over the marble floor, stopping occasionally to stare pointedly at the chronometer on the wall.

The late night budget meetings were taking a toll on the honourable gentleman. Now the Grand Master was making demands of his time too. The last four years had aged the minister considerably. He'd lost weight, hair, he'd grown jowls and his eyes were dark and sunken. Still he kept going, toiling for the public, unappreciated as he was. He was a great man, intelligent and fair, not prone to letting his emotions control his mood. He wasn't angry now. More frustrated than anything else. It was already too late to go home and see his children before bed. Waiting around for the Grand Master was just one more frustration in a long line of irritations. He wanted to move past the meeting and on to making provisions for the consequences.

A knock at the door.

The minister composed himself, then called out, "Enter."

The Grand Master moved slowly into the room, clicking the door shut behind him. He came closer, stopped and bowed.

"You have news of some importance, Master Aegis?" the minister asked. Straight to the point. He hadn't offered a seat, either. He was making sure the meeting remained brief.

"I do," Aegis replied. "And thank you for agreeing to meet with me, Minister."

"Not a problem, Master. I know you wouldn't request my time unless necessary."

"To the point," the Grand Master said. "As you know, I came here to give you an update on what we've discovered in Aratta."

"Principal Hootan has news from the old capital?"

"He does. About a third location that kidnap victims are being taken to."

"The mountains. Yes. Baxter informed me of it. Have we discovered why they're being taken there?"

"We have a pretty good idea. Order men dressed in furs have been abducting people with academic or scientific backgrounds. We believe they're being taken to the mountains so they can work on a portal that Lord VorMask is building there."

"A portal?"

"We're not sure how it's been achieved, or even if it works, but you can trust that it will be thoroughly investigated." The Grand Master paused. "May I sit?"

The minister's jaw clenched, but he nodded and perched himself on the corner of his desk.

The Grand Master sat in a chair opposite Baxter. "The portal was not why I came to talk to you tonight. I have … bigger news." He waited before going on.

The gravitas was not lost on Baxter. He found himself leaning forward in his seat.

The Prime Minister shifted on the edge of his desk. The Grand Master wanted to make sure he had their attention. This was going to be big. Something major. Baxter had never seen him act like this before. Perseopia was changing. Even in the capital, way out in the Khushk plains, he could see it. The lower yields of food, the fear in the traders eyes when they returned from the Fungi Forest. Was the Grand Master going to impart information that would explain what was happening to the realm?

"An event has occurred since Hami left Aratta. And we're trying to understand the significance of it." The Grand Master edged forward in his seat, maintaining eye contact with the minister. "A visitor from the Mother World has entered Perseopia."

The minister said nothing. He got up, walked around his desk and sat down. "When?" he asked.

"About four days ago."

"Why were we not told?"

"We felt a fluctuation in the fabric of our realm, but we didn't know what it was. We speculated that it was someone arriving, but we didn't know who it was or where they came from."

"And you know now?"

"Principal Hootan found her. A young girl with yellow hair, wandering the Fungi Forest alone."

The minister crossed his arms and waited for Aegis to go on.

"Lord VorMask knew she was coming before she arrived."

"What does that mean?"

"It means he knows more than we do. And the implications are significant."

"Because of this girl?"

"They're the actions of a desperate creature. He believes she'll bring his reign to an end. Perhaps even bring about his death. And he's scared enough that he's been constructing the black column, building a portal and amassing an army of crabman for the past thirty years in preparation for this event."

The minister remained quiet for a time, seemingly deep in thought.

"Where is Hami taking the girl?" he said after a time.

The Grand Master broke eye contact and stared into his hands. "He was bringing her here." He took a deep breath. "But then he dropped off the network and I haven't heard from him since."

–SIXTEEN–
Karkadann and Cart

Sammy lay in the back of the cart next to Victa. She stared up at the narrow strip of purple sky in between the glowing mushroom undersides. They'd been bumping along the pothole-ridden forest track for almost two days now and it'd been near impossible to sleep. Calven had wanted to keep off the well-travelled paths, as crabmen were known to use them, but that meant they'd wasted the first afternoon fighting their way through thick vegetation and creepers. They'd made such little progress that eventually Sammy had convinced Calven to divert back onto the path. She reasoned that Harsoot, Calven's karkadann, could take on most crabmen they came across, and she'd pick off the stragglers with Victa's lightning staff. She'd saved a fully-fledged magus from multiple crabmen at once, after all. She could handle it.

Calven had murmured several complaints under his breath but ultimately it had worked.

Yet even the forest path was too slow. Sammy recalled the journey to the fire temple with the thirty Marzban as being a lot faster, and they'd been travelling through thick forest.

They camped in the tents the first night, but not the second. They'd lost too much time already. From that point onwards, they ate and slept on the go. Sammy even convinced Calven to let her have a go riding Harsoot, so he could take a shift sleeping in the cart. It turned out that it wasn't so hard to steer a karkadann. The animal pretty much led itself. All she had to do was sit in the saddle and tug the reins every so often when it veered off the path. It was quite fun, actually. Like riding a giant, hairy horse ... that had a six-foot horn and ate flesh instead of hay. Thankfully, Calven had uncoupled it from the cart when he'd taken it to feed. Sammy hadn't had to watch it attack or eat the pig-dog it caught. But she'd heard it. The cold, murderous look in its eyes along with the blood dripping from its chin hair had chilled her enough that she wasn't going to take her tenuous relationship with the animal for granted.

Calven pulled the beast to a stop.

Sammy sat up and twisted round in the cart, careful not to pull her stitches. "What's the hold up?"

Calven had his compass out and was consulting a map. "I think we've veered south," he said. "Do you think you might've taken a right-hand fork while I was sleeping?"

"I don't know. It's hard enough to figure out what's path and what's a gap in the mushrooms. Isn't there a better track we could've taken?"

"There was, and if you'd paid attention to where you were going we'd be on it. That big hill we passed several stadia ago. That was supposed to be on our right."

"So what does that mean? Do we go back?"

"No, we can carry on this way. It just means we're going to be south of where we should be when we exit the forest. We'll have to travel north up the Cataclysm several stadia."

"Are we going to make the fire temple before Hami?"

"It depends how fast they're going. We had a half day lead on them."

"They were going pretty fast."

"*Were* going pretty fast?"

"You know what I mean. Victa made it sound pretty urgent, whatever it is they need me for." Sammy smiled innocently. "Just trust me. They'll be there."

Calven sighed audibly. "We're getting close to the edge of the forest. I guess we'll find out how fast they *were* soon enough."

–SEVENTEEN–
Catching Up with the Past

Hami ran to the edge of the Cataclysm where the bridge had been. Part of it remained, jutting out from the land like a huge diving board.

He slowed.

A black arm shot up at the far edge of the rocky protrusion, scrabbling for purchase. It was followed by a second and then a third arm.

Ramaask hauled his head and chest above the ridge. Steam billowed from his body. His cloak had been incinerated and his armour had melted to his body, still glowing orange and red in places. He pulled his helmet off with his thin rear arm and threw it aside, exposing his bald, smouldering head.

"You've made a grave mistake," he said with a wheeze.

"It is you who made the mistake," Hami said, lowering his staff to point it directly at him, "when you attacked my partner."

Ramaask managed a strained chuckle. He pulled the rest of himself up and onto the end of the bridge. He remained on all fours, his broad chest rising and falling. "You can't kill me," he said.

"I can't," Hami replied. "But the Cataclysm can." And he lowered the staff further to point at the ground between them.

"No!" Ramaask yelled.

Lightning slammed into the rock, disintegrating the last of the bridge and sending Ramaask careening backwards.

"You need me!" he screamed as he fell.

Hami watched him fall and catch fire. He continued watching well after he'd disappeared.

When he could no longer stare into the light, he turned from the Cataclysm to see the last of the crabmen fleeing into the forest.

Ramaask had finally gone.

Hami re-joined the magi network. It was the first time he'd done so in days. He took a moment to communicate to the Grand Master, told him where he was and what had happened to Ramaask. Then he disconnected before the argument started. His dressing down could wait for another day. He was dead on his feet. He wanted to collapse where he stood, to tuck himself into a ball and sleep.

But he couldn't rest yet.

The earthquake hadn't stopped. If anything, the tremors were building. He went to the edge of the Cataclysm but could see nothing in the harsh light. No pterodactyls, no slaves. Most of them would be dead.

He would need to find a way over to the fire temple. Near impossible, now that the bridge had gone. The bridge had spanned a gap of several stadia, and though the mountain widened towards the base, the distance was still too great to cross. Even if he could descend the side of the Cataclysm to the point where the distance was shortest, he'd never survive the temperature down there.

Hami's stomach was churning again. He let its contents force its way up and onto the ground. He wiped his mouth and kicked dirt onto the black, oil-like vomit.

He'd almost got used to the illness. It had become a routine. Puke, wipe mouth, bury the mess. He wasn't sure where the endless vomit was coming from. He'd snacked intermittently since leaving the old capital, but he hadn't eaten properly in days, he couldn't keep anything substantial down, and had been running on adrenaline only. He wasn't sure how long a person could go without proper food, but it felt like he was close to finding out.

The earthquake raged on. Vibrations came up through the ground, increasing in intensity. Hami moved away from the edge, spread his legs and braced himself with his staff as a crutch. The rumbling was building to a crescendo, to an almighty climax.

The shockwave hit his chest, knocking him back a few paces, as it raced away across the plain behind him. He staggered, managing to remain upright as plumes of fire and lava flew into the sky.

Then the mountain shifted. And it was falling, coming towards him.

Hami ran. He cleared almost half a stadion before it hit the plain.

The collision took the ground from under him and he landed hard.

He rolled onto his back but remained where he lay, trying to suck air back into his lungs.

When he was able to breathe again, he eased himself up and coerced his body back into a standing position.

The mountain had sheared off its base and fallen forward, coming to rest up against the Cataclysm wall, where Hami had been standing moments before. Where the bridge had been.

He walked back towards it, approaching the edge and the Fifth Azaran Fire Temple, now significantly closer than it had been and leaning towards him at a shallow angle.

It wasn't far down to the mountaintop below, perhaps a single storey, and although the temple was on the far side of the plateau, it was still close enough that he could see lights on through the first floor windows.

Sammy had broken the column just like Behnam said she would. But how? She couldn't have known the Temple of Paths would be in there. Mehrak wouldn't have known either. Could they have learned it from Esther's sister? He'd interrogated her hard and she hadn't let anything slip. What about Esther herself? She'd been a deserter. It wasn't beyond the realms of possibility that she'd given their secrets away too.

He sensed a fluctuation. A burst of energy deep in the mountain. Was that Sammy leaving? He closed his eyes and reached out to her. He couldn't feel her, but that didn't mean she'd gone. There was a considerable amount of rock between them that could be blocking him.

She couldn't have left Perseopia. She'd crossed the seal, that part was obvious, but she wouldn't know how to use the Temple of Paths. Not even the magi knew which portal pearl took you to the Mother World.

Except Esther had known, apparently.

Sammy had only met the woman briefly at the Mother World market. There wouldn't have been time for Esther to fully describe how to find the portal pearl and escape the realm. No. He was jumping to conclusions. Sammy didn't know how to return. She'd been in tears when he'd told her she was stuck here. She didn't know anything and that meant she was still here. She had to be.

The rumbling stopped.

It took a moment for Hami to acclimatise to the quiet. An eerie stillness asserted itself, a deficit of movement and noise filling the vacuum that the battle and seismic activity had left in its wake.

As Hami's ears adjusted, he heard whispering. Hundreds of voices, hissing in earnest. He turned on the spot, but saw no one. Had the whispering started before or after the earthquake had ended? He couldn't tell. And where was it coming from?

Then, faint hoof beats from the plain. Two Marzban on karkadann were emerging from the darkness. Narok and Eva. The relief at seeing them alive was overwhelming and it took all Hami's resolve not to break down and cry in front of them. He smiled.

Blood had soaked Narok's turban. It was down the side of his face, neck, and in his beard, but he returned a weary smile. Eva was uninjured but looked dishevelled, an errant twirl of hair dangling out from under her turban. "What's that noise?" she asked.

Hami shook his head.

"The crabmen have fled into the forest," Narok said. "Where's Ramaask?"

"At the bottom of the Cataclysm," Hami answered.

Eva's eyes widened. "You defeated him?"

Hami shrugged. Could it really be over? He didn't dare hope.

He edged closer to the precipice.

A black vapour had begun drifting up out of the Cataclysm on one side of the mountain. A thin line of smoke as if something was burning below. It became more substantial as it snaked up out of the light, a thick heavy smoke, almost liquid, an upside-down waterfall flowing up into the clouds. Globs of it were sluicing off the main column as it rose, dropping back into the crevasse or slopping onto the mountain. The magenta clouds were darkening where the liquid smoke reached cloud level. The whispering was getting louder.

A separate tendril of the substance broke off the main column and arched over onto the mountaintop, pooling outside the fire temple, forming a growing black mass.

Smaller wisps spiralled out towards Hami. He dodged as they continued past, disappearing into the darkness of the plain.

"What is that?" Narok asked.

Hami had no answer to give. This was all new, unprecedented.

The column of smoke broke off from the Cataclysm at the bottom and continued up into the sky. As the last of it disappeared, the clouds flushed black, in a single ripple movement starting at the point of entry.

The sky had gone. No swirling smog, no movement, just a dark, yawning void.

Narok and Eva had gone pale in the light of the Cataclysm, now the only significant light source, bar the faint glow coming from the Fungi Forest way off behind them. What must be going through their heads?

Hami turned back to the Cataclysm, to the black mass of liquid smoke that had gathered outside the Fifth Azaran. It was coalescing, forming something in the middle. Tentacles of liquid slithered in and around each other, coiling over and under like enormous snakes. A mass grew in the centre, solid yet liquid and gaseous at the same time. Hami couldn't make out what it was, but it looked organic. It looked alive. He realised now that it was also the source of the whispering.

The karkadann backed up. Hami moved away from the edge too, while keeping his eyes on the blob. He glanced over his shoulder to check on Narok and Eva.

Both were wide eyed and trembling.

Narok raised a finger, pointing past Hami.

Hami sensed the movement late and spun around, lowering his staff.

A Marzban guard staggered out of the darkness. A lone survivor from the battlefield, but something wrong with him. It took a moment for Hami to figure out what that something was. Then he realised, and panic threatened to reduce him to a quivering heap. He couldn't feel the man's life force. An impossibility. A dead person didn't just get up and walk off the battlefield.

The Marzban's skin had taken on a greyish aspect and his eyes stared motionlessly ahead as he walked. Hami recognised the man's face but didn't know him well enough to know his name. He reached out to touch him, to grab him by the arm and shake him, but he stayed his hand. The man's arm was missing, severed below the shoulder. Most of the blood had clotted but some still oozed from the wound, soaking the clothes down the side of his body.

The guard kept walking, approaching the Cataclysm. When he reached the edge, he stepped off.

There was a crunch as he hit the mountaintop below. The sound of bones breaking.

Hami moved back to the edge to take a look, his heart rising in his throat.

The fall had done little to stop the man. He was still going, albeit slower, crawling one-armed and one-legged, dragging a freshly broken ankle behind him, the foot of which pointed out at an ugly angle.

He was heading towards the roiling mass of liquid smoke.

This was the thing Behnam had warned him about when he'd communicated across the network. The worst case scenario.

Panic made him impotent. He didn't know what to do. Had no order to give Narok and Eva. They'd know the individual. He'd be a colleague, a friend maybe. He might even be a relative. Hami should tell them something, comfort them or lead them away. He'd put them through enough. He looked to them now, to try and reassure them, but they weren't looking at him. They were staring out across the plain.

Other bodies were emerging from the darkness, silhouetted by the light of the Fungi Forest. Hundreds of shadowy figures shuffling towards them.

Crabmen.

Hami tensed, but could tell the creatures weren't as they had been in life. They were like the Marzban. Changed. Their eyes were as lifeless as ever, yet their grey bodies had darkened further to an almost black with red joints. They moved towards him in their stilted, jerky fashion, but it was slower, almost lethargic. There were darkened karkadann among them. A lava pterodactyl too, dragging itself across the plain on burnt wings. The crabmen outnumbered the Marzban and the other creatures interspersed between them but all walked together heading towards the Cataclysm. They shuffled in between Narok and Eva's trembling karkadann, past Hami, stepping around him, yet at the same time strangely unaware of his existence, not making eye contact. They all walked up to the Cataclysm and in turn toppled over the edge to the mountaintop below.

The first guard had gone now, consumed by the black mass. The crabmen followed him in. Corded tentacles of liquid smoke slithered in and out of each other, growing as more bodies entered.

112

The bodies kept coming, dropping onto the mountaintop below, then crawling or dragging themselves onward. Hami jumped back as a karkadann pitched itself over, narrowly missing taking him with it as the edge collapsed, sending an avalanche of rubble down the slope.

Humans and animals alike were entering the black mass, becoming consumed by it. The oily liquid tugged at their bodies, tearing limbs apart, pulling off skin and re-grafting it together. Ripping, moaning and crying accompanied the whispering voices.

Then they stopped.

The few that had already fallen to the mountaintop below kept going, heading towards the heaving mass of smoke, shell, flesh and fur. Those that hadn't made it to the Cataclysm edge remained where they stood. Stationary, expressionless and unseeing.

"We should get out of here," Narok said.

His voice seemed strangely out of place in the stillness. Hami waited, he'd caused this, he was going to see what happened next, record it for the brotherhood and commit it to memory. He could do that for them, at least.

The tentacles of liquid smoke continued to slither over and around each other inside the oily black mass, breaking bones and tearing flesh. The bodies whimpered and cried as the mass grew. Then it was morphing, forming a shape and standing up.

Two glowing red eyes opened near the top.

Hami had seen enough. "Okay. Let's go," he said as he ran to Narok's karkadann, Indomit. He leapt onto its back, landing behind the general, and they were off.

They fled towards the Fungi Forest with Eva in pursuit, galloping through the trance-like crowds of crabmen, knocking them down and crunching them underfoot. The creatures made no protest as their bodies were destroyed, didn't flinch from the karkadanns' paths as Narok and Eva ploughed through them.

They tried to avoid the bodies of other Marzban where they could, but in the darkness they were near impossible to spot in time. Like the crabmen, they stood their ground as their fragile bodies were pulverised by the weight of the giant mammals.

The karkadann soon left the last of the resurrected bodies and emerged into the centre of the plain where the battle had taken place. There were no dead remaining, only miscellaneous body parts.

They kept going, heading for the Fungi Forest. Fear driving them onward.

It wasn't until they reached mushroom cover that Hami remembered that Sammy and Mehrak were still inside the fire temple.

−EIGHTEEN−
The Reunion

Hami was struggling to rationalise what he'd seen. What he'd done. The series of events he'd set in motion by his actions.

He'd done it to save Behnam. To absolve himself of guilt for killing his best friend's sister. To put one small thing right in this broken and corrupt realm. If another magus had been captured, would he have done anything different? If his judgement hadn't been impaired? It was true that he'd been spurred on by the notion of saving his friend, but the objective had always been to lure Ramaask out of Aratta. To destroy him and save Perseopia. Hadn't it? It wasn't an entirely selfish plan. Behnam was a convenient excuse to rush the objective through to completion. Not that it would've carried weight with the brotherhood. Given the opportunity, they'd have dithered, considered options, and then deemed the plan too risky.

He should try to put it behind him. It was done now, and he'd have to live with the consequences. All that mattered is where he went from here.

The Temple of Paths thing with Sammy, that was unexpected. He still couldn't get his head around the fact that she'd found it. It was such an unlikely scenario. And yet she'd used it, somehow. He was pretty certain about that now. He wasn't convinced before, but he'd had time to reflect on it and there was no other explanation for the sensation he'd felt.

He wondered where she was now. If she'd chosen the right portal pearl.

115

He desperately wanted to see her again and his thoughts turned bitter at the prospect that she'd truly gone.

Mehrak had helped her. That pathetic little peasant had sent her back to the Mother World and Hami would get the blame for it. Mehrak could remain in the bowels of the mountain for all he cared. This was his fault. Let him find his own way out. Or not. He wasn't Hami's problem anymore.

The brotherhood would see this mess as his fault. He'd lost the girl and initiated the apocalypse. His career as a magus was over.

That wouldn't stop him rescuing Behnam, though. But first he'd return to the Fifth Azaran to observe the corpse monster. He still had a responsibility to the brotherhood. The magi had to know the extent of the disaster he'd caused if they were to have any chance of combatting it, with or without his help. He'd transmit whatever information he could, then he'd leave the Cataclysm and the network before they arrived and arrested him. He'd have to go into hiding. Perhaps find a small village near the boundary to live out the rest of his life in obscurity.

Hami walked to the edge of the Fungi Forest.

The Marzban Sasan was leaning against a mushroom, watching the fire temple with a telescope. He was one of two other surviving Marzban they'd found on the way back to the forest. A quiet, straight-faced individual with an impressive moustache. The other, Rougetta, was a tall, gangly woman. She was currently at the top of a high mushroom, using it as a vantage point, while Narok and Eva swept the surrounding forest for straggling crabmen.

Both Marzban had been waiting at the edge of the forest with Harz and one of his men, Jokram. They'd given chase to the fleeing crabmen, followed them to the forest, then had held back for reinforcements. Hami, Narok and Eva were the only ones that had turned up. Unsurprising, considering what they'd been up against.

Hami held his hand out for Sasan's telescope. The guard handed it over.

The congregation of dead creatures was too far away to see properly. They'd need to get closer. As much as he wanted to leave the area before the magi reinforcements got there, he couldn't allow them to run into this debacle without at least letting them know what they were up against.

Narok and Eva returned from their recce and gave the all clear.

At least the living crabmen had gone.

Hami gave the nod and leapt onto Indomit, landing behind Narok. Harz boarded his chariot with Jokram. Eva climbed onto her karkadann, and Sasan and Rougetta climbed onto a third riderless karkadann they'd found near the edge of the forest.

They set off slowly across the plain. Hami planned on getting close enough that they'd have a clear view with the aid of the telescope, but plenty far enough that they wouldn't be seen in the darkness of the plain.

As they neared their position, a flurry of lava pterodactyls erupted from the Cataclysm. A swirling vortex of dark wings spiralling up into the air. They took to the skies, circling around the assembled dead.

Hami snatched up the telescope and leapt from Indomit. He landed into a forward roll, then up and back onto his feet. He got the telescope to his eye in time to see the swirling mass of flesh and gaseous liquid crest the ridge of the plain. Smoke unfurled from it, rushing along the ground through the legs of the congregated bodies. Then the indistinct shape raised itself up on two legs, turned to its right and lumbered north along the Cataclysm edge, dragging itself forward.

The army of dead creatures turned to their left in unison, falling in alongside the undulating core of liquid darkness that contained the corpse monster. The pterodactyls swarmed above in a whirlwind of leathery wings.

Hami set off towards the Fifth Azaran at a slow jog. The others followed.

By the time they reached the Cataclysm, the army of dead creatures had moved on.

Hami surveyed the area. It was much as it had been after the mountain had first fallen, with nothing more to be seen.

"The magi will be here soon," he said. "I'm going to meet them. Narok, can I take Indomit?"

Narok paused. "Can't you tell them whatever you need to over the magi network?"

"I want to talk to them in person. I'm worried about a breach in the network," he lied.

"But …" Narok was stalling. He didn't want to hand over Indomit's reins. "Shouldn't we rescue Sammy and Mehrak first? Surely that's more important."

Narok was right. He wouldn't have questioned Hami if he'd asked for one of the other karkadann. He should've known how protective Narok was over Indomit. Now if he made excuses about leaving Sammy and Mehrak, they'd know something was up. Still, the magi wouldn't be here for a while. He'd have to be quick, but this was okay. It was good, in fact. He could put his mind to rest that Sammy had truly gone and he'd be doing the decent thing by rescuing Mehrak. Not that the guy deserved it, but it was one less death on his conscious. Then he'd go. There was time.

The smoke demon had pulled down a large quantity of earth and rock when it had dragged itself up over the ridge, but Hami would still need to shift more to make a decent ramp to get Louis and Golden Egg Cottage out.

Hami stood there, distracted by what he'd done and the emptiness of what lay ahead. He was so tired. His efforts may have brought about the end of the realm, but all he wanted to do was lie down and sleep. Then a sensation came to him. Faint. The merest flutter of feeling, barely a thought.

Sammy. She was still here! Could she still be down inside the mountain?

Narok interrupted him then. "Another one of our guys made it. Look!" He pointed.

A Marzban riding a karkadann was approaching from the south, following the edge of the Cataclysm towards them. Hami didn't care. He needed to reach Sammy.

"Wait," Narok said. "It's … Calven?"

Something in Narok's tone stopped Hami and he turned to watch the Marzban draw close.

The guard wore the standard issue purple uniform and pink turban, not the navy combat fatigues worn by the Marzban that Hami had brought with him, and his karkadann was pulling a cart.

Hami gasped as he recognised the sensation of two people he knew. Neither of them should be at this location right now. His heart raced and a cool sweat beaded his forehead. He staggered towards the karkadann and cart. It couldn't be.

"Calven?" Narok said as the Marzban pulled to a stop. "What are you doing here?"

Then Sammy climbed out of the cart.

–NINETEEN–
RETURN TO THE TEMPLE

Hami was just as she remembered him. Not a day older than when she'd left. The dark, tangled hair to his shoulders, the lean corded arms and intense stare. A young man's face with eyes that had seen too many terrible things. But there was hope there too, an intensity that hadn't been diminished.

He faltered when he saw her. The hope vanished and he looked as if his world had come crashing down around him. The drop of his shoulders, the air leaving his lungs. Everything he knew was wrong and his brain would be desperately trying to catch up with what his eyes were showing him.

Around him, only four Marzban remained sat atop three of the thirty karkadann they'd left Honton Keep with. Along with Dirty Santa on his chariot. She'd forgotten about him. He and one other member of his gang had survived. Everyone else that had been with them, along with all the crabmen, had gone. Dead, she presumed, although bizarrely there were no bodies present.

Calven cleared his throat. "General Grotta? Sir?" His voice cracked. "The magus told me to bring her to Hami ..."

Narok was staring at her. "I don't understand," he said to no one in particular, ignoring Calven's question. "She went into the Fire Temple."

Hami's eyes didn't leave hers for a moment. "You're ... older."

"I'm two years older," she said. She walked towards the giant temple on the fallen mountain. The shimmering golden dome, the minarets. "I was inside the Temple of Paths when this happened," she said. "I remember the tremors, the ground tilting. All the pearls fell off the shelf when the mountain slammed to a stop." She gazed up past the dome into the darkness above. "Did the sky go black when Ramaask died? I thought it would've gotten lighter."

"You shouldn't have come back," Hami said.

"Did you actually kill him?"

"What are you doing here?"

"I thought you'd be pleased to see me. Wasn't I supposed to be trained as a magus?"

Hami approached her, he leaned in close and took her arm. "How did Mehrak figure out how to get you into the secret part of the temple?"

Sammy pulled away from him. "He didn't figure it out. I did. And you can take your hands off me! I'm not the same little girl you could intimidate last time."

Hami's hand shot back like he'd been burned. "I ... didn't—"

"You did and you should feel bad for it. You used me and you're upset I figured out how to escape."

Hami shook his head. "I never meant—"

"Yet despite how badly you treated me last time, I've done you a solid."

"Sammy, I ... You've done me a what?"

"I saved your pal, Victa," she said. "I even brought him here to you."

"Victa ..."

"The magus," she said. "He's in the cart."

Hami walked around to the back of the cart. His face remained passive but he was breathing hard. He steadied himself on a corner like he was about to collapse.

"We patched him up as best as we could," Calven said. "But he's in a lot of pain. Sammy said we should bring him to you."

Hami nodded. "You did right." He moved further round to Victa's head and held his hand over the young magus's forehead. When he finally removed his arm and turned to Sammy, he'd gone pale.

121

"You were the recruit Victa went to pick up?" he said. "You appeared on the network …"

"Yeah, I heard an enrolment whisper, apparently. Victa said that's why he came to find me in the forest. But then we got attacked by crabmen and he got his legs chopped off before I could save him."

"*You* saved him?"

"Well. He got a couple of the crabmen, I suppose. I killed the rest. Then I went to get help and found a Marzban outpost. Calven went back to collect Victa, brought him to the outpost and patched him up. I persuaded him to bring us both here. He's actually supposed to be on leave. I told him you'd reimburse him for his holiday. So he gets the time back. That's okay with you isn't it, Narok? I mean, General?"

The question seemed to catch Narok by surprise. "Yes, I'm sure we can work something out."

Sammy winked to Calven to let him know matters were sorted.

"How did you know to come here?" Hami asked.

"I figured out the portal pearls, didn't I? I'm not as stupid as I look."

"I never said you were—"

Sammy waved his apology away. "One of the Marzban that swapped over with Calven at the outpost said you were at Honton Keep with a yellow-haired girl, a man and a gastrosaur. It wasn't too hard to figure out I'd come back to the same moment I'd been here before. Although it took me a while to get my head around it."

Hami's eyes widened. "That's why there were no other ripples in the barrier around Perseopia, and why it was larger than normal. You and your previous self arrived at exactly the same time." Hami became silent a moment before going on. "This means the portal pearl on your midnight bracelet is time and date specific. But why this exact time? Were you brought here to prevent all this happening? Or were you sent here to cause it?" He glanced at her warily. "And who else is here? The fluctuation was three times larger than the one when Ramaask arrived, which means that your bracelet is only ever used three times. We know you've used it twice already. Theoretically, there could be a third version of you here … Or else there's someone else."

"Borzin arrived at the Keep several days ago with a boy he'd found in the Fungi Forest," Eva said.

"Borzin found a boy?" Hami asked. "Why was I not told?"

Sammy shrugged. "I heard about him."

"Who is he?"

"We don't know," Calven said. "Borzin found him in the Fungi Forest not far from the outpost. Creepy-looking kid."

"Was he like Sammy?" Hami asked.

Sammy raised an eyebrow. "I'm not creepy."

"He had yellow hair," Calven said. "That's all I know. Borzin took him to Honton Keep with him. He would have arrived at the Keep just before you did."

Hami was quiet for a time, then turned to Sammy. "You figured out which portal pearl takes you to the Mother World?"

"Of course," she said.

"And you got home okay?"

"It was like I'd never been gone. It took me back to the exact moment I left."

"That makes sense. The pearls of portal paths won't be time specific. Only in as much as they'll return you to the same time you left."

"Hold on," Sammy said. "If the battle has only just finished, and my past self just left, then Mehrak is still down there in the fire temple!" She ran to the edge of the Cataclysm. "We need to rescue him."

———

And like that, Sammy was back in his life. The same excited and enthusiastic girl that he'd said goodbye to moments before, now a woman or near enough, and now only six years younger than he was. Her hair was longer and tied up. Her body curved in places that hadn't been quite so curvy that morning. He felt his face flush when he realised that he was looking at her. He couldn't help himself. She was an attractive woman. Soft clear skin, golden hair.

He turned away. Fatigue was causing this lapse in judgement. He was weak, run down. He was better than to succumb to such base urges.

"Careful near that edge," he called out. He sounded soft. "It's further down than it looks. Stand back." That was better. Commanding. How he should sound in front of civilians.

Sammy moved away from him, went back to the cart, grabbed Victa's lightning staff and started back towards the edge.

"What do you think you're doing? That's a magus's staff."

"Relax. I know how to use it."

"I don't care. You aren't properly trained."

"The tall thin monster in the black cloak is in there with Mehrak. I need to save him."

"The one from the forest? It was down there with you?"

"Yeah."

"And you still escaped?"

"Wouldn't be here if I hadn't."

Hami walked over and took the staff off her. "You still aren't taking that staff. It's a liability. I'll come with you. You'll be safe with me." He tossed Victa's staff to Harz. "Look after this until I get back."

Harz nodded and stashed it in his chariot.

"Narok?" Hami said. "Can you wait here with Victa? The magi may arrive before I return." They wouldn't. "Explain what has happened if they do. We're going to find Mehrak and we'll be back shortly."

Hami held his hand out towards the edge, clenched his fingers, and concentrated. Earth and stone came loose and dropped to the mountaintop below, forming a slope. He sent another five mini avalanches of stone and sand sliding down until the slope looked gradual enough that Sammy could get down without hurting herself. Yet despite his best endeavours, she almost fell the moment she launched herself down the incline, skidding and tripping as she went.

"Careful!" he called as he plunged down after her.

Sammy carried on regardless, but seemed to be gripping her waist as she powerwalked across the mountaintop.

"Are you okay?" Hami asked as he caught up.

"I must've pulled my stitches sliding down the hill."

Hami stopped her and removed her hand from her stomach. "You're bleeding."

"I got stabbed by one of the crabman." She took her hand back and pressed it against her stomach. "It's fine."

"Let me see."

Sammy lifted her t-shirt enough to expose her stomach.

"Hold still." Hami concentrated on the ragged molecules around the edges of the wound, pulling them together and reforming bonds between one side and the other. Sammy sucked in air through her teeth as he worked, but otherwise made no protest.

"How's that?" Hami asked when he'd finished.

Sammy twisted back and forth at the waist a couple of times. "That's brilliant, thank you." She continued walking.

"It's not perfect," Hami said as he walked alongside her, "but you'll be almost back to normal in a couple of days."

"Awesome," Sammy said, stopping as she reached the temple doors.

Hami stopped next to her. He held out his arm, concentrating on the large bolts that he could feel were securing the door on the other side. He gripped each one mentally and raised them with a flick of his wrist. He heard them clatter to the floor inside, then locked onto the doors and thrust his hand out, forcing them open.

Sammy's eyes met his with sparkling delight, her mouth stretched into a wide grin. "That was cool," she said.

How was it that she could be more impressed with him unbarring a door than stitching her flesh back together? Yet despite her disproportionate excitement, a warm contentedness spread in his chest. The realm was in the toilet, but with Sammy beside him, he was ... what? Happy? But only for a moment. A tsunami of guilt crushed the flicker of joy under its weight. How could he be so consumed with this girl when the dead were reanimating and Behnam was still imprisoned? And Jamileh. What of her? Was she so easily forgotten? It sickened him, the ease with which he'd filled the hole she'd left with Sammy. It was an affront to her memory and he had no excuse for it. Still, Sammy would be gone soon. He'd make sure of it this time, and when she had, he would be free to save Behnam without distraction.

"Let's keep going," he said as he marched ahead across the threshold.

The atrium inside the fire temple was deserted.

He took a moment to take in the vastness of the space, the marble columns, the polished floor mirroring the golden dome above, and something else. Movement in the reflection, circling and birdlike.

He looked up.

A lava pterodactyl banked and came at them. Hami dragged Sammy to the side as the winged beast barrelled past and out through the temple doors. It was gone in a streak of crimson, but Hami had seen enough to identify a harpoon shaft protruding from its chest.

Sammy shivered as she watched it go. "That was dead the last time I was here," she said, her voice trembling. "We shot it through the heart."

It wasn't the only creature in the area that should've been dead.

Hami walked off ahead, climbing the sloped floor towards the back of the atrium and the hall that would lead them to the Temple of Paths.

–TWENTY–
DÉJÀ VU

Sammy absentmindedly opened and closed the locket at her throat. Would it still work after sitting in her mother's jewellery box for two years? Presumably it didn't have an expiry date. She seemed to recall that the head priestess had owned it since childhood so it was unlikely that travelling to and from her world would've damaged it. Even still, she couldn't quite believe it would work again.

Sammy tucked the locket back inside her t-shirt collar as they neared the rear hall. She didn't want to lose it. Not yet, anyway. The head priestess could have it back when they'd rescued Mehrak.

At the doors to the back hall, Hami repeated the manoeuvre he'd used to open the main entrance doors, forcing them open and toppling the furniture that had been piled up behind them.

The hall was dark, lit faintly by fire light. Men and women were hiding in the shadows. They emerged clutching broken pieces of furniture, pew legs and sharp planks like they intended to defend themselves with them.

"It's okay," Hami said, holding up his staff and lighting the end. "I'm a magus."

The scent in the room dragged Sammy back through time to when she'd been there before. The exotic spice and lemon triggering memories, erasing the intervening years, re-inserting her back into that moment. The gilding on the marble columns, the battles in the paintings on the ceiling representing good versus evil, the red and white chequered floor, burning pews. Every individual piece of debris and speck of dust exactly where it had been. A perfect recreation of the stage she'd stepped off two years ago.

Nothing had moved forward in the intervening years. She was literally picking up from where she'd left off. Sammy experienced a weird, out of body, kind of déjà vu when she stopped to consider that her other, previous self, had been through this hall moments before her. She paused to let that sink in, and to try to wrap her head around it.

Two bodies covered by white sheets lay over to her left. Sammy re-experienced the overwhelming dread she'd suffered the first time around, as if her previous self had hung it aside, ready to be picked up and placed back onto her shoulders. The tall thin creature had killed those people and was here, deep underground, waiting.

One of the female priests stared at her. "How did you get out?" she asked. The woman looked vaguely familiar. "Aren't you supposed to be …" she trailed off and glanced to a pile of furniture over to her right.

One of the men stepped forward. "Lila-Maryam told us—"

"We're going down," Hami said. "Keep the hole covered after we've gone. Don't let anything out."

Then he stopped. He pointed to the bodies under the blankets. "What happened to them?"

The priest that answered him looked dreadful. His eyes were raw, hair dishevelled and face pale. "There was a tall thin demon," he said and gulped back a sob.

"Are they definitely dead?" Hami asked. "You've checked?"

"Look at them," one of the others said.

"I apologise if this sounds insensitive," Hami said, "but you might want to think about disposing of the bodies. Or at least keeping them behind a locked door." Then softer, "I'm sorry for your loss."

He waved his hand to the side and the piled up furniture scattered across the polished marble floor. Then he gripped his fist and looked to be concentrating. The red tile that had until that moment been under the furniture wobbled and lifted.

The entrance to the maze.

Sammy concentrated on the tile too. Picturing the atoms trembling in their rows. Imagining them getting lighter, shifting. The tile came up. And Hami let go.

The slab fell, landing on the hole but askew so it didn't drop in and sit flush.

"What happened?" Sammy asked. "You let go."

"When did you learn to do that?"

"I've been gone two years. I've had time to practice."

Hami broke eye contact. He got down on his knees and dragged the tile to the side, then he dropped into the hole.

He'd already gone by the time Sammy had lowered herself into the small room below the hall. She made for the archway and the spiral staircase that led down into the mountain.

For someone that didn't care much for Mehrak, Hami was setting quite a pace. Sammy had to jog to keep up with the stretched shadows cast by his staff light. If he went much faster, she'd lose him and end up stumbling down in the dark.

The stairs were never ending. Sammy had forgotten just how far underground they went. She was tiring, legs becoming wobbly and clumsy. How could anyone have tunnelled so deep through solid stone?

Hami was waiting for her when she staggered out of the large pillar that housed the staircase. He acknowledged her arrival, then pressed on through the towering stone columns filling the cavern.

"I've still got the locket," Sammy said as she jogged after him.

Hami didn't look back. "What locket?"

"The one that shows where you're going."

Hami stopped. "Show me."

Sammy slumped up against one of the stone columns to catch her breath. She pulled the locket out from under her collar and held it out to him.

"Where did you get that?" He brought his face close to inspect it. She could see all the pores in his skin. The prickling of stubble. The strained muscles in his neck.

"The head priest lady gave it to me last time I was in here," Sammy said while trying to slide away from him round the column.

Hami lifted his eyes and they met hers. "The locket of desire," he said.

Sammy had nothing to say to that. She stared blankly into his blue eyes.

"They say it can be used to find anything," he went on. "It looks into your soul to determine the object of your desire. But what the locket leads you to is often not something you should have. It isn't especially powerful. You have to be close to the object you want before it will start working. Even still, it's a dangerous artefact. I'm surprised a priest came to own it. Make sure you give it back when we return to the surface. Or better yet; throw it in the Cataclysm."

"Don't we need it?"

"I know where I'm going."

"You've been here before?"

"The magi have. I'm following directions on the network."

Every so often, Hami would stop and pull Sammy close. His strong callused hands brushing her arms, leaving warm, rough patches. The closeness of him numbed the threat of the tall creature. Sammy had shed the fear she'd acquired in the hall above. She was safe with Hami. He'd defeated Ramaask. This lesser monster would pose no threat.

She reminded herself that she could handle herself, too. Her and Hami together. Side by side, they'd be a force to be reckoned with.

Sammy sent out her mental feelers. The signal was faint, but she could sense the creature. A bitter and burning anger. It was out there somewhere, hiding in the columns, waiting. Biding its time. But for what?

They reached the wall that blocked the tunnel to the Temple of Paths without drama. The creature seemed to be keeping its distance. For what reason, Sammy couldn't determine, but it was probably a sensible move. It was bound to be able to sense how badass she and Hami were.

Sammy stepped out of the stone columns into the barren track that ran the length of the wall. The tunnel that led to the temple of paths was blocked with rubble.

Hami surveyed the damage.

"That tall thin creature did this," Sammy said.

"Blocked up the tunnel?"

"It was aiming for us."

"It blocked you in so the only way forward was through the Temple of Paths."

"But ..." Sammy stopped herself. The creature had been trying to kill her. Yet it had been pretty lucky how they'd escaped. And come to think of it, why was the mound of rubble undisturbed? It appeared that no attempt had been made to shift any of the rock.

"Find a wide pillar and stand behind it," Hami said, interrupting her train of thought.

Sammy ran into the columns, found a large one, and waited in the dark behind it.

Without Hami beside her, she was on edge. It was too easy to feel safe in his presence. And she hated that. That kind of mentality was holding her back. She should have more confidence in her abilities. She was powerful. She didn't need Hami babysitting her. She didn't need anyone. To be fair, the tall thin monster wasn't just some run-of-the-mill college bully. She wasn't sure how she'd fare in a one-on-one fight. But the more she thought about it, the more convinced she became that it wasn't the creature making her tense. She was nervous at the prospect of seeing Mehrak again. And more than that, worried that he'd jumped into the portal already.

The explosion was incredible. A concussive blast raced through the columns turning Sammy's stomach upside-down and sucking the breath from her lungs. Rubble bounced along the floor either side of her column and stone dust filled the air.

When echoes of the blast quietened, she stepped out into the dust cloud and made her way towards the beacon of Hami's staff light.

She coughed as she inhaled airborne stone particles. "Did it work?"

Hami had his mouth and nose in the crook of his elbow. He pointed at the gaping maw of the tunnel with his staff.

Sammy's palms were sweaty. This was it. Would Mehrak still be there?

She ran for the hole, stumbling over the blocks of rubble that got in her way and into the black tunnel on the other side. She opened the locket and the tunnel filled with light. The object of her desire was close. The portal that would return her home? Or something else at the end of the tunnel?

"Hold up," Hami called as he negotiated the rubble behind her, but Sammy had already broken into a sprint.

She flew out of the tunnel and into the long rectangular cavern on the other side. She slowed briefly as she neared the scary angel statues guarding the Temple of Paths, and the broken disc in the entrance. No earthquakes erupted when she approached this time so she carried on through.

"Mehrak! Hello?" she yelled as she ran.

Silence. Had he chosen a pearl and taken the plunge? Sammy slowed. Her heart beating hard, her pulse pounding in her ears.

Then a faint, "Hello?", a pause and, "I'm in here!"

–TWENTY-ONE–
BACK WITH MEHRAK

Mehrak assumed his ears had been deceiving him. Sammy had gone home. She couldn't still be here.

Then she staggered back into the temple chamber.

She was frantic a moment, then spotted him on the floor in his pool of portal pearls. She seemed to relax then and slumped against the curved temple wall, bracing herself with hands on knees and holding her head low while she caught her breath.

Mehrak watched her with something akin to mild amusement. He couldn't quite get his head around seeing her again so soon. She'd dropped through the hole in the floor, swapped her clothes and re-emerged sometime later from the tunnel that led back to the column maze. He accepted this illogical circumstance in the same way he'd accepted all the other illogical experiences he'd been through over the last several days. An explanation was sure to be forthcoming, but for now he would savour Sammy's company again for as long as it lasted.

She straightened up then and Mehrak noticed that it wasn't just her clothes that had changed. Her hair was longer and tied up. An obvious difference, but there were others. Smaller, subtle things. Her face had shed some of the chubbiness of youth, yet other areas of her body had filled out.

"You don't have to stare," she said.

Mehrak looked away. "You've only just left—"

"It probably seems like that." She took a long breath. "I'll explain once we've rescued you."

"We've?"

Hami ducked into the low temple chamber behind her. "Mehrak," he said by way of greeting.

"Hami," Mehrak replied. The name tasted bitter in his mouth. Silence.

"So we should probably get going," Sammy said.

"No," Hami said. "You're going back to the Mother World."

"I've only just got here. I've not seen Mehrak for two years. We need to catch up."

Two years? Mehrak found himself almost unable to focus. His brain was imploding. If he hadn't been sitting he might've collapsed and fallen into the pit.

He slumped against the wall. It couldn't be that long. She'd only been gone a moment. He didn't want to believe it. He wanted to fight it, but when he looked at her, he knew it to be true. She was different. Mature.

His mind churned with the imagined experiences she'd had without him. It made him upset, jealous even. Others had enjoyed her company, spent time with her. She'd have forgotten about him. Moved on.

"What do you need to catch up about?" Hami said. "He's not done anything since you left."

The comment cut even though it was true. "Did you bring water?" Mehrak asked, at a loss for anything else to say.

Hami frowned. "Is that really the first thing you want to ask? You aren't interested in the fact Sammy has returned?"

"I've been down here a long time and it's hot." He stuffed his hands into the portal pearls around him so Hami wouldn't see them shaking. "Sammy said she hasn't seen me for two years. She obviously reused the Midnight Emerald bracelet to come back, and although I'm thrilled to see her," he made eye contact with her, "I think it was reckless to return. I risked my life to get you home." He was acting petulantly. He didn't want Sammy to see him like this, but he'd meant what he said. He tried to relax. "I would like to catch up, though."

"So it's agreed," Hami said. "Sammy's going back to the Mother World."

Sammy's eyes widened in indignity, then when Hami showed no sign of backing down, they moved to Mehrak and became pleading. *Mehrak,* they said. *Let me stay.*

He had to look away to muster all his resolve. "I can't believe I'm siding with Hami," he said, "but he's right. You shouldn't have come back. It's too dangerous."

"I thought you'd be pleased to see me," she said as she marched around the glowing portal pit to the area of shelf that had held the green pearls.

"I am," Mehrak said. "I don't want you to leave, but those crabmen tried to kill you."

"The pearl's not there," Sammy said. She turned back to face them and shrugged. "I can't go back."

"It popped back onto the shelf after you left," Mehrak said. "It rolled off onto the floor. You'll have to search for it." He got up onto his knees. "I'll help."

Sammy crouched and half-heartedly swooshed the pearls side to side with her hand. "This is going to take ages."

Hami came over to help. "Sweep all the pearls into the pit."

Multi-coloured bursts flared to the ceiling as the pearls cascaded into the portal. Many landed back on the shelf as they popped back into existence. Others missed their divots and bounced back onto the floor.

Amid a flurry of green pearls re-appearing and rolling off the shelf, one remained as the others fell.

It held, floating in mid-air.

Then it flew to Sammy's hand.

"This is it," she said. "Definitely."

"How did you do that?" Mehrak asked.

Sammy grinned. "I've had practice."

Mehrak experienced another pang of jealousy. What else could she do now that he didn't know about?

136

"Let me go back later," she said to Hami. "Ramaask is dead. The crabmen have gone. There's no rush. Besides, I want to hang out in Golden Egg Cottage with Mehrak and Louis."

Hami deflated and his eyes became distant. "I promised that if I lived through the battle I'd return you home."

"Can't I at least accompany Mehrak up to the surface to see Louis?"

"We don't have time to debate this. I wish things were different, but there's a new threat and it's very likely worse than Ramaask. You have to go. Now. Don't make this any harder than it needs to be ..." He stopped. "What was that?"

"What was what?"

"Stay here," he said, pointing his finger at Sammy. He made eye contact as he did so, as if to reinforce the order. Then he dashed back up the corridor.

"Let's go with him," Sammy said, walking around the outside of the portal pit.

Mehrak remained on his knees. "He told us to stay."

"So now you do everything he tells you?"

"It could be dangerous."

"That tall thin creature is still down here," Sammy said. "We'll be safer with Hami than on our own. Come on." Then she tossed the green pearl into the pit, pulled him by the collar and dragged him into motion.

Mehrak impulsively followed. He hadn't begun to consider the consequences of what they were doing, but he found himself blindly following her anyway.

He heard the portal pearl pop back into existence behind him, and most probably roll off the shelf and onto the floor.

"Why did you throw the pearl away?"

"I don't need it. Besides, it's safe enough where it is."

She flicked open Lila-Maryam's locket, lighting up the corridor ahead, as they sprinted from the Temple of Paths and back into conflict.

–TWENTY-TWO–
BIG MISTAKE

The locket retained its continuous beam of light as Sammy staggered over the rubble outside the tunnel, then began blinking as she crossed the barren track and sprinted into the stone columns.

Mehrak lagged behind her, sweating. She recalled that he'd dragged her through the stone columns last time. Now he was struggling to keep up. All the football she'd been playing had given her the physical edge. She'd grown stronger and faster while Mehrak had remained frozen in time.

She slowed so he could catch up.

She'd been self-conscious when she'd stumbled into the portal chamber and he'd looked her over. But the feeling had been fleeting and she'd relaxed back into his company. The intervening years collapsing to a dreamlike interlude as if she'd woken from her distant Sheffield dream back into this more real existence.

A distant moan.

Mehrak gasped. "Is that Leiss?"

The big Marzban guard that had travelled with them in Golden Egg Cottage. Sammy had forgotten all about him. He'd been attacked by the tall creature like Borzin had. But his departure hadn't been dramatic. He'd just gone. Borzin had been brutally murdered in front of her. She'd lived through the gruesome aftermath. Leiss had been a footnote by comparison. There one moment, gone the next.

Surely he couldn't have survived.

Sammy slowed. Witnessing the mess that had been made of Borzin had permanently scarred her. A raw wound that had endured. With time, the memory had faded, but a small part of it never left. Those lidless and unseeing eyes, the aroma of cooking meat. She couldn't go through that again.

"We're almost there," she said, sounding braver than she felt, letting her adrenalin carry her forward. "I can see Hami's light."

No sooner had she seen it than they were upon him.

Sammy squinted, flinching in preparation for the horror.

There was none.

She relaxed. The big Marzban was on his back in a pool of Hami's staff light. His clothes were singed, his face was red and blistered in places, and his pink turban had partially unravelled, but otherwise he wasn't in such a bad state. Nothing like Borzin had been in.

Hami's eyes were wild. He rounded on Sammy. "I told you to stay put!"

"It's fine," Sammy said, kneeling beside Leiss and attempting to ignore the scary look on Hami's face. "We can go back later."

"I'm sorry," Leiss groaned.

Hami grabbed her by the arm and pulled her back to her feet. "No, it isn't fine."

"I'm sorry," Leiss said again. "I tried not to call out. It made me …"

Hami let go of her, and his face became ashen. "Please tell me you brought the portal pearl with you?"

Sammy's eyes met his. In them she saw true fear. An emotion she'd once thought him incapable of. She shook her head.

Hami opened his mouth wordlessly. Blinked. Then ran.

Without the steady glow of Hami's staff, they were intermittently plunged into darkness as the light from Sammy's locket blinked lazily on and off. Each pulse lit up their surroundings before plunging them into nothingness. The shame of what she'd done made her covet the dark each time it returned.

Those fleeting moments of 'in between' time where she didn't exist and couldn't be seen or judged.

Leiss looked to be in some pain. He remained on the floor gripping his left leg. A thin trail of blood led away from him into the columns.

Leiss followed her gaze. "The creature made me crawl here so you'd hear me call out," he said as he squinted up into the light.

Sammy used the following dip into darkness to angle her body away. She couldn't look at him. Couldn't face what she'd put him through.

She fell under Mehrak's scrutiny during the next surge of light. He said nothing, but he didn't have to. He and Leiss had risked their lives to send her home and she'd thrown it back in their faces.

They waited some time for Hami to return.

When he did, the only thing he had to say was, "It's gone."

–TWENTY-THREE–
Back to the Surface

Sammy trailed Hami and Mehrak as they supported Leiss through the stone columns. The pulses of light from her locket grew further apart as they walked, and soon stopped altogether. She continued to follow from behind, wallowing in the long shadows cast by Hami's staff light.

She was stuck in Perseopia.

She didn't want to go home, yet having lost the option forever filled her with dread. She'd never see her mother again. Would she be okay without her? What if the tall figure entered the portal later, once they'd left the fire temple? It could get teleported to her home in Sheffield. The realisation set off a mild panic attack and left her hollow. She supported herself against the columns as she staggered between them. The creature would kill her mother and burn their house down. All direct consequences of her actions.

Hami hadn't spoken to her since announcing that the pearl was missing. His silent disappointment worse than anything he could have said.

She lagged further behind, her will to keep moving diminishing with each step.

Ascending the staircase back to the fire temple was a slog. Hami and Mehrak took turns helping Leiss up the stairs and numerous breaks were taken.

And after an eternity of staggered climbing, they reached the top and the low room below the hall.

Leiss slumped up against the wall, then slid down to his bottom.

Mehrak rolled over on the floor and remained where he lay. He groaned as he stretched out. "Ooh, my ribs." Then, following Sammy's quizzical expression, added, "Where the crabman hit me. You probably won't remember."

Hami moved past them to the area below the entrance to the hall above.

The tile was missing.

In a single motion, he leapt up through the hole and was gone.

A moment went by, then he called down to let them know the hall above was clear. He pulled Sammy up first, then together they helped Mehrak, then Leiss. Leiss was easier to lift than she thought he'd be given his size. She could only assume Hami was using some kind of magus trick to lift him as she still hadn't figured out how to move people.

The furniture that had been piled on top of the entrance to the secret room was scattered nearby. Most of it was either smashed, burning or both.

"Where is everyone?" Sammy asked.

Hami pointed. "Over there."

More dead bodies. The priests they'd spoken to before descending into the mountain had been reduced to charred husks.

Mehrak looked to Sammy, and she nearly lost it. She felt suddenly conspicuous. Like everyone was judging her for this even though it wasn't her fault. The tall thin figure was always going to come back this way. She hadn't ordered the priests to man the entrance. She hadn't caused their deaths.

She looked away and concentrated on not freaking out. She didn't know them. If she could distance herself from thinking of the blackened shapes as once having been human, she might be able to avoid a breakdown.

"We need to leave," Hami said. He took his cloak off and put it over Sammy's shoulders. "Stay hidden and try not to let anyone see you." He pulled the hood over her head.

"Why?"

"So no one discovers that you've stayed. If we can keep you hidden, there may be an opportunity to return you to the Mother World at some point in future."

"Maybe I don't want to go back." The words came out without consideration, and she couldn't take them back.

Hami's eyes flashed with anger, but he kept his voice even. "If you hide now, you'll be able to make that decision later. If my brothers find you, then you've lost the option."

Sammy opened her mouth to say something, but the look Hami gave her ended the conversation. He turned to Mehrak.

"Mehrak? Find Louis and bring him into the atrium. Get him as close as you can to this hall, then back him up to the doors. We don't want Sammy seen and we need to make it quick."

"Why quick?" asked Mehrak. "And what right do you have to tell us what to do? You've lied and manipulated us. I think you should leave us to make our own way from here."

Hami bristled. He seemed to be straining to keep his voice measured. "I tried to send Sammy home just now. You agreed it was the right course of action."

Mehrak frowned and looked to Sammy.

"The magi will be here soon. And they *will* take her. *If* they find her. No one knows Sammy is still here except us. I want to keep it that way until we figure out what's best for her."

"What's best for her? As if you'd know anything about that."

Sammy wasn't interested in their bickering, but that last part caught her attention. "The only person that's going to be deciding what's best for me, is me."

"Wrong," Hami said. He was becoming increasingly agitated. "The magi will be making the decision for you if we're not quick. We're running out of time. Let's get out of here first, then have the debate."

Mehrak looked to Sammy.

Sammy shrugged. "Whatever. I'm still getting the deciding vote."

There was a brief standoff between Mehrak and Hami.

"Fine," Mehrak said. "I'll fetch Louis." And he made for the atrium.

Hami guided Sammy a short way from the hole in the floor to a secluded area by the back wall. He sat her in the shadows behind a row of pews. "Until we ..." He stopped himself, made eye contact. "Until you and I, and maybe Mehrak, figure out what's best, let's not let anyone know you're still here," he said, then got up and walked back over to Leiss.

Sammy crouched down and waited. It wasn't long until the doors opened, spilling light across the darkened hall. Mehrak had returned and was arguing with a squeaky-voiced woman. Sammy lifted her aching body enough to peer out from her hiding place. She recognised the woman as the head priestess.

The stout lady bustled in with her breasts gathered up in her arms.

"Not until you explain this to me," she said.

"Lila-Maryam, I've told you, I don't know anything," Mehrak replied. "Ask Principal Hootan over there."

Hami made his way towards them, supporting Leiss under the arm. "Did you bring Louis?" he asked. "We need to get Leiss into bed."

Lila-Maryam cried out. She ran towards the freshly dead bodies, staggered, then stopped. "No. Please no."

"The magi will be here soon," Hami said. "They'll explain everything."

Lila-Maryam turned on him, her face burning with rage. "How dare you!"

Sammy ducked back into the shadows as the priestess berated Hami and her strangled crying moved out into the atrium.

The hall darkened and the tirade softened to a murmur as the doors closed.

Sammy's legs ached from the staircase climb. She was drained both physically and emotionally. The dead priests, the loss of the pearl and her general fatigue caught up with her and weariness took over. She embraced the quiet dark and a respite from conflict and pain. She lay down on the hard marble floor and pulled Hami's cloak around her. Resting her head in the crook of her elbow, she closed her eyes.

She started awake in the dark. Someone was nudging her to get up.

"It's me," Mehrak said. "Come on." He was trying to coax her to her feet.

Her legs were heavy useless objects vaguely connected to her body. She recalled that too many stairs had been climbed and she groaned as she stood, stretched and arched her back.

"Hurry up. We haven't got far to go. You can go back to sleep when we're aboard Eggie."

Sammy perked up at that. Eggie? Were they boarding Golden Egg Cottage?

Mehrak whisked her along the hall, through the pews, past the burnt and burning furniture, and towards the atrium.

"Keep your head down and stay close." He stopped her when they reached the doors. Sammy waited behind him while he peered through the gap.

"Go," he said. And they were moving. He bundled her into the light, bright and dazzling. She raised her hands to block it out as she was moved into position atop a platform that boosted her up and through a hole. She alighted a staircase leading up a narrow tunnel.

"Keep going," Mehrak called from behind.

Sammy climbed, half-asleep and disorientated. Then stopped.

A collage of multi-coloured shapes swirled at the end of the tunnel.

She was inside Golden Egg Cottage!

The sleep haze vanished as she scampered to the top of the stairs and emerged into the kitchen.

Sammy's dream fantasy home restored to reality. She closed her eyes and breathed the place in, picked out the faint aroma of mushroom soup, and of smoking mushroom strips in the stove. Memories bubbled to the surface. Those of cupping steaming tea at the kitchen table. Mehrak making himself busy, whether washing dishes at the sink or stirring a casserole on the hot plate. The intervening years that she'd been away drifted from memory like X-Factor winners after their Christmas number ones left the charts.

Sammy took her time taking in the atmosphere, savouring everything. She moved to the table, ran her hand over its uneven green surface. Traced a finger along the polished copper work surface, over the sink and under the misaligned kitchen units.

She tapped one of the multi-coloured birds in the mobile above her. A red one that until then had been coasting lazily above her head. It soared away, pulling its friends along with it, altering their trajectories and creating spiralling patterns in the complex paper and wire structure that filled the ceiling.

This cramped but beautiful little capsule, that she'd spent less than a week of her life in, had dominated her dreams over the last two years. Not all the memories she'd made inside it had been pleasant, but she'd built it up in her mind as a refuge from her life in Sheffield. All her problems and responsibilities were outside these curved walls. Now she was safe.

"Is it as you remember?" Mehrak asked, severing her from her reverie. He closed the trapdoor they'd come up through. "I still can't believe you've been away." He looked away, and laughed awkwardly. "We were both here in the kitchen this morning. You were angry we'd tried to lose Hami."

Sammy smiled. "I remember."

"This feels strange," Mehrak said.

"What?"

"Us," he said. "We were best friends earlier today. Now you don't know me."

Sammy wasn't sure what Mehrak expected to hear. She shrugged. "I know," she replied. "It's weird."

He nodded. "You know you can still stay here as long as you like?"

"That's kind. Thank you." Sammy made for the stairs that led up around the outside wall. It was what she'd wanted to hear, but voiced aloud it came across sounding awkward. She'd not forgotten that the last time she'd been here, she'd kissed Mehrak. To him it had only just happened. To her it was a lifetime ago, figuratively. She hoped he wasn't looking to rekindle something between them. He was still technically married, even if they were now a lot closer in age.

She'd figure something out if she needed to. For now, she was going to enjoy being home.

"Hami says you shouldn't go out onto the balcony," he said. "Someone might see you."

"Okay," Sammy replied as she continued up the stairs.

Leiss was in Mehrak's bed. He watched her climb out of the hole in the centre of the room, then looked away to the ceiling.

Sammy closed the railing gate at the top of the stairs. A natural, subconscious action that she only became aware of after performing it. It pleased her to think she was already tuning back in to the harmony of Eggie.

The bedroom was exactly as it had been. A smaller space than the kitchen with blue walls and a red doughnut-shaped carpet around the spiral staircase down to the kitchen. Mehrak's bookshelf still contained its small collection of books, there was the green wardrobe, and the red curtains that covered the arches to the front and rear balconies.

The only object out of place was Leiss, lying sullenly on his back and taking up most of Mehrak's four-poster bed. He said nothing and kept his eyes fixed firmly on the wrought iron chandelier in the apex of the ceiling.

"I thought you were dead," Sammy said.

"I deserve to be." He was still not looking at her.

Sammy cast her mind back. "You left us to go after that tall thin creature." Too much time had passed for her to feel angry about what he'd done. "I made it home," she said. "And none of us died, so I wouldn't feel too bad about it."

Leiss said nothing more and rolled over.

The floor lurched and Sammy caught hold of a bed post to steady herself as the cottage rose up beneath her. Louis was getting to his feet. She held on until the cottage settled in to a gentle, side to side rocking motion.

The sensation made her feel oddly queasy. After congratulating herself for quickly acclimatising to life aboard Eggie, she was disappointed to have lost her sea legs, or, she supposed, Louis legs.

Sammy tentatively edged towards the front balcony and the curtain that separated it from the bedroom. The pull of the forbidden balcony was strong. She desperately wanted to see Louis again. Hami had told her not to go out onto it, and she wouldn't, but a quick peek couldn't hurt. She wanted to see where they were going, to relive previous travels. Leiss was facing the opposite direction. He wouldn't see. No one would know.

Holding the centre of the curtain closed with one hand, Sammy parted the top to make a gap just big enough for her face.

Louis had already covered most of the atrium in the short time it had taken for her to cross the room. As they reached the open temple doorway, Sammy glimpsed a young female priest on the gallery above the doors. Their eyes met and the girl's mouth dropped open.

Sammy tugged the curtain closed and waited. Was this bad?

Maybe the girl was looking at Louis. She might've never seen a gastrosaur before. Priests probably didn't get out much. If the girl had seen Sammy, she'd only have seen her eyes and nose. No blond hair. And there'd been a decent distance between them. It could have been anyone peering out.

Sammy still had an uneasy feeling about it, though. She parted the curtains again, just enough to see out with one eye, but by that point it was too late. They'd already passed through the temple doors and she found herself looking up at the ridge of the Cataclysm and the black sky above.

–TWENTY-FOUR–
MAGI INBOUND

Hami scrambled up the piled earth back to the plain where Narok and the others were waiting. At the top, he stumbled and dropped to one knee. And for a moment couldn't get up again. Every physical exertion was an ordeal. His body was precipitously close to shutting down, but time for recovery wasn't a luxury he could indulge.

He rose slowly and set about organising for Louis to get up the incline. The gastrosaur could probably make it alone, but he instructed the Marzban to tie ropes around his waist anyway and secure the other ends to their karkadann.

Mehrak came out for moral support and talked the animal through each step.

Louis heaved himself and the cottage up the earth mound as the karkadann backed away, keeping the ropes taut enough to keep him moving forward.

When Louis reached the plain, the relief was strong enough that Hami fell to his knees again and then forward onto his hands. He was mentally and physically spent, and not entirely sure how his body was still going. If he were to lie down now he could pass out that very moment. But he wouldn't allow it. Not yet.

They needed to leave, to begin moving before the magi got there. He was surprised they weren't here already. Perhaps they'd been held up. Perhaps his luck would hold out one last time.

He'd give Narok an excuse, then they'd be on their way.

Eva had seen the tall thin creature crest the Cataclysm and head north following the direction the demon and bodies had gone. He could use that as the basis for his excuse. He'd ask the Marzban to wait for the magi while he took Sammy north after the thin creature. Then, once they were out of sight, they'd detour west. If he could get Louis into the Fungi Forest with Sammy on board, they'd be concealed enough to sneak away and he'd be able to sleep. He'd figure out everything else when he woke.

But as he raised his head from where it hung, he saw a herd of greenbuck bouncing towards him. Landing and rebounding like fleas. The twenty-strong magi reinforcements had arrived. And he was too late.

———

The thin figure moved through the darkness between the dead crabmen and Marzban, zigzagging its way through the shuffling corpses. They were nothing more than puppets. All of them reanimated shells, devoid of the souls that had previously piloted them. Some of their memories remained, personality traits that distinguished their behaviour from the others around them, but they were echoes of their former selves, ghosts haunting flesh and bone vessels.

As the figure made its way towards the front of the crowd, the density of bodies became tighter. Their faces and exposed skin bubbled and melted as he passed them but they made no protest, they felt nothing.

His master existed where the bodies were thickest. The core of everything dead and polluted.

A deep gargling voice emerged from the amalgamation of animal and human body parts. "Ramaask has gone?"

"At the bottom of the Cataclysm," replied the thin figure. "Trapped beneath the column."

"You must return to the city. To the gate."

"There is nothing to be done there."

"Guard it. Nothing else can be allowed through until the time is right."

151

"That's unnecessary. Nothing can—"

"Do you defy me?"

"Never, master. Everything I have done has been in preparation for your arrival. The death of my brother. Leading the Mother Worlder across the seal to release you."

"You have been loyal."

"But not yet loyal enough for you to return me to my true form? To release me from this half-existence? I've restored you to the realm of the living."

"Patience. You must protect the portal in the old capital while I travel through the portal in the mountains."

"As you wish, my master. May I at least make a detour? I have someone to collect from the city of Honton Keep. Someone that may prove useful to us."

"Go then," said the voice. "But be swift. Do this thing for me and I will return you to your true, terrible form."

–TWENTY-FIVE–

STOWAWAY

Hami remained on all fours. He no longer had the energy to get up. He'd failed spectacularly. A new plan was needed, but his brain was too slow to come up with one. He sifted through the fog that clouded his head, searching for the barest shred of an idea. There had to be something he could do. He was a lost cause, but perhaps he could save Sammy.

"Mehrak!" he called.

"What?" he asked as he came over. "Are you okay?"

"Head back into Eggie and stay with Sammy. Make sure she stays in the kitchen where the walls are thickest, and keep her there. She's giving off too much energy. If the magi find her they'll take her away. Tell her to close off her mind if she can. Tell her not to reach out to the magi network and to focus on a simple object like a cup or a spoon. She needs to picture it in her head and concentrate on it. Tell her to think of nothing else and to keep it in her mind's eye. Go now and don't make it obvious."

Mehrak turned away and walked off in an exaggerated nonchalant manner that he must've assumed looked casual. *Idiot.*

The greenbucks came out of the darkness, bouncing to a stop like balls losing their elastic energy. Hami recognised Master Salazar Piruzan at the front. It was the last magus Hami wanted to see. The man that had vetoed his request for the status of Master. A battle-scarred monster of a man whose power far exceeded the intelligence he could muster to control it. He was the only magus in recent times to have fought Ramaask and survived. An accolade Hami now realised that he shared. Piruzan hadn't come away from his fight lightly, having lost half the skin on the left side of his face, exposing his jaw and giving the impression that he was constantly sneering.

He leapt off his greenbuck over the top of its head. He landed in a crouch, stood and approached Hami slowly. He licked the area his lips had been. A mannerism he'd adopted since his injuries, presumably out of necessity to stop his exposed gums drying out.

Hami lowered his head to face the floor. "Louis," he whispered. "I need you to wander off a little way. Not too far as to make it obvious, but I need you to put some distance between Sammy and the magi." He hoped the effects of Ramaask's past presence, the shadow that the corpse creature had left in its wake, combined with the thickness of Golden Egg's walls, would inhibit the magi from sensing her. But they were all rested, alert. He struggled to sense her, but he knew her individual entity frequency. It could go either way.

Louis began moving.

"Master Piruzan," Hami said.

Salazar Piruzan watched Louis move away. "Principal."

Hami couldn't bring himself to his feet to face him. So he remained where he was on the floor, and said nothing.

Piruzan returned his attention to Hami. "What a mess," he said, then gazed up at the sky.

"We need to—"

"We, Hami? There is no we. Not now. There is us, and there is you. You are to be escorted directly to the Grand Master in New Ecbatana."

"Master," Hami said as politely as he could manage. He couldn't provoke Piruzan. Not if he wanted to appeal to the man. He had a history of pettiness, but he was still a master magus and would serve Perseopia in what he believed would be a fair and just manner. Hami would have to appeal to his conscience. "May I speak?"

Piruzan wasn't looking. He'd fixed his gaze on Eggie. "Perhaps, we could talk inside the gastrosaur caravan," he said. "Meet your friends."

"She's gone, Master."

"Has she?" Piruzan said. He didn't sound convinced.

"You can feel her echo," Hami said. "The resonance of the Mother World is strong. Much stronger in her than in any of us."

"I feel the power, Hami. It's still here."

"It's not hers." Hami got to his feet with a groan. "I can help you."

Piruzan said nothing.

"Please," Hami said. "Let me show you." He walked to the Cataclysm and waited close to the edge, where it was possible to see down past the mountain. "Can you feel it?" he asked, once Piruzan had joined him. "You of all people should be able to."

Piruzan said nothing for a time. He licked his exposed teeth and gums. "He's really down there, isn't he?"

"He really is. You're feeling his echo. Like Sammy's."

"Tell me what happened."

Hami told Piruzan of how he'd used Sammy to lure Ramaask to the Cataclysm, how he'd fought the crabmen and defeated Ramaask while Sammy had remained inside the temple. He explained how she'd used the Pearls of Portal Paths to return to the Mother World, how the mountain had fallen and the skies had turned black. He went into detail about the creature in the liquid smoke and the bodies getting up and walking away.

"We felt the creature arrive. It was like nothing else that has ever arrived in Perseopia. Not even the girl when she created that larger rift." Piruzan stopped himself. He lowered his voice. "I appreciate that you're cooperating, Principal, but our orders are to deliver you to Grand Master Aegis."

"Why wouldn't I cooperate?" Hami said. "I'm still a magus … for the moment. Tell me you wouldn't have done the same thing if it meant ridding the realm of Ramaask?"

"I wouldn't have risked the entire realm for Master Baktash. The realm comes first. It always has."

"You lost your partner, Siamak, to Ramaask. You only survived because he gave his life so you could escape."

Piruzan's hand went to the ruined side of his face but said nothing.

"I had the realm's interests at heart. I had an opportunity to lure Ramaask out of Aratta, and I seized it. You can at least understand why I did it."

"I understand more than anyone. But it doesn't mean I condone it."

"I know we've never seen eye to eye," Hami said. "But you need me if you're going to take this thing on."

"There are eighteen of us, Hami." Piruzan gestured at the magi and greenbucks congregated behind him.

"That's not enough." Hami paused. "I was told you were twenty."

"We were."

Hami stared down into the light. "Who did you lose?"

"Aran." Piruzan paused and took a deep breath. "And Taj. I'm sorry, I know you two were close."

Taj had been a teenager when Hami trained him. He'd been given the boy to train as an apprentice despite being only five years older. He'd not known the boy long, yet the loss still caught him unexpectedly, and for a moment he was unable to talk. "Crabmen?"

Piruzan nodded.

Hami let the moment pass. "We have another casualty." He led Piruzan to Calven's cart.

Calven looked up as Hami approached. Hami was quick to dismiss him. "Could you leave us a moment," he said before Calven could open his mouth and ruin everything.

"Okay, but I was wondering—"

"I'll explain later," Hami interrupted. "Just give us some space. Head into the golden caravan, ask Mehrak, the traveller, to make you some tea. Please."

"But my karkadann …"

"I'll make sure he doesn't run off."

Hami took Piruzan round to the back of the cart while Calven dismounted and headed over to Golden Egg Cottage.

"Victa?" Piruzan shook his head. "Poor boy."

"I need to take him to the magi garrison so he can be treated."

"I can't allow it, Hami. I have my orders. You're going to New Ecbatana. Victa can go with you. You were always a passable healer, you can patch him up on the way."

"With respect, Master, I believe he needs proper help. He's lost both feet. I can't match the healers at the garrison and those at the capital aren't much better than I am."

Piruzan gazed at the boy, his eyes full of sorrow, then they narrowed. "How did he come to be here?"

Hami shrugged as nonchalantly as he was able. "He registered briefly on the network when he got injured. I told him I was coming here. He must've told the Marzban that saved him from the crabmen."

"You told Victa you were coming here? A new recruit that you barely know. You must've told him a while ago, because he's travelled quite some distance to be here. Yet Aegis, our Grand Master, you've only just told. Why is that?"

"Taj trusted him."

"You need to start cooperating, Principal." Piruzan began marching towards Eggie. "I'm going to have a chat with your friends."

"I am cooperating," Hami said, catching up to Piruzan. He had to stop the man entering Golden Egg Cottage. "What have I got to hide? I contacted the Grand Master voluntarily to tell you I was here. Why else would I do that?"

"There's more you aren't telling me, Principal. You're only telling me what's convenient." Piruzan fell silent, his eyes widened and fixed on something beyond Hami.

Hami turned.

Victa was out of the cart and almost at the Cataclysm. He stumbled towards the edge on the stumps of his legs, blood soaking the bandages as he walked on them. No pain registered on his face and he moved as if in a trance.

He looked like he was about to jump, but at the edge he stopped and raised his arms and head to the skies.

Hami ran for him. Piruzan close behind.

Hami got there first and grabbed Victa by the arm. The boy spun round, his face pale grey and drawn, but there was fire in his eyes. He looked at Hami, and for a moment there was recognition, a grin, then his eyes became dark. The whites and irises became black and vacant, the grin widened until it became a grimace, and he dropped to the ground. His body began seizing, thrashing wildly on the floor. Hami tried to hold him down, keep him from falling over the edge of the Cataclysm.

Piruzan took the boys legs and together they dragged him away from the precipice.

Victa seemed to calm the further they took him from the fire. He shook once more, hacked up a lungful of black, purple sputum, then fell still.

–TWENTY-SIX–
Infected

Hami and his brothers congregated around the back of the cart. Victa was pale and sweating. His black eyes were partially open and he looked dreadful. Whatever had happened to the other dead bodies was happening to him, too. Except his body wasn't dead enough yet.

The magi were all pale and nervous in the boy's company, and a couple had knotted pieces of cloth over their faces as if he were contagious. And that gave Hami the plan he needed. He felt guilty exploiting the opportunity, but he had little choice.

"There's more you need to know," he said to Piruzan as he led him away from the cart, leaving the other magi to watch over Victa.

"We need to get moving, Principal. So do you."

"Behnam's still alive."

Piruzan inclined his head. "Then why hasn't he re-joined the network?"

"He's worried he'll infect us. He contacted me directly in order to dissuade me from trying to draw Ramaask out by taking Sammy to the temple."

Piruzan raised his eyebrows, but said nothing.

"Ramaask predicted this event. He knew this would happen if Sammy was brought here." He took a deep breath. "Ramaask knew about the enrolment whisper and he explained its meaning to Behnam."

"Explained it?"

Hami spoke the rhyme that came so freely to him. The passage that Piruzan and all his brothers could recite mechanically, being as it was, etched into the collective memory of all magi.

"Seek out the path, cross the river of light,

"Descend through the depths and when you alight,

"Take a trip through the gate, where the mountain will fall,

"And that's when the realm becomes darkest of all."

The half of Piruzan's face that still had skin went white and then slack. He opened his mouth but nothing came out.

"Seek out the path: Temple of paths," Hami said. *"River of light*: Cataclysm."

"And that's when the realm becomes darkest of all," Piruzan uttered.

"Ramaask was predicting the end of times. The Ahriman rising, his body being made flesh."

Piruzan said nothing for quite some time. "I'll have to communicate this to the Grand Master. The council will have to decide what happens next."

"And while they're planning and deliberating, you'll lose this creature of flesh and smoke as it heads north. You need to follow it."

Piruzan held up his hand to stop Hami. It was clear he was attempting to contact the Grand Master.

Hami waited. It would all come down to this. If Piruzan got through to Aegis, then the plan would fall through, Sammy would be captured and he'd be incarcerated. But he may yet be lucky. Aegis was often unavailable. Unless he was waiting for Piruzan to check in. It could go either way. Hami took a deep breath.

"I can't get through," Piruzan said at last. "I know you'd prefer to cut out the council and go ahead with your gut instinct, but that's not the way we operate."

"You don't need to break your orders. As long as you don't engage the creature, you're still just investigating and providing useful intel. The magi need to keep track of it, losing it isn't an option. The only real decision you need to make now is what to do about Victa."

"Whether to send him to the garrison or with you to the capital?"

"How many men to send to the garrison with him. He'll need protection through the Fungi Forest. Sending Victa to New Ecbatana is out of the question. He's contaminated. I don't know if he's part way to becoming one of those reanimated dead things, but you can't send him to a highly populated city. He needs to go into quarantine at the garrison."

Piruzan gritted his teeth and licked his gums. "Five men to take Victa to the garrison. Five to take you to the capital, and eight of us to follow the shadow."

"You'll need more than eight. And you need to station a few men here."

"Why?"

"Ramaask's creature, the thin one, stole the Mother World portal pearl from the Temple of Paths after observing Sammy use it."

"Great Ahura." Piruzan shook his head. "This just keeps getting better, doesn't it?"

"Four men with Victa. Four stationed here. And ten to track the demon."

"I'm still waiting for a reason why I need to take so many men north with me?"

"Where do you think the shadow demon is heading?"

"I don't have time for this, Hami."

"What happens in the prophecy of the chosen children?"

"Don't talk to me of prophecies …"

"One to bring life and hope. The other brings death and the end of all things."

"Get to the point."

"… and thus the darkness was too big to be contained and spilled into the Mother World."

"I fail to see how that's relevant."

"The demon is consuming our dead. Possibly our living, too." Hami nodded to Victa. "Certainly the weaker ones. And soon, who knows? Maybe the healthy, too. We don't know how contagious this thing is or how the infection is spread. And it's getting too big to be contained."

Piruzan stared at him. "You're saying it will spill into the Mother World?"

"What is directly north of here?"

"The Naziarabad Monument at Ameretat." Piruzan's eyes widened. "The staircase to the above. But the smog precludes anyone using it."

"What smog?"

Piruzan glanced at the black sky.

"The smog precludes any human using the staircase. But this thing? It could well be immune. The white column is where we'll make our last stand. And you'll need more than eight men for that. We'll have to call over everyone we have within range. Everyone we can spare from the garrison. Send Victa to the garrison with four men, and hope they don't run into any more crabmen. I'll come to the column with you."

"Aegis wants me to send you to New Ecbatana in the company of five magi."

"The crabmen have fled into the forest. I don't need protection. Victa does."

"It's not about protection, Principal, it's about enforcement."

"You're the boss out here. You can't get through to Aegis. Make the call."

"We have magi at the white column. I'll communicate with them and prep them for battle."

"You need more. You haven't grasped the enormity of the situation or what you're up against. Aegis is hundreds of stadia away in the capital. Behnam is trapped in Aratta. How many top tier magi do you have at your disposal for when this thing hits the column?"

"Hami—"

"You need me. I'm the most powerful magus you have here."

"You aren't that powerful."

Hami maintained eye contact. Piruzan stared back, unflinching.

"Fine," Hami said at last. "My orders are to head to New Ecbatana so I will, but I'm going to be communicating with Aegis as soon as he's back online to convince him I need to turn around and join the rest of you. You're going to need me." He turned away and walked towards Eggie. "You'll be seeing me again sooner than you think. Aegis will understand."

Hami could feel Piruzan's eyes on him. Was he buying it? As long as Piruzan didn't get through to Aegis, he'd be okay.

"Go then, Hami," Piruzan said at last. "But this is your last chance to redeem yourself. Don't do anything else stupid."

"And don't you get too close to the demon," Hami said. "Ten men can't fight it. And one more thing. Can you keep me informed of your location and what you're seeing? In case Aegis gives me the go ahead to join you." He added that last part to give Piruzan the impression that he'd remain connected and accessible to him, but the moment Salazar was out of range he'd disconnect from the network and would leave it for good.

Piruzan watched him walk all the way to Louis before calling his men to action. Four of them took charge of Victa's cart. Four moved towards the fire temple. The rest mounted their greenbucks and sprang off to the north.

–TWENTY-SEVEN–
STRAINED RELATIONSHIPS

Sammy closed her eyes and inhaled the steam coming off her mushroom tea. She hadn't been especially fond of the drink when she'd been here before. It was an acquired taste that she was only now beginning to appreciate. A warm, comfort drink that germinated memories with each sip. Fleeting moments. That first sensation of safety after Mehrak had rescued her from the Fungi Forest. Coming down the tower staircase in the mornings to be greeted with a mug of tea on the kitchen table while Mehrak prepared breakfast.

Not all glimpses of the past were laced with joy. They'd been drinking tea when Hami had told her she'd never return to the Mother World. The recollection constricted her chest. Best not to dwell on thoughts like that. Concentrate on the mug like she'd been told to. A trickier job than it had any right to be, seeing as the drink it contained brought back so many memories.

The back door hatch slammed and Hami climbed up out of the hole in the floor.

Mehrak threw his dishcloth over his shoulder and turned to face him. "Did you get away with it?" he asked.

Hami ignored the jibe. "Are you still planning to head north to the snow base to search for your wife?" he asked.

Sammy looked up from her tea.

Mehrak glanced at Sammy. "Er ... Yeah."

"Then this is your lucky day. We're going after her, but first we need to make a detour. Are you ready to leave?"

"I suppose."

"Sammy. Are you okay with that? Spending more time in Eggie? I know you wanted to make the choice regarding what happens to you. Is this an acceptable option for the moment?"

Sammy tried not to smile too hard. "Really? I can stay?"

"Yes. So there'll be plenty of time to catch up with Mehrak. Not that you have any choice, after losing the portal pearl back to the Mother World," he added with a surprising amount of bitterness.

"What about me?" Calven asked as he got up from the table.

"You're coming with us," Hami replied.

Calven paused. "But I need my karkadann. And all my stuff is in the back of the cart."

"Master Piruzan's men are taking the cart and karkadann to transport Victa to the garrison. I'll make sure everything is returned to the Keep when they're done."

Calven sat again. "And what about my leave?"

"You can go back to the Keep with Narok and Eva in a day or so. Right now I need you to stay put and enjoy Mehrak's hospitalities."

Mehrak gave Hami the side eye, but made no complaint.

"It's because I've seen Sammy, isn't it?" Calven asked. "And you don't want me to talk?"

"Correct. Are we good to go, Mehrak?"

Mehrak shrugged. "I suppose. What's happening with Leiss? Is he staying?"

"Leiss?" Calven asked. "Not Leiss Rustam?"

"Upstairs," Mehrak said. "Why?"

Calven seemed to shrink to half his size as he expelled air from an overly protracted sigh. "We have some history," he said. "I'd better get this over with." And he took to the stairs.

He wasn't gone long. He returned to the kitchen with slumped shoulders and an expression of tired resignation. "Let's just say he's not exactly thrilled I'm coming along for the ride," he said.

"Why not?" Sammy asked.

"He still blames me for the breakdown of his marriage."

———

They left the Fifth Azaran Fire Temple and set off south along the Cataclysm. Dirty Santa and his mate on the chariot, Narok and Eva on their individual karkadann, and the two other Marzban, Sasan and Rougetta, sharing a third rhino. And, of course, Golden Egg Cottage leading the way.

While Mehrak refilled the tea, Hami excused himself and went upstairs. Sammy gulped down the rest of her cup, then went up after him.

She found him alone on the front balcony.

Sammy walked out onto the long ship's prow-like balcony for the first time in two years. She ran her hand along the railing and leant over to watch Louis trundling along below, ears panning left and right, scanning the ground in front of him as he walked. She'd missed her big gentle buddy. "Hi Louis!" she called down. "It's good to see you again."

Louis wagged both his ears back and forth and shook his head enthusiastically. He probably didn't know she'd been away and even if he did he wouldn't be able to see any difference in her. Would she smell different? She hoped not, unless it was for the better. Though not many things smelt better with age. Especially bodies that hadn't showered in days. She wished then that she'd had a chance to wash before coming outside. Louis didn't seem to mind, though. Or if he did, at least he was polite enough not to show it. The perfect gentleman. He was a known quantity, a reliable friend, tirelessly carrying them onward, putting the miles behind them without complaint. What a legend.

Hami remained silent as they followed the white snaking light of the Cataclysm on the left. To the right, black nothingness, and above the same.

Sammy would have to initiate the conversation. "Is this my fault?" she asked, tilting her head towards the sky. "The blackness?"

Hami kept his gaze firmly forward. "You made it happen by crossing the threshold of the Temple of Paths, but it wasn't your fault. You weren't aware of the consequences. I take full responsibility."

It was what she'd wanted to hear, yet she still felt some guilt. Perhaps it was wasting Mehrak and Leiss's efforts in getting her home. Or the fact that it had been pretty obvious that something wasn't right as she approached the Temple of Paths seal. The earthquakes themselves should've been enough of a clue. She'd destroyed the realm whether she'd known she was doing it or not. "I'll help put things right," she said. "If you train me up as a magus I'll fight for you."

Hami said nothing in reply.

After a time, Mehrak joined them on the balcony. No one spoke until Hami asked Louis to veer away from the Cataclysm into the plain, heading west, back towards the Fungi Forest.

As the light and the temperature dropped, Hami left the balcony to go downstairs. Mehrak followed. At the curtain, he turned back. "Are you coming in?" he asked.

"In a moment," Sammy said. She smiled.

Mehrak dipped his head. "Take your time," he said, and left her to her thoughts.

Sammy remained at the railing as they crossed the black void between Cataclysm and Fungi Forest. The darkness seemed to permeate her soul, chilling her with a remorseless emptiness. Yet she stayed. She couldn't have said why, exactly. The warmth of the kitchen stove was calling and she was tempted to follow Mehrak downstairs, to have another mug of mushroom tea, to tell him all the things she'd been up to back home, but an intangible force kept her where she was.

A stillness had pervaded the plain, a deficit of life. Something terrible had swept through here. A joyless entity that had sucked everything hopeful, leaving a hollow husk. An echo of the presence remained. A shadow that Sammy couldn't draw away from. It was seeping into her now, making her drowsy. She fought it, but her eyes were getting heavy. Sleep was coming, trying to drag her away.

A jolt jarred Sammy awake. She came around, bleary-eyed into the light, still stood up and still clinging to the balcony railing, which was now tilting to the side.

Louis was slumped on the ground below, stretching out flat on his belly. They were back in the Fungi Forest.

Her last lucid memory before succumbing to unconsciousness was of the forest being little more than a thin line of light on the horizon. And now she was here and somehow still upright.

Harz pulled his chariot up while the Marzban dismounted their karkadann. Mehrak came around the side of Eggie carrying the paraphernalia Sammy recognised as his food-gathering equipment. Then he bustled off into the undergrowth in his typical enthusiastic manner. Like old times. Sammy smiled. This was what she wanted. Reunited with her unique travelling family again, on the road and back in the Fungi Forest having adventures. The emptiness she'd surrendered to on the plain was being filled, her body sponging up the energy released by the living, breathing ecosystem around her. She was already feeling more awake and alive.

Hami and Calven appeared at ground level. Calven went to help the other Marzban unpack the karkadann. Hami made for Narok. Both men distanced themselves from the rest to hold their conversation.

Narok stole a glance up at Sammy.

Hami was making plans for her again. Just like he had done last time. Why wasn't he including her in whatever they were discussing? It was because he wanted to send her home this time and knew she didn't want to go. She wouldn't go back. There was nothing for her to return to. She felt harsh on her mum, thinking that way, but it was true. The woman cared about her, but Sammy was in the way. If she stayed in Perseopia, her mum wouldn't have to worry about her grades, wouldn't have to feel guilty when she inevitably kicked her out of the house. Mama could enjoy a stress-free life with Jerry, without the financial burdens of feeding and housing a surplus adult that did nothing but get in their way. They could go out to dinner, take romantic walks in the country, visit a spa or whatever. The boring stuff old people enjoyed.

The only thing that got to Sammy was that she hadn't said goodbye, but then time had technically stopped back in the Mother World, like it had the last time. Her mum was frozen in time. If Sammy ever went home, then she would pick up right where she left off. Which was a depressing thought. The argument with her mother would be a distant memory to her, but to her mum it would be like it'd only just happened. That wouldn't be much of a reunion. The portal pearl had gone, though. Hami couldn't send her back.

Leiss joined her on the balcony. He hobbled over to the railing and gripped it with his big hands. "When you head down to get some food, can you bring me some up?" he asked.

"Sure," Sammy said. She paused. "Do you think I've made a stupid mistake, coming back here?"

Leiss shrugged. "Mehrak and I both risked our lives to send you home to your family. And look what I got for my troubles." He held up the arm he had in a sling. "You came straight back, throwing our efforts back in our faces. I'd do anything to keep my family together, but you've left yours twice now. I suppose people from the Mother World have different priorities."

Sammy hadn't had different priorities two years ago. But since then she'd learnt you couldn't rely on anyone. She remembered that Leiss's wife had walked out on him, and recalled him breaking down in front of her. So why did he still want to put himself through the pain of being part of a family again? A small part of her was jealous that he could nurture such child-like optimism.

She'd love to indulge a similar naivety and she had done once. She'd believed her father had been a hero, a tough, strong man, but he wasn't any of those things. He was angry, abusive, and had beaten her mother on several occasions. The signs had been obvious, but somehow Sammy hadn't noticed at the time. It was amazing, the extent to which you could fool yourself when you didn't want to believe something. She felt her face burn with the shame of remembering it. Her father was scum. And Leiss was a fool. Families were messed up. If he wanted to indulge himself in silly fantasies, that was up to him.

Sammy left Leiss at the railing. "I'll grab you some food," she said, and tossed the curtains out of the way as she entered the tower.

–TWENTY-EIGHT–
The Plan

Baxter dismissed the messenger and rose from his bed. He pulled on his clothes, picked up his satchel and was soon hurrying through the darkened streets towards parliament square. He deeply regretted his former aversion to the purple hue that had once saturated his city. The colour he'd previously found so abhorrent would've been a welcome respite now that everything was dark.

He ran through the black centre of a square where the streetlights no longer penetrated. The city's dim gas lamps were no longer sufficient to fully light up their surroundings and would have to be turned up. More gas would be needed. Taxes would go up.

Fear had taken hold of the people of New Ecbatana. This wasn't the city he'd grown up in, the safe, optimistic capital of their realm. Seemingly overnight it had become a ghost town, absent of the vitality and hope that made him proud to be a resident.

The minister was already dressed and sitting at the desk in his personal quarters when Baxter arrived. Grand Master Aegis paced opposite him.

Baxter bowed to the men, then took up a stool in the corner and fetched some parchment from his bag.

"And this demon of smoke and bodies is heading north?" the minister asked.

Baxter looked up. "Demon?"

"We'll fill you in on the details later." The minister was clearly in no mood to recap for his benefit. "Master Aegis?"

"Yes, Master Piruzan's unit is tracking it," answered the magus. "He is of the opinion that this demon is travelling to the Naziarabad Monument at Ameretat to escape Perseopia and gain access to the Mother World."

"As Lord VorMask was attempting with his black column?"

"Indeed."

"But surely this demon would need the key," the minister went on. "The item you told me is needed to leave Perseopia."

"Perhaps it already has it. Or perhaps it's powerful enough to open a portal without the need of one. We know next to nothing about it."

"Where's Hami?" Baxter asked.

The Grand Master paused. "He's allegedly coming here."

"Allegedly?"

"He's left the magi network again and has not re-joined."

————

Sammy lowered herself onto Louis's tail as she exited Golden Egg Cottage's back door, and kept her balance admirably on the way down to the forest floor. She strolled around the side of the cottage and into the campsite with a spring in her step, happy with her disembarkation.

The camp effort was already in full flow. Calven and Eva were digging a fire pit. Hami, Harz and Jokram were erecting tents. Mehrak was off somewhere still hunting and she couldn't see Sasan or Rougetta either.

"Is Leiss coming down?" Eva asked as Sammy approached.

"I don't think so. He asked me to bring him some food up."

Calven kicked at a scrawny root sticking out of the fire pit wall. "It's because I'm here."

"Give him time," Eva said. "He's been through a lot. And still blames himself for Borzin's death."

Calven shrugged. "I know." He picked up his shovel and continued to dig. "I still can't get over what happened to Borzin. And I wasn't even there."

Eva put a hand on his shoulder. "He'll come around," she said. "I'll go check on him in a bit."

Sasan and Rougetta appeared then, carrying armfuls of twigs and bits of dead bush. They waited for Eva and Calven to vacate the pit, then tossed everything in. Sasan set about lighting a fire using a flint and steel type contraption. Sammy wondered if she should light it for him using her powers. But she didn't want to show off or emasculate him—if he happened to be the kind of man that got upset at such things. Instead, she watched and waited.

Mehrak returned from his forest expedition with five rats hanging from a stick. He took a seat on a rock nearby and began filleting the little animals. Sammy tried not to watch, but the speed at which he turned the animals inside out and gutted them was impressive. She still wasn't a fan of blood and guts, but she was slowly becoming desensitised to it. Which may or may not be such a good thing.

Hami came over with Dirty Santa and Jokram, left them by the fire pit, then wandered off towards Golden Egg Cottage. He returned not long after with Leiss in tow, nodding for the big guy to join everyone else around the fire, then he cleared his throat to get their attention.

"Sammy, Mehrak and I are heading north," he said.

No one said anything in reply. Mehrak seemed not to be paying attention. He brought his rats closer to the fire, which was now beginning to take.

"I have asked a lot of you ladies and gentlemen," Hami was heading into formal speech mode. "Although you didn't know it at the time, you were fighting for the realm. And because of your efforts, we won that battle. You should be proud of yourselves." He gave everyone a moment to reflect on this. "You all helped destroy Ramaask. He's at the bottom of the Cataclysm thanks to you and I want to apologise for dragging you all into this fight. But also to thank you for putting your trust in me. Especially when none of us knew how this would end."

Mehrak carried on preparing the rats and threading their disgusting skinless carcasses onto a spit.

Narok was the first to speak. "We were going against the magi's orders," he said. "And you're going to ask us to do it again."

Hami looked him in the eye. "I did what I thought was right."

"But what you thought was right has killed many of my guards and jeopardised the people of Perseopia. It might even have doomed us all."

Hami dipped his head in what appeared to be silent acknowledgement. "That's why I need your help now more than ever. I may not have always been honest, but this thing we've released—"

There were murmurs around the campsite, and a few raised eyebrows.

Hami held up his hands. "This thing *I've* released—I take full responsibility." He took a deep breath. "This thing looks to be a worse threat than Ramaask. We're talking the fate of the realm again. But this time I'm not ordering anyone to do anything. I'm asking you."

"A favour?" Narok sounded sceptical.

"You're free to say no. Your debt to the magi has been repaid. You can go home if you wish."

Sammy watched Hami. His shoulders were stooped, his eyes were red. She remembered him as being much more forceful and demanding last time.

"What exactly is it you want from us?" Leiss asked. "Are you asking us to follow you into battle again? To join Master Piruzan and engage this demon that can raise an army of the dead?"

"No." Hami paced around the fire. "I'd like you to travel north with me to Ramaask's snow base in the Atrabiliars."

"Why?"

"Because I believe it's the real location the demon is heading to. There's a portal there that it intends to use."

Mehrak put his knife down. "How does that corpse monster know of the snow base?"

"The tall thin figure knows about it. It betrayed Ramaask to release the demon."

"Betrayed Ramaask how? It was trying to kill Sammy for him."

"That was an act. It was chasing her towards the Fire Temple so she would cross the seal to release this demon, its master."

"It was trying to kill me," Sammy said, but she didn't truly believe it anymore.

"It wasn't trying to kill you," Hami said quietly. "When it found you in the Fungi Forest, it chased you without catching up. Remember? It shepherded you towards Mehrak and Louis knowing you'd be safe with them and that they'd take you out of the forest. It also scared us into leaving Honton Keep earlier than planned, knowing I'd try to draw Ramaask out of Aratta. And then it led you to the Temple of Paths."

"That sounds like a bit of a stretch," Mehrak said. "Why didn't it just drag Sammy to the temple instead of using an elaborate plan that could've easily gone wrong?"

"I don't think it can. It comes from the same place Ramaask does, but it's not like him. I overheard them talking in Aratta. Ramaask entered the realm whole. This other creature didn't. It exists in some kind of half form. Maybe because Achaemen Mantis called Ramaask here via an incantation. I don't know. But Ramaask refused to return the thin creature to his true form because existing on multiple planes and in multiple dimensions allowed it to find Sammy. I'm guessing that also means it can't physically touch you, Sammy, hence having to herd you. It might not be able to control its heat either and might've accidentally killed you if it got too close. Think about it. It killed Borzin right in front of your eyes, even going so far as to torture him until he begged Leiss to help you get home. I know it's been two years, Sammy, but I bet you haven't

175

forgotten how Borzin acted when you found him. He didn't sound like himself when he made Leiss promise to help you, did he?" He looked to the big man. "That's right, isn't it, Leiss?"

Leiss nodded without making eye contact. "Yeah."

"You were listening to the thin figure's voice through Borzin. The whole time he was guiding Sammy towards the seal of the Ahriman so she could release his master."

"That's why it missed us with the fireball," Mehrak said.

"Excuse me?"

"I wondered how it managed to miss us right outside the Temple of Paths. It shot a fireball over our heads and caved the roof in. I figured we'd been lucky at the time, but it left us no choice but to continue along the tunnel to cross the seal." Mehrak put down his rat. "And it lifted the floor tile in the back hall of the Fifth Azaran. We would never have figured out how to get to the temple if it hadn't shown us the way."

Sammy had nothing to say to that. She'd been convinced they'd outsmarted the thin figure. But it had been one step ahead of them the whole time.

"If you truly believe this monster is heading to the snow base," Narok said, "then why did you send Master Piruzan to the white column in Ameretat? You're putting the realm at risk again."

"Because I didn't want him to know about the portal." Hami looked away. "It's a gateway to the Mother World."

Mehrak stood up. "You knew there was another, safer way home for Sammy and you took her to the Fifth Azaran instead? You used her as bait, risked her life and everyone else's in the realm?"

"We've been through this already. I told you my reasons." Hami spoke through gritted teeth. He opened his mouth to continue, stopped himself, then took a deep breath. "This time is different," he said at last.

"And how's that?"

"Because this time I'm putting Sammy first. I promised that if I survived the battle outside the Fifth Azaran, I'd help her get home to the Mother World. I tried to send her home in the Temple of Paths but she refused to use the pearl."

"You're still putting the realm at risk by deceiving the magi," Narok said. "You've sent them to the wrong location. I want Sammy to go home as much as the next person, but you can't risk the very existence of the realm for her."

"I'm not. I've informed Grand Master Aegis about the portal. He's bound to figure out that's where the demon is actually going, if he hasn't already. When that happens, the magi will travel there and shut it down. We have a narrow window to get there before they do. Now that the Mother World portal pearl has been taken, we have no other option if we want to return Sammy home."

"Perhaps I don't want to go home," Sammy said.

"Hold on," Mehrak said. "Why doesn't the demon use the portal pearl instead of travelling to the snow base? The thin figure presumably stole it for his master."

"That is a very good point," Hami replied. "And one I don't have the answer to. My best guess would be that it can't use the Temple of Paths and that the portal pearl has been stolen to stop anyone else using it."

"Sending the magi to the wrong location at a time like this is still incredibly reckless," Narok said.

"This is the best way," Hami said. "The monument at Ameretat is directly in the path of the snow base. Piruzan and the magi will engage the demon outside the city to protect the civilians that live there. If they can't hold the demon back there, they won't be able to hold it back at the snow base. At least this way the people of the citadel will get the full might of the magi to protect them. And it will buy us enough time to get to the snow base, to send Sammy home and destroy the portal so the demon can't use it."

"But there are only eleven of us. This portal is going to be heavily guarded. What chance do we have of getting Sammy home and destroying it?"

"The snow base is way up on the freezing slopes of the Atrabiliar mountains. Which means crabmen can't survive up there. It's desolate. Security shouldn't be high."

"They could have domesticated karkadann like ours," Narok said. "Or manticores, banded wolves or silverback bears."

"They may have some of them," Hami said, "but you have me. And you have Sammy."

–TWENTY-NINE–
INTO THE DARK

They followed the edge of the Fungi Forest north. On the left, mushrooms and glittering light. On the right, nothingness, the end of the world. Each time they stopped to make camp, Sammy would test her nerve by walking out into the darkness. And each time, she would be unable to sense anything ahead of her, no life and no structure. Occasionally there would be other mushrooms that had grown apart from the others. Single beacons of light out in the black. Sammy would walk out to these islands of light, these safe havens in the sea of shadow, and stand under their luminescent canopies, allowing their glittering spores to drift down on her. The further from her companions she ventured, the heavier the sense of dread became. She'd not witnessed the corpse demon Hami had told her about, but she could tell it was out there. She couldn't feel it exactly, but there was a cold emptiness left in its wake. A vacuum devoid of life.

She experienced the emptiness each time she strayed from camp, yet something drew her to it. A curiosity maybe, or a nihilistic urge to approach the abyss and plunge into its depths. She wanted to leave everything behind, embrace the nothingness.

She had no tangible purpose in Perseopia other than for Hami to babysit her to the portal in the mountains. To him she was little more than a burden. Someone he felt obliged to help after making rash promises to send her home.

That didn't bother her. Perseopia had Golden Egg Cottage, lightning staffs and excitement. It had Mehrak too. Even if she didn't want a relationship with him, he at least cared for her.

But there was more. Something separated her from the others. Something intangible. She could feel it. She had a feeling Hami could too. She acknowledged this with unemotional resignation. That was fine. She was happy in her own company and already had a long history of being different.

The thing that stopped her from walking away and giving herself to the nothingness completely was that Hami had begun to teach her. She could sense a reticence in him, like he didn't truly want her to explore her abilities, but he would need her for the fight at the snow base, and that meant she got trained. It was important that she become strong enough to take on whatever they came up against. Which sounded ominous, but it meant discovering more about who and what she was. She learned to feel for objects without having to see them first, to latch on and keep them airborne while concentrating on other things.

Her powers grew daily. Hami even let her adopt Victa's lightning staff, once she'd convinced him she could use it responsibly. She practised lighting it up and firing off shots, and took it with her whenever she went out into the darkness. She would shine beams of light out into the void often, but there was rarely anything to see other than a distant rock or boulder.

It was on one of Sammy's solitary wanderings that she saw the flames. She'd wandered further than normal, leaving her staff dark and testing her bravery by feeling the way with her senses. The edge of the forest had become a distant shimmer behind her, and she could no longer see the camp.

Sammy closed, and then opened her eyes. The difference between them being open or closed was negligible. A perpetual night with no stars. She could just about see her hands and staff when she moved them, there seemed to be some ambient light, but not much.

Sammy walked further still, pushing her boundaries, and there it was. A single point of orange flickering in the distance. Instinctively, she carried on towards it.

She'd been walking for some time when she heard Hami calling after her.

"What are you doing?" he said as he caught up. He illuminated his staff, dazzling her, despite him keeping the light low.

"There's an orange light in the distance," Sammy said while shielding her eyes.

"And you just walked towards it? It could be anything."

"I've got Victa's lightning staff. And there are stones on the floor I can use as bullets."

"Your threat sensing ability is still underdeveloped. You couldn't sense that I was approaching."

"That's unfair. You cloak yourself from me somehow."

"Let's have a look at this orange light, then," Hami said and extinguished his staff.

Sammy's eyes took a moment to adjust and relocate the light. She couldn't see Hami. She could sense him now though, which meant he was letting her. It was unnerving to be in such close proximity to him in the dark. No one else could've made her feel this way. She could sense a little of what people were feeling, but not Hami. Hami was a blank.

"What is it?" she asked, breaking the silence. "The orange light."

"There's a village in that general area. It might be a fire. We should probably investigate."

"It could be the magi. Master Piruzan and those other guys."

"They might've come this way. But they're way ahead of us now."

"How do you know?"

"A couple of the lower order magi in Master Piruzan's team aren't securing their communications properly. I'm only picking up snatches of conversation but I've worked out they're keeping pace with the corpse demon as it heads towards the eastern shore of the Kuchak Sea."

Hami lapsed into silence again. Sammy wondered what else he knew. "Did you find out anything else?"

"Nothing worth knowing. I can't pick up anything between Piruzan and the Grand Master. They'll be using their own secure channel, which will be locked down and virtually impossible to crack. I'm certain they've been discussing me, among other things. And they'll be wondering why I haven't checked in with them on my way to New Ecbatana."

"What will they do?"

"Not much they can do now. How will they find me?"

———

Mehrak was stacking empty dishes when he noticed Sammy return with Hami.

Hami had gone after her, to see if she was okay. Which, of course, she would be. Louis could smell a threat several stadia away. Not to mention the karkadann they had with them. They'd be on top of an attack in moments. Nothing would be able to get within twenty stadia.

Mehrak watched them. Sammy was talking animatedly. Hami was smiling, which was unlike him. Then Hami said something and now Sammy was smiling.

"Where have you guys been?" Mehrak called over, his voice sounding jealous in his head.

"Nowhere," Sammy said.

"You've obviously been somewhere."

"Obviously," Sammy said, and wandered off towards Eggie.

Hami came over but didn't sit down. "We saw a light out in the dark," he said. "A fire, most likely. I think there's a village out there, so we'll take a look."

Leiss, who'd been sat, staring into the fire until then, perked up. "I'll come with you."

"Fine," Hami said. "We'll take Harz's chariot."

Calven was putting up a tent nearby. "Can I come too?" he called over as he continued to stretch guy ropes and hammer pegs into the soil.

"Sure," Hami shrugged, but his attention was on the forest and Harz clambering out from between the mushrooms. Hami set off towards him. "I'll be right back."

Leiss got up from the fireside and walked over to Calven. He moved in close and bent until they were eye to eye. "I think you should stay here," he said.

Calven stepped back. "I, er … if that's what you'd prefer?"

"Leiss, can you find Sammy?" Hami asked as he and Harz walked back into camp.

Leiss continued to stare at Calven. "No problem," he said at last, then broke eye contact, turned away and shouldered his way past Harz on his way towards Golden Egg Cottage.

"What's his problem?" Harz said as he went to sit down by the fire. He held out a skewer with the mangiest looking rat Mehrak had ever seen. It looked like it had been run over by the guy's chariot and then dried out for several days. Mehrak would never have served something that looked so disgusting, but then he prided himself on his cooking, and enjoyed the compliments he received.

Everyone appreciated Mehrak's food, yet he always found himself clearing up alone. His fault. Calven tried to help, but he never quite put the plates and cutlery in their correct places. It was just easier for Mehrak to do it himself. There was nothing wrong with striving for perfection. He was proud to be a domesticated man, and being able to maintain a clean and tidy home. But being surrounded by physically impressive human beings like Leiss, Eva and Calven made him feel inferior and unmanly. Hami was the worst, with his commanding attitude, and his ruggedness and muscles. And Sammy was becoming like him. A fighter.

He would watch them train every day. The two of them spending time together. Shooting lightning staffs or moving objects with their minds. And the funny thing was that Hami seemed genuinely in awe of her. Sammy appeared entirely unaware of it. It was only when Hami's stolid expression would slip that Mehrak could appreciate how quickly she was progressing. For the briefest moments, Hami's eyes would betray shock, and on occasion, even fear.

All Mehrak ever taught Sammy was the correct drawer to put the spoons in or the best way to dice a roan shrub root.

He was still clearing up when Hami came over to talk, striding with his wide, manly gait. He stood over Mehrak, hands on hips, practically dripping manliness all over him.

"Sammy and I are going to investigate the burning village," he said.

"Now?" Mehrak asked as he scratched at a speck of gristle that had attached itself to a plate.

"Yes. Why not?"

Mehrak didn't want to go. He'd had enough of adventure, of being scared for his life, but he wasn't about to let them go by themselves. "Can I come?"

"If you want. I thought you'd want to finish off the rest of these dishes. Put them in their correct drawers."

"Why would I want that?" Mehrak said, flinging the plate he'd been holding into the bushes. "Let's go."

He'd go looking for the plate when they got back, when no one was watching.

–THIRTY–
The Burnt Village

The light grew from a dot on the horizon to a blazing fire during the time it took to cross the plain on Harz's chariot.

Flames leapt up behind the stone wall surrounding the village, carrying glowing ash and smoke into the sky. The wall was high, yet misshapen and uneven, like it had been built in a hurry. Most likely a recent addition to keep crabmen out.

Harz steered the chariot through the broken gates and past the strewn furniture that had likely been the barricade behind which the villagers made their last stand. It had been woefully inadequate against whatever they'd been trying to keep out.

Houses and shops huddled either side of the dirt road running through the centre. The place was silent but for the fire that snapped as it consumed the roofs of the houses at the far end of town.

There were no bodies.

Mehrak was regretting the decision to step outside his comfort zone.

Hami moved to help Sammy off the back of the chariot, but she brushed past him and walked ahead into the village. She was upset that he'd stopped her from bringing Victa's lightning staff.

Mehrak smiled at the slight and walked after her, leaving Harz and Leiss to tie the silverskins to a hitching post.

She crossed the street and looked through the window of a shopfront.

Hami entered a building on the nearside.

Mehrak wasn't about to squander an opportunity of having Sammy to himself so hurried to close the gap between them.

"We've hardly spent any time together since you've been back," he said when he caught up.

"We've spent time together."

"It's just that you feel distant to me, like you're shutting me out for some reason. I know you aren't doing it on purpose. I suppose I must seem like a stranger to you." He stopped talking. There were so many things he wanted to say, but he couldn't figure out the best way to do it. She'd had two years to get over him and move on with her life. And what was he actually trying to achieve? He was married, and acting like a lovesick teenager.

"Is this about the kiss?" Sammy asked.

The question came out of nowhere and Mehrak wasn't prepared with an answer. He'd thought about it often over the last few days, but he was no closer to knowing how he should feel about it.

"Because you know that was two years ago—to me, anyway. I can't really remember why it happened. I guess I was just being a silly sixteen-year-old with a crush on an older man. It's not like I've been thinking about it all this time. It didn't mean anything, did it? After all, you're married."

Mehrak's heart rose up in his throat and it felt like he was choking on it. "I just ... wanted to make sure there was no awkwardness." He feigned a smile and mumbled something else about going to check on Leiss and Harz.

Sammy let him go.

As he walked away, he told himself that it was for the best, that the kiss should never have happened, but as he approached the chariot, the world seemed to be spiralling away from him.

———

Sammy felt bad for saying what she had. She liked to think it was for the sake of Mehrak's marriage, that she'd been 'doing the right thing'. But in truth, she'd probably done it out of pettiness.

She'd lied about not remembering the kiss. It had been her first, and she'd thought about it for longer than had been healthy. She'd fallen, a little bit, for Mehrak back then, and it had taken her a year to get over him. And she resented him making her feel that way. Her undying love, which she realised now was just a crush, had hardened and she'd become bitter. Now she could see him for what he truly was. Just a lonely guy desperate for a companion. She was still attracted to him, weirdly. But not in love. And it was for the best that it remained that way.

Hami, on the other hand, was available, seeing as his girlfriend had died. Although that had probably piled on a load of emotional baggage, it also made him complicated and interesting. She could nurse his broken heart back to health. Show him what it was to love again. Yeah, right. She smiled to herself. He also happened to be tall, dark and muscular. That helped.

Sammy went after him.

"Hey," she called out as she ran across the street to meet him coming out of a house. "What are you looking for?"

"I'm not sure. Survivors. Supplies."

Sammy followed him as he entered a small hardware store. Trays of varying sized nails were lined up on the wall behind the counter. Saws and hammers hung from the ceiling, and spades and pickaxes leant against the wall.

Hami, still silent, picked up a stone mason's hammer and turned it over in his hands.

Sammy latched onto it with her mind and tugged it out of his hand so that it flew to hers. She smiled as she caught it and wiggled her eyebrows up and down.

Hami didn't crack a smile, so she handed it back. "Why couldn't I shift Victa with my mind?" she asked.

Hami looked up.

"When we were in the Fungi Forest. I was trying to drag him to the Marzban outpost but I couldn't lift him or even make him lighter. My powers don't work on me either. I've tried. Like if I wanted to jump really high. Or fly. I can't get it to work."

"Bodies are too complex."

"It worked with the crabmen."

"Crabmen are different. They have large sections of shell that are composed entirely of the same repeating molecule, like a rock. It makes them easier to latch on to. That's how you managed to stop that crabman's arm from running you through, and why you're so adept at firing stone projectiles. Humans are more complex, but it's possible to latch on to bone if you can see through the surface layers of skin, tissue and muscle in your mind's eye. Not many magi can do it and it takes many years to perfect the technique."

Hami lapsed into silence, then he left the storefront through a back door that probably led to a storage room or living quarters. Forget him. If he wasn't going to be sociable, Sammy would explore somewhere else.

She went outside. The village brought to mind a small outpost town that you'd get in an old western. The sort of place two men would draw guns at high noon.

She spied Mehrak sat on the steps of a building further down the street. He looked up, but Sammy turned down an alley and walked away. She was going to have some alone time. She turned down another side street and found herself in a darkened part of the village away from the fire. She sat down on a porch. She shouldn't have been so awful to Mehrak. He at least cared for her, unlike Hami. She still wouldn't encourage his advances, though. The guy's wife would be devastated if she knew another woman was making moves on her husband. Sammy would stay strong. For her sake as much as Mehrak's.

There was a flash of light accompanied by a warm gust of air. The roofs around her were beginning to catch. She should go.

Sammy got up from the porch. And stopped.

A large hyena blocked the way. One with razor spines down its back.

Fear rolled off it in waves. Its spines rose and fell with its rib cage as terror made its movements erratic. It was panicked and aggressive. A combination that didn't bode well for an unarmed Sammy. Thanks for that, Hami.

She would have to tackle the beast like she had the pig-dog. But this thing was a whole new threat level, a proper predator. She scanned the ground for stones and found none. Everything else was nailed down. Could she reach the nearest door before it reached her? How would she barricade it?

She concentrated on the hyena's emotion. It was scared. And hungry. That much was obvious, but she could feel more. It had come here looking for bodies, had smelt death but found nothing to feed on. Now it was trapped and had found Sammy. It was preparing for an attack. There was no time!

Sammy sent calming thoughts to the beast. And it paused.

Had that worked? She kept going and the beast's stance eased. It was working! Somehow, unbelievably, it was relaxing, and she was making it happen. Its anger ebbed. Its breathing slowed. It regarded her warily.

Sammy held her breath and took a step closer. No sudden moves. The hyena barked at her and snapped its jaws.

She kept the calming thoughts flowing. Moved closer.

And held out her arm.

————

Mehrak got up off the steps. He shouldn't have let Sammy go off alone. Even if she could handle herself better than he could. Perhaps Hami had said something to upset her. He would see if she was alright. Comfort her if she needed it.

He turned the corner and stopped.

Sammy was crouched in front of a hyena, stroking its head. And not just any hyena, a particularly ferocious breed of its type.

The creature growled and he flinched back behind the corner. "What are you doing?" he called.

"Making a new friend," Sammy replied.

"That's a slicer!" Mehrak whispered loudly.

"A what?" Sammy ruffled the hair on its head. "You're going to have to come closer. I can't hear you all the way from that wall you're cowering behind."

Mehrak tentatively edged out from his hiding place and took a few steps closer. "I said it's a *slicer*."

"Because of these razor spines down his back?"

"Some large breeds of hyena can be ridden. But not ..."

"... a slicer, because you'd get sliced in half?"

"And they're notoriously vicious and hard to tame."

"Can't be that hard. I've done it." Sammy lifted its big head and looked it in the eyes. "He's so cute. What shall I call him?"

"Scary killing-machine?"

"Hardly rolls of the tongue."

"How about Spike? You know, because—"

"... he has spikes on his back?" Sammy said. "Good effort. Original. I'm calling him Kimbo Slicer. Because he looks tough. Kimbo for short."

"I don't get it."

"You wouldn't."

This was Mehrak's chance. He was going to say something. "Sammy?" He looked away, worried that if he made eye contact, words would fail him. Worried that he'd see her roll her eyes and embarrass him. "In the Temple of Paths before you left. The thing that happened between us ..." There was no going back now. "It wasn't nothing. To me, anyway. I care about you. I know two years have gone by for you and feelings change over time, but—the thing that happened—it's only just happened to me and the time we've spent together has been special and—"

"Great Ahura! What is that?" Leiss exclaimed as he hobbled over.

"It's Kimbo," Sammy replied cheerily. She got up and led the monstrous beast over.

Leiss had the worst possible timing. At least Mehrak had managed to get some of what he wanted to say off his chest. She knew he cared about her. That was good enough for now.

Leiss backed up a couple of paces as Sammy brought the hyena close. "That is one scary looking animal," he said. "Are you sure you should be so close to it? He's not a pet you know."

"He's my pet."

"That thing can't stay in Eggie," Mehrak said. "He's too big."

"We can keep him, though. Right? He can jog alongside Louis."

"What if he attacks us? Hami won't like it."

"You can talk him round though, can't you?" She smiled at him and touched his arm. "If you *care* about me ..." She pulled a pouty face like a child would when it wanted to be indulged.

Mehrak wasn't stupid. He knew he was being mocked, but there was no cruelty in it. "I'll talk to him," he said.

"Thank you," she said, and jogged off with her new 'pet'.

He watched her go, a warm feeling of contentment spreading in his chest.

"You're a mug," Leiss said. He laughed and slapped him on the back.

Mehrak didn't care. Sammy didn't necessarily return his feelings, but she was at ease with him. They were on good terms and she'd touched his arm. That had to count for something.

"Wait for us, dog whisperer," Leiss called ahead to Sammy. He jogged to catch up.

She stopped and turned back. "Dog whisperer? Seriously?"

–THIRTY-ONE–
THIRD PERSON ADVENTURE

Behnam watched his body stagger down the street from behind, using Ghobad's eyes.

Both men stopped so Behnam could adjust the dressing over his own ruined eyes. From the guard's viewpoint, he watched his hands adjust the bandages and tighten them around his head.

He wasn't entirely accustomed to this voyeuristic out-of-body experience yet. He could feel his hair with his own fingers, could feel his head being scratched, but it was a strangely disconnected sensation, seeing it from a location outside himself.

Ghobad the person had long gone, his consciousness imprisoned, locked away deep within his brain. Behnam was disgusted with himself for having done it. It was a heinous act, unforgivable by the magi, and if it weren't for the fate of the realm, he would've sooner died than put another human being through it. Even scum like Ghobad, a man that had pledged his allegiance to Ramaask.

Behnam sighed, he wasn't able to rationalise his actions, even to himself. He stirred himself back into motion. Was he really as old as he looked through Ghobad's eyes? He'd lost weight from his incarceration, explaining his slack skin. But when had his hair become grey?

It had taken time to get used to this new way of controlling himself. When Ghobad had first unlocked his cell and dragged him to a safe place, he hadn't been able to walk unaided. He'd barely been capable of feeding himself.

While Behnam recovered, he inhabited Ghobad's head, piloting the man's body, sending it out for food and supplies, eventually becoming adept at remote-controlling it.

After several days of lying low, Behnam's own body was finally fit enough to walk under its own steam. At first it made him ill, watching himself from a location outside his body. A kind of motion sickness. Similar to when he'd first learned to ride a greenbuck. He figured it was due to the input from his new set of eyes not synchronising with what his inner ear balance was telling him.

It took some trial and error, but he managed to get both Ghobad and himself to the area where he and Hami had tied their greenbucks. Both animals had long since depleted their food reserves, were malnourished and close to death. It would be days before they were strong enough to move, let alone ride. Behnam had Ghobad feed them, then untie and shoo them away. The poor creatures could barely stand. He wasn't sure how much longer they'd live but they might survive if they made it to the Fungi Forest.

Ghobad's first task was to find some healthy animals for them. The guard possessed a detailed knowledge of Aratta, so by tapping into that, Behnam was able to guide the man to one of the Order's stables where he stole a pair of horses. Food supplies came next, then they were ready to leave.

Behnam needed to catch up with Hami as soon as possible. If he was still alive. The last location he'd been at when they'd connected was the Fifth Azaran Fire Temple. It was unlikely Hami would still be there, but it was as good a place as any to start looking for him. And yet, as Behnam stared up at the black sky using Ghobad's eyes, he knew it was too late.

Had Ramaask been right in his fears? Behnam had unintentionally connected with the demon when he'd tried to read his mind. He'd gazed through the window into Ramaask's head, seen things that no human should ever see. He almost hadn't returned from the experience. Something had returned with him though, a shadow that strained at his sanity. Damage had been done, he'd been changed, traumatised. He couldn't allow himself to infect the wider magi network and, by extension, his brothers. He wouldn't connect again, he'd go to Hami in person.

Still, there were questions that needed answering. Had the Ahriman been unleashed on Perseopia? Or was this darkening of the sky something else? And what of Ramaask? Had he died like he'd feared?

Behnam and the guard led the horses from Aratta, taking the eastern trade route out into the Fungi Forest towards New Ecbatana. The route hadn't been frequented for its intended purpose for more than a hundred years. Occasionally, a brazen thief would use it to sneak into Aratta to scavenge treasures from abandoned houses, but mainly it was used by Ramaask's henchmen and crabmen to enter and leave the city.

Mushrooms had grown up on some parts of the route, but it had been used frequently enough that it remained a usable path through the forest. Hopefully, with Ramaask's apparent demise, they wouldn't run into anything dangerous coming the other way.

–THIRTY-TWO–
Target Acquired

Sammy helped Mehrak collect the soiled dishes from around the fireside. She gathered them up in a stack, then set off towards Eggie. Halfway there, she paused to look back at the Fungi Forest. Now just a thin strip of green, way off in the distance.

After the burning village, they'd collected Louis and the Marzban and struck out across the plain. That first decimated village was a long way back now. They'd passed another two since then, before they made camp out in the darkness of the plain.

Hami had been listening in on the magi's communications. Apparently they'd followed the demon north and witnessed the deaths of villagers along the way. They'd tried to intervene at first, but two of them had been lost to the dead army and so they'd retreated. Each village that fell in the path of the demon was consumed, the inhabitants were killed and their bodies joined the ranks of the dead to grow the demon's army.

Despite her frequent journeys out into the dark alone, Sammy missed the vibrancy of the Fungi Forest, the duality of calming beauty and lurking danger. Now that they'd left it behind, she realised that she might not ever see it again if Hami got his way and returned her to the Mother World.

He was heading for disappointment if he thought she'd go willingly. She was exactly where she wanted to be; back on the road with Mehrak and Louis.

An uneasy feeling hitched in her chest then. The purpose of their mission was to travel to the snow base for Mehrak's wife, as well as sending her home. Two scenarios she didn't relish coming true. It was selfish, but she didn't want Mehrak to find his wife. She didn't want the woman to spoil what they had, whatever that was.

As she passed Kimbo, she shifted the plates she was carrying to one hand so she could ruffle the hair behind his ear with the other. They'd made him a makeshift collar and leash to tie him up away from the other animals. For their safety as much as his. Slicers could chew their way through plate armour, apparently, which meant he'd be able to deliver significant damage before they could take him down. Narok was especially concerned about what he might do left alone without Sammy around to keep him calm. But Kimbo was a big softy. Sammy could see inside him. He was a simple creature but he was loyal to her. If she told him not to attack the other creatures, then he wouldn't.

"Come on dog whisperer," Leiss called from the back door hatch. "Pass me those plates."

Sammy dragged her heels towards him. "I thought we'd dropped dog whisperer."

"I like it."

"Can't we swap it for beast master? Or ..." Sammy shrugged, "... monster tamer?"

"Monster tamer sounds dumb."

"I'm trying to think of one on the fly."

"You ridiculed me for Spike," Mehrak said as he came over with his plates.

"Spike is still worse." Sammy yawned.

"You should get some sleep," Mehrak said. "Maybe your new nickname will come to you in a dream."

"I think bed is a good call."

"Sleep well then, dog whisperer," Leiss said, then disappeared back into the cottage.

Sammy couldn't summon up the effort to respond. She stepped onto Louis's tail and was boosted up and onto the stairs.

She nodded an acknowledgement to Hami, Leiss and Eva when she reached the kitchen, but then headed past them and took the steps to the tower. The day had not been an especially hard one, they'd done no more walking than normal, but the excitement of finding the village and taming Kimbo had left her drained. She climbed into the bed and within moments she could feel her consciousness drifting away as sleep dragged her under its veil.

Sammy experienced an almost dreamless sleep. She was vaguely aware of being asleep, but it was a sleep of sensation and shapes, without tangible substance, until she heard the words;

"Seek out the path, cross the river of light,

"Descend through the depths and when you alight,

"Take a trip through the gate, where the mountain will fall,"

Then it stopped. Hands were on her. Shaking her awake.

Sammy came around to the view of Hami standing over her, his expression stricken.

"What are you doing!" he yelled.

———

Baxter was at the minister's desk, poring over the particulars of funding the military presence in Ameretat, when the Grand Master burst into the room unannounced.

The minister looked up. "To what do we owe the pleasure, Master Aegis?"

Aegis composed himself and took a breath. "I have news."

"That couldn't have waited until the morning?"

"I believe there's a second child from the Mother World here in Perseopia."

The minister put down his papers. "Explain."

"A number of days ago, a potential magus recruit registered on the magi network not far from where Sammy was found in the Fungi Forest. The recruit we sent Victa Wild to collect."

"And you think it's this recruit? But how could that be? Victa ran into a group of crabmen and dropped off the network before he found the person?"

"We *assumed* Victa dropped off the network before he found them. But then the same recruit has just connected to the magi network again. This time near the village of Kath in the plains of Al-Biruni. Hundreds of stadia from where they had first appeared."

"How do you know it's the same person?"

"Every human has a unique brainwave signature. Like a fingerprint. As a magus, you get to recognise the characteristics of these signatures like you'd recognise a face. This person is the same one that connected in the Fungi Forest, and they've coincidentally travelled hundreds of stadia across Perseopia to a location just north of the Fifth Azaran Fire Temple, only a day and a half behind Master Piruzan."

"Are you implying that the Marzban that found Victa also found this potential recruit and took them both all the way across the Fungi Forest to Hami at the Cataclysm?"

"That is exactly what I'm implying."

"Which means Hami is hiding this person."

"The evidence suggests it. He's left the network, and we know he's listening in on conversations between the lower order magi in Piruzan's unit. He's checking their location and that of the demon. Probably so he doesn't stray into either by accident."

"But what makes you think this potential recruit is from the Mother World?"

"Piruzan sensed something when he met Hami at the Cataclysm."

"Something?"

"Something not of this realm. Hami explained it away as being the residual essence of the first child from the Mother World, Sammy. The one that left. And because Lord VorMask's presence was still overpowering, it helped to mask it. Hami also happened to be forthcoming with information and seemed eager to assist, so

Piruzan didn't press further. But it seems Hami was merely telling Piruzan what he needed to hear in order to escape with this person unknown."

"And Piruzan fell for it?"

"Piruzan didn't completely trust him, and after dwelling on the unusual sensation he'd experienced at the Cataclysm, he communicated to the magi he'd assigned to the Fifth Azaran and had them interrogate the Hirbod."

"And?"

"At first, not much. No one had seen Hami enter the temple and the Hirbod that had been protecting the opening to the Temple of Paths had been killed. Burned to death by what we believe was one of Lord VorMask's creatures. However, the custodian Lila-Maryam and several others were around when Hami left with the traveller in the golden caravan. She reported that they'd both acted cagey and had backed the caravan up to the hall that led to the hidden temple, as if they were smuggling something or someone out. Then as they left, one of the young priests spotted a face peering out of the curtains of the caravan."

"What sort of face?"

"She couldn't make it out from her vantage point, so couldn't give us much to go on other than she thought the person looked like a young woman."

"It's not likely to be a potential magus recruit if it's a girl though, is it? And you haven't convinced me that this child is from the Mother World. Or whether it is still the first child being smuggled back out of the temple."

"It could be the girl, Sammy, but I think that's unlikely. The mountain fell and the skies have darkened so we know she definitely crossed the seal. However, the sensation Piruzan experienced upon meeting Hami at the Cataclysm was powerful. And in hindsight, he believes it was most likely a child from the Mother World."

"In hindsight? Most likely?"

"I know it's not much to go on, but why would Hami keep a normal magus recruit secret? I realise that this may sound far-fetched, but given the gravity of the situation we find ourselves in, I'd rather make preparations for it being another Mother Worlder than assume it's not and suffer the consequences. Piruzan sensed the essence of someone not from here. He believes Hami had someone with him, someone he was hiding. I know for certain that Hami didn't want an escort back to New Ecbatana. He told Piruzan that he wanted to go north with him, to follow the demon."

"So let's assume you're right in your hypothesis. Why would Hami want to risk the life of another Mother Worlder by following the demon to the Naziarabad Monument?"

"Unless he's not going to the monument. If you carry on past Ameretat and travel far enough north, you hit the Atrabiliar Mountains."

Baxter felt his head beading with sweat. "The snow base with the portal."

The Grand Master nodded. "A portal, if Hami is to be believed, that Ramus VorMask intended to use to travel to the Mother World. And I believe it's this snow base that the demon is heading to."

The minister's mouth opened but nothing came out. Baxter found himself similarly at a loss for words.

"Hami knows something we don't about this potential magus, and I think he is taking him—or her—to the portal in the mountains to send him or her home."

"Why didn't he send them home the same way as last time, using the Temple of Paths?"

"I can't go into detail but that avenue to the Mother World has been lost."

"This is a disaster." The minister held his head in his hands. "Should we move our armies to the snow base?"

"Ameretat is too heavily populated. It's out of the question that we lose all those civilian lives. This demon is destroying every town and village in its path, killing all their inhabitants and building its army of the dead. We've been lucky that thus far its path has contained low population settlements. We can't lose the citadel too. We already have the bulk of our military forces assembling at the column. As you know, my magi and many of your pachycephalosaur riders are already there, minister. Marzban from Honton Keep are on their way over too. None of them are prepared for low temperature or high altitude fighting. We should continue with the plan as it stands."

The minister nodded. "Very well."

"The Naziarabad Monument will be our last stand against the demon. If we can't defeat it there, we won't be able to defeat it anywhere else."

"But what of the snow base? If we don't stop the demon in Ameretat, then what happens when it reaches the portal in the mountains?"

"Alleged portal. I've sent magi into the mountains to investigate. If the fight against the demon begins to slip, then they'll be given instructions to destroy the equipment, the portal, the entire base if necessary."

They sat in silence while the Grand Master paced.

"And what of Hami, and this other potential Mother Worlder?" the minister asked.

"Piruzan is sending some men south to retrieve them. Hami has been cloaking his location since he left the network, but this potential magus, this magi-sensitive person, can't block theirs. They've recently connected to the network again and we're using that signal to track them down. We're closing in. When we have them, we'll know more about what's going on."

–THIRTY-THREE–
OFF THE GRID

Mehrak placed a steaming cup of mushroom tea in front of Sammy. "This will keep you awake while Hami teaches you to cloak yourself from the magi," he said. "I'm going to finish packing up outside. I'll be back in a little while." He smiled, then descended the stairs to the back door.

Sammy cupped the tea in her hands, closed her eyes and inhaled. She wanted to go back to bed. But there were worse things in life than being woken up to drink Mehrak's mushroom tea. She opened her eyes and watched the multi-coloured birds circle above. She hadn't truly appreciated Golden Egg Cottage last time she'd been here. Something she fully intended to remedy from now on. If Hami was going to force her to go home, then she was going to soak up every moment of being here. It wouldn't come to that. She'd dig her heels in when they got to the portal. Or maybe she'd destroy it before Hami could send her back. She'd do something, anyway. Then he'd have to find some other purpose for her. And magus recruit was the obvious solution.

Sammy sipped the steaming brew, savouring the subtle aroma. There wasn't much flavour, kind of like celery, although it didn't taste of celery. It didn't even taste like mushroom. The closest she could liken it to was a mixture of parsnip and toasted almonds.

Sammy wondered if everyone in Perseopia made tea the same way. Because if Mehrak found his wife at the snow base and Sammy suddenly found herself homeless, would she lose mushroom tea too? That would be a disaster.

But seriously, what would she do if Mehrak found his wife? The thought left her reeling and she gripped her cup tighter. She wasn't ready to leave Golden Egg Cottage yet. To leave Mehrak.

She was getting worked up again. No one knew what would happen when they finally reached the snow base or what they'd find. Hami said it would be a number of days before they got there anyway, she'd worry about it later.

She took a long draught of mushroom tea. She savoured the mouthful, then gulped it down as Hami climbed out of the staircase hole in the floor into the kitchen.

"Are you ready to learn how to block your brainwaves from the magi network?" he asked.

Sammy looked up. Shrugged. "Remind me why we're doing this again."

"So the brotherhood can't locate you."

"And that would be bad, wouldn't it?"

"This is serious." Hami sat down opposite, his jaw set.

"Okay, let's do it."

Hami let out a long, slow breath. "Your brain has been attempting to connect to the magi network. Which is normally the first step to becoming a magus."

"I want to be taking the first step to becoming a magus."

"I understand, but if you connect to the network the brotherhood will be able to track you down, which means they will be able to track me down. I know you don't want to return home, but if you allow us to get caught, we'll fail to close down the portal at the snow base. So regardless of which decision you ultimately make about your future, please will you learn how to block your location for the time being?"

Sammy shrugged. "Sure."

"I should've thought to teach you this earlier," he said. "You heard the enrolment whisper before I woke you, yes? The same rhyme you heard shortly before Victa arrived to collect you?"

"Cross the river of light ... something, something ... along the path, tower will fall ..."

"Close enough. The magi normally retrieve a recruit shortly after they've heard the whisper for the first time, then we help them set up a connection to the network. Because neither Victa nor I set you up and it's been a while since you first heard the whisper, your brain will have polled the network again, trying to establish a connection. Both times you tried to connect, you sent out location markers. It won't have slipped the magi's attention that you've somehow travelled all the way from the depths of the Fungi Forest to where we are now, the approximate area that the demon was last spotted in, and all in a reasonably short amount of time. The magi aren't stupid. They'll have figured out I'm behind this, and Piruzan will have sent some of his men back to fetch us. Hence why Mehrak and the others are outside packing up camp and why I'm here teaching you how to close your mind off from the network."

"Let's do this then."

"Okay. First we need to connect you to a simple network before you can learn to block it. But because we don't want you to transmit your location across the whole magi network, we'll set up a local network, just you and I."

"How do we do that?"

"I'll initiate the connection. You'll experience a slight tingling in your brain."

"I don't like the sound of that."

"It's not unpleasant. It's very slight, and you can ignore it easily enough or even block it. Don't try to block it in this instance. Try to concentrate on it and open your mind to allow the sensation in."

"You want me to surrender my brain to you?"

"You're not surrendering your brain, or even giving me access. All you're doing is allowing me to speak to you."

He made it sound almost pleasant, yet Sammy wasn't convinced.

"It's not hard. You'll pick it up straight away."

"You've already started, haven't you? I can feel a strange tingling. I felt it after you first woke me, but I thought I was still half asleep so I ignored it."

Hami's face went pale. "That's not me. Push it away! I haven't started yet."

Sammy blocked the buzzing from her head and it gradually receded. "Gone," she said.

Perspiration glistened on Hami's forehead. "The magi are trying to talk to you. If you initiate a connection, you'll send out another location marker. We need to go. Now." He got up from the table. "I'm going to chase up the guys outside. Wait for me upstairs in the tower." Then he left down the stairs to the hatch.

Sammy drank more of her tea while she listened to Hami call out orders through the open kitchen window. Mehrak, Leiss and Calven entered the kitchen soon after.

Golden Egg Cottage rose up, then shifted, and settled back into its easy side to side rhythm over Louis's hips.

Sammy placed her cup in the sink and climbed the stairs to the tower.

Hami caught up with her in the bedroom. "They're going to try to communicate with you again," he said. "The next time they do, I want you to concentrate on their signal and try to answer it. They may ask you some questions. But I need you to act dumb, like you don't know what's going on. Don't tell them who you are and don't tell them you're with me. Keep the conversation as brief as you can, then disconnect mid conversation so it sounds like you disconnected by accident."

Sammy didn't like the sound of connecting to a strange magus. "Why do you want me to talk to them now?"

"Because we're going to give them false information."

"We're going to lie …?"

Hami held up his hand. "We must do everything in our power to ensure success."

Sammy kind of understood why he was doing this, but she didn't have a good feeling about it.

"I'll tell you what to say," Hami went on. "But first we have to prepare you, and make sure you know how to block your brainwaves when it comes time."

Sammy moved to the bed and sat down on the edge.

Hami pulled up a chair. "You aren't sensing any tingling right now, are you?"

Sammy shook her head.

"How about now?"

Sammy could feel it now, the tingling sensation again. This time it was different to the last signal. This time it was Hami. She could tell. The frequency of it was the same as the feeling Hami gave off when he was close. He was inside her somehow, filling her head. Sammy opened herself up to him and heard his voice.

Hello Sammy, can you hear me?

Yes, she replied.

That was easy enough, wasn't it?

It was okay. Sammy didn't trust herself to think anything. Didn't want Hami to know her intimate feelings. *Can you hear everything going on in my head? Everything I'm thinking?*

No. Only what you project towards me. Do you want to try and disconnect?

Sammy closed off her mind and Hami disappeared. She experienced a slight feeling of detachment. Hami filling her mind had been a pleasant sensation. Him becoming a part of her, yet at the same time she hadn't felt truly comfortable with it. The intimacy of it made her want to withdraw from him. She didn't trust herself with him being so close.

Sammy experienced the sensation of Hami trying to connect again. She let him back in and his voice filled her head.

That was good, he said. *Now we're going to teach you to block me. Okay?*

Why do I need to block you?

You're only going to block me temporarily. You need to learn how to block a signal in case your mind accidentally reaches out to the magi network again while you're asleep. This part is more complicated but not hard. You can tell the difference between me and the other signal you felt, can't you?

Sammy nodded.

Okay. Concentrate on the frequency of my signal.

How do I do that?

I suppose you concentrate on the way my mental voice sounds. It's unique only to me.

I'm not sure I have it.

You probably do, you just don't realise it. Brain functions are subtle.

Okay, Sammy said.

You're probably experiencing the signal reverberating in the centre of your head. Take that signal and move it to the back. Place it away. Mentally put a lock on it.

How?

Imagine yourself locking it in a box and tucking it away where no one will find it. Hami said nothing more. He'd gone.

"Did it work?" Sammy asked.

"You tell me? I'm trying to communicate with you right now."

Sammy felt nothing. "I think it worked. I'm not getting any signals."

"Good. I need you to mentally retrieve that locked box and open it again. So I'm not blocked anymore."

Sammy raised an eyebrow. "Maybe I like you being blocked."

Hami responded with a wry smile. "As soon as we've finished, you can block me for good if you really want to."

"I was just kidding," Sammy said, a little too desperately. She liked the way they could talk in secret.

Hami held up his hand. He was serious again. "We don't have much time and we need to get this right. I need to connect you to the magi network, then you need to block it so your brain stops calling out to it while you're asleep. Security on the network is high so only a magus can give you the correct key to connect you. Are you ready?"

"I don't think so, but let's give it a shot."

"This is serious."

"I know."

"After I connect you to the network you need to concentrate on the signal, then disconnect and lock it away like I taught you. Okay?"

"Okay."

"I won't talk to you while you're connected in case you accidentally mention my name or broadcast my signal onto the network and give me away. Alright?"

"Alright." Sammy retrieved her mental box and concentrated on Hami's signal.

Excellent. You're back, Hami said. *I'm going to connect you to the magi network now. You'll hear faint whispering and voices. It sounds a little strange but they're just conversations travelling back and forth. Anything you mentally project into the network can be heard by any magus so be careful what you say. Perhaps just ask if anyone's there. And ask why there are voices in your head. Before anyone answers, disconnect and then lock away the signal. Then we'll be safe.*

Grand Master. Wake up!

Master Aegis sat up, momentarily disorientated. He was in a strange bed. The room was empty. It took his sleep-addled brain a moment to realise he was in the Grand Master's suite at the magi consulate.

And he was receiving a communication over the network. Principal Emmes. What was he doing calling at this hour? And why was he being so forceful? Ordinarily a communication wouldn't have woken him, but Emmes was bombarding him over multiple frequencies.

Aegis opened his mind.

Master Aegis. She connected to the network. The recruit Victa went after. It's another girl, like the one Hami found.

Where did the signal originate? Aegis asked. *Have you located it?*

Yes. She's not far from where she was last located. She's still heading in the same direction. Towards Master Piruzan.

Thank you, Emmes. I will contact her now. Relay the message to Master Piruzan's men and send them the location. We've got them now.

———

Sammy was getting a new signal, not the same one she received after the enrolment whisper. She sat up stiff, turned to Hami. He was calm. He looked her in the eye and nodded.

Sammy accepted the call.

Please don't be alarmed, said the voice. *My name is Master Aegis. I only want to talk.*

Who are you? she asked. *Why are you talking in my head?*

I'm a magus, came the reply. *I'm a protector of this realm. The one you find yourself in. I imagine everything must seem very strange and scary to you. But we can help you.*

I don't understand.

Why is Hami hiding you from us?

The question caught her off guard. *Hami?* she responded, but too late.

He's breaking his orders, and putting you in danger.

I don't know any Hami. Please leave me alone. And Sammy disconnected, then blocked the signal. "Done," she said. She gave Hami the thumbs up and tried to look optimistic.

Hami got up and walked over towards the front balcony. He parted the curtain and leaned out. "Okay Louis, change course. Take us north west away from the magi."

–THIRTY-FOUR–
CRABBY PATOIS

Behnam and Ghobad had been travelling through the Fungi Forest for less than a day before they ran into crabmen. In typical fashion, the creatures announced themselves ahead of their arrival with loud chattering, providing plenty of time for the two men to lead their horses off the forest track and into the mushrooms.

They tethered the animals to a rock and headed back towards the road. A short way off, they veered away, creeping through the bushes and vines parallel to the path.

It wasn't long before Ghobad's eyes picked out the crabmen. Five of them, moving slowly, chattering as they went. They slowed as they neared the men's location.

Then stopped.

Behnam froze. And waited.

And then a realisation. He could understand what the crabmen were saying.

Not him, but Ghobad. The guard could understand their language. His brain was processing everything they were saying and converting it into something Behnam could understand.

"Enemy. Hidden," one of the crabmen said.

Behnam's skin prickled. Had they seen him? Or one of their horses? He remained still, out of breath, breathing hard, trying to slow down his intake of air. He was panicked, but the thrill at being able to understand the crabman language had him excited. The brotherhood had undertaken multiple missions over the years to try to understand the way crabmen communicated, yet no progress had ever been made. After fruitless years of investigation, it was assumed that crabmen were incapable of conventional speech.

But there was language there. Hopelessly basic, but there. The chattering they made was a decoy. Instead, the almost inaudible grunts in amongst the noise formed their words. No wonder the brotherhood had never deciphered it. Ramaask must have given some high up workers the ability to understand the creatures because only through processing the noises via Ghobad could Behnam understand what they were saying. Almost like it was a power bestowed, and not something you could learn. Behnam believed he would eventually be able to absorb it, but it would take time. Ghobad would have to be kept alive until then.

"Home. New orders," one of the crabmen said.

"Enemy. Hidden," the first repeated.

"Master dead. Demon come. New orders. Hurry."

But the crabmen didn't move on. They remained, scanning the forest with their stalk eyes, flinching with their jerky unnatural movements.

Behnam watched the crabmen from Ghobad's viewpoint while his own body lay prone and sweating. He could tell the guard was well hidden, but himself? There was no way of telling without turning Ghobad's head, and he didn't want to risk the movement. There could be a part of his body sticking out of the undergrowth. And if the crabmen spotted it, he wouldn't be able to defend himself. He had barely mastered walking both his body and Ghobad's at the same time.

Taking out five crabmen would ordinarily be an easy proposition for a master magus. Without a working set of eyes, they posed a serious threat. The creatures moved with the speed of insects. If you mistimed a strike or a lunge, it meant death.

Several tense moments passed while the crabmen searched the area.

When they eventually moved on, Behnam's left leg was cramping spectacularly.

The creatures were heading back towards Aratta, the direction Behnam and Ghobad had come from. No longer did they dwell in the bottomless lake of their ancestors. Ramaask had re-engineered them, upgrading the existing species, turning them into killing machines and making the old city their new home.

'Master dead. Demon come', they'd said, confirming what he'd already suspected. That the girl had crossed the seal, Ramaask had perished and the Ahriman had been unleashed. Did that mean Hami had died too? He surely would've stopped the girl if he'd been able to. Behnam had made the consequences clear.

With difficulty, he worked his way through the vegetation to where he and Ghobad had left the horses. He contemplated heading straight to New Ecbatana. Grand Master Aegis had been heading there, and he could do with some of his friend's sage advice right now. But Aegis wouldn't condone how Behnam had taken over this guard's mind. Even though it had been out of necessity to save his own life, and even if it meant learning the crabman language too.

The sensible plan would be to head to the garrison for treatment. Ghobad had cleaned Behnam's eye sockets with alcohol, but he needed proper medical attention. He needed Ramaask's shadow exorcised from his mind too. But first he needed to use what he'd learned when he and Ramaask had joined minds. He knew things now. Things that no one else did.

Ramaask had planned to go to the Cataclysm to kill the girl. Then from there he was going to the portal in the mountains. But that hadn't happened. The most likely set of events was that Ramaask's brother had betrayed him, as he'd suspected, by orchestrating the release of their master. Both master and servant would be well on their way to the portal by now.

Behnam couldn't communicate any of this to his brothers, he couldn't risk some trace of Ramaask spreading across the network. He had tried several times to purge Ramaask from his head himself, but always some part remained. During sleepless nights, dark and twisted visions would fill his head. Tortured and mutilated bodies sewing themselves together. He'd spend each night drowning in dead bodies and black liquid. And then there were the eyes. Two burning spheres of hellfire that found him wherever he hid. The Ahriman was coming and it was going to take him with it.

Behnam had seen the snow base in his visions. He'd seen the sprawling buildings on the mountaintop, the dark castle in the centre. Every night at the point where dream met consciousness, he would be running. Escaping the smoke and dead bodies that threatened to smother him. Always towards the snow base. A perceived safe haven. Is that what Ramaask had believed? Would the portal have saved him from the girl breaking the seal that ended his life?

Behnam needed to find Hami, to ensure his safety and to put things right between them. His health would have to wait.

He felt his way up onto his horse. Then controlled Ghobad onto the other.

The snow base was his new destination. Ramaask's memory had been pushing him there, but the crabmen had confirmed his worst suspicions. If Hami had survived the battle, he'd be heading there too. He knew how important it was to shut down the portal. Even more so now that the Ahriman had been released. If the worst case scenario had come true and Hami had perished, then Behnam would need to shut down the portal himself.

He didn't truly believe Hami had died, though. He'd be okay, he had to be. Behnam would find him and release him from the burden of his sister's death. Then they'd destroy the portal together.

Behnam kicked his horse on, but turned it from the road they'd been travelling, picking a new path through the mushrooms. One that led towards the mountains in the north.

–THIRTY-FIVE–
Evading the Law

Hami had remained on the front balcony all day. Sammy spent some time with him when they'd first made the detour, but with Louis's headlight lanterns extinguished so as not to alert the magi, there wasn't a lot to see. Not a problem for Louis with his echo location, or apparently Hami, as he seemed to know exactly where they were going, but a big problem for Sammy. Sightseeing in pitch blackness got old fast. It wasn't like there was any conversation to be had, either. Hami said nothing, other than when he whispered directions down to Louis.

The rest of the day Sammy spent downstairs with Mehrak, Leiss and Calven. And Leiss and Calven said nothing to each other.

Calven had initially acted civil towards Leiss, but Leiss had pretty much ignored him from the beginning. Now neither spoke to the other. Eventually, Calven made an excuse to go upstairs and left them.

Mehrak, on the other hand, moved about his kitchen with a spring in his step. He boiled water for tea, chopped vegetables for a large batch of soup. He seemed to genuinely relish cooking and looking after everyone. Sammy could literally think of no other guy in their early twenties that was as comfortable as Mehrak was in the kitchen or carrying out domestic duties. It was weird, but there was something about it she liked. The guy showed no pretence to excessive masculinity. He seemed completely at ease with who he was and she liked that.

As he busied himself with the soup, he asked Sammy all about what she'd been up to since she'd left. About what had brought her back here. Why she'd left her mum and why she didn't like her mum's boyfriend, Jerry.

Sammy mumbled that her mum and Jerry weren't really interested in her. She explained how she couldn't talk to anyone about Perseopia because of how crazy it sounded. Her mum, the only person she had told, didn't even believe her. She also told Mehrak of how embarrassing Jerry was and how he often wore a cravat and that made her want to slap the moustache off his face.

"None of those are valid reasons why you chose to come back here," he replied.

Sammy shrugged. "Can I have another cup of tea, please?"

"What have you got here that you haven't got back in the Mother World?"

She looked up and saw him watching her. "It's not that life is bad back home," she said. "I've been in trouble a few times for fighting. But nothing terrible has happened. I guess I'm just bored."

"You've been fighting like your dad?"

"How do you know about my dad's fighting?"

"You told me about him a few days ago … sorry, two years ago to you. You told me he never let anyone disrespect him and got in fights because of it."

Sammy stared into her tea. Had she really become like her father? The thought of it disgusted her.

"I'm sorry." Mehrak was backtracking now. "I shouldn't have said that."

Sammy sighed. "It's a fair comment. My dad was a thug. And it took me way too long to realise it. I do get in fights, but I'm always defending myself, not starting them. I guess I can be quick to take the bait, though. I should probably learn to chill."

"You aren't like him at all … I assume. Obviously, I've never met him. But I've never seen you aggressive. You're a lovely person." Mehrak cleared his throat and turned away to make Sammy's tea. "You don't see him anymore?"

Sammy shook her head. "My dad turned up drunk to one of my football matches and punched one of the dads supporting the other team. The son had been hassling me all game, then fouled me in the box. The referee missed it, so I didn't get the penalty I deserved." She sighed. "My dad took matters into his own hands. Or rather, fists."

"Football's that game we played in the forest with the chunk of mushroom, isn't it?"

Sammy couldn't help smiling as she recalled the game they'd played so long ago. "Yeah. That's it."

"Punching an opposing player's father seems a bit extreme."

"It was. He got in a lot of trouble for it. I never invited him to watch me again. He barely ever came as it was, and I had to beg him to come that one time, so it wasn't hard to keep him away. He did that himself."

"You didn't come back here to escape your dad?"

"No. I haven't seen him in months. I don't know why I came back, in all honesty. I think I just like the idea of being here. My life back in the Mother World is uneventful."

"Uneventful?"

"Dull, boring, I have to go to school, next year I'll have to either do more learning or get a job. I want a more exciting life than that."

"And there's no occupation of magus back in the Mother World?"

"Exactly."

"So you're dead set on becoming a magus?"

"What else would I be? I have magi skills. I can shoot a lightning staff. I can talk to Hami without opening my mouth."

Mehrak flinched. "You can communicate with him telepathically?"

"Yup. It's great. He showed me yesterday when you were packing up camp. Shall I show you? I'll ask him something now."

"No. I don't want you talking …" Mehrak's jaw tightened. "I mean, I believe you."

The room fell silent and Mehrak returned to chopping vegetables.

"You don't want me to become a magus?" Sammy asked after a time.

Mehrak stopped chopping. "It's probably my grandfather's prejudices coming out in me. The magi are … well, I suppose they're trying to help the realm, and their ethics are admirable. I just think they wield too much power. They're only human, and they make mistakes." He took a deep breath. "I'm sure you'd make a fine magus, though. It's about time there was another female magus. The first in decades."

"Assuming I didn't become a magus, what would you prefer I did instead? I can't travel with you in Golden Egg Cottage after you get your wife back."

"Why not? You're part of our Golden Egg family now. I can't just kick you out."

He stopped as Hami arrived at the top of the stairs. Louis was slowing down. Apparently they'd reached their destination.

———

Baxter caught up to Aegis as he marched through the parliament building.

Aegis gave no indication of acknowledgement, but said, "It's Sammy, the same girl as before."

"How? You mean she didn't leave?"

"She did. But she came back."

"That doesn't make any sense."

"She arrived back at the exact moment she previously did. An older Sammy arriving in Perseopia and overlapping with her younger self."

"How can you tell?"

"The fluctuation in the fabric of our realm when Sammy arrived was three times the size as when Lord VorMask arrived. Indicating someone either three times as powerful …"

"Or three separate people."

"Exactly. But there was a missing piece of the puzzle. How did the second visitor from the Mother World happen to be in the centre of the Fungi Forest one moment, then all the way over near the Cataclysm the next? Hami said that he told Victa where he was going. But I wasn't convinced of that. He wouldn't have wanted to risk anyone stopping him. He only informed the brotherhood of what had happened after the fact."

"You're saying the girl found him."

"She figured out she'd returned to the same moment she was here last time. Probably after talking to some of the Marzban at the outpost. Knowing she'd returned to the same point in time, she knew exactly where Hami was going to be. Think about it. It was a coincidence Hami stumbling across the first visitor. A second visitor travelling hundreds of stadia across Perseopia so that Hami could stumble across them too?"

"I can't deny there's some logic to your hypothesis," Baxter said. "What about the third person?"

"We don't know. We hope to know more when we apprehend Hami."

"You haven't found them yet, then?"

"No. Magi Hogir and Fuad have backtracked to pick them up but they aren't where they should've been. My brothers have discovered gastrosaur and karkadann footprints, which means that the girl is back with the traveller in the golden caravan."

"One big happy reunion."

"Indeed. My magi are following their tracks. But it appears Hami has figured out I'm onto him. I contacted the girl after she connected to the magi network, she acted like she didn't know who Hami was then disconnected from me. I think Hami had her connect to the network in order to block it so she doesn't connect again by accident or while she's asleep. Because when my magi reached the location they would've been when I'd spoken to her, they found that the tracks changed direction shortly after."

Baxter nodded. "They know. Hami must've had the girl speak to you to send out a location marker, before getting her to disconnect and take a detour."

"Yes. But we're following their tracks now. My magi will track them down. The net is closing around them."

–THIRTY-SIX–
The Lake

They spent the night on the banks of the Kuchak Sea.

The next morning, Mehrak popped out to collect drinking water from the 'sea', which wasn't really a sea, but an enormous freshwater lake. He returned with the water and a small catch of eyeless fish courtesy of Rougetta. The fish were grilled, washed down with tea brewed from Kuchak 'seawater' then the cottage crew joined everyone else outside where they congregated near the water's edge. Everyone except Harz and Jokram, who were absent along with their chariot, tent and possessions.

Hami stood further down the shore looking out across the gently undulating surface of the lake. Dark water stretched out ahead, the horizon barely visible as a dim glow in the distance.

"I'm guessing you already have a plan," Mehrak called to him.

"I do," he said without turning. "We're splitting up."

Mehrak shook his head and smiled. "Let me guess, you and Sammy head off one way around the lake, while the rest of us act as decoys and head the other."

"You're mostly right," Hami said, without a hint of sarcasm. "You'll all head west around the lake. Sammy and I are taking a karkadann across it."

Mehrak lost his smile. "Funny. What are you actually doing?"

"Exactly what I just told you."

"You can't cross the lake on the back of a karkadann," Narok said. "It's too far. Even here at the narrowest part. It's still faster to go around than to cross."

"I know you're a desperate man, Hami," Mehrak said. "But this time you've gone too far."

Hami remained calm. "We aren't at the narrowest point," he said. "We're slightly further west. You don't recognise that faint glow out in the water?"

Mehrak moved down the bank, away from the campfire and towards Hami, where the water was lapping against the shore. "Is that …?"

"Archipelago City."

Mehrak snorted out a laugh. "You've got to be kidding me."

"I don't understand," Sammy said.

"The lights on the horizon are from Archipelago City," Hami said. "It's a city made up of interconnected islands. Islands that are connected to the mainland on the far side by Marvo's bridge. If we can reach the southern-most point—Jonubi Island—we can island hop our way to the other side."

Mehrak shook his head.

"We need to gain some ground," Hami continued. "Sammy and I need to get to the snow base ahead of the magi. We can't allow them to close the portal before we get a chance to use it."

"You can use it," Sammy said. "But I'm not."

Hami pinched his lips together. "We still need to get there before the demon and we're running out of options."

"You're insane," Narok said.

"If you have any other suggestions then I'd like to hear them," Hami replied. "We're way behind the demon and the magi, but they have to travel around the lake. This is our chance to get to the snow base before anyone else."

Narok sighed heavily and stared out across the lake.

"Louis and I are coming too," Mehrak said.

"Me too," Leiss said.

Hami frowned. "How will that work?"

"Louis can swim."

"With Golden Egg Cottage?"

"It floats. My parents had the hatch at the bottom built to be watertight. In case they needed to cross a river or lake. I've never put it to the test, because of the sort of creatures you generally encounter in large bodies of water ..." Mehrak stopped. "Oh wait." He paced away, several steps back from the shore. "Are there lake monsters like the ones you get in the Fungi Forest?"

"One lake monster," Hami said. He gritted his teeth. "A big one."

Mehrak's head fell to his chest. "The biggest, right? The leviathan? I remember now. The Kuchak Sea is commonly known as Leviathan Lake." He exhaled loudly and watched the water. "Is the leviathan even real?"

"Let's hope we don't find out."

Mehrak raised his eyebrows. "At least be honest."

Hami shrugged. "Okay, yes," he said. "It's real. But there's only one of him, or her, and it's a vast body of water so our chances of avoiding it are good. And you don't have to come."

Mehrak looked at Sammy, smiled. "I'm coming." He puffed out his chest. "Someone has to look after our Mother Worlder."

Sammy smiled back. Mehrak always had her back. Or liked to think he did. "You know it'll be me looking after you, don't you?" she said. "Against this ..." Sammy stopped. "What is a leviathan?"

Hami had returned to staring out across the water and didn't volunteer an answer.

"I don't know," Mehrak said, answering for him. "The stories I've heard depict it as a giant fish, reptile creature, and that it's gigantic and filled with teeth."

"That's all you really need to know about it," Hami said. "Other than the lake is a thousand stadia long and the leviathan is the only one of its kind, allegedly. So our chances of running into it are slim."

"I don't think I can allow you to take this risk with my Marzbans' lives," Narok said. "I'll come. Not for you, but to save the realm for my children. My Marzban must be free to make their own choices."

"That's fair," Hami said. "I won't ask any of you to put your lives in danger again. For Sammy and I, I think the risk is worth taking. Crossing the lake will allow us to escape the magi and buy us enough time on the opposite side to get to the portal first. Whoever remains here and circles the lake will get tracked down by the magi. They'll question you, but all you've done is follow my orders. Stick to that story and they'll leave you alone."

The group lapsed into silence.

"Harz and Jokram left us last night," Hami said. The chariot isn't able to make the crossing so they're heading west around the lake. I doubt they'll make it round in time to be useful, but they're on their way. Anyone else who wants to continue the fight but doesn't wish to cross the lake should set off as soon as possible. The rest of us need to make preparations for the crossing."

Mehrak sighed. "You can stay on Eggie with Sammy and me, if you like."

"Thank you," Hami said. "That's very generous. You're sure Louis can handle it? Carrying us all and doing it all silently? Sound travels quickly through water and it's possible the cottage may amplify noise."

"Louis can be quiet when he needs to."

Hami gave a tired smile. "I know he can," he said. He paused, collected himself. "The distance across isn't great." He looked each of them in the eye. "Under normal circumstances it's possible to make the crossing in half a day, but we'll take our time and aim to take the full day, hence why I've left it until the morning so we'd be well rested. We don't want to risk making waves or splashing. Strong powerful strokes. No animals panicking. No breaking the surface. All lights need to be extinguished. Not just the head lamps like we've been doing, but the internal lights too. Until we make it to the other side."

"I'm coming," Leiss said.

Hami opened his mouth to speak out but Leiss held up his hand to silence him. "I'm not leaving Sammy's side until I've either sent her home or avenged Borzin's death. This is my fight now too."

"I figured that was probably the case," Hami said. "Thank you."

"I'm coming too," Eva said.

"You aren't obliged to," Hami said. "You've done more than enough for us. You can leave now with your head held high."

Eva shook her head. "I've come too far to bow out now. I want to see how this ends and you'll need a decent fighter. Leiss isn't going to be as handy with his dodgy leg. Not that he's as good as me even when he is fit. Besides, us ladies have got to stick together eh, Sammy? Why should the men have all the fun?"

Sammy smiled. Eva was a total legend.

Sasan spoke next. "I'm going to sound pathetic after Eva's display of bravado, but I'm done. I almost lost my life fighting an unnecessary battle. A battle that's damaged our realm, probably to the point of irreparability. I've seen most of my friends die. I'm going home." He looked to Rougetta.

Rougetta dipped her head. "Me too."

Calven looked to Eva, the guilt plain on his face.

Eva put her hand on his shoulder. "Go with them," she said. "You've done enough."

"My mother hasn't got anyone else."

Eva pulled Calven into a tight hug. "Go," she said.

"Yes, go," Leiss added. "My wife needs more consoling and we don't need you here."

–THIRTY-SEVEN–
The Swim

Sammy knelt in front of Kimbo. She cupped his muzzle in her hands and lifted it to her face.

"This is goodbye, big guy. It's too dangerous for you to come with us."

Kimbo tilted his head and whined.

"I know it's not fair. But life isn't fair. Us humans have to fix the damage we made to your realm."

Sammy hadn't spent long enough with Kimbo to get too emotional over his departure, but she'd still miss the big softie. She took several steps back and connected to him mentally. He seemed confused. She planted an image of a human in his head and then fear. Kimbo backed up a little way. Sammy concentrated on the fear and raised it tenfold. She lunged at the animal and screamed.

Kimbo ran.

She watched his cowering body scamper away into the dark, feeling the weight of bad karma on her shoulders. She'd probably scared the poor animal away from humans forever. Not necessarily a bad thing. It might keep him alive in the future. She dragged her feet as she walked back towards the campsite that had been partially packed away.

Mehrak was following Eva as she cleared away her things.

"Make the crossing in Golden Egg Cottage," Mehrak said. "You'll be safer on board with us."

Leiss heaved a rolled tent onto his shoulder. "I've asked her already. You're wasting your time, Mehrak."

"We need to ride the karkadann," Eva said. "Who else is going to keep them calm during the crossing?"

"Excuse me?" Calven had been sharpening his sword nearby, but dropped it and came over. "You're riding your karkadann across the lake? I thought you'd be travelling in the caravan."

"We can't risk the karkadann making waves," Eva replied.

"And if the leviathan attacks you?"

"There's more chance of it attacking if the karkadann panic and churn up the water."

"I'm not leaving now," Calven said. "I'll ride your karkadann across."

"Don't be ridiculous."

"I'm not letting you do it, Eva."

Leiss dumped the tent he'd been carrying. "You've got to be kidding me," he said to no one in particular as he marched away towards Eggie.

Mehrak went after him. "Leiss. Wait up."

Calven watched them go. "It wasn't my fault his wife left him."

"I know," Eva said. "He's still in a bad place. Give him time."

Calven shook his head. "Forget about him. What about you? I don't want you in the water."

"I know you're trying to be chivalrous, but you aren't taking my place."

Calven held his hands up. "This isn't about chivalry. I know you're twice … maybe *three* times the fighter I am, but I'm better with animals. I'm a better rider, too. I'll keep Bludget calm. Better than you could."

Eva scowled.

"You know I'm right. We've known each other since childhood. You know how good I am." He took hold of her hands. "Do you really think I'm offering so I can prove my masculinity?"

Sasan and Rougetta said their goodbyes, hugged everyone, then left on the nameless karkadann they'd found on the battlefield. Narok mounted Indomit and Calven climbed onto Bludget.

"I've tightened the back door hatch," Mehrak said when he joined everyone else on Eggie's front balcony. "The lights are out in the kitchen and bedroom. And so is the stove, so there won't be any hot food today. Here's the rope," he said as he handed it to Hami. "It's all we've got."

"It'll be perfect," Hami said. "Thank you." And he took the rope and carried it into the tower.

Sammy went after him, feeling her way through the black bedroom, and following him out onto the back balcony.

Hami tied the rope to the railing and threw the loose end to Narok, who tied the middle to Indomit's saddle horn before throwing the rest to Calven so he could tie the end to Bludget's saddle.

Mehrak was pulling up the oil lanterns when Sammy returned to the front balcony. He'd temporarily lit them while they cleared camp, to help everyone see what they were doing, but now he lifted them over the railing, opened their glass casings and blew out their flames.

The balcony became dark. Only the faint light from Archipelago City brought any kind of relief from the cloying black, lighting up the horizon and reflecting off the water.

Sammy could just about see everyone when her eyes acclimatised. Mostly as black shapes, but that was enough to quell her nervousness from panic to merely being 'on edge'. The sky wasn't completely dark, anyway. More slate grey with lighter patches here and there. But no purple. If the smog still existed above them, there was no sign of it.

"Let's go, Louis," whispered Mehrak. "Take it nice and slow."

Louis pulled forward, edging down the sandy shore and into the lake. He shivered as he inched into the water and the cottage shuddered.

Eggie sank further as Louis pulled forward. It seemed for a moment that they would go under, but as the water level neared the kitchen window, they stopped their descent.

Louis's head remained above the surface as he slithered snakelike forward, cutting through the water.

Sammy passed back through the bedroom and onto the back balcony. Below, Louis's tail swept side to side as he swam. Narok and Indomit were already in the water, and Calven and Bludget entered soon after, trailing behind on the rope.

As the shoreline shrank into the gloom, Sammy returned to the front of the cottage. She couldn't keep still. She was terrified but excited too. The water ahead lay still like polished obsidian, rucking up and peeling back as Louis dragged Golden Egg Cottage through it. Her nerves tingled, waiting for something to happen, for the lake monster to burst from the water. But nothing happened. And the morning ebbed away with Sammy slumped over the railing.

Louis swam on. Not only was nothing happening, but there was nothing to do either. At least with the lights off, it wasn't possible to play Chaturanga.

Mehrak stood by her, nervously tapping out a rhythm on the balcony railing. Leiss hung back near the curtain, straight and alert as always, even with his injured leg. Eva stood next to him, equally as alert.

Hami was down in the kitchen. Puking silently in the dark, most likely. Even in the darkness he'd somehow managed to look peaky and had been battling his gag reflex. He'd gone downstairs early into their journey and had not returned.

"It's funny how quickly you can become bored when the monster you're expecting to attack doesn't show up," Sammy whispered.

Mehrak pushed himself off the railing. "I've got an idea ..."

"We can't play Chaturanga," Sammy said.

"I wasn't going to suggest that." Mehrak left the balcony and returned carrying a handful of pillows and some blankets. He lay the blankets out on the floor and placed the pillows along one edge. Then he lay down with his hands behind his head on top of the pillow, and motioned for Sammy, Leiss and Eva to do the same.

Sammy wondered if she should fetch Hami to join in. There wasn't actually enough space, but she didn't want him to feel left out. Then again, he might not want to be disturbed while he was spewing. Either way, Sammy wasn't going to creep downstairs in the darkness to find him. She'd let him make his own way up when he was ready.

Sammy and Eva lay down on either side of Mehrak. Leiss took Eva's side of the blanket—no surprise there—and shuffled up close to her. He so obviously fancied her, it was ridiculous. It was quite sweet, really. Eva didn't seem to mind either, and made no move to rebuff his advances.

"Is this similar to what the sky looks like at night in the Mother World?" Mehrak whispered.

"On a cloudy night," Sammy whispered back. "When the stars and moon are hidden. You ever heard of stars?"

"Describe them to me," Mehrak said.

Sammy knew he'd have read about them. He just wanted to hear them described by someone that had actually seen them. He wanted to know what she saw when she looked to the heavens. "They're like pin pricks of light twinkling against a large black … er … blanket." She wasn't exactly doing justice to the staggering majesty of the universe, a spectacle Mehrak would never see in his lifetime. At least he wouldn't be disappointed by her description.

She kept going. "Some stars are spaced out, some are close together. They're arranged in constellations millions and billions of miles away—or stadia to you guys. Further than anyone can travel in a lifetime."

"It sounds beautiful," Leiss said.

Really? Sammy didn't think her description was deserving of the word 'beautiful'. Perhaps anything sounded beautiful to Leiss when he was lying next to Eva.

"It is beautiful," Sammy said.

"Do you miss it?" Mehrak asked.

"Not really. I live in a city with too much light pollution so I don't get to see stars often."

"I still can't understand why you'd come back here."

Sammy lapsed into silence as pale light from the islands rippled across Eggie's golden surface, and a fine breeze carried mist off the water, prickling her skin. The warmth of Mehrak pressed against her. This was why she came back. Life was perfect in that moment. Too perfect. It was a hopeful but naïve glimpse of a reality that she would never enjoy. And a seed of darkness began germinating in her heart.

"You're determined to get your wife back, aren't you?" she said, destroying the moment for herself. If the happiness she'd been enjoying was a sham, then it was better to end it rather than letting it linger.

"Of course," Mehrak said.

Sammy said nothing else. The breeze off the lake now seemed cold rather than fresh and the sky assumed the murky void of nothingness it had always really been.

"I mean. I suppose I am," Mehrak went on.

"You suppose?" Sammy could almost feel Leiss and Eva cringe in the darkness. They'd gone quiet and were probably wishing they were somewhere else.

"I want to rescue her and for her to be safe," Mehrak said. He seemed to be picking his words carefully. "But I don't want what we have to change. I don't want you to leave the cottage and become a magus."

What did they have? It didn't seem like an awful lot right then. "But I won't be able to stay here when your wife comes back."

Eva got up. "We should probably go check on Hami," she said, pulling Leiss up off the blanket. "He's been alone downstairs for a while."

"Er … yeah. He has, hasn't he?" Leiss said. "See you guys in a bit."

And they disappeared into the tower.

"Gisouie and I," Mehrak said after they'd gone. "We weren't always happy. Not all the time. She was my childhood sweetheart and we married early, but she had a terrible temper. She made a lot of enemies back in Dungalor. We would've been kicked out of town eventually if we hadn't left when we did. That was one of the motivations for us leaving to go on the *Rule book* adventure. I suppose I spoke more fondly of her to you because I felt guilty about not loving her more. Especially after she was captured. Maybe I was overcompensating. I knew we weren't right for each other." Mehrak was babbling. He sighed. "This is coming out all wrong. She had moments when she was really thoughtful and she could be a kind person. I care for her, a lot, and want to make sure she's safe. I love her even, just not in *that* way …"

"But you're still married."

"Marriage is just a simple union where I come from. You can annul your marriage quite easily."

"What are you trying to say? That you're going to cancel your marriage and I'm going to move in with you? What are you going to do about your wife? Just drop her off somewhere in the forest? What if you get bored hanging out with me too? Would I get annulled?"

"That's not what I meant." Mehrak tried to take her hand, but she pulled it away. "The way you light up Golden Egg Cottage, just by being here …"

"So I'm supposed to hang out with you and your wife, lighting up Eggie? Like a lamp?"

"Sammy—"

A thud reverberated through the cottage and threw Mehrak against her.

Then a splash and the balcony pitched forward.

231

Sammy pushed Mehrak off and leapt to her feet and to the railing.

In the distance, three islands were clearly visible now, with huts on their banks and their connecting bridges lit up with hundreds of twinkling lights.

Below them, Louis was floundering.

"What is it, buddy?" Mehrak asked as he gained his feet.

Louis waved his ears.

Hami came running out onto the balcony. His hair was dishevelled and his eyes were puffy. "Calm down, Louis. Stop splashing."

He stumbled over the blankets on the floor on his way to the railing. He glanced down at the wadded bedding, bleary-eyed, then looked up at Sammy and Mehrak in confusion. His guard was down a moment, but he snapped out of it quickly. He leant over the railing, scanning the water below.

Sammy ducked into the bedroom as Leiss and Eva squeezed past her coming the other way. She fumbled in the dark for her staff, found it near the bedside and brought it out to where everyone had congregated at the railing.

She lit up the orb.

The brilliance of it temporarily blinded her, and probably everyone else on board, but it was enough to see what Louis had bumped into.

Hami shoved her staff down. "Turn it off!"

"It's just a boat," Sammy said, extinguishing the light. "Why didn't Louis see it coming?"

"He's not been using echo location," Mehrak said. "We don't know what sounds are audible to the leviathan. It might navigate using a similar frequency to the one Louis uses. To be safe, Louis's been swimming blind."

"Wait ..." Hami said.

They waited. Louis had calmed but he continued to shiver as he floated in the water. In the quiet, smaller sounds were amplified.

The water lapping against the cottage, the staccato breathing of those on the balcony.

After the brightness of the staff light, it took a moment to re-acclimatise to the dark.

Leiss was the first to see something. "Over there," he whispered.

Ahead, a large object rose on a swell of water.

Hami ignited his staff this time, keeping the light low. The dim glow revealed the smashed hull of a ship. A large green mushroom-planked vessel, upturned with a jagged hole in the bottom.

The relief on the balcony was palpable.

"There are others," Hami said, shining a beam around at the other smashed and broken vessels they found themselves surrounded by.

"What's the matter with Louis?" Leiss asked. "He's shaking."

"He's smelt something," Mehrak said.

Sammy squeezed her eyes shut and wished she could go back to being bored. "Not the—"

"No," Mehrak interrupted. "Not the leviathan. Louis can't smell underwater. He can smell dead people, though."

–THIRTY-EIGHT–
LEVIATHAN GRUB

Hami narrowed his beam of staff light, focusing it on a single hull. "The boards aren't rotten," he said. "This boat was destroyed recently. And look. The Regent's insignia. These fishermen are from Honton Keep."

"They risked their lives coming here for some fish?" Sammy asked.

"Just some fish?" Leiss said. "The white sturgeon that live in this lake fetch ridiculous sums back at the Keep. They're the Regent's favourite. You should see the security detail we provide a shipment of sturgeon on its way through the forest. I used to know a couple of the fishermen that worked this lake. Crazy guys. They'd make a fortune every time they came home, then spend it all on alcohol and women. I guess you have to be a certain kind of person to risk your life crossing this stretch of water."

It was an obvious dig at Hami, but the magus ignored it.

Narok and Calven brought their karkadann around Louis. They bobbed alongside as Narok edged Indomit closer. "Do we double back and go around?" he called up in a raised whisper.

"I'm not sure—" Hami began.

Then Louis thrashed out.

The cottage surged backwards. Louis back-paddled frantically, dragging Narok, Calven and the karkadann with him. His ears twirled up and down holding poses independent to each other.

"It's okay, buddy. Calm down," Mehrak said.

"Stop moving!" Hami whispered loudly. Hami aimed his staff beam down into the water.

The swollen body of a man floated face down in front of Louis.

Louis stopped but continued to sign and shiver in the water, while large, steaming breaths of air unfurled from his open mouth.

"It touched him," Mehrak said. "He got spooked, but he's fine."

"We're not fine," Hami said. "These ships have all been dragged here. To this one place." He cut the light.

"You have *got* to be kidding me!" Sammy said. "You've brought us right into the leviathan's lair?"

"Quiet. It could be below us."

"For the love of Ahura," Mehrak said. He lunged at Hami, scooping up handfuls of the magus's cloak. "You've doomed us all!"

"Get a hold of yourself," Hami said as he nudged Mehrak away. "Everything will be okay as long as we remain calm. We've been unlucky. That's all. I picked a bad place to cross, but we can get through this if we're smart about it. The main objective right now is to get out of here. If there are still bodies in the water, the leviathan may be back. Louis, you'll need to be quick, but take it steady. We can't allow ourselves to get tangled up in sails or rigging."

A large swell of water raised Golden Egg Cottage. Sammy felt the momentary weightlessness flip-flop her stomach and they came down bobbing and bumping into the karkadann.

"What the hell was that?" Leiss said.

Sammy lit up her staff. She hovered the beam over an expanse of water where bubbles were breaking the surface. "Over there! One of the boats has disappeared!"

"Put out your staff!" Hami snapped.

Sammy disconnected from the orb and it became black again.

A large body launched itself from the lake ahead of them.

Everyone panicked. Nervous energy crashed around the balcony. Sammy shoved and got shoved. She took hold of Mehrak.

"It's just a boat," Hami said. He sounded as breathless as everyone else. "Keep still. And quiet. Especially you, Louis."

Sammy let go of Mehrak and clasped her hands together to stop them shaking.

The boat slowly came to rest, eclipsing the lights of the islands ahead and drowning everyone on Eggie in shadow.

No one moved.

A small swell buffeted Eggie and several of the boats bumped into each other, making hollow thuds.

When there was no further movement, Hami whispered down to Louis. "Slow strokes. Aim for that gap between the two ships ahead." Hami moved along the balcony railing to the point closest to the karkadann. "Narok. Keep close."

Louis pulled forward. He shivered as he brushed past the dead man again.

Another large whoosh and a ship ahead creaked and splintered.

"Stop!" Hami whispered loudly.

Louis stopped. The ghostly shapes of ruined vessels floated all around them, creaking and knocking against each other. All large foreign objects in the dark.

Then one submerged.

"Another ship's gone down," Sammy rasped.

"That wasn't a ship," Hami said.

"That had to be a ship," Mehrak whimpered. "It was too …"

"… big?" Hami finished.

"It's here?" Sammy was entering panic mode. "It's really here?" Her head seemed to be contracting, her eyes expanding in her head. The leviathan had come for them and they were dead. Mehrak was right. She should've stayed at home.

Hami moved to the front. "Listen."

They waited in silence again. Another swoosh through the water. Way off, behind Eggie. The cottage bobbed up and down again.

"It's circling us," Hami whispered. "It knows we're here."

"We need to make a swim for it," Leiss said.

"No. The islands aren't as close as they look. Even if the distance were halved, we wouldn't make it."

"So what then?" Leiss said. "We stay here and wait to die?"

"We wait," Hami said. "And hope we don't die. We're still alive, which means the leviathan doesn't know exactly where we are."

Another movement, the rush of water being displaced, and another object submerged.

"There it is," Sammy said.

"No," Hami said. "It was another ship. The leviathan is systematically working its way through all the floating objects in the area."

"Great Ahura!" Leiss said. "We could be next! We can't stay here and wait to die."

"It can't tell which object is us." Hami's eyes were alive. "It must use motion to track its prey. It felt Louis's ripples when he panicked but because we're still, it can't triangulate our exact location."

Another ship plummeted into the black abyss.

"Hami!" Mehrak squawked.

"I've got a plan," Hami said. "Louis, there's a gap opening up ahead, between two of those wrecked ships. When I call 'go', swim as hard, but as quietly, as you can. You guys, too. Narok. Calven. Did you get that?"

Narok held up an arm.

"Sammy," Hami said. "I need your help. We're going to create a diversion. Follow me."

He took her through the bedroom to the back balcony and pointed down to the silhouette of the dead man in the water. He had drifted a little way behind, but was still close.

"When I nod my head I want you to concentrate on his belt. We haven't moved organic matter in our lessons so far, so we'll go for the belt. It should be sufficient if we work together. The plan is to hoist him slowly from the water, then fling him as far as we can in that direction." He pointed out behind them.

Sammy stared down at the dead man.

"Are you okay to do this?"

Sammy nodded.

Hami placed a hand on Sammy's back. It was warm. One of the few times he'd touched her without gripping her. She was ashamed to admit it, but it felt pretty good.

She snapped out of it. She had a job to do. She concentrated on the belt, imagining it in great detail, and picturing it on a molecular level.

They lifted. The man's bottom came up first, poking out of the water. Sammy could feel herself straining, her mind pulling at the seams. It was hard, but they kept going.

The man rose up into the air, water pouring off his clothes.

Hami pointed to the man, then in a sweeping movement of his arm, the direction they were going to send him.

Then he held up his hand indicating that Sammy should wait.

They waited, keeping the body suspended over the water. Time was dragging out. The strain was beginning to hurt. A headache was pounding in her temples.

A ship to the left went under. Sammy could hear the remaining wrecks move around in the resulting eddy.

The alignment of the hulls must've come good because Hami gave the command, "Go!"

Sammy dug deep. She could feel Hami do the same, and they launched the man.

The body spiralled away into space.

"You're becoming powerful," Hami said as they lost sight of the body.

Sammy slumped on the railing. She couldn't see his face but she could hear the pride in his voice. The effort had taken a lot out of her, but she'd done good. That smallest of compliments warmed something inside her. Not enough to make the boat trip of death a worthwhile experience, but it gave her the boost necessary to rise from her metaphorical foetal position and enter a zen-like fight-for-your-life mode.

A distant splash. The body had landed. Something large below shifted and the lake seemed to drop away as water was displaced beneath them.

"Go Louis!" Hami called. "Smooth, powerful strokes. No splashes."

Louis pulled forward hard. The Marzban on their karkadann followed, but the gastrosaur was pulling hard enough to drag them along with him.

Sammy followed Hami through to the front balcony.

Two ships hit each other as Louis approached. The hulls shattered, throwing up splinters.

"Go right!" Hami yelled.

Louis leant right but got caught in the undercurrent and was pulled into a ship, slamming the cottage hard and knocking everyone into each other.

Mehrak was thrown across the balcony and hit the railing. "My ribs," he moaned. "Again."

"Keep going!" Hami called.

Louis forged on past the ships. He cut through the water, pulling the karkadann with him and out into open water.

Behind them, a thunderclap splash followed by a roar that boomed out like an oil tanker's horn.

"He sounds like a big boy," Eva said, matter-of-fact. If she was scared, she didn't show it.

"That's not funny," Mehrak replied.

"Louis. Stop!" It was Hami. "Narok, Calven," he called out. "You guys too. You have to stop!"

Louis and the karkadann floated to a stop.

"He's heading back," Hami said. "We need another distraction. Sammy, with me." He led her back through the tower and out onto the back balcony again. The others followed this time.

The wrecked ships had been left behind, but were still visible in the light from the islands.

Hami levelled his staff and the orb lit up. He fired a bolt of lightning at one of the ships and blew a hole in it. Planks flew in all directions, then fell, splashing into the lake. Off to the left, a series of serrated dorsal fins broke the surface of the water, cutting a line for the ship.

"It's working," Leiss said.

"Go Louis!" Hami shouted. He fired another shot at a different vessel. Another explosion. "And don't stop!"

Louis pulled forward.

Sammy exploded a ship using Victa's staff. The pure violence of her action mesmerised her. She marvelled at the destruction and resulting carnage of flaming planks. She blew up another. And then another. This was totally metal! Burning mushroom timbers rained down like mini comets, lighting up the ship graveyard like a fireworks display.

A curved mound broke the surface of the water in between the shipwrecks. Scales on its surface shimmered in the light of the flames. It was as vast as an island and ridged like a dragon's back. Then it was gone.

Hami snatched the staff off her. "That's enough," he said before handing it back. "The diversion will only work for so long. Mehrak, do you know if Louis's echo location works underwater?"

"I believe so."

"Get him to start using it. See if he can scan the underwater topography. Get a landscape for us. The leviathan will realise we've gone sooner or later and will cast its net further afield. Get Louis to look for anything that might hide or protect us. Shallow areas, rocks just under the surface of the water. Anything we can put between us and the leviathan. The water should start getting increasingly shallow as we reach the islands and that might give us the edge we need."

Mehrak dashed through the tower.

They left the ships behind, receding into the darkness. Hami launched two more bolts from his staff, blasting apart another ship.

Amidst the burning wreckage, Sammy glimpsed a silver mound with white eyes. The leviathan was looking for them.

Until then it had been difficult to gain a true sense of scale of the creature, until its head rose further from the water, placing it alongside a broken hull. There wasn't a lot of difference in size between them.

The beast turned its ship-sized head towards her then, and their eyes and minds locked. Sammy gasped at the cold bloodlust projected towards her and her friends. This creature was an apex predator. There was no fear, no fury, just a calm and calculating motivation to kill. Louis and the karkadann were in its sights and it knew there was no escape.

The head submerged.

"It's coming for us!" Sammy screamed.

Hami sent bolts of lightning at the remaining ships, setting off a cacophony of explosions, but when he stopped nothing moved.

"It's coming!" Hami shouted.

Eggie pitched and they changed direction.

"Louis's found something!" Mehrak shouted from the front balcony. "A sandbank. A wide one just below the surface. He's heading for it now. The water should be too shallow for the leviathan to follow!"

"How far?" Hami shouted back.

"About two stadia!"

Hami stared out across the water. He was breathing hard, his eyes wild.

"We're not going to make it, are we?" Leiss said. Voicing what Sammy could already surmise from Hami's expression.

"What about Calven?" Eva screamed. She seemed genuinely panicked for the first time. "We have to save him!"

Trailing way behind, Eva's karkadann, Bludget, was panicking and Calven appeared unable to calm her. The beast's legs were churning water, the rope was taut. Its flailing was slowing them down and Louis was having to drag them.

"Calven!" Hami shouted. "You don't have long. Don't panic and do exactly as I tell you!"

Calven stared back, his eyes wide and fearful, but he nodded, his jaw set.

Hami fired a lightning blast into Bludget, where its neck met its shoulders. The karkadann screamed as a patch of hair and skin flapped open and blood gushed out of its neck. The terrified animal began thrashing harder. It roared in pain and panic.

"Bludget!" Eva grabbed Hami by the throat, but he elbowed his way out of her grip.

"I'm saving your friend's life," he growled. "So I'd appreciate you keeping your hands off me."

"By killing my karkadann?"

Sammy couldn't believe the calm manner in which he'd mortally wounded the animal. There'd been no hesitation, no weighing up options. *Bam.* Sentenced to death.

"Untie the saddle!" Hami shouted. "But keep hold of the rope. Whatever you do, don't let go!"

Calven fumbled with the rope, struggling to untie it. It had been pulled tight by Louis forging ahead and he couldn't get it undone.

A swell rose up in the distance behind the karkadann. A vast submarine mass, racing towards them, displacing water around it. The leviathan was coming, closing the gap unnaturally fast.

Then it went under.

"Use your blade!" Narok screamed.

Calven unsheathed his sword as the top and lower jaws of the leviathan broke the surface either side of Bludget. Huge crocodile jaws that kept coming as rows of shark-like triangular teeth sawed their way out of the water.

Calven gripped the rope with his free hand and slashed the knot with his sword. With a snap, he was yanked from his saddle as the huge jaws closed on Bludget and dragged the karkadann down.

Sammy recoiled, but there was nothing to see. No gore or horror. No screaming. Leviathan and karkadann had gone.

Calven remained, at the end of the rope, dragging through the water behind Narok and Indomit.

Hami reached his hand out towards the flailing Marzban.

Realising what he was doing, Sammy latched on to the rope and helped raise it from the water. The rope came up, arched over like a fisherman's rod, Calven dangling from the end like a prize carp. They directed the rope over Indomit's back and placed him in the saddle behind Narok.

Hami's plan had worked. Ending Bludget's life had saved Calven's. Maybe all of theirs. Sammy didn't like it, but it'd been effective. How did you reach a point in your own life when you could make snap decisions about ending something else's?

"Are we safe now?" she asked. Her voice cracked as she spoke. "I mean, the leviathan's eaten now, right?"

Hami said nothing. He pointed.

Way off, a serrated ridge of vertebrae broke the surface, slithering snake-like through the water as it came at them.

Hami began firing lightning bolts at it. Sammy instinctively joined in. Water exploded upwards with each blast. The leviathan writhed each time it was hit, but didn't slow. Then it went under.

"Narok! Calven!" Hami shouted. He lit up his staff. "Take hold of the rope ..."

Then Eggie slowed, bumped, and lurched upward, tipping Sammy into Hami, Leiss and the railing.

"We've hit the sandbank!" Mehrak yelled from the front.

Golden Egg Cottage rose from the water as Louis staggered upright.

Narok and Calven came up behind on Indomit.

Sammy lit her staff and shone it down into the water.

The sandbank wasn't visible through the stirred-up silt and shimmering staff light, but it couldn't have been far below the surface as Indomit's belly remained above the water.

"Are you okay, Calven?" Eva called out.

Calven's face was pallid and waxen in the staff light but he managed a shaky smile. His sopping turban had partially unravelled, sagging at the side.

"Can it get us here?" Mehrak asked as he walked out onto the back balcony.

"No," Hami replied. "It's too heavy. It wouldn't be able to lift its body from the water."

"Stalemate then?" Narok said.

"Not necessarily. It depends on how long the sandbar is and how close it takes us to the island. If there's any significant stretch of water to cross, we might be in trouble. You and Calven should come aboard Eggie in that event."

Narok held Hami's gaze. "I'm not sacrificing Indomit. I can keep him calm."

"As you wish," Hami replied. "Lights off, Sammy. The leviathan will be tracking our movement through the shallows but let's not make it too easy for him. Let's hope this sandbar takes us the rest of the way to the islands."

———

On the way back from luncheon with his old department, Baxter called in on the Prime Minister in his office.

"We need to delay the council," the minister said, by way of greeting.

Good afternoon to you too, Baxter thought. "And why is that, minister?"

"Aegis's men have lost Hami."

Baxter found himself at a loss for words. "How exactly did they manage that?" he asked after a moment. "They're on greenbucks. Hami is in a gastrosaur caravan. It's not as if he can outrun them. They're on the plains of Al-Biruni, there isn't anywhere to hide."

"Their tracks end at the shore of the Kuchak Sea."

"End?"

"It appears that they entered the water and swam for it."

"That makes no sense," Baxter said. "Hami wouldn't risk their lives crossing Leviathan Lake."

"Apparently he would. Judging by their point of entry, they'll have been hoping to reach Jonubi Island. It's not a long stretch of water, but as you know it's a perilous one. Aegis didn't allow his magi to go in after them so they're heading back to Piruzan."

"If Hami survives the crossing, he can use the bridges between the islands to island-hop all the way to the other side."

"Correct," the minister said.

"So we've lost them?"

"Aegis has an old friend in Archipelago City. Ex-magus I think. He'll keep a look out. There are also magi heading from the garrison towards Ameretat that are passing by the northern shore of the lake, so there's still an opportunity to apprehend them."

"If they survive."

"Aegis seems to think they will. He doesn't say so, but he has a certain admiration for Principal Hootan. I, on the other hand, think we should prepare ourselves for the possibility Hami gets the girl killed, and formulate a plan for how we're going to deal with the Ahriman without her."

–THIRTY-NINE–
The Shallows

The sandbar took them a significant way towards reaching the archipelago, yet not far enough, and there remained a sizable expanse of open water between Eggie and the closest island. Too great a distance to outswim a streamlined killing machine in its own back yard.

They were so close. Close enough to distinguish beach huts and campfires on the shore. People, too. Indistinct but there, milling around, doing whatever it was archipelago islanders did.

The disappointment aboard Eggie was palpable.

"This can't be as far as it goes," Leiss said. "There must be another sandbank branching off this one somewhere, maybe further back ... or a rock or something."

Louis lowered his head into the water, moved it in a slow arc from left to right, then lifted his head and signed to Mehrak.

"There's another sandbank between here and the island," Mehrak said. "A bigger one. But it's a way off."

"Can we make it?" Leiss asked.

"I don't know," Mehrak said. "The leviathan's lying in wait. Louis thought it was another sandbar at first. Until it moved."

"We know it's big," Leiss said. "How does that help us? By reminding us how futile our chances of survival are?" He was rattled, twitchy. He was breathing hard, hyperventilating. He hadn't snapped into elite Marzban mode like he'd done in the fire temple. Probably the thin figure had stripped him of his confidence or perhaps the leviathan seemed too vast and insurmountable. Whatever the cause, Leiss wasn't coping.

Hami reached out and put a hand on the big man's shoulder. "Why don't you go downstairs?" he said. "Sit this one out."

"I can't leave you guys to face the leviathan without me." He spoke quietly. It was a weak objection without conviction.

Hami let him off the hook. "We can't fight the leviathan," he said. "And you're a fighter, Leiss. The only way to survive is by outmanoeuvring it. You can't help with that. And, honestly, you're only going to get in the way if you stay up here."

"I can't sit around downstairs in the dark knowing that at any moment Golden Egg Cottage is about to get crushed around me and dragged to the bottom of the lake. I can't deal with that."

"I'll come with you," Eva said. "I'm guessing you don't need my fighting skills either?" she asked Hami. "As good as I am, even I'd struggle against the leviathan." She smiled and took Leiss's hand. Then she turned to Hami and her expression became grave. "You dragged us into this, and you killed my Bludget. You better get us out of it."

Hami met her gaze, nodded once.

"Figure something out," she said, then led Leiss away.

He made no protest as he allowed himself to be taken inside.

Hami gave them a moment, then went to the railing. "Louis, is the leviathan sounding underwater?"

Louis's ears flicked straight up, signing, *yes*.

"Do you think it's using those sounds to navigate? Like you've been doing?"

Another yes.

"Good," Hami said. "That's useful."

"Good in what way?" Mehrak asked. "Good that we have even less chance than we thought? Leiss was right. This is futile."

"Do you want to go downstairs too?"

Mehrak clenched his teeth. "You need to start showing me some respect. You're aboard my house. And we're helping *you* clear up the mess *you've* caused."

"Don't you think I know that?" Hami said. "It's all my fault. The black skies, the demons, the legions of dead rising up. And now this situation. I know what I've done to the realm, Mehrak. I'm aware every moment of every day. But I'm trying to fix it. No one else is heading to the snow base to shut down the portal. We're on our own. The fate of Perseopia in our hands. I knew this crossing was a risk, but honestly, I believe there was no other choice."

Mehrak clenched his jaw but said nothing more.

Hami coughed, retched, and took several long breaths to get his gag reflex under control before speaking. "Louis navigates using soundwaves to bounce off objects. He waits for the returning echo to tell him where objects in front of him are. If Louis can recreate similar sounds to those made by the leviathan, then we might be able to disorientate it. Or even bombard it with multiple signals. The effect would be similar to one of us having a bright light shined in our eyes. The leviathan won't be able to locate us and will be swimming blind. And that might give us enough time to make it to the next sandbar."

Hope rose in Sammy's chest. She didn't want to get too carried away but she needed something to cling on to. "Will that work?" she asked.

Mehrak shrugged. "It's a plan. I wouldn't say I'm entirely happy about it, but it seems like our best shot. We can get Louis to transmit disinformation too, to send the leviathan in the wrong direction. But that's assuming it can't see or smell us."

"It couldn't pick Louis out from the ships we were amongst earlier," Hami said. "That leads me to believe that its sense of smell isn't as well developed. Its eyes were white too, which would seem to suggest that it's blind."

"It saw me," Sammy said. "It looked right at me."

Hami shrugged. "Even if that's the case, Perseopia is far darker now than it was a few days ago. I'm willing to bet the leviathan isn't used to this level of darkness. It'll be relying almost entirely on sound."

"What about heat detection or movement?"

"I'm not worried about heat as the leviathan couldn't differentiate between us and the ships. Movement? I don't know. We'll just have to stop whenever it's close."

Sammy's earlier spark of hope was diminishing. "I don't have a good feeling about this," she said.

Louis raised his head and signed a brief sentence to Mehrak.

"The leviathan has begun circling our sandbank," Mehrak said. "We should set off immediately after it's gone past in order to give us the maximum amount of time before it returns."

"Agreed," Hami said. "Then once it comes back round, Louis can start blinding it with noise."

Louis added some further ear semaphore to the discussion.

"We need Narok and Indomit to pull us backwards," Mehrak said.

"We can't," Hami said. "That will drastically reduce our progress."

"Louis needs to be facing the leviathan and sending sound waves when it rounds the sandbank. If there's any gap in transmission, the leviathan will be able to see us."

"Does that matter? We only need enough of a head start to reach the next bank."

"Louis seems to think it will. He can't swim and keep turning around to distract the leviathan. He needs concentration to reflect sound off the large rocks and underwater structures so they hit the leviathan right. You can't aim noise directly at it, because it'll be able to trace it back to us."

"If Louis can hear the leviathan's noises then it must be able to hear ours too," Sammy said. "So it will know we're tracking it."

"Not necessarily," Mehrak answered. "Louis says the leviathan is only using a narrow frequency band, which would imply that it can only hear in that range. Louis has been using a much lower frequency to monitor its movements. Which means it probably doesn't know we're watching it. It won't be aware that we know it's circling the sandbank. That gives us an advantage."

"Do you think it's that easily fooled?" Sammy said. She'd been staring out across the oily water, attempting to locate the source of niggling doubt that she couldn't quite pin down. "We connected. The leviathan and I. I experienced its thought processes, its intentions. This creature's intelligent. Not as clever as Louis, but a lot smarter than Kimbo or the karkadann."

"We don't have a better plan," Hami said.

"I can tell it's biding its time, calculating ..." she trailed off.

"You know, there were once magi who practised the discipline of establishing sympathetic links with animals," Hami said. "It took them years of study to learn what you've picked up in a matter of days."

"But I can't control the leviathan. It's too big and strong willed."

Hami watched her. "You're capable of more than you know. I have faith in you. And if you're not ready, be sure to keep your staff close." He paused. "I doubt we'll be able to hurt the leviathan, but we might be able to slow it down. Don't light up until we have no other option. It may not have decent eyesight, but let's not give it anything to aim at."

–FORTY–
BACK IT UP

Narok led Indomit into the shallows, guiding Louis backwards down the bank. The rope between Eggie and Indomit's saddle had been doubled up with the surplus that had previously connected them to Bludget. A third line ran alongside the first two. A thin piece of twine linking Eggie's back balcony railing with Calven's wrist. This third line would be used for communication.

The plan was for Sammy to man the rear balcony—which for the next segment of the journey would be travelling forwards—and to use the line to relay messages to the gents on the karkadann. If the leviathan was deemed to be getting too close, Louis would sign to Hami, who would communicate a halt command to Sammy over their special network. Sammy would then give a quick tug on Calven's twine, Calven would squeeze Narok, and Narok would stop Indomit. It was convoluted, but hey, that was the plan.

Sammy, Mehrak and Hami waited in silence as Louis waded further out and stopped. He sunk his head under the water and twisted round to scan the direction they were going to be heading in.

After a time he raised an ear from the water and gave the signal. The leviathan had gone past and was on its way to performing another circuit of the sandbank. Sammy crept quietly through the bedroom to take up her position on the back balcony. She waved to Narok, and Narok took Indomit forward until the rope tightened. When the line tugged, Louis edged backwards, allowing Eggie to slip into the water.

Mehrak came out onto the back balcony to join Sammy as the cottage and an inert Louis floated backwards out into the water. He stood close, his arm touching hers, no doubt showing solidarity against the perils ahead. Sammy tried to ignore it, while she stayed focused on the islands in the distance, their haven of light just out of reach.

They travelled in silence, bar the intermittent slosh of water each time Louis raised his head from the lake to gulp down air. Indomit was working hard, pulling against the bulky mass of the cottage, dragging them towards their goal, but progress was slow, seemingly negligible, as if the islands themselves were swimming away from them. It created an almost paralysing dread that numbed Sammy's senses. The islands were falling out of focus as she stared into their light, the darkness encroaching on all sides like the leviathan's jaws closing over the top of her.

Then she felt Hami's mind reach out to her. *Stop!*

Sammy snapped back to the present and gave Calven's twine a tug.

They floated to a stop.

Mehrak flinched but held himself firm. He was trying to remain calm for her. A rock to cling to. But his petrified shivering shattered the illusion of stoic optimism and instead served as a reminder of how tenuously their lives hung in the balance.

What's happening? Sammy asked Hami.

The leviathan came round the sandbank, then dived to the bottom, he replied. *It either knows or has a suspicion of what Louis's capable of and is trying to catch him out by swimming under his detection. Louis's struggling to track it against the lakebed terrain and keeps losing it.*

Should we swim for it? Sammy asked.

No. Do nothing.

Sammy waited for further instruction, but none came. Time passed. She had no idea how much.

Fear was rolling off Mehrak in waves. He was struggling to keep his nerves under control and was practically spasming. Sammy put her hand on his to reassure him.

Then Hami was back. *Sorry for the gap in communication. Louis is signing incredibly slowly as he doesn't want to create vibrations. The leviathan's directly below us, about three stadia down and sending pulses in all directions. So far all have missed us. So we remain quiet and wait for it to pass.*

Mehrak was getting increasingly agitated beside her. "What's going on?" he whispered.

Tell Mehrak to be quiet! Hami yelled in her head.

Sammy raised her finger to her mouth, staring at Mehrak pointedly.

Mehrak tightened his grip on the railing and turned his gaze to the islands while continuing to shake.

They waited.

Eventually Hami came back online. *All clear,* he communicated. *The leviathan's moved on around the sandbank.*

Sammy gave Calven's twine a quick tug, waved to Narok, and Indomit pulled forward again. She let out a long breath and smiled to Mehrak. He tentatively smiled back. She returned a reassuring hand to his. Then Hami fired back the order, *Stop!*

They'd barely begun moving again, yet Sammy tugged the rope. Indomit stopped.

It's back and searching the area again. It knows we're making a run for the other sandbank.

Mehrak took hold of her arm. He looked pale even in the orange fire light from the islands.

Silence. Unbearable silence.

It's found us!

Sammy wasn't sure how to process that information. *What now?*

Hami burst through the curtains. "Go!" he yelled to Narok. "Just keep going and don't stop."

Indomit surged forward. Eggie shifted, but not by much. They were moving again. Slowly. Way too slowly, like they were swimming through treacle.

"Come with me." Hami dragged Sammy away through the dark bedroom to the front balcony. "I need your help to divert the leviathan."

"But it's already seen us."

"Only for an instant. Indomit is dragging us away from our last known position and Louis's filling the whole region beneath us with noise. The leviathan's blind. It'll have to surface if it wants to see where we are." Hami leant over the railing. "Louis. Do you know where the leviathan will surface?"

Louis pointed his ear out.

"How far?"

Louis signed.

"That's less than a stadion," Hami said. "Sammy, I need you to splash the water way off over there." He pointed. "Draw the leviathan to that point so that when it breaches I can go for its eyes, forcing it back underwater."

"But I can't latch on to fluids," Sammy said. "We've tried before—"

"You have the power to do this. You just need to calm yourself and concentrate."

"Can't I fire the lightning staff?"

"No. If the leviathan is given enough time to locate us visually, we're dead."

Louis flicked an ear up.

"Now, Sammy!"

Sammy concentrated on the water, but couldn't bring the molecules into focus.

"Sammy?"

She mentally teleported her microscopic self to the area of lake she was supposed to affect. But just the smallest of ripples on the surface were moving molecules vast distances on a relative scale.

As soon as Sammy tried to latch onto one, she lost it. "I can't do it!"

"I need a target, Sammy. You have to act now!"

It was too much pressure. Sammy couldn't concentrate, couldn't think. And then she realised. The surface molecules remained mostly together. Hydrogen bonds creating a surface tension holding large groups of molecules together as they slid up and over the ripples. She took a mental step back and focused on a larger array. Then she latched on.

The water began to swirl. She was doing it!

A bigger ripple, then a splash.

The water exploded as the leviathan's jaws burst through the surface. Just the top and bottom jaw at first, but rising, reaching high out of the water before clapping together with devastating force.

The resulting shockwave travelled across the lake and up through Eggie into Sammy's feet.

The beast groaned, as lightning slammed into its head, and it dropped back beneath the water.

Hami extinguished his staff. "Good work," he said. "You've bought us more time. But we need to go again. Make a splash off to the right this time."

Sammy picked a spot and made the surface churn. Like He-Man, she *did* have the power. And she was getting good at it. They were going to make it!

The water burst upward again as the leviathan breached, and again Hami hit it in the head with searing lightning, forcing it back under.

"Again Sammy!"

Sammy splashed a patch of water off to the left. Nothing. She tried again, but no leviathan. "Why isn't it working?"

Then she saw the silhouette. A way off from where she'd splashed the surface. The leviathan's eyes and the top of its head were above the water. It hadn't fallen for the decoy a third time. It was watching them. Hami blasted at the leviathan as it submerged, but it was too late. It had seen them.

"We have to get out of here, Louis. Now!" Hami shouted. "It's coming."

Louis started pumping his legs, heaving them backwards while intermittently submerging his head, presumably to keep bombarding the leviathan with underwater noise.

"I can see the top of the sandbank," Mehrak shouted from behind. "We're almost there!"

"Get ready to splash the water again," Hami said. "Do it closer to Louis where we were a moment ago. The leviathan will still have to breach to confirm our location."

Sammy focused on the water a little way off and churned it up.

There was a lull as Louis frantically back pedalled. Then the lake erupted as the leviathan launched its entire body out of the water. A cruise-liner-sized crocodile with flippers instead of legs. It roared with a deep vibrating bass that turned Sammy's internal organs to trifle. Time seemed to slow as the leviathan hung in the air like a vast zeppelin. Sammy realised then how Princess Leia must have felt when the Star Destroyer descended on her rebel ship at the beginning of A New Hope.

Together, Sammy and Hami fired screaming arcs of lightning into the leviathan's belly before it came down.

Even at a distance, the resulting lake displacement nearly sucked Golden Egg Cottage under. Swathes of water beat down on them, knocking the passengers to the floor, before a swell rose up and pushed Eggie on towards the sandbar.

Sammy dropped Victa's staff when she hit the deck and for a frantic moment thought she'd lost it. She spotted it drifting through the balcony railings and caught it just before it went over the edge.

She pulled herself up, body battered and bruised, clutching Victa's staff as the leviathan's dorsal scales cut a line away through the water. "Why is it leaving?"

Louis raised himself up out of the water. They'd made it to the second sandbank!

Sammy let out a nervous giggle.

Louis staggered on shaky legs, shook water from his head and began signing frantically to Hami.

Mehrak came running through onto the front balcony. "We made it!"

Hami waited for Louis to finish. "Go then!" he called down. "And don't stop!"

Louis turned to face the islands and surged past a drenched Indomit, and shivering and ragged Narok and Calven. He plunged back into the water and began pulling towards shore.

"What's going on?" Mehrak asked.

"The sandbank was a long crescent," Hami replied. "We've just crossed the middle. The leviathan will have to swim around. If Louis's quick we can make it to the island before the leviathan can get all the way around and back to us."

The oasis of sand, beach huts and lights lay ahead. A few of the islanders had stopped what they were doing to watch Louis and crew approach.

"Can we make it?" Sammy asked. It seemed too good to be true.

"I don't know," Hami said. "It'll be close. We should be ready to defend Louis just in case."

Sammy followed him through the bedroom and onto the back balcony. Mehrak went with them.

The three of them stood together watching a distant shimmer of ripples out in the darkness.

"Is it turning?" Mehrak asked. He paused. "It is. It's turning. It's rounded the sandbank already! We aren't going to make it."

Hami shook his head in disbelief. "It's too fast."

Sammy clutched the railing. "It's gone under!"

Louis's swimming became frantic. Golden Egg Cottage creaked as it dragged through the water. A wide 'V' shaped wake rolled out to the sides. Narok was struggling to turn Indomit forwards, but the beast was floundering and creating drag. Louis's breathing was becoming laboured.

Sammy's mind was numb. She couldn't think, couldn't call anything to come into her head. Her brain had shut itself down to protect itself from impending doom.

Out in the water the surface bulged. A hill of water steadily grew as it raced towards them.

Sammy and Hami lit their staffs.

The bulge in the lake grew bigger still, higher and broader, like a foothill growing into a volcano.

It erupted as the leviathan's top jaw lanced out of the water, and over Indomit. The creature's mouth yawned wide as multiple rows of teeth sailed over Sammy's head, dripping water onto the balcony.

This was it. The jaws would snap shut over the cottage and they'd all be dragged to the bottom of the lake. Sammy hoped it would be quick. No pain. No drowning.

She concentrated on the leviathan, raised her hand and reached out. She felt the confidence the beast exuded, the satisfaction of knowing it had won, that it would be consuming its prey imminently. She tried to send calming thoughts to stop it, but it was too powerful. It paused, but that was all. Its brain had decided on a course of action and it was carrying it through. But she was confusing it. She sent more sensations, conflicting thoughts. Sowed seeds of doubt, and told the leviathan they'd moved, that they were behind it, that it should turn around.

The leviathan slowed. Turned. The jaw swung off to the left.

"Now!" Hami shouted, and let forth a screaming blast of lightning down the beast's throat.

Sammy let rip too, firing directly into the mouth.

The jaws slammed shut, barely missing Indomit. The karkadann got caught in the surge of water, spinning him wide. Louis stalled, caught in the eddy, then carried on, taking them forward. And then they were slowing.

The leviathan had stopped.

Golden Egg Cottage rose slowly from the water.

Louis pulled them up the beach. He kept going, dragging Indomit, Narok and Calven up the shore, then sunk to the ground, dropping his head to the sand.

The leviathan screamed behind them, churning the lake into foam. Sammy could feel the rage boiling off it. It roared and brought down its tail with a sound-barrier-bursting crack. She giggled nervously. They were alive!

Hami was white-faced, shaking. Mehrak, too. The strain of the journey had taken its toll on them. And when she saw Mehrak failing to keep it together, she burst into tears.

–FORTY-ONE–
Archipelago City

Thousands of tiny lanterns illuminated the island. Each sat atop a pole planted in the sand surrounding the beach hut dwellings that huddled further up the beach. The huts were basic structures, fabricated from mushroom staves and braced with circular steel bands at the top and bottom like barrels. The roofs were mushroom canopies. Some were dead and dark. Sammy figured those were the sleeping quarters. Other huts had live, fully-lit mushrooms growing up through the centre. Those buildings seemed to house most of the activity, and it was out of them that islanders were cautiously exiting to come and stare. First at the strange menagerie of travellers that had washed up on their beach, then at the leviathan writhing offshore.

"You crossed the lake," one of the men stated as he came down the beach. "I don't know whether to applaud your bravery or mock your foolishness."

Indomit snorted at the man, making him jump and stumble away up the sand.

"Do whatever you feel is most appropriate," Narok said as he jumped down and walked Indomit up the beach. He held up a hand to Calven.

Calven ignored it and leapt off himself, landing in the sand and rolling over onto his back. The sand stuck to his wet clothes, but he didn't seem to care as he made sand angels and whooped loudly.

Leiss and Eva staggered out onto the balcony. Leiss burst into half-laughter, half-tears and scooped Eva up into a hug. Eva seemed initially startled, then beamed and hugged him back.

Hami led Sammy into the dimly lit bedroom. "We don't want any of these people to know we're magi," he said as he took Victa's staff off her.

"Why not?"

"Yeah, why not?" Mehrak asked as he followed them inside.

"Sagus Virgil lives here, he's an ex-master magus. He retired to these islands a number of years ago, but he's remained on the network as a magus point of contact. It won't be long before he finds out we're here, if he doesn't know already."

Mehrak climbed onto the bed and, holding on to one of the bed posts, stood on his toes to fetch a candle from the chandelier.

He held it out to Hami.

Hami lit the candle with a fine beam from his staff orb. "Aegis will inform Master Virgil about us so he'll be on the lookout."

Mehrak began lighting the other candles in the chandelier from the first.

"Mehrak?" Hami asked.

Mehrak paused.

"Will you do me a favour and go out there and explain to the islanders that you were being pursued by crabmen and you had to escape across the water. Say you've lost several days travel because of it and now you're in a hurry to move on. Sammy and I will remain in here while you get rid of them."

Mehrak stopped what he was doing.

"Please."

Mehrak climbed down and handed Hami the candle. "Fine. But can you light the other candles for me?" And he went back out onto the balcony.

There was a muffled exchange outside at which Hami rolled his eyes. He could obviously hear a lot better than Sammy could.

Mehrak came back into the tower. "All sorted. All we have to do is meet their leader Duke Boyanta, then we're free to go."

"We can't do that. Master Virgil has retired from magi duty but still keeps council with the Duke. The Duke will know why we're here. We can't see him."

"Well that's going to be a problem," Mehrak said. "Because we aren't allowed off the islands until we've met him."

"I didn't risk our lives crossing the lake only to get captured as soon as we dragged ourselves back onto dry land," Hami said.

"What then?"

"The islanders know we're in a hurry. We'll agree to see him and head towards the Duke's island, but at speed. It won't take long to leave these guys behind, then we'll take a detour and escape." Hami paused. "Although we aren't exactly inconspicuous, are we? We'll just have to move quickly and hope for the best."

A horn rang out. Then another further away, and another further still.

"They're calling ahead." Hami said. "We'd better go."

"Shall I tell Narok?" Mehrak asked.

"He'll figure out what's going on soon enough. Can you cut the rope at the back?" Hami said. "Louis. Let's get moving."

It still amazed Sammy how good Louis's hearing was, as the floor pitched and Louis shakily got to his feet. She could feel his feet unsteady as he moved forward, could feel him. Her breath caught as they connected. She experienced the fatigue that racked his body as he straightened his legs, and the accumulation of each physical hardship he'd endured on the journey to get them to this point. But there was no unhappiness. When Sammy dug deeper she experienced a warmth, a contentedness that he was with his family, and that they were safe because he'd protected them. A flush of shame reminded her how often she'd taken Louis for granted as he tolerantly carried her wherever he was told. He wasn't just their mode of transportation, their pet. He was a compassionate, intelligent creature. He was their friend.

Sammy closed the connection. Reading Louis was wrong. She made a promise to herself that she wasn't going to invade his privacy again. He'd put up with enough from her already. Looking into his head was way beyond the line.

Golden Egg Cottage moved forward, picking up pace.

There were a few raised voices outside. Sammy guessed the islanders were complaining that they couldn't keep up. But it wasn't long before the clamour faded and Louis began crossing solid ground that reverberated with his footsteps. Probably the first of the bridges to the other islands.

"Can I go outside?" Sammy asked.

"Not yet," Hami replied.

Louis's footsteps returned to sand.

"Come on. We're past the first island."

Hami sighed, but didn't say no. Which was practically a yes.

Sammy went out.

The first several outlying islands had giant mushrooms growing in their centres. They were surrounded by huts, lanterns on poles, and beach. The further they travelled, the larger the islands became, each containing larger groups of buildings and more mushrooms. Some islands held pens and livestock. Some were devoid of houses and had fields of wheat growing under uniformly spaced lines of mushrooms that appeared to have been planted to provide light for the crops to grow.

Mehrak explained that the islands accounted for much of the agriculture in Perseopia due to being protected against crabmen attacks, from the mainland by fortified gate houses, and from the lake due to the fact it was freshwater. Crabmen needed a high saline concentration, apparently. Another of Mehrak's hugely fascinating facts.

Islanders leapt out of the way as Louis and Indomit charged past. The elderly peered out from their beach huts. Parents snatched up their children. And all were wide eyed as the alien creatures tore through their neighbourhoods.

The bigger islands had multiple bridges branching off and Hami would call out directions as they went. The terrain became rockier as they traversed the archipelago. The first of the rocky islands possessed stone outcrops between beach huts, but the further Louis went, the more these rock formations transitioned into small mountains, with mushrooms sprouting from their peaks and dwellings clinging to their sides.

"Head to the right," Hami called down as they reached the black shale beach of the first significantly mountainous island.

It was dark in the shadow of the shear rock faces with only small patches of mushroom light illuminating the narrow strip of beach.

They travelled around the island in near darkness until a towering mountain island came into view, linked by a stone bridge. Before the bridge sat a gatehouse complete with portcullis and guards positioned at the top.

"Keep going, Louis," Hami said. He spoke the words softly but with urgency. "Go for the gate."

The lookouts clearly expected challengers to rush the gatehouse from outside the archipelago, because no one reacted to Golden Egg Cottage until the top of Eggie clipped the keystone of the gatehouse archway.

The guards flew to the walls as the sound rang out, but they were too late. Louis and Indomit were halfway across the bridge when the portcullis dropped.

"Halt!" one of the men called after them. "In the name of the Duke, I command it!"

Horns were blown. Distant horns echoed back, but no one came running.

Louis led the way across the stone bridge, over the water between the two islands and up the beach, joining a narrow track carved into the side of the rock and through the mushrooms that blanketed the lower slopes of the island.

The clamour of horns had quietened by the time they left the mushroom cover and the remaining trek to the summit was a silent one. It was a long climb on uneven ground, and Louis was shaky by the time he reached the peak. He staggered to a halt at the top to catch his breath.

Below, the whole of Archipelago City lay beneath them. A glittering mosaic of light against the black lake. Each island linked to its neighbours by thin bridges, appearing string-like from the heights of the mountain as if the islands were balloons that would float away if the lines were severed.

"I can see why that magus chose to retire here," Leiss said to no one in particular. "I think I would have done the same."

"It's certainly beautiful," Eva said. "I didn't know places like this existed in our realm."

Sammy hung over the balcony railing, letting the clean mist blowing up the side of the mountain wet her face. That moment cemented Sammy's decision to stay in Perseopia. The Fungi Forest, Archipelago City, these were the places she belonged. Not in the grey reality of the Mother World with its lack of opportunities. Her mum had Jerry now, and there was no place for Sammy in their lives. Her resolve hardened. Maybe her mother would believe her if she were here to see this sight. Sammy closed her eyes and relaxed. She wouldn't let that old argument rile her up again. She wasn't a child. She could be grown up about this and be happy for her mother. Jerry was a total dork, but he was kind and—more importantly—gentle. Her mum deserved to be treated well after being beaten around by her pathetic father, and Jerry treated her like a goddess. He respected her and they would take care of each other. Sammy would miss Mama, but she wasn't going back. It was the natural order of things. You grew up, moved out, moved on. She wiped an errant tear that had traced a line down her cheek.

When they got to the portal in the mountains, she'd destroy it. Perseopia was her home now.

Hami pointed to the largest island, where the lights shone brightest. "That's the heart of the city," he said. "And that smaller island to the north is the Duke's palace. See how the main bridge linking the city district to the mainland passes close to the palace?

That's so the Duke is always aware of who's entering his city. And those towers along the bridge? Along with the heavily fortified gatehouse in the middle? One of the Archipelago's first Dukes, Marvo Priess, had it built in the centre of the bridge so that enemies would have to funnel onto the bridge before arriving at the gate, putting them at a disadvantage and reducing the number of men that could attack the city at once."

"Where does the magus live?" Leiss asked.

"Ex-magus," Hami said. "I'm not sure. Hopefully a long way from where we are now."

"Are we off the archipelago?" Sammy asked.

"We're still on one of the islands. But we're past security. There are three routes onto the Archipelago Islands from the mainland and three bridges with gatehouses that restrict those routes. The one running past the Duke's palace is the original. Marvo's bridge. It's still the main route. There's another, over to the West, *way* past it. And then there's the one we crossed. A minor service entrance that links Fisherman's Wharf at the base of this mountain to the archipelago proper."

"Aren't the two smaller bridges security risks?" Eva asked. "The one we passed through wasn't exactly heavily manned."

"That's true, but we came at it from behind. The guards aren't there to stop people leaving. The two smaller bridges are narrow enough that you'd struggle to get an army across and you can lock the portcullis down like you can on Marvo's bridge. The eastern bridge, the one we came across, was built for fisher folk to get their catch off their boats and onto the mainland conveniently. It was built after the Association Battles, during a time of relative peace and before Ramaask created his crabmen. The same goes for the western gate. There's been talk of dismantling them because of the security risk they pose, but the crabmen never come here and both entrances have decent sized gatehouses if they did."

They descended the mountain into the mushrooms that grew on the north-eastern slopes. At the bottom, they emerged from the vegetation into a crescent bay surrounded by shear rock faces encircling five ramshackle stone houses and an impressive network of mushroom-board jetties. Boats were moored alongside the jetties and lights were on in a couple of the houses, but there was no one around outside, and no movement in the buildings.

Hami instructed Louis to take a route round the outside of the settlement along the northern edge of the bay. At the far end, a narrow path led around the corner of the black cliff face.

On the other side a lone jetty extended out into the darkness. It was constructed from mushroom boards like those in the bay, but there were no boats moored alongside.

"Fisherman's Bridge," Hami said. "It will lead us all the way to the mainland." He breathed out and gave a relaxed half chuckle. "We actually made it."

The boards creaked as Louis and Indomit eased themselves onto the bridge. Mehrak re-hung the lanterns from the balcony railing, partially shuttering them so they didn't draw too much attention.

Louis slowed up. He signed a message.

"There's a man ahead," Mehrak said, turning to Hami.

"Alone?"

Louis responded with a yes.

"It's him."

"Who? The magus?" Mehrak asked. "It might not be."

"A guard or lookout would be two or more," Hami said. "Proceed with caution."

"Should I keep out of sight?" Sammy asked.

Hami shook his head. "You can't hide from Master Virgil."

Louis took his time crossing the creaking bridge, and it was many long minutes before they reached the lone hooded figure that stood in their way.

The person was hunched over, seemingly frail and small at Louis's feet.

A gnarled pair of hands slid from the opening of the cloak and lifted back the hood revealing a bald crown surrounded by a wreath of wispy white hair.

The old man was aged beyond anyone Sammy had seen before. His face was scored with deep wrinkles and a patchy beard sprouted from the sagging wattle of skin beneath his neck, yet there was strength behind the pale grey eyes that took in Louis and the caravan. The man straightened his back and set his jaw as he fixed his gaze on the crew members high up on the balcony.

"Master Virgil," Hami said. He gulped and Sammy caught the tremble of uncertainty in his voice.

"You no longer need to address me as Master, Principal Hootan," the old man replied. "I gave up that title when I left the brotherhood. That was a long time ago now. Sagus will do fine."

Hami said nothing.

"You didn't wish to sample the Duke's hospitalities?"

Hami shifted restlessly on the balcony. "How did …?"

"I may be retired, but I remain on the network and have regular contact with Master Aegis. He told me you'd be travelling by here in a gastrosaur caravan. Who else would be foolhardy enough to brave crossing the Kuchak Sea?"

Hami remained quiet.

"That the girl?" Sagus asked. He looked her in the eye, dipped his head, but continued to speak to Hami. "You should talk with Aegis before you take her to the mountains."

"He knows?"

"He's no fool." Sagus paused. "Do you have a reason for taking her to the portal? Have you learned something that you should be sharing with the rest of the brotherhood?"

Hami stared down at the old man wide-eyed, but kept his mouth tight.

The silence drew out until it became uncomfortable.

Eventually Sagus spoke. "I no longer possess the strength to stand in your way, Principal Hootan. And I don't work for the magi. But you are still a magus and you swore an oath to the brotherhood. Zubin Aegis is a wise man, you should hear what he has to say." He stepped aside, and held out his arm to usher them past. "Don't make the same mistake Master Bruche did."

Hami broke eye contact as Louis carried them past Sagus and away from the archipelago. Sammy stopped him as he tried to leave the balcony.

"Who was Master Bruche?" she asked.

Hami paused but didn't look at her. "He was one of the greatest magi that ever lived," he said. "But he left the network to help a young woman … and lost his life for it."

–FORTY-TWO–
A GIRL IN HIGH DEMAND

For the first time since Sammy had arrived in Perseopia, it rained. It beat down on Eggie like ball bearings on a tin roof and didn't let up all day. Louis struggled on until well into the evening, carrying them through the dirt turned mud, across undulating and slippery terrain. The cottage jerked as Louis lost traction climbing the rises, and wobbled as he slid into the trenches. It was slow going and, in the end, the final straw that broke the gastrosaur's back. Louis collapsed to the ground.

Hami protested that they weren't far enough from Archipelago City to be safe, but Louis was done in. Mehrak was able to coax him a short way further, to a valley deep enough to conceal them from a distance, but even that was a struggle and Louis slumped back down after.

Narok and Calven came in out of the rain, joining everyone else in Golden Egg Cottage. They hung their cloaks and clothes over the stove and stood close to the fire, shivering in their undergarments.

Hami covered the porthole with tea towels while Mehrak prepared an unspecified casserole of animal parts and plant stuffs.

Sammy took a place at the kitchen table and waited to be fed. Despite surviving the lake crossing and escaping the Duke, the atmosphere inside Eggie was as dreary as the weather outside. Hami moved sullenly about the kitchen extinguishing lamps, leaving one for Mehrak to prepare food by, and a second on the table for everyone else. He had nothing to say to anyone and Sammy could only guess at what he was brooding over. She liked to imagine it was remorse for fatally wounding Eva's karkadann, Bludget, or maybe risking all their lives by crossing the lake. But most likely he was worried about getting tracked down by the magi or the Archipelago City watch. Then there was the thing Sagus said to him. That would be a large part of what was playing on his mind. But in all honesty, Sammy had no idea what went through the guy's head. Half the time she couldn't decide if he was deranged. There was an alarming trend of living in mortal danger whenever you spent time with him. If she had any kind of self-preservation, she should be trying to convince Mehrak to break off the search for his wife. They should try to escape Hami and go on an adventure in search of the magical book he was so interested in. It was unfair on Mehrak's wife, perhaps. Certainly very selfish on Sammy's part. But they weren't going to find her now. She'd been gone too long. Mehrak wouldn't appreciate being told that, but it was time he faced up to that reality. Sammy wasn't so unfeeling as to drop that opinion on him, but keeping up the pretence of optimism was a waste of time.

Hami wouldn't let them escape anyway. She recalled what had happened the last time they'd tried to sneak away, on her first visit to Perseopia. Not only had he predicted they'd make a run for it, but he'd practically orchestrated it.

No. She wasn't going to attempt an escape. She'd indulge Mehrak's fantasy of finding his wife and then Hami's fantasy of her willingly stepping into the portal. They could all travel to the mountains together so that Mehrak could discover his wife wasn't there and then Sammy would destroy the portal before getting forced into it. A lightning staff blast would surely do the trick. There may be more to it than that, but she'd work out the finer details when they got closer.

It took until midmorning the next day before Louis was capable of carrying them onward towards the mountains. The rain had lightened up, but the ground remained sodden and the going was slow.

Hami maintained his tense demeanour as they made their way north-east, but the more distance they put between themselves and the archipelago, the more he seemed to relax, and that night, as the terrain became rocky, Hami actually looked at ease.

"Look at this place," Leiss called from the front balcony.

Sammy threw on one of Gisouie's waxed animal-skin coats and went outside to join him and Mehrak at the railing.

The temperature had dropped and a thin mist hung in the air cooling Sammy's skin and soaking her hair. With Eggie's headlight lanterns partially shuttered she lit Victa's staff and directed the beam ahead to see where they were going.

The landscape consisted entirely of black, glass-like rocks. Thousands of monolithic crystals jutting up from the ground, angular, multi-faceted, and many covered in wet lichen or moss.

Louis slowed further from his already laboured walking to cross the slippery terrain with care.

"It's a lot damper here than in the Fungi Forest," Sammy said.

"What is this place?" Leiss asked.

"The outcrops, I think," Mehrak said. "I believe my grandfather came here once."

"No one purposely comes to the outcrops," Hami said as he joined them on the balcony. "It's treacherous, and time consuming to traverse. There's nothing worth coming here for, but it should keep pursuers off our backs."

"My grandfather told me Achaemen Mantis had a secret base out here. Or there was a hidden underground temple ... or something."

"Utter rubbish," Hami said, and went back inside.

Mehrak ignored him. "And there are giant frogs. They live in these rock pools and eat creatures that pass by."

"Seriously?" Sammy asked. "Just when I thought we were over the worst of what Perseopia had to offer. Is there anything here that doesn't try to kill you?"

"Relax. The frogs are only the size of small dogs and they're harmless to humans."

"In that case, I want to see one."

Sammy didn't see any. Typical. The only creatures in Perseopia unlikely to kill you and there weren't any to be found.

As Louis moved through the outcrops, it became wetter still and he found himself wading through pools of water and weeds. A splash in the dark had Sammy wheeling around to shine her staff light across a pool. There was nothing to see, only the ripples of something—probably small-dog-sized—disappearing below the water.

The rain let up as they reached higher terrain. It remained wet underfoot, but Louis found it easier going and was able to pick up the pace.

When they stopped to make camp, Mehrak caught up with Sammy who was trying to enjoy some solitude away from everyone else.

"Why do you think Hami's taking you to the portal?" he asked as he walked over to the flat black stone she was sat on.

She looked pointedly at him.

"I mean, why is he *really* taking you to the portal?" he continued. "The magi know about it and they don't want you to go. Sagus said so."

Sammy wanted to say something to defend Hami, but she couldn't think of anything. He'd endangered her life multiple times. And he'd been wrong to do so on at least one of them. He was probably wrong to take her to the portal, too. Mehrak, on the other hand, was on Team Sammy, thus validating her choice of remaining in Perseopia and proving beyond reasonable doubt that it was the right decision.

"I know you like Hami," Mehrak said, shuffling uncomfortably, "but I care about you and want what's best for you."

"I care about you too." The words slipped out unconsciously. She hadn't realised she'd said anything at first, but when Mehrak perked up she carried on unprompted. "I don't want to leave you again. I want to stay in Eggie."

Mehrak smiled. "I think we should talk to Hami then."

They found him on the back balcony staring out into the void.

Mehrak cleared his throat. "We have something to say."

Hami didn't turn around. "I had a feeling you might."

"The magi know about the portal."

"And?"

"Have you spoken to them yet?"

"No."

"Sagus seemed to think you should."

"I know what they'll say. They don't want to lose Sammy." He sighed. "The Grand Master is of the opinion that she should stay and fight our war against the darkness. To fight this demon."

"And you don't?"

"I promised I'd get her home," Hami said simply.

"But what will that achieve? Sammy will be gone. The demon will still be here, and you'll get punished. You'll lose everything."

"I've already lost everything. At least Sammy and the outer Mother World will be spared."

"But I don't want to go home," Sammy said.

"I made a promise."

"A promise that *literally* no one wants you to keep." Sammy paused. "I'm contacting the Grand Master."

"No!" Hami and Mehrak chimed in together.

Mehrak's eyes were wide. "Just because you want to stay in Perseopia doesn't mean you should give yourself up. Let's figure out a plan first. We still need to destroy the portal whether you go through it or not."

Hami turned to Sammy, but couldn't bring himself to make eye contact. "I promised I'd get you home, but that isn't the only reason I want you gone." He took a deep breath. "None of the other magi have spent time in your presence. They don't know you, what you're capable of. You're fragile, you can be childish, and I've seen you act out of anger and pettiness."

All the words that Sammy wanted to projectile vomit at him coalesced into a blockage that she was unable to dislodge from her throat.

"The thought of you remaining in Perseopia scares me," Hami went on. "You possess too much power. After you left Perseopia the first time, you unleashed this black plague on us."

"You said that wasn't my fault," was all Sammy could get out.

"I'm not saying it to make you feel bad. I know it wasn't intentional. You possess more power than you know, but you're young and corruptible. In the wrong hands you'd—"

"I'd what?" Sammy managed at last. "I'm not stupid. I won't just turn to the dark side."

Hami looked her dead in the eyes. "What if you're tortured? What if your friends and family are threatened? What would you do then?"

Sammy stared back. He was trying to manipulate her again. But it wasn't working. She wouldn't turn bad. That sort of thing didn't happen in real life.

"The demon is heading to the portal in the mountains," Hami said. "To escape to the Mother World where it will accumulate more bodies and more power. The disease has already spread here. We can't allow it into the Mother World too. The magi know this and they've sent some of my brothers to close the portal."

"Let them close it," Mehrak said. "They're better equipped to fight the Order than we are. Sammy doesn't want to leave. She isn't a liability and you've risked our lives enough already. Leave the job to the professionals."

"You're not understanding what I'm trying to tell you. What do you think this demon will do if the portal gets destroyed and Sammy isn't on the other side of it? Bearing in mind that it's on a quest for power and Sammy has an abundance of it?"

"How will it find her?" Mehrak asked.

"How did the tall thin demon find Sammy before? How did it keep finding her? In the Fungi Forest, at Honton Keep, at the Fifth Azaran Fire Temple. Ramaask used it to hunt her down and it found her every time. This thing will too. The magi wanted to train you to fight Ramaask, and now they want to train you to take on this demon. I can't protect you forever. The demon will overpower us, and it will take you for itself. I want you gone not only for your own safety, but for ours too."

–FORTY-THREE–
How Do You Solve a Problem Like Sammy?

Mehrak tried to calm her down, tried to tell her it didn't matter what Hami had said, and that they'd figure something out, but his words lacked conviction. He knew nothing about how powerful she was supposed to be, or what kind of perceived threat she represented. He realised then that he didn't really know an awful lot about her or the place she came from.

She was different to how she'd been the last time she came to Perseopia though. Older, obviously, but something else. Her childlike optimism had gone, some amount of happiness too. But it was more than that. Part of her was missing. Like it had been shed between her leaving the last time and returning to Perseopia again. Mehrak couldn't place exactly what that something was, but the absence in her was disconcerting.

The atmosphere inside Eggie remained tense over the days it took to skirt the outcrops and exit onto the plains in the north. One evening after they'd stopped for the night Mehrak found Sammy alone in the kitchen, sat perched on the edge of the kitchen bench with her head in her hands.

"The magi might've already shut the portal down before we get there," Mehrak said, hopefully.

Sammy lifted her head. "Do we have to go to the mountains? Can't we run away instead? I'll stay in Eggie and live with you."

Mehrak wasn't sure what to say to that. "You know you're welcome to live here …" he said, and trailed off.

"But?"

"I still have to rescue Gisouie. Whatever happens between us, I could never see her hurt or in danger. When she's safe we can talk to her."

"And if she says I can't live here?"

"We'll deal with that situation if it arises."

Sammy got up and walked slowly towards him. She narrowed her eyes as she stared into his. "Do we have to save her?"

"Sammy?"

She sighed and carried on past him. "I know ... I just hate that you're married."

Mehrak held out his hand to her, but she didn't take it. "Do you want me to talk to Hami?"

Sammy picked up Victa's lightning staff from where it had been leaning against the wall and took the stairs down and out of the cottage.

When the back door hatch slammed, Mehrak went to find the magus.

He found him on the front balcony watching Sammy walk towards the fire pit.

Mehrak watched with him. The pit had been dug deeper than usual in order to conceal the fire light from a distance. Sammy stood on the edge with her back to Eggie, but her body language was clear. She kicked at a loose stone in frustration, then wandered away out into the darkness.

"Hami," Mehrak said as he joined him at the railing.

"You're not going to talk me out of it," Hami said by way of greeting.

"She doesn't want to go."

"She's too dangerous to stay."

"Is she? I think you're making excuses."

"And why would I do that?"

"Because you like her."

Hami's jaw set. "I think you misunderstand—"

"There's no misunderstanding. I see the way you look at her. You feel guilty about having feelings for someone so soon after your friend's sister lost her life."

"Her name was Jamileh."

"I'm sorry you feel such guilt. But sending Sammy home won't make everything right."

Hami's eyes burned. Mehrak inched back, but no attack came.

Then Hami became distant. "Go ahead. Turn it around on me if it makes you feel better. You clearly aren't trying to keep Sammy here for your own selfish reasons."

A flash of light preceded a concussive boom out in the darkness. Then the pattering of pebbles raining down.

"Sammy!" Hami yelled. "That staff is not a toy!"

They stood in silence for a time. Hami's eyes were vacant.

Mehrak wasn't sure where to go from there. "Whatever happens, it's got to be Sammy's choice," he said at last, figuring that was the only thing left to say.

Louis turned his head to the west. Hami followed his unseeing gaze out into the darkness.

"We know what Sammy wants to do ..." Hami said, then trailed off.

"What?" Mehrak asked.

Hami gripped the railing. "That stupid girl!"

"What?"

"She's given us away."

Mehrak looked out into the darkness. There was nothing there.

Below, Louis signed: *Antelopes*. A moment went by and then: *Greenbucks. Magi.*

While Mehrak was still processing what Louis had signed, Hami dragged him into the bedroom. "If Sammy and I are captured, will you still go to the snow base? You're not going to abandon your wife, are you?"

Mehrak mustered all his indignation. "What sort of person do you take me for?"

"I know you're an honourable man, but I also know you want to keep Sammy in Perseopia."

"Yes, but I'd never—"

"You must carry on to the portal. If Sammy and I don't make it, it's down to you to shut it down."

"But—"

"Mehrak." Hami held him at arm's length. "Sammy's just ruined her chances of returning home and in the process has jeopardised the realm. Our only way out of this is for you to convince the magi you're ignorant of my plans so you get to go free. The fate of Perseopia is now on your shoulders. Will you do it?"

Mehrak nodded, barely aware of what Hami was talking about. He steadied himself against the bed. His chest was constricting and his guts were turning to water. It was as if his life was ending, and in some ways it was.

He was losing Sammy again.

–FORTY-FOUR–
BUSTED

The Marzban around the fire pit shielded their eyes as the greenbucks came springing into camp and the magi ignited their staffs, illuminating the surroundings in stark white light.

Until that moment, Hami had never tired of witnessing a platoon of battle-ready greenbucks coming in to land. It was an impressive sight and ordinarily a relief, as it typically signified back-up. This time was different.

The magi took their time interrogating everyone. Mehrak, for all his faults, put on an excellent performance and was spared for his efforts, along with Narok and the Marzban.

Hami couldn't have been a wanted man, they'd explained, because Master Piruzan wouldn't have let him go if he was. Mehrak's indignity worked. Although it was probably his tears that sealed the deal. Real tears for the loss of Sammy. Hami had never got on with Mehrak, but he felt genuinely bad for the guy. He was contentious and meddling, but underneath it all, he was a decent human being. Hami knew that after they'd gone, Mehrak would do everything in his power to close the portal like he'd promised.

The magi confiscated Hami and Victa's lightning staffs, then transferred Sammy to the back of Kouros's greenbuck. Hami climbed onto the back of Zand's.

The remaining crew of Golden Egg Cottage watched them depart. Louis, Mehrak, Leiss, Narok, Eva, Calven and Indomit. All there one moment, then the greenbucks took to the air and they'd gone. It was unlikely Hami would see any of them again.

The magi had been on their way to Ameretat to defend the monument when Sammy gave Eggie's position away. Now he and Sammy found themselves headed there too. Most likely they'd be held somewhere while his brothers fought the demon. If they won the fight, Sammy would be taken to the Grand Master in New Ecbatana, and he would be transferred to the garrison to await trial. If they were unsuccessful and the citadel was compromised, they'd likely wind up dead.

They travelled in semi darkness. Some of the brothers had their lightning orbs low, to give enough light for the greenbucks to see by, but not enough to draw attention to them.

Hami caught sight of Sammy every few jumps. Kouros and Zand's greenbucks weren't quite in sync so she would be bouncing alongside him one moment, then gone the next.

They stopped often for Sammy to empty her stomach. Hami recalled how awful jump sickness had been for him when he'd first learned to ride. Sammy was doing admirably, considering. Most recruits complained more than she did. She looked miserable, though. And he guessed that was unlikely to be purely sickness.

She didn't eat a lot when they made camp that night, and sat for most of the evening in silence, staring at her hands in her lap.

I tried to keep you hidden, Hami spoke in her head.

I know, she replied. Then she disconnected from him.

———

They came from downwind.

Whoever these people were, they'd discovered Behnam, Ghobad and the horses before he'd sensed them, and now they came without stealth, not bothering to conceal their approach.

Behnam had Ghobad raise his eyes from skinning the rabbit so he could use them to guide him to his horse. He picked up his staff and walked shakily to the animal. When he reached it, he took hold of the reins and placed one foot in a stirrup in preparation for escape. Then he turned Ghobad's gaze to the forest.

He heard the heavy footfalls before Ghobad saw them. One karkadann and two Marzban riders. Their lanterns dazzled the guard's eyes so Behnam raised the man's hand to shield them.

The beast was battle-ready and laden with supplies and camp equipment, the Marzban were dressed in navy fatigues. One man, one woman. Ragged and weary as if they'd ridden straight from a fight.

"You're a long way from the Keep," Behnam said.

"We're on our way back," the woman replied. Then, "You're a magus." It wasn't a question.

"You've been fighting at the Cataclysm." Behnam took his foot from the stirrup and dropped the reins. "You fought with Hami."

The Marzban looked to each other, at Behnam's back, and then at Ghobad who sat by the campfire, mute.

"I'm Hami's partner," Behnam said.

The man spoke this time. "Principal Hootan lost his partner in Aratta. He was captured and—"

"I was." Behnam turned to face them. He saw the puzzlement on their faces via Ghobad as they looked at him and the blood-stained bandage covering his eyes. "I was not treated well," he said by way of explanation. "But my companion here looks after me. He guides me where I need to go." He paused. "Is Hami … okay?"

"He was when we last saw him," the woman said. "But then, he was just about to cross the Kuchak Sea in a gastrosaur caravan."

Behnam felt tears soaking into his bandages. He wondered at the fact that his tear ducts had somehow survived the blunt trauma that had blinded him, even though his eyes hadn't. Then he realised none of that mattered because Hami was alive. He allowed himself a smile.

"He's heading north, then? Heading for the mountains?"

The Marzban looked at each other again. They were no good at deception, these two, the answer was plain on their faces.

"And what of Ramaask?" Behnam knew the answer but wanted it confirmed.

"Dead," the woman said without hesitation.

"Then you must help me get to the portal before Hami makes the second worst mistake of his life."

"This isn't our war any longer," the man said. "The magi have asked enough of us already."

Behnam grinned. "I believe I can convince you."

–FORTY-FIVE–
The Sky Citadel

Sammy had never felt so belly sick. She wasn't typically prone to motion sickness and hadn't suffered it while travelling in Eggie, but bouncing across Perseopia on a greenbuck was something else. The rapid acceleration when the creature jumped, the gradual slowing, stopping, dropping, then harsh deceleration as they hit the ground. It was causing her guts no end of trouble. She hadn't been able to stomach much of anything after leaving the others behind and she'd spent the time in between in a daze of sickness and dizziness. But that was the least of her problems.

She missed Mehrak. She no longer cared that he was married. She just wanted to stay with him and Louis. To have adventures with them. And if she'd kept her emotions in check and resisted firing off the lightning staff, she still could've been. Hami, for all his good looks and bulging muscles, wasn't much company. Each time they stopped for the night, he would try to talk to her, to make her feel better, but he was socially awkward and never said anything that helped.

It took two long days of rollercoaster sickness before they saw the Naziarabad Monument. A brilliant white thread connecting the heavens to the earth.

"Why have we stopped?" she asked Hami when they made camp that night. "We're nearly there."

"It's not as near as you think," he replied. "Another day at least."

"It doesn't look that far away."

"That's because it's so large. It stretches from this world to the next, up through the smog … And now that black cloud. Whatever it is."

"How long did it take to build?"

"No one knows."

"*No one?*"

"It was discovered by a traveller in the first century. At the time, people believed that angels had created it. Others said that the column was created by Yima when he sealed Perseopia from the Mother World. At the top is a staircase. Some say you can climb it to the Next World."

"The Next World?" Sammy had heard of that place before, but she couldn't place where.

"Where angels live," Hami explained. "The place you go when you die."

It was after lunch the next day when they reached the outskirts of the vast encampment that surrounded the monument's base. The column had grown larger throughout the day as they got closer. Perfectly straight, brilliant white and shimmering. It wasn't hard to see why the people that discovered it believed that divine beings had created it. Sammy had been sceptical at first, but she was beginning to believe the same thing. She'd seen images of skyscrapers on the internet, but this thing was on another level.

The greenbucks touched down and jogged to a stop. Kouros jumped off, helped Sammy down, and led the way into the sprawling city of temporary canvas residences surrounding the column.

As they wove their way through the tents, it became clear that the site was comprised of many separate camps. Each formed a distinct suburb with its own variety of tent and branded with its own banners. Different attire went with each camp and the citizens of each. Some were dressed in matching uniforms of luxurious cloths that suggested royal guards. Some campers wore basic infantry uniforms, and others were formed of ragtag groups in mismatching clothes.

And everyone carried a weapon. These people were fighters, called to the monument to defend it against the encroaching monster. Perseopia versus the demon.

As Sammy walked and her sickness faded, some of her earlier despair seeped back in. And yet it was mild compared to what it had been. In this hive of bustling activity, it was easy to be distracted from the loss she was feeling for Mehrak and Louis. The people here were unified in defending the realm. There was an overwhelming sense of hope and camaraderie in the air. Camps were mingling with each other, joking and sharing rations, and it was infectious.

And then there were the animals that accompanied these disparate people. The large majority were horses. But there were other creatures, exotic beasts that you'd never get back home.

The bandit-looking group had silverskins, the same silvery, sharp-toothed horses that pulled Harz's chariot. Some fighters had brightly coloured ostrich-like creatures with hooked beaks. There were giant warthogs and karkadann dotted about the place. But it was the royal-looking dudes that had the most awesome creatures. They rode dinosaurs. A two-legged variety, lightly feathered in white and black. A pair of them were sparring by slamming the domes of their heads together. Heads that had to be solid bone given the force they were bashing them together with. Sammy could practically feel her teeth rattle each time they came together.

She was beginning to feel more hopeful. Mehrak wasn't lost, she knew where he was heading and she wasn't leaving Perseopia any time soon. They'd find each other again. Somehow. The magi couldn't imprison her forever. She hadn't done anything wrong. And in the meantime, she'd make the best of her current situation. Perhaps she could even use her new found magus abilities to fight the demon alongside these other people.

"Nice hair!" called a lean woman with a shaved head. She winked at Sammy and held up a large mug. The glazed look on her face suggested that the beverage in her hand probably wasn't her first. The others in her party held up their drinks too, took long draughts, then cheered. Sammy couldn't help but smile.

The encampment took the remainder of the day to cross and all the while the monument dominated the skyline above the tents. An endless white pillar from earth to heavens, shimmering with almost ethereal pearlescence, and birds circling at the top, thin slithers of white drifting lazily beneath the black sky.

The campsite closest to the monument consisted of a ring of tents surrounding a herd of greenbucks hitched to a post in the middle.

Sammy got led into the centre through a gap in the tents.

"So we finally get to meet this chosen child."

Sammy turned towards the voice.

A magus strode towards them from one of the tents. He'd lost part of his cheek on the left-hand side and his teeth were bared through the gap. His facial disfigurement made him look both maniacal and furious at the same time.

Hami's eyes dipped, his shoulders slumped, and all the fight went out of him. "Master Piruzan," he said.

"Principal." Piruzan sucked saliva in through his teeth and smiled a sadistic smile. "You thought you could lose us?"

"Master, I—"

"I'm not interested. You'll have plenty of time in confinement to work out your excuses. You can tell them to Aegis when you're brought to trial in New Ecbatana."

"I thought I'd be tried at the garrison."

Piruzan ignored him and turned to the magi that had brought them. "Your team has done well, Zand, but I'll take the fugitives from here. I'm heading up to the citadel shortly to speak with the Air Chief Marshal. I'll take them to the cells where they can wait out the battle."

Hami stepped closer. "Let me help."

"With what?" Piruzan held his arms out and turned a slow circle. "I have an army."

"I'll fight alongside you. Take Sammy up to the citadel. Let me stay and regain your trust."

"My trust for you has long since waned," Piruzan said. "You had your chance." He raised his staff above his head and illuminated the orb, pulsing the light on and off several times.

At first nothing happened. A few of the magi glanced up, but Sammy couldn't tell what they were looking at. Then she noticed that several of the birds that had been circling the top of the column were closer than they had been. They were coming down, spiralling lazily in the light of the citadel, growing larger as they descended.

Piruzan led everyone to a wide space, away from the greenbucks, where the magi lit their staffs and spread out to create a circle.

Broad shadows swept over the camp, eclipsing the light above as gigantic birds passed over. Their vast wings beat air down as the creatures came in to land, whipping up dirt and flinging Sammy's hair and clothing into disarray. She shielded her eyes against the airborne debris as canvas flapped against tent poles and guy ropes were pulled from the earth.

Four of the gigantic creatures stood in the settling dust, shaking out their feathers, screeching and rolling their shoulders. They were more dinosaur than bird. Similar in appearance to the lava pterodactyls but covered in white feathers on their heads, backs and wings. Pale pink and grey scales lined their throats and bellies, and their yellow beaks were filled with triangular teeth. Crests adorned the back of the animals' heads, like the lava pterodactyls but shorter and rounded at the end like hockey sticks.

The men and women riding them were dark-skinned, dressed in white, and wore leather flying hats and goggles like Biggles.

Sammy was led to one of the pterodactyl birds, helped up onto the saddle behind the rider and strapped in.

"Hold on tight," said the woman holding the reins, and they leapt into the air.

Sammy snatched hold of the woman's billowing shirt as the dino-bird heaved its wings and they surged into the sky. The rapid acceleration was more violent than that of the greenbuck's, and for a moment Sammy's stomach turned. But as they climbed higher, the breathless joy of flight took over. The rush of air in her face, the effortlessness of riding the thermals. They banked, cut in close to the tower and then soared out over the camp.

Hami followed behind on the next bird down. She glimpsed him as they banked and a moment later had lost him. Further below, the campfires spread out around the base of the column for miles in all directions. A vast shimmering tapestry of twinkling lights. Only from this height could Sammy truly appreciate the number of people invested in the battle. There had to be tens of thousands of people down there. Surely enough to be able to stop the demon. They'd win out. They had to.

Above her, the light of the citadel projected from the column like a lighthouse of the gods, blazing into the darkness that hung low over the realm.

They turned then, sliced back across the tower, and out in the other direction.

Each time they banked they rose higher, zigzagging up the tower and putting more distance between themselves and the ground. Other dino-birds were patrolling the skies nearby. A few were out by the fringes of the camp, but most were congregated around the top of the column.

Sammy's bird took them higher still, to the occupied section of the monument.

Citizens of the citadel were carrying out their daily duties on the other side of the circular windows in the column's façade. The residents, like the dino riders, appeared to be predominantly dark-skinned, and dressed in white. On each pass of the column, Sammy got a snapshot of them working, then the bird would beat its wings and carry them up and away to the next level where she'd see a different set of people performing different tasks.

The top of the citadel was dino-bird central.

Long, straight runways projected from wide arches around the column circumference and dino-birds were taking off from and coming in to land on them. Sammy's rider sent their bird out and around in a wide arc, then it swept back to join the back of a queue coming in to land.

They touched down on the protruding platform and moved along to free up the runway for those coming in behind. Sammy's rider climbed down and led the dino-bird forward by the reins. Behind them, another bird landed, then the one carrying Hami, and lastly the one carrying Piruzan.

They entered the citadel through an arch, where Sammy climbed down from the saddle and was, for a moment, light-headed. She wavered while her rider departed with the bird towards some stables nearby.

Sammy bent over, bracing her arms against her knees.

"Breathe in through the nose, and out through the mouth," Hami said as he came over accompanied by Piruzan. "We're high up. You'll need to acclimatise to the altitude."

Sammy nodded, but remained in the leapfrog stance. She breathed deeply, emptying and refilling her lungs.

It didn't take long for the dizziness to pass and for her to regain a posture upright enough to take in her surroundings.

The interior of the citadel was hollow and vast. Wide walkways and staircases joined opposite sides of the column, crisscrossing each other above and below. Pod-like dwellings hung from the walls, walkways and staircases. They were bulbous and smooth like they'd grown organically from the column itself and was what Sammy imagined the inside of an alien spaceship might look like.

"I want one of those dino-birds," she said, nodding back towards the stables, where the bird that had carried her up was getting preened by a stable boy while a girl threw it meat scraps from a bucket.

"A rook?" Hami replied.

"Aren't rooks black?" Sammy asked. "And a lot smaller?"

"Not here they aren't."

"Can magi ride them? Could I get one if I became a magus?"

"You're not a magus," Piruzan said. "And you aren't likely to become one ..." He trailed off as his gaze focused on something behind her. He smiled. "Here they are."

Ten armed guards dressed in white arrived. Their uniforms were trimmed in gold and at their waists hung hook-shaped swords that possessed Sheffield stainless steel levels of shininess.

"Lead the way," Piruzan said to the guards. "But not too fast. Our guests are still acclimatising to the altitude."

The guards spread out, encircled them in a neat, swift movement, and led them from the entrance archway and into the citadel proper.

The place was a throng of activity. Carts were loaded with supplies brought up by the rooks, street vendors were touting their wares, and other assorted tradespeople were generally rushing about. Many stopped to watch the visitors in their midst, but none stopped for long and each of them dashed off soon after.

The guards forged ahead, clearing a path through the crowds as they led Sammy and the two magi onto the first walkway.

Hami hung back with Piruzan. "You know about the portal at the snow base?"

"No thanks to you, Principal."

"Ramaask was going to use it to get to the Mother World. I think the Ahriman ... this demon, is trying to do the same thing."

"We figured that out for ourselves," Piruzan said without looking back.

292

Hami grabbed him by the shoulder. "Aren't you interested in knowing what I have to say?"

Piruzan stopped. "Do you expect us to believe any of it? You only tell us what suits you in order to further your own machinations."

"I'm captured. What good will it do me to lie now?"

"I don't know, Principal. I'm not familiar with the game you're playing and, as I've already told you, I'm past caring. I know what my orders are. Master Aegis can decide what's to be done with you."

Hami paused. "I can't access him."

Piruzan sneered. "You can't access anyone. I've had you blocked from the network."

Sammy?

I can still hear you.

Piruzan smiled at Sammy. She turned away. "I assume you've just figured out that you can still communicate with each other. The girl's never been properly registered so we can't block her, but you can forget trying to convince anyone else to set you free. They can't hear you."

"You've sent magi to the mountains, haven't you?"

"Of course. Ankar and Morris."

"Just those two?"

"They'll be reporting back when they find out what's there."

"They don't need to find out what's there. They need to destroy the portal."

"Perhaps you could've divulged what information you had back at the Cataclysm when there was still a chance I might've believed you."

Hami took a long breath. "Are you taking me to see Queen Jorj?"

"The Air Chief Marshal isn't interested in every petty criminal that enters the citadel. You're headed for the cells."

The guards led them over a second walkway, ascended two flights of stairs, across a wide bridge lined by market stalls and up a final staircase to a large bubble of a building clinging to the inside of the column.

They entered a foyer area filled with mushroom-green chairs, and at the far end, a desk also fashioned from mushroom. The furniture looked strangely out of place in the white, almost futuristic environment of the citadel.

A man behind the desk looked up from the parchment he'd been reading as they approached.

"Two prisoners," Piruzan said. "And one of them a magus so you'll need to be careful. No entering the cell. No visitors." When the man failed to reply, Piruzan followed up with, "Let's go."

The man nodded hurriedly, got up from his chair and beckoned them to follow. Piruzan ordered the guards to wait in the foyer, then nudged Hami and Sammy after the man as he led them down a corridor.

There were iron cell doors spaced out along the corridor with a significant distance between each. Behind the third door, something screamed and crashed around.

"What's wrong with that person?" Sammy asked as they passed the door.

"That was the head of the citadel guard," the prison warden said. "When the purple smog disappeared and the sky went black, he climbed the stairs through the ceiling to see if the path to the Next World had been reopened."

"Path to the Next World …" Sammy turned to Hami.

"And had it?" Hami asked without looking at her.

The prison guard shook his head. "Let's just say the black stuff is worse than the purple stuff. He came running back down the stairs with glowing red eyes and chewed out the throat of the first person he saw. It took ten men to restrain him and drag him here to be locked away. He hasn't eaten anything for seven days and he's still as ferocious as when he turned into whatever he is now."

Sammy experienced what she imagined was the feeling movie characters experience when they say, "I have a bad feeling about this."

At the fifth door, the warden paused and peered through a narrow letterbox-sized aperture. Evidently satisfied, he fished a hoop of keys out of his pocket, slowly picked through them until he found the right one, then unlocked and opened the door.

It was a large room, split across the centre by a fence of vertical metal bars. On the far side were two beds, in between which sat a box with a hole in the top. Sammy guessed it was the loo. A narrow horizontal window filled with yet more bars sat in the wall near the toilet.

"I've got a present for you, Principal," Piruzan said. He flashed one of his wicked smiles as he fished in the pouch at his belt and drew out a pair of glass handcuffs.

"Magi-cuffs?" Hami said. "You can't be serious."

"Brought these all the way from the garrison for you. Picked them up when I got the call from Aegis." He held them out to Hami. "Somehow I knew you'd be needing them."

Hami took them. Held them in his hands. "You don't need to—"

"Put them on."

Hami's eyes were dark as he clicked the cuffs into place around his wrists.

What are they? Sammy asked.

Hand cuffs made of a special tetra-silicate, a glass-like material with a semi-crystalline structure that's really hard to latch on to or manipulate because of its unusual arrangement of molecules. Supposedly developed by ancient sorcerers to restrain magi.

Sammy tried to concentrate on the cuffs but couldn't. The molecules on the surface of Hami's wrists were there, the proteins in the hairs of his arms. But the hand cuffs didn't seem to exist, like there was an area devoid of matter where matter should be. She glanced at Piruzan.

Piruzan smiled. "Magic," he said, and licked his exposed teeth. He nodded to the prison warden.

The man unlocked a door in the centre of the bars. He let Hami and Sammy inside, then locked it behind them.

"Stand back," Piruzan said. He lit his staff and concentrated a beam of light on the lock in the cell door. The metal sparked, turned red, then quickly transitioned through orange to fiery yellow. The heat coming off the metal was incredible. Sammy took several steps back and looked away to stop the heat drying her eyes.

When she dared to look back again, the lock had returned to a dull red, but still radiated a significant amount of heat.

"Just in case you think about picking the lock with your powers," Piruzan said.

"What happens if the Ahriman reaches the tower?" Hami asked. "What happens to Sammy?"

Piruzan turned to leave. "You better hope it doesn't come to that."

"I need to speak with Master Aegis."

"You had ample opportunity, *Principal*."

"Master—"

"Anything you need to say to him you can say to me now. But make it quick, the demon is approaching and I need to help rally the army."

"Close the portal."

"You've said that already."

"I'm serious. That thing can't be allowed to get within a hundred stadia of the snow base. There's no point fighting for the people of Ameretat if that portal remains open. If the Ahriman gets through, it could destroy the realm."

"My men will find the portal."

"It's on the northern slopes of Dev's Peak."

Piruzan paused. "Honestly?"

"I swear it on my life. Please, Piruzan."

"Master Piruzan," the magi master said. He sneered. "Wish us luck. Your lives depend on it." Then he turned and led the prison warden out of the room.

–FORTY-SIX–
BANGED UP

Hami went to the window. He remained there for some time, staring out into space. Eventually he stepped back and went to sit on his bed. He fiddled listlessly with the cuffs at his wrists, gave up, then looked over at Sammy.

"I had to tell them to close the portal," he said.

She shrugged. "I don't want to go home. I told you." Her voice cracked slightly as she said it and wondered if she was coming across as indifferent as she hoped.

"I'm not sure you fully understand the alternative," Hami said. "Look out of the window."

Sammy stared back at him. He didn't look away, so she got up from her bed and looked out of the thin letterbox window. Outside, a black stormfront approached. It was hard to make out in the darkness, but she was just able to see movement in the swirling smoke drifting towards them.

It was a menacing sight, but still a long way off.

"I can't risk the Ahriman escaping to the outer Mother World," Hami said. "We need to contain it."

"It's fine." Why did he keep going on about it? Sammy wasn't entirely comfortable about losing her way back to the Mother World, but everyone had reservations when it came to major decisions. If she really had to go home one day, there'd be an amulet, a potion or some kind of magical hat.

"This isn't it though, is it?" she asked.

"What do you mean?"

"You've got a plan. We aren't really stuck in this cell until the demon gets here and attacks us?"

Hami shrugged. He lay down on the bed, resting his cuffed hands on his stomach, and stared at the ceiling.

Sammy remained at the window. The creeping smoke rolled ever closer, behind it the faint glow of the Cataclysm on the horizon. Above, dino-birds circled the citadel, below, the campfires twinkled. The world ostensibly at peace. How far removed Sammy was from everything. From the battle below. From Mehrak. And from her family in Sheffield.

Imprisonment had stripped her of responsibility. All their problems were now someone else's. Even if she wanted to help there was nothing she could do.

When Sammy turned back, Hami was asleep. It was one of the few times she'd seen him in that state. He was usually awake when she fell asleep and was always up when she woke. Perhaps being forced into incarceration and handing over responsibility to Piruzan had eased some of the stress he'd been suffering. A frown fleetingly distorted his expression, then he returned to peace.

Sammy decided she'd let him sleep and lay down on her own bed.

She listened to the former head of the citadel guard screaming down the hall and wondered if there was any part of his consciousness that remained. Had the intangible essence that made him who he was died when he entered the black smoke? Did some other entity possess his body now? She shivered. Whatever it was controlling the noise coming from him had pitched the sound just right to spook anyone that heard it.

Sammy figured she'd never sleep with the zombie scream soundtrack, but she started awake sometime later when the lock in the outer steel door clanged and the prison warden entered the room carrying two trays of nondescript yellow mush.

"Dinner," he said as he approached the bars. He placed the trays on the floor and slid them through the narrow gap under the door with his toe.

Hami got up from his bed. "I'd like to see Air Chief Marshal Jorj," he said as he collected the first tray and placed it at the foot of Sammy's bed.

"You heard the magi master," the prison officer replied. "No entering the cell. No visitors."

"He didn't say you weren't allowed to deliver a message for us, though, did he?"

The prison officer was silent. It was almost possible to see the cogs in his brain processing Hami's request.

"It's a very simple message," Hami went on. "I'm not trying to trick you. All I ask is that Queen Jorj is informed that Hami Hootan is being held in one of her cells."

The prison officer paused. "Principal Hootan?" He lowered himself to one knee and dropped his head.

"You don't need to bow," Hami said.

"It is an honour," the man said. "Truly. But my orders—"

"Are still being obeyed," Hami finished for him. "You won't be breaking them by passing on my message. I won't get you in trouble."

The man seemed to consider this a moment, nodded, then scurried from the room.

Hami collected the remaining tray from the floor and took it back to his own bed.

Queen Jorj? Sammy asked.

Hami chose to voice his reply. "The Regent's niece and Air Chief Marshal of the citadel's air force. Technically there can be no royalty in Perseopia since the Sultan was killed, but Marshal Jorj is so well loved that many people call her Queen Jorj."

"Why?"

"She was born to one of the citadel's wealthiest families, and donated most of her inheritance to humanitarian causes. She worked her way to the top of the air force by starting at the bottom. She has influence with the controlling families, and yet listens to the people. She'll work a day in the mines north of here, a day lifting freight, serving in a kitchen, you name it. Every once in a while she'll even spend a day in sewage processing. She's also always the first person to fly into battle."

"That's pretty cool."

"It is, but her courageous attitude almost cost her her life about a year ago during a hunting trip. Thankfully, I was visiting the citadel at the time and had joined her security detail for the day. We were set upon by crabmen, and as it happens, I saved her life. And the lives of everyone else there that day."

Sammy jumped up. "So she owes you one?"

"You could say that."

"I knew you had a plan. We're busting out of here!"

Sammy had eaten her lunch and was beginning to doze off again when Queen Jorj arrived.

She came in through the outer steel door taking two big strides into the room.

"I'll call you when I need you," she told the prison officer over her shoulder.

The prison guard dipped his head and left, closing the door behind him.

Queen Jorj wore no crown. Her clothes were white and simple like every other inhabitant of the citadel, yet she radiated royalty with every movement she made. She had deep brown skin, short cropped hair, and was the most flawlessly beautiful person Sammy had ever seen.

"Guests of the citadel," she said as she bowed. She maintained eye contact with Hami and then Sammy as she spoke.

Hami lowered his head. "Air Chief Marshal," he said.

"You sent a message informing me you were here."

Sammy involuntarily stepped back as Queen Jorj came closer.

"I did, Air Chief," Hami replied.

"Which was unnecessary as I'd already been told."

Hami seemed genuinely surprised. "Really?"

"Master Piruzan suspected that you might try to contact me. In fact, I've just come from a meeting with him." She approached the bars. "We've been discussing the impending battle, but he did mention you." She paused. "And the trouble you've caused the realm."

Hami grimaced. "I want to put things right."

"Piruzan said you'd say that."

"But you came to see me anyway?"

"I felt I owed you as much for … the assistance you gave my hunting party last year."

"I saved their lives. I saved your life."

Queen Jorj held up her hand to silence Hami. "I will hear what you have to say, but I can't promise I'll act on any requests given what I've learned."

"My plan was to lure Lord VorMask from Aratta and defeat him," Hami said. "And it worked. The rest … I never meant for Sammy to cross the seal that unleashed this demon."

"The Ahriman."

"That's what people are calling it."

"And you … according to Piruzan."

Hami looked away.

"Regardless of your good intentions, you have unleashed something far worse than VorMask and many of my people are going to die today as a result."

"You know I would never have done this deliberately."

"I know it. Piruzan does too."

"He does?"

"He's contentious and aggressive, but underneath he's a good man."

Hami sat on his bed and put his face in his hands.

"He thinks you're misguided," Queen Jorj said. "He thinks you're in the early stages of smog sickness and will continue to make bad decisions from this point forward. The fact you're unwilling to talk to the brotherhood is compounding that assumption."

Hami removed his hands and looked the Air Chief Marshal in the eye. "You remember my partner? Master Baktash?"

She nodded once.

"He was captured by Lord VorMask recently. He communicated to me during the battle outside the Fifth Azaran, told me things about Sammy that he'd learned from VorMask. Things I can't repeat to anyone."

Sammy turned to him. *What things?*

Later, Hami communicated, then shut himself off from her.

Queen Jorj smiled, then turned to leave. "I will talk to the magi. Perhaps I can persuade them to send more men to the portal."

"The demon isn't interested in your citadel," Hami called out before she could leave. "It's only passing on its way to the portal. Have the magi told you that they're using the Naziarabad Monument for their last stand? A barrier against the demon?"

Queen Jorj turned to face Hami again. "They have asked my assistance in dealing with the creature. I've consented."

"I've seen what this creature can do. All the towns between the Fifth Azaran and here have been destroyed. It's decimated them and collected their bodies. That's all it wants from the citadel. More dead bodies to build its army. Then it will continue past to the portal. Evacuate your people from the ground. Bring them up here until it passes. You'll save lives."

"The brotherhood know what's best for the realm."

"In this instance they don't. They've only dispatched two magi to the portal. Two middle tier brothers that are likely to wind up dead."

"I have faith—"

"Have faith in me! I saved your life. I'd never ordinarily call in that debt, but you leave me no choice. You owe me."

Jorj bristled. "I'm grateful you were there that day, Principal, but I'm tougher than I look. I could've handled those crabmen."

"Maybe. But what about the rest of your hunting party? What about your friends? How many of them would still be here if I hadn't been with you that day?"

Queen Jorj began pacing. "I can't go against the magi."

"Everything I do, I do for Perseopia. It's my duty to protect and serve. Let me save the realm."

Queen Jorj stopped and approached the bars. She gripped them tightly, stared at Hami. "What would you do if you were to escape from here?"

Hami stood. Took a step towards her. "I'd take Sammy to the portal in the mountains and return her to the Mother World."

"The brotherhood don't want that."

"They want to use her power for themselves. She's only eighteen. She has a family."

"Then after you've sent Sammy home?"

"Then I'd destroy the portal so the Ahriman can't use it."

"You wish only to send Sammy home, then destroy the portal?"

"Just that. The demon can't be allowed to escape into the wider Mother World. We can contain it here. Out there ..." Hami shrugged, "both our worlds die."

Jorj remained quiet for a time. "You're sure there are no other undesirable outcomes that you could inadvertently set in motion? No seals that can get crossed? No further demons that could get unleashed? And no apocalyptic events that might get triggered?"

"Please."

"And you're sure you can close this portal down?"

"I'm not sure of anything. But I have to try. The alternative is a lot worse."

Queen Jorj walked to the outer cell door, then stopped.

She didn't turn back to face them. "If the citadel came under attack causing this cell to become unsafe. Unsafe enough that you had to be transferred. And if it so happened that during that transfer you escaped, would you swear to go to the portal and destroy it?"

"I would," Hami said.

Queen Jorj nodded once, then left.

–FORTY-SEVEN–
THE BATTLE OF SMOKE AND WINGS

Sammy pressed her forehead between the bars in the window. Giant, Perseopian-style rooks circled above and below. At times seeming to fly in choreographed formation, and at others completely at random, spiralling and dancing on the thermals, cutting across each other, but never colliding. The riders themselves were primed for battle, armoured in leather and carrying hook-shaped swords that matched the shape of the dino-birds' crests. Sammy imagined the design choice had been deliberate.

The demon's black smoke continued to advance along the ground. Crawling ever closer, until the lights at the far edge of the camp flickered and went out.

The demon had arrived.

A call went up and the rooks dived into battle.

There were flashes of light and loud cracks where smoke met camp, but Sammy was too high and too far away to see individuals.

Then the blackened lava pterodactyls from the Cataclysm came slicing up through the air. A swirling hurricane of leathery wings.

Sammy glimpsed Air Chief Jorj in amongst the dino-bird riders, then she swooped into battle followed by twenty other rooks and she'd gone.

The rooks and pterodactyls cut through each other, striking out as they passed, the rook riders with their hooked blades, the pterodactyls with their claws. Every so often there'd be a full on mid-air collision and the combatants would fall.

Queen Jorj reappeared nearby, hovering. She made eye contact with Sammy, then vanished into the mass of winged bodies again.

A moment later, the limp body of a pterodactyl came careening towards the window.

Sammy leapt back as the creature hit the outside of the column, sending cracks racing through the clean white wall.

Hami leapt up and pushed past her to the window.

Sammy elbowed her way in next to him.

Queen Jorj hovered outside. "Call for the guard!" she shouted. "Tell him your cell is unstable." Then she dived away.

Hami left the window and went to the bars dividing the room. "Hey!" he shouted. "Warden!"

No response.

He called again. When no one came, he closed his eyes. He was concentrating on something.

The outer cell door rattled in its frame. Then the lock clicked and the door swung open.

The screaming citadel guard in room three became louder.

"Hey!" Hami shouted again.

Still nothing.

Sammy returned to the window to watch the battle while Hami continued to yell for the warden. The battle had moved lower and Queen Jorj was nowhere to be seen. More camp lights at the fringes flickered and went out as the shadow spread closer.

A scream startled Sammy. A large white object careening towards her, flapping, squawking. It hit the outside wall below.

The impact shook the room. Large fissures raced through the floor below Sammy's feet. Cracks in the wall spread.

Then the window frame and surrounding wall fell out.

Sammy dived towards Hami, but too late.

The floor disappeared, along with the beds and toilet.

She caught the remaining section of floor across her chest, then fell back catching hold of the edge with her hands.

Hami was still up against the bars.

"Sammy!" he called down and took a step towards her.

The ground at his feet cracked and the flooring under Sammy's right hand fell away. She screamed as she hung on with her left.

Hami stopped. "Hold on."

She felt him concentrating on her belt. Holding her steady with his powers. Cold air blew in through the hole in the outer wall.

A rider-less rook floundered in the rubble below, one floor down. It screamed up at Sammy as she dangled by one arm.

"Hami!"

"I can't come any closer. The floor will collapse. If you drop down I can slow your descent. I've got you by the belt."

"It's too far!"

The rook screamed again and snapped its jaws. Sammy could sense the animal had an injury.

She swung her right arm up and grabbed hold of the floor.

Another crack, and the area she clung to tilted.

"Sammy!" Hami shouted. He lowered himself to the floor and carefully spread his weight, reaching out to her with both cuffed hands.

The pain coming off the rook was acute. The beast shook the rubble off its wings and screamed again. Sammy traced the pain to a broken leg. She concentrated on quelling the animal's fear like she'd done for Kimbo, but the intensity of the pain was blocking her ability.

She focused on the leg.

Hami reached closer, but she couldn't pull herself up to take his hand. The mortar was giving way.

The rook stopped screaming. Shook out its feathers. Sammy urged it closer. And it moved, labouring over the rubble below, flinching as it transferred weight onto its damaged leg.

Sammy soothed as far as she was able, but the creature was becoming increasingly agitated. It raised its head as it drew close. *Keep going. Almost there.*

The floor gave way.

Sammy opened her legs and landed across the giant bird's neck. She slid down the smooth white feathers, feeling for the saddle with her feet.

The half-dinosaur, half-bird raised itself to full height, then beat its wings together.

One moment they were inside the tower, the next they were outside, as if sucked out backwards through the hole.

Then they were in freefall.

Sammy became weightless, disconnected from everything. She caught a fist full of feathers in one hand, but the rest of her hung in space. She pulled herself in, guiding herself towards the saddle hoping the feathers she held wouldn't come loose.

The leg straps whipped around in the rushing air. Sammy manoeuvred herself in close, fumbled with the buckles. She managed to guide her legs into the loops, secure the straps. Then communicated for the rook to pull up.

Nothing.

Panic had taken hold of the dino-bird's brain and it'd closed itself off to suggestion. The ground was fast approaching, close enough to be able to pick out individuals.

Sammy panicked too. She needed to rein it in, to calm herself so she could calm the bird. She held her breath, slowly filled her lungs and sent soothing thoughts. The rook's muscles loosened. Its mind opened. And Sammy gave the order. *Pull up!*

The rook spread its wings, raised its head, and gravity re-asserted itself at abdomen-crushing levels of deceleration. For a moment everything blurred and Sammy almost blacked out.

She clung on, slumped against the rook's neck. She forced herself to take short, shallow breaths. Then she opened her eyes.

They were skimming the top of the campsite. Air rushing through her hair. Tents and fire lights whipping by below. Passing over men, women and beasts as they swept towards the approaching blackness. Above her, rooks and lava pterodactyls engaged in aerial dogfights. Below her, men and women rode into battle.

Then Sammy was above the undead army. Grey men and women this time. Dark crabmen and other beasts too. All of them drained of colour and all advancing on the column, with dead eyes and blank expressions.

Sammy adjusted course as a crabman lunged with its sword arm. The movement happened instinctively. She had maintained her connection to the dino-bird and was in control. If she wanted the rook to move, it did so. No independent thought was required, just an impulse and the creature moved like it was an extension of her own body.

They were rapidly approaching the heart of the darkness now. A mass of black liquid and smoke coiling in and around itself. A giant's silhouette in the centre, formed from pieces of man, crabman, and animal. Part flesh, part shell. The creature's burning eyes fixed on her and it reached out an arm.

You are mine, dark princess, it said in her head.

Sammy banked hard, turning her rook back towards the column.

You are mine, she heard again, quieter this time, fading.

And she was back over friendly territory again. Lights and tents flashing below. War cries, chanting.

The demon couldn't have been talking about her. She wasn't a princess, dark or otherwise. What did it mean? Although perhaps she didn't want to know. For now she was going to rescue Hami and get the hell out of there.

Hami! she communicated.

Sammy! You're alright? he replied.

Get to the hole in the wall. I'm on my way back.

My hands are still cuffed.

I'll find you something to break them, just get to the wall.

Sammy slowed her rook to scan the campsites below.

She sensed the threat late, but banked hard as an undead lava pterodactyl came barrelling past.

It hit the ground, tumbled through a tent and a camp fire and sent sparks flying.

The beast righted itself, shook itself off, and turned towards Sammy exposing the harpoon end protruding from its chest.

The pterodactyl from the fire temple.

It launched itself back into the sky and came at her.

Sammy turned her rook and fled.

The other rook riders—the professional ones—were fighting the pterodactyls with their hooked blades, swinging them in a hacking motion, landing the hooks then dragging them through their enemies. Sammy needed a weapon too.

A burst of lightning flashed off to the side catching her attention. She banked towards it and picked up pace.

The harpooned pterodactyl followed.

A group of magi were fighting undead crabmen, taking them apart with lightning blasts. One of their group had already been killed. He lay in a pool of blood, arms and legs splayed, eyes staring lifelessly into the sky. His staff was by his side.

Sammy came in from above.

She concentrated on the staff and it flew to her hand. She cornered sharply and set a path for the column.

A rook chased by another pterodactyl came in from the side. Sammy ducked underneath, then banked as her pursuer swooped in from above.

She chanced a look behind. The pterodactyl was gaining.

Sammy turned in her seat and lit up the staff orb. This time she'd put him down for good.

She misfired as another pterodactyl clipped her rook, sending them into a spiral. She fumbled, almost lost the staff, but managed to catch it as they righted themselves.

She needed space. She forced her rook down towards the ground, out of harm's way, below the swarm of flying reptiles. The pterodactyl with the harpoon followed.

This time she'd be quick.

They cleared the battle, she ignited the staff orb, and turned.

The pterodactyl opened its jaws, screamed.

And Sammy let rip.

The blast hit like a megaton. The creature disintegrated, raining chunks of its barbecued flesh on the tents below.

Relief and something like elation flooded Sammy's body. She'd taken on a monster and won. One nil to the Mother Worlder!

Her victory was short lived. She took a metaphorical step back and gazed upon the scale of the aerial battle playing out above her. The monster she'd defeated was one of several hundred that now circled the column.

Below her, the grey army's foot soldiers were closing in on the tower. And huge swathes of the campsite had already gone dark.

Sammy aimed her rook at the citadel and took it up.

They weaved in and out of the aerial combatants around them. Sometimes ducking, sometimes banking, but always rising.

At some point in the journey they picked up another pterodactyl on their six. A big one. It followed them from the battle and around the column, in and out of the other fights.

Sammy needed to gauge where she was in relation to Hami. She struck out from the tower to get a better look, circling higher still. She was high above the camp now. Everything below just black shadow.

She spotted the hole in the column, and a tiny figure standing at the base. It was still a long way up, but she knew where she was heading. And Hami was waiting for her.

She barrel-rolled through the centre of a dogfight and powered back towards the column, pterodactyl in tow.

Forget becoming a magus. If Sammy was going to be stuck in Perseopia, she was becoming a rook rider. She whooped as she ducked below an incoming foe and zigzagged in between others.

She flew to the side of the column, coming in tight around the back and luring her pursuer behind her. She could sense Hami's presence rapidly approaching.

Sammy flung the lightning staff up, guiding it to where she knew Hami would be.

And there he was, soaring from the column. He seemed almost suspended in mid-leap. Time slowed as Sammy tilted in his direction and dipped under him. He caught the staff in his cuffed hands as Sammy pulled up and he landed on the saddle behind her. Hami bounced and almost went off the back, but he snatched at a leg strap and clung on.

Sammy cut away from the tower. A lightning burst behind her separated Hami's hands and a second larger burst accompanied a reptilian scream.

One down, Hami communicated to her.

Two, Sammy replied. *You're late to the party.*

Sammy took them into battle as Hami secured himself in the saddle behind her. Lightning blasts screamed into lava pterodactyls left and right, and charred body parts fell from the skies.

"Take us up!" Hami shouted. "Over there." He pointed ahead.

A rook and its rider had become separated from the others and a pterodactyl was closing in.

Sammy went for it, taking them in on an intercept course. Her rook caught up quickly and Hami vaporised the pursuing pterodactyl.

The chased rook slowed up and turned, revealing Queen Jorj on its back. She swept round in an arc and fell into formation alongside them.

"Hami?"

"Twice I've saved you now," Hami called to her. Then, "Look."

Below them, the grey army had reached the base of the column and was passing around it, heading north.

The Air Chief Marshal looked pointedly at Hami.

Hami maintained eye contact when he spoke. "I'll keep my promise." Then to Sammy: *Take us north.*

Which way is north?

Past the tower.

Sammy nodded to Queen Jorj, then peeled away setting course for the column. "Let's go, White Lightning!"

"White Lightning?" Hami shouted behind her.

"I just thought of it. There was a guy that sat outside the off-licence by my dad's house. He drank bottles of the stuff. I figured it was a cool name for the beast master's ride."

"Concentrate on the flying, beast master."

Sammy banked hard round the side of the column, thus proving her extreme flying credentials. She actually cut in a little too close and set her heart racing, but she kept her cool. Hopefully Hami hadn't noticed.

I know what you're doing. It was the demon's voice again.

Sammy glanced down.

The dark centre of the undead army had reached the column. Liquid smoke slithered around the base. Black tendrils licked up the sides like shadowy flames. Sammy couldn't see the creature inside, she was too high, but it was there, watching. Coming for her.

Behind them, a tsunami of beating wings crashed around the tower in their wake.

They had company. A lot of it.

The demon has sent them after us, Sammy communicated to Hami.

Hami unstrapped his legs and swung round in the saddle to face backwards. *Keep White Lightning steady.*

Sammy stole a look backwards.

The pterodactyls were coming in fast.

Hami began dropping them in rapid succession. Each blast of his staff connected, and each target went down. It was like watching Wayne play the Call of Duty Zombie maps but on timelapse. Wayne spent all his summer playing and wasn't close to being this good. But for all Hami's skills, the pterodactyls were too many and too fast. They were overtaking, coming in from the sides.

Sammy ducked, weaved and banked, but it was getting hard to avoid the flying lizards.

A collision put them into a spin.

Sammy pulled Lightning out the freefall, but Hami had gone. She reached out mentally and found him struggling against a pterodactyl, both of them falling together.

Sammy went for them, stooping into a dive to catch up.

Hami was clinging onto the pterodactyl's wing as it twisted around on itself, snapping at him.

As Sammy neared, Hami let go. He dropped backwards and aimed his staff. A powerful blast destroyed the pterodactyl, then he rotated himself as Sammy swooped underneath and caught him for a second time.

The other undead pterodactyls didn't let up. Scaly bodies were piling in from all directions. Hami continued to blow them out of the sky, but he was tiring and they'd lost too much altitude to survive another fall. It couldn't end like this. They'd been through too much.

A battle cry from behind scattered the pterodactyls.

Ten rook riders sailed in with Queen Jorj at the head.

"We'll hold them off," she shouted as she held up her sword. "Get to that portal and shut it down!"

Sammy took Hami and White Lightning away.

The rook riders peeled off into the pterodactyls, raking their hooked swords through the leathery flesh of their foes.

Hami mopped up the occasional stragglers that followed, the few that made it through the Air Chief's defences, but soon the column and battle faded, and they set a course for the mountains.

–FORTY-EIGHT–
The Good? Or the Greater Good?

Sammy could feel the weariness spreading through White Lightning. The sensation was slight at first, but as time went on she could feel his wings weighing heavy and it took increasing effort to keep him going.

There wasn't much to see below as they flew north. Occasional clusters of light indicating small settlements, but not a lot else. Sammy wondered if any of the people living in those settlements knew why the sky had turned black. Or whether they had any inkling that an army of dark creatures approached from the south to murder their children, take their souls and enslave their bodies.

Sammy experienced a desperate need to fly down, to warn everyone. To tell them to leave their towns before the demon arrived.

They're all going to die, aren't they? she asked Hami. *All those people in the villages below us.*

If we can shut down the portal quickly, there'll be no need for the demon to come this way.

But we won't be quick enough to save the towns closest to the column. And even if we shut down the portal, the demon will be stuck here in Perseopia and will continue killing.

Hami didn't reply. That was answer enough.

Sammy felt the situation spiralling out of her control. She'd been god-like while fighting the pterodactyls. A superhero soaring through the sky. Now she was helpless and all her powers were for nothing to these innocents who were going to die because she'd happened to cross a golden disc two years ago. She couldn't cope with that. She might've unleashed the demon unintentionally, but these people would still die. Manslaughter rather than murder, but death was still death. Last time she'd been here she'd been desperate to be important, to be the hero, but she'd somehow unleased darkness and death on Perseopia, worse than anything they'd ever known.

The demon said she was his dark princess. It was easy to see why, when you considered the facts. Was that why Hami wanted to send her back to the Mother World? Because she caused nothing but death? What did he know about her that he wasn't telling the magi?

Sammy leant forward against White Lightning's neck. She didn't want to see any more villages, to count houses, or to guess at death counts. If she'd only stayed in Perseopia the first time she'd arrived, the seal would never have been crossed and this whole disaster could've been avoided.

But Hami would've still taken her to the fire temple to draw Ramaask out of hiding. And if the outcome had been different and she hadn't crossed the seal, Ramaask would've killed her, Hami, Mehrak, and probably everyone else.

Hami had created the unwinnable situation. Not her. Yet, she didn't hate him for it. He was moody and controlling, but underneath it all there was a semi-decent man trying to make the realm a better place, however misguided his efforts were. And despite everything, she liked him for it.

It was a shame things had worked out as they had. It was a shame that Perseopia was not more like Fillory or a post-white-witch Narnia, rather than the dark and polluted place it had become. And the word 'shame' probably didn't do justice to the fact everyone would eventually hallucinate on toxic smog before going insane and asphyxiating. That was unless their bodies weren't enslaved by the Ahriman demon first.

She should stop thinking about it. There was nothing she could do. For the moment, she'd absolve herself from responsibility and relax into the flight.

Her respite didn't last long.

The next collection of lights they flew over was a large one. A town, most likely. Sammy tried to calculate how many people lived there based on the number of lights she could see. Several hundred lights meant several hundred houses. Three or four people in a house, perhaps. A thousand lives?

Something had to be done. She couldn't fly past knowing that all those people below were going to die and she could've prevented it.

Sammy sent White Lightning into a dive.

What are you doing? Hami sounded panicked.

Saving these people.

You can't!

Sammy pulled up short of the roofs and hovered in place.

Sammy, please don't!

She'd aimed for the area where the lights were brightest, which turned out to be close to the main square.

The few townsfolk that had been milling around parted as Lightning descended. Sammy tried to land carefully but the poor animal collapsed when it put pressure on its lame leg. The pain was excruciating and took Sammy's breath away.

Lightning slumped and passed out.

Sammy nearly blacked out too. She broke the link between them and was for a moment woozy. She unfastened her leg straps and half-climbed, half-fell to the ground. When she'd pulled herself together she called out to the people gathered around them.

"There's a demon coming!"

The townsfolk looked at each other, then back at her.

"A demon?" one of them asked.

You foolish girl, Hami communicated. Then he stood up on the back of Lightning and lit up the orb of his staff. "This woman is right!" he shouted. "I am a messenger from the magi and I bring a warning. The Ahriman has been made flesh and walks the realm of Perseopia. It is the cause of our dark skies."

There were a few gasps, some panicked murmuring.

Hami took a deep breath. "And it's heading this way."

Several of the townsfolk cried out. A woman close to Sammy snatched up her son and hugged him to her chest.

"There is no need to panic if you do as we say," Hami continued. "You must gather up your children and elderly and head west. Tell everyone. You have half a day's head start. Leave your possessions, the Ahriman has no need of them. Take only two days' provisions. Once you've exhausted them, you can return. The Ahriman will have passed."

There was silence.

"Go!" Sammy shouted.

The townsfolk dispersed, dashing in all directions.

Sammy turned back to Hami and smiled. "You saved their lives."

Hami watched a father gather up his three children, put them in a wheelbarrow, and roll them away. "I've only postponed their deaths."

"But—"

"How are we getting to the snow base now?"

"White Lightning …" Sammy looked at the prone beast. Its eyelids flickered.

"… is not going anywhere."

"But if he has a quick rest …"

"He's going into shock. Do you honestly think he's getting back up again?"

There wasn't much Sammy could say to that.

"You've saved this town and simultaneously killed everyone else in the realm, *and* in your precious Mother World. In half a day we're dead too. We should find some horses and get out of here before the demon arrives."

"But we need to get to the portal."

Hami turned on her. "Yes we do!" he shouted. "And yet again you didn't listen to me and have ruined everything."

"I didn't know the magi would see that lightning staff explosion."

"But why take that risk? You were blasting stones, for Ahura's sake! What exactly was the point of it?"

"I was angry."

"And now the realm and the Mother World will die because of it."

"Don't turn this around on me! You're the one that took me to the Cataclysm. You led me to the Temple of Paths."

"I didn't tell you to cross the seal."

"What was I going to do? Remain your captive? Get killed by Ramaask? You lied and manipulated me."

"Yet you still came back."

She had come back. She'd come back and she'd looked for him when she'd reached Perseopia. Even though he'd treated her badly previously. What did that say about her?

Hami clenched his fists and the corded muscles in his arms tightened. "I'm going to find us some horses," he said, and ran off.

A cold wind blew through the town square. Sammy looked up past the lampposts and burning torches into the black void above. She still couldn't quite believe she'd caused all this by crossing the seal.

You are mine, dark princess, the demon had said. It was coming for her. She could feel its legion spreading. Its darkness seeping into the world and her nihilistic urge to embrace it rekindled. The desire to lie down and let the darkness consume her was all-encompassing.

She wanted to drop to the floor and curl into a foetal position. She was weary and felt unable to fight any longer. The escape from the leviathan, avoiding guards on the islands, the sickness of travelling by greenbuck, imprisonment in the citadel and dogfighting pterodactyls.

She bent over, hands on knees, and closed her eyes. Everything seemed futile. Lying down seemed to be the best course of action. She could rest while she waited to die.

She missed Mehrak. And then the realisation dawned. Mehrak would never quit on her. It took a surprising amount of effort but she straightened up, stood tall and opened her eyes. Mehrak wouldn't quit. Right now he'd be on his way to the snow base to shut down the portal. It needed to be done and he'd do it. Sammy knew this categorically. He'd never let her down. And she wasn't about to do the same to him, either.

Sammy approached White Lightning. She put her hands together and began channelling her energy.

————

Hami leant on the stable door. Empty. Same as the last two places. The townsfolk had been quick. They'd taken their families, their food and horses, and cleared out.

That ridiculous girl. Why did she never listen to him?

She frustrated him greatly, but he was already dreading losing her.

He couldn't explain why he wanted her so badly. She wasn't interested in him and he was still grieving for Jamileh. Could it be that he just wanted a friend? While it was true he was lonely, that wasn't all it was. There was something about her.

No. He had no choice but to send her away through the portal. Not just for Perseopia's sake, but for his too. He didn't want her to go, but he couldn't cope being around her, to be tempted, all while she was indifferent to him and favouring Mehrak.

The name was bitter on his tongue. He should've sent Mehrak on his way after the battle and taken Sammy himself.

Hami left the empty stable and ran off to find another.

But Sammy wasn't a possession to be won. He couldn't force her to be with him, still the notion that he had no control over her or the situation drove him crazy. He wanted to rage at her for her ridiculous flights of fancy and her lack of accountability, yet at the same time he wanted to pull her into an embrace and not let go.

He reached a dimly lit cross roads.

As he contemplated which direction to turn, a flash of white streaked over his head.

There you are!

Sammy?

Sammy came back, slowing the rook and hovering above his head.

"Time to fly, Principal Hootan," she called down. "We have a portal to shut down, and I can't land Lightning on his bad leg again."

She was a vision, sat erect in her saddle, White Lightning's wing beats whipping up her hair. She had complete mastery over the beast. And of him too.

A powerful downbeat sent the rook off again. It raced away across the houses.

Sammy was bringing it around.

Hami waited as she flew out and began banking, then he ran across the road, leapt onto a gate post, using it as a stepping stone to propel him higher and onto a low awning. He ran up onto the roof and along the spine.

Sammy came in from the side and he leapt.

Hami caught the rook's saddle straps, yanking his arm hard but he held on. And they were away, striking out from the town and towards the mountains.

–FORTY-NINE–
BASE CAMP

Hami clung to the back of her, almost like an embrace. Sammy tried to absorb some of his warmth and enjoy the sensation, but she was distracted. It was taking significant concentration on her part to numb the pain in Lightning's leg. She'd been doing it since they'd left the town, and that had been a while ago now, days it seemed like, but it had scarcely been one. She was drained and needed to rest.

They saw no other villages. A relief that there would be no further fatalities, but simultaneously a problem. Without their light to guide them, it was difficult to gauge how high they were. Yet Perseopia wasn't completely black, despite the dark cloud cover above. A faint aura edged the mountains ahead like there was a dim light far away over the horizon. An ambient light, enough to pick out silhouettes, although not much else.

"We've reached the foothills of the Atrabiliars," Hami said after a time. "If we want to get another day out of your rook, we should find somewhere to make camp."

Sammy hadn't told Hami she'd been blocking the animal's pain receptors, feeding him energy to keep him going. Yet even with her help, Lightning was struggling. His breaths were coming out in ragged gasps and he was attempting to glide between wing beats to reduce effort. When the time came for them to stop, they wouldn't be taking off again.

"Are you sure I'm allowed to take him down this time?" Sammy called back.

"I think he's likely to fall out of the sky soon if we don't."

Relief flooded Sammy. "Can I bring him down now?"

"Not yet. We've only reached the foothills. If we can reach a reasonable altitude, we'll be able to make camp and acclimatise while we sleep. In the morning we can carry on to Dev's Peak."

They flew higher as the foothills grew, working their way up the slope of the mountain range, and it wasn't long before the air became thin and cold. Sammy buried her fingers in Lightning's neck feathers to keep them warm.

They dipped then and Sammy had to release more energy to keep Lightning steady. His muscles were seizing, becoming shaky. He couldn't go on much longer on such thin air.

"I think we've pushed it far enough," Hami said. "Let's find somewhere to land."

Sammy slowed Lightning and took him in at a glide.

Hami lit his staff and indicated a flat area under a tall cliff face. "Over there."

They landed awkwardly. Sammy untied her leg straps, rolled off, and dropped to the floor where she sprawled out in the dark. For a moment she couldn't break the connection to Lightning. He wasn't letting go. And then he did, and relief filled her body.

Lightning cried out as he inherited the pain Sammy had been blocking from him. He whimpered once, then fell quiet as he shivered against the chill.

It was black and cold in the lee of the cliff face. Sammy was fortunate to have been wearing substantial clothing when she left Eggie. Thick trousers, boots, a light, fur-lined leather coat, but it wasn't enough to keep her warm so high in the mountains.

Sammy squinted up into Hami's staff light as he came around Lightning's slumped body. She staggered to her feet and brushed the rust-red dirt she'd been laying in off her clothes. She swayed light-headed a moment and went back down to one knee.

"You numbed his pain, didn't you?" Hami asked.

Sammy nodded. She didn't look up.

"You mustn't do that again, okay?" Hami didn't sound angry. Just concerned. "It's dangerous. Magi have died letting others feed off their energy."

"Really?" She was uncommonly weary, but she found it hard to believe she'd die of tiredness.

"If you feed the wrong type of creature, they can become dependent on you. And if the connection is strong enough they'll drain you of life."

That wouldn't happen to Sammy. She was too powerful, probably. Still, she wasn't going to test her limits.

White Lightning was in bad shape. He remained where he'd landed, chest heaving, body shivering. His eyes stayed closed when Sammy approached and he didn't respond to being stroked.

Hami went around to the other side. "His leg is ruined," he called over.

Sammy followed the light to where Hami was crouched and recoiled when she saw Lightning's bone protruding through his leg.

She looked away. They'd flown all the way from the white column without treating the poor animal. Sammy had forced him to land on his bad leg back at the town and had only covered up his pain to keep him going. Now that he was no longer useful, she'd saddled him with the full payload of pain. If she was a better person she'd keep helping him, but selfishly she didn't want to, couldn't bear to be drained any further. She was barely coping with the bone-deep weariness as it was.

Surely saving that town full of people had redeemed her somewhat? Lightning's life for all of theirs?

An easy trade to make when it wasn't your life on the line.

"We should make camp," Hami said as he stood up. He stretched. "Your rook's done well. We're way beyond where we would've been if we'd taken horses. Maybe further than we would've been if we'd stuck with your friend Mehrak." He gazed out into the darkness.

Sammy didn't like the way he'd said 'your friend Mehrak', but the notion Mehrak and Louis might be on their way towards them at that very moment was enough to cheer her.

"What about Lightning's leg?"

"I'll see what I can do once we've made camp."

"How do we make camp?" she asked. "We haven't got any stuff."

Hami scanned the area with his staff light, then set off along the base of the cliff.

Sammy followed.

A little way along, Hami stopped near a boulder. It was about the size of a large old-style TV, the sort of square, deep-backed old relic her granny still watched Antiques Roadshow on.

He fired his staff at it. Sammy stepped back as Hami applied a constant stream of pure energy directly into the boulder and kept it going as steam rose off it.

When it became red, they both had to take several paces back, such was the immense heat being given off. By the time the stone glowed orange they were standing several metres away and Sammy could still feel the warmth as if she were next to a campfire.

Hami stopped as the boulder neared yellow. "I'd keep well back," he said. "The rock's close to melting. If you get too close at this temperature, your hair and clothes may catch light."

Sammy had been freezing a moment ago. Now the whole area was so hot there was steam coming off the stones around her. She stood with Hami in the dim orange glow of the boulder, both of them holding their hands out to absorb heat.

After a time, Hami announced they should probably eat and sleep to give them the energy necessary to carry on up the mountain in the morning. And he departed.

He returned sometime later with two large tail-less rodents with short noses and strange toes that looked like fingers. He skinned them, placed them on a flat, plate-shaped rock and used his magi powers to float the rock over to the heated boulder, where he placed it on the ground just short of it.

The tiny bodies looked disgusting and cadaverous, but in moments the sweet fatty smell of barbequed meat filled the air and they began to look more appealing.

The rodents cooked quickly and Hami brought them back through the air and over to a low boulder between them.

They tasted amazing. Sammy was almost ashamed of how mercilessly she devoured Bugs Bunny's short-eared cousin. The meat was dark, fatty, rich and salty, and she stripped the bones clean, flicking them into the darkness when she'd done with them. When the food had gone, she licked her greasy fingers, lay back in the dirt and closed her eyes.

She wondered how Mehrak and Louis we getting on, and where they were now, but it wasn't long before exhaustion overwhelmed her and she fell asleep.

She woke once to the sound of Hami re-heating the boulder.

White Lightning's screams woke her the second time.

–FIFTY–
ON FOOT

Sammy leapt up. Everywhere was dark.

She wheeled around blind. Stopped.

Floating in the black nothingness ahead of her, two golden eyes burned.

A deep growl reverberated beneath them, then Hami's staff orb lit up beside her, flooding their camp with light.

The light dazzled Sammy, but not enough that she missed the giant red beast drop behind White Lightning and disappear.

I must've overslept, Hami said.

What was it?

A tusked manticore. Like the one we saw in the Fungi Forest.

It had been two years, but Sammy would never forget the beast Hami had fought the last time she'd been here. A giant red tiger with sabre teeth growing up from its bottom jaw.

The manticore circled them. An indistinct silhouette stalking the shadows just outside Hami's staff light.

Sammy closed her eyes and reached out to the animal. She could feel its tension. It was gearing up to pounce.

"It's going to attack!"

I'm ready, Hami replied.

Sammy tried to calm the creature but it pounced before she had time.

The beast seemed to appear before them in mid-air, jaws wide, claws extended. It arrived headfirst into a burning column of Hami's staff lightning, then its motionless body dropped at their feet.

Sammy watched the creature's chest rise and fall.

"Just like before," she said. "But you finished this one quicker."

"I was showing off last time. There was no need for that fight to last as long as it did. I was putting on a demonstration of my powers for Mehrak. In any fight you should try for a swift, clean finish. You're risking injury when you don't put your opponent down quickly. Now, step back. I need to finish off our would-be assassin."

"What do you mean finish off?"

"Kill. What do you think I mean?"

"Can't we leave him alive like the one in the Fungi Forest?"

"It killed your rook."

"So you're getting even?" Sammy looked across to the motionless body of White Lightning.

"No. What I mean is, we've lost our transport, so our progress is going to be slow. This isn't like it was in the Fungi Forest where we had Louis to carry us away. We're on foot and climbing a mountain. We won't get far before this big cat wakes up again and comes after us. Next time it will be one of us killed in our sleep instead of Lightning."

Hami had a good point. "But it's a living creature."

"Like those hyraxes we ate last night?"

Somehow a large majestic beast like the manticore seemed above the rodents and small creatures they'd murdered for food. Which made no sense, really. A life was a life.

Sammy turned away and moved towards Lightning.

A burst of light cast her shadow on the cliff face in stark relief, before their temporary campsite returned to the dim steady glow of Hami's staff light. She felt the life essence leave the manticore, but didn't stop walking until she reached her deceased rook.

She placed a hand on Lightning's chest. He was still warm but entirely still.

The animal had served his purpose and now he was dead.

Sammy couldn't muster up an emotion fitting for the end of Lightning's life. Sadness would be appropriate, but too much had happened since the start of her journey, and she wasn't able to spare any.

They left their temporary camp once they'd gathered their supplies.

Hami had the manticore pelt over his shoulder. He reasoned that it would be getting colder as they ascended the mountain and that they'd need it to keep warm. On the other shoulder he had one of Lightning's saddle bags filled with chunks of manticore meat. It looked like the spoils of a slasher movie antagonist. Disgusting. Blood dripped through the fabric as they walked. Probably attracting more manticores, but Hami didn't seem overly concerned.

Sammy carried the staff and Lightning's other saddle bag, even though it contained very little. A small flask of water, a light blanket, some fingerless leather flying gloves and matching leather riding cap.

Sammy put on the gloves and cap and wrapped the blanket over her shoulders. She must've looked ridiculous, but she didn't care. Anything to reduce the biting cold that cut through her clothes and chilled her bones.

It was half a day before they reached snow.

Sammy's head ached from the relentless icy wind striking her forehead. The water flask had long since been emptied and her lips were getting chapped.

She scooped up a handful of snow and melted it in her mouth.

"You shouldn't do that," Hami said. "It cools down your core temperature."

Sammy shrugged. Her legs ached and she was hungry and thirsty so she took another mouthful of snow, and received the mother of all brain freezes. She sat on a boulder and hunched over to wait out the pounding headache.

Hami brought over a rock with a concave face. He took the lightning staff off her, melted some snow into the shallow recess using a narrow beam of staff energy and handed it back. The water was hot, but two sips and it had gone.

Hami repeated the process several times, until Sammy could feel the warmth of the liquid spreading throughout her body and her headache receding. Then he placed the manticore pelt over her shoulders and set about melting snow in the area around them. He exposed a large rock, not far from where Sammy sat, and concentrated a stream of lightning on it until it began to warm up.

Hami hadn't taken any water yet. He'd provided for her, but not himself. Whatever reason he'd come up with to take her to the portal and send her through it, it wasn't because he didn't care.

"We'll warm up for a little while," he said. "I'll cook some of the manticore meat, then we'll carry on, okay?"

"Okay."

Hami didn't look at her when he spoke. He'd barely looked at her since they'd left the citadel. It was almost like he was nervous around her. This muscular, hardened warrior that killed animals and spoke with authority to regents and air marshals had become timid in her presence.

When had that happened? It could only have been recent. The battle at the column, maybe. Was her new-found badassery turning him on? She'd rescued him like a knight on her noble White Lightning, swooping in to pluck him from the tower like he was a damsel in distress. She'd rescued him from the pterodactyl too, the metaphorical red dragon. And it wasn't only Hami that she'd saved, she'd saved everyone in the town they'd landed in. She'd even gotten White Lightning air bound again when all had seemed lost. She'd more than proven herself to him. She'd been vindicated.

And perhaps that intimidated him.

Sammy smiled inside. She left her seat, handed the stone with the shallow concave to Hami and moved closer towards the glowing boulder, wrapping the manticore pelt more tightly about her. It was weighty, but warm, and she was glad of it.

Steam filled the air around the boulder creating a humid atmosphere and she was careful not to allow her clothes to get wet. Damp clothes on top of a frozen mountain would be incredibly dumb.

Hami drank a few shallow stones worth of water, then set about cooking the manticore meat on a hot rock. Sammy wanted to object to eating the tiger's flesh, even though it had killed White Lightning. There was something wrong about eating giant cat. Yet it wasn't like they'd gone out with the intention of hunting it like that dentist that killed Cecil the Lion. Their killing had been in self-defence, at least.

Hami wasn't one for presentation. Mehrak would've found a sprig of some random herb to garnish the meat with. Hami merely slapped it down on top of a dirty rock. Sammy didn't care, though. She was too hungry. She brushed off the grit and set to devouring it.

They continued walking when they'd finished. The small circle of Hami's staff light followed them up the mountain. It seemed to contain their entire world, like nothing else existed but a continuous, inclined and snow-covered treadmill. It could've been afternoon, it could've been the middle of the night. Time had lost any meaning.

Sammy slipped behind. She was already struggling. Her legs were like someone else's, no longer part of her body, numb and heavy. She was slowing Hami down. Asking for more breaks and for more water.

"We have to keep going," Hami kept saying, but Sammy was done in. She'd used up too much energy on White Lightning and hadn't fully recovered. She had nothing left. The thin air was making her light-headed and she kept drifting off into daydream.

Swirling colours and dancing figures took shape in the darkness ahead. Victa was there. He was walking on his shortened legs carrying a sword. Then she saw Mehrak and a woman. She closed her eyes. Opened them again and the visions had gone. She was back on the mountain. Then the mountain pitched and she stumbled.

"Thank you, Mehrak," she murmured as he caught her.

"It's Hami," came the reply, and she flopped to the ground where she drifted into an uneasy sleep.

–FIFTY-ONE–
ALL ABOARD

Sammy got pulled, lifted, carried, dropped.

During the period this went on, she became semi-aware of light shining in her eyes and faces crowding around. Then everything receded and went dark again.

As she resurfaced from unconsciousness, she found her legs were sore, but overall she was comfortable and more importantly, warm.

She opened her eyes.

An open four poster bed canopy framed a small chandelier swaying in the peak of the ceiling where curved blue walls met at the top.

Eggie.

She should've been shocked to find herself back in Golden Egg Cottage, but she was too tired to register surprise. She accepted it like she accepted that Mehrak was always coming for her. Louis would have sniffed them out, and he would've led Mehrak to her. And Mehrak would've come willingly. She realised then that he would do anything for her.

She tried to roll to the side, but something heavy on top of the covers pinned her down. She coaxed her aching limbs to move into a position where she could see what the thing was.

It was Mehrak. Of course. He had his back to her, still fully clothed and turbaned. His chest rose and fell with the peacefulness of sleep.

Sammy shuffled closer under the covers and put an arm over him.

———

Hami stood by the stairs watching them sleep. It almost caused him physical pain seeing them together. And when Sammy put her arm over Mehrak, his heart withered inside his chest. It was torture, but he couldn't look away. Sammy would never appreciate what he was doing for her and she'd never love him for it.

The magi wouldn't take him back now, either. Not anymore. He'd thrown his life away for this girl. He'd betrayed the memory of Jamileh and he'd betrayed her brother, leaving him at the mercy of his captors.

He took a deep breath. All wasn't lost though. He'd fallen for this girl, but that didn't matter. What mattered was that he took her to the portal. Behnam had virtually said as much before he left the network. They had to get rid of her somehow. That was the priority. He felt guilty for not going after Behnam first, but as always the realm came first.

Sammy sighed and pouted her lips as she slept. He wondered what or who she was dreaming of. He wanted to reach out and touch her. To hold her hand, to make skin contact. Even though she had her arm over another man, even though Hami was nothing to her.

A calm settled over him. He would still sacrifice his life for the realm. For all the people that cared nothing for him and would accuse him of wrong doing. And for Sammy.

He forced himself to look at her and Mehrak one last time. To memorise them together, and to feed off the hurt inside. Anything that would give him the strength to do what came next.

–FIFTY-TWO–
Together and Yet Apart

They continued up the mountain the following morning.

Louis found the snow and scree hard going, and despite a considerable portion of his body being covered in furry feathers, the cold was getting to him and multiple breaks were required. Each time they stopped, Hami would heat up boulders in the vicinity to thaw him out, and when he'd been warmed sufficiently they'd progress further up the mountain.

During Louis's downtime, Narok would patrol the area with Indomit to scare away any threatening wildlife that ventured too close. Visitors that included a manticore and then later two wild karkadann. All three animals had been white, unlike the rust-red variety that lived further down the slopes and who shared their fur colour with the terrain found at lower altitudes.

That evening they made camp in the shadow of Dev's Peak.

Sammy climbed out of Eggie's back door hatch, onto Louis's tail, balanced as he lowered her to the ground, then fumbled through the darkness behind him and emerged into the light of the fog lanterns that hung from the balcony.

Hami had already melted most of the snow from a large circular area around them. He looked up, but didn't acknowledge her and carried on with his task in silence.

Sammy pulled the hood of her fur coat up and joined Eva, Calven and Narok by the steaming boulder Hami had heated for them.

Eva was packing snow into tin cups and melting it on the rock. Calven was heating a batch of Mehrak's casserole surprise. The surprise, he'd told her, was mushroom. She could imagine there were worse surprises than mushroom in there, and she was happy to leave them as such.

Hami finished clearing the snow, then wandered off behind Louis. Sammy didn't hear the back door hatch open, so could only guess that he'd gone to puke up or have a toilet break. She couldn't tell with Hami anymore. He didn't appear as ill as he once had. It seemed more like he was sulking. And it was probably because they were back with Mehrak. Whatever it was, Hami no longer wanted to spend any time with her. He clearly didn't have the feelings she'd assumed he had, but then she'd always been terrible at reading people. She didn't have that intuition that women were supposed to have. And Hami could block his feelings from her even if she were tempted to use her powers on him.

Sammy had lost Hami's respect. That was it. He hadn't taken her for any training sessions since the whole White Lightning debacle and they'd not even spoken on their secret brain frequency thing.

She needed to stop thinking about him. He'd been grumpy the last time she was in Perseopia and he'd been grumpy most of the time since she'd returned. Different flavours of grumpy, but essentially the same thing. Once they'd closed down the portal, she and Mehrak would leave and they wouldn't have to put up with his moodiness.

The back door hatch clunked and Mehrak strolled out around the side of Louis. He looked about as cheerful as Sammy had ever seen him. He sidled up beside her and brushed his hand against hers. She couldn't help smiling back. It was a big toothy grin that no doubt looked goofy, but she didn't care. She was happier than she would've thought possible, shivering on the side of a dark mountain.

The moody magus didn't make an appearance until later that night. He ate barely anything and said even less. He stayed long enough to reheat rocks for everyone, then went inside. None of the others seemed to notice a difference in his behaviour so perhaps Sammy was reading too much into it.

Eva and Calven spent most of the evening chatting animatedly about who they would visit first when they returned to the Keep. Leiss and Narok mostly concentrated on their food.

Sammy remained beside Mehrak. She wasn't sure exactly what had changed since she'd been away, but he couldn't have been more attentive towards her. It was a struggle to stop herself from reaching out with her mental feelers to find out what he was feeling. She'd told herself she wouldn't do it to any of her friends. And it turned out that she didn't need to, because despite Sammy's inadequacies in reading facial cues, Mehrak was making it pretty clear what his intentions were. And they were making her blush.

She surreptitiously shifted her hand so her fingers touched his. One of his fingers moved on top of hers and stroked up and down. Heat flushed her cheeks. She wanted to be with Mehrak then. Sitting so close, only making finger contact was excruciating. She wanted more.

After dinner, Sammy helped Mehrak melt snow into buckets for Louis, then they refilled the buckets and brought them inside Eggie to fill the water tanks under the sink.

The kitchen was quiet. Hami was asleep at the table, his head tucked into the crook of his arm. The Marzban were all still outside.

Mehrak placed the evening's dirty plates and cutlery in the sink *without washing them*, then announced that he was heading up to bed.

Sammy's heart raced as she practically chased him up the stairs.

Mehrak shook off his shoes and climbed into bed. Sammy did the same. They found each other under the covers and wriggled in close, entwining their arms and legs.

Sammy pressed her lips into Mehrak's as lust consumed her. She pulled herself closer. And for a moment was content. But the act of acknowledging her contentedness diminished its intensity.

She began running through the scenarios of what might happen when they found Mehrak's wife. And she went cold.

Mehrak's hand slipped down from her waist and came to rest on her bottom.

Sammy took his hand off her.

"Is everything okay?" he whispered.

She shifted back to look him in the eye. "What's going to happen when we find your wife?"

Mehrak sighed. "She might not even be at the portal. Hami probably lied about her being there. Like he did about her being at the Cataclysm."

"But what if she is? And you're reunited with each other? You're married."

"Marriage is only a simple ceremony performed by a priest. A tradition."

"It might be, but that doesn't change anything."

"No one even came to our wedding. The priest that performed it was ancient. He's probably passed away by now, or would have no recollection of us so there'll be no witnesses. We can travel back to Dungalor, tear up the certificate, rip out the relevant page of the marriage register and we're good. Job done. We don't have any children together. There'll be no complications."

Sammy said nothing. She watched the chandelier sway in time with Louis's breathing.

Mehrak rolled onto his back. "The realm is being destroyed around us and you're upset about an archaic and outdated ceremony. I went through it because Gisouie asked me to. She wanted our union recognised in the eyes of the Great Ahura Mazda. You know I'm not a believer."

"After everything you've seen?"

Mehrak shrugged. "Witnessing demons rise from netherworld and meeting one of the chosen children from the Mother World changes your perspective somewhat, but I'm still sceptical about organised religion."

"You still cared enough about Gisouie to go through with a tradition you didn't believe in for her. And even if it meant nothing to you, it obviously meant something to her."

Mehrak deflated and looked away. "You're right," he said. "Gisouie's out there somewhere, scared and alone. And I'm in bed with another woman." He turned back to face Sammy. His eyes were glassy with sorrow. "I want her to be safe. Truly. I know I may seem selfish and callous to you, but I never felt the way I feel with you about her. I didn't think it was possible to … I thought the poets were being dramatic when they spoke of … matters of the heart."

Mehrak sounded like he was about to declare his undying love. Fortunately, he stopped himself and climbed out of bed. "I'm glad we've talked about this," he said. He took some blankets out of the wardrobe and began setting up his bed on the floor. "I don't think we should rush anything until we close down the portal and rescue Gisouie. It's disrespectful to her and it's unfair to you. I need to make a clean break and hopefully then I can prove my commitment to you."

Sammy wanted to live in his house, and she did fancy him. But commitment? That was a stretch. They should at least spend longer than a couple of weeks together before they got to that point.

She turned to the side so she could pretend to fall asleep. And to hide her smile. It wasn't like she wanted to marry Mehrak, but the fact he was so into her was pretty cool. It felt way better than Wayne's gormless dependency.

She pulled the covers up over her head and settled into the nest of sheets, rolling with the movements of Louis's breathing. Warm, safe, desired and hidden. This state needed to be preserved. No expectations to fulfil, nowhere to be and no responsibilities. But that wasn't entirely true. Sammy's fleeting contentedness was slipping. The cold, grasping claw of obligation was dragging her from the warmth.

The portal was looming heavy on the horizon.

Hami stared at the top of the kitchen stairs, to where they tightened into a corkscrew within the tower, at the hole Sammy had departed through. He'd seen the hunger in her eyes as she pursued Mehrak to the bedroom and this time his heart truly died in his chest. He could picture the look on Sammy's face even now.

He wanted to rage at her for choosing Mehrak over him. But he couldn't summon the anger. He mostly felt empty. Weak. Utterly used up and rejected. Even breathing was giving him difficulty.

He again committed the feeling to memory. He would use it to numb himself, to give him strength enough to rid Perseopia of her.

–FIFTY-THREE–
There's No Base like the Snow Base

The snow base lay on the other side of the mountain, a short climb down from the summit. It was a sprawling network of buildings covering a broad plateau with shear slopes on all sides.

In the middle, dominating the skyline, an imposing black structure loomed above all others. It was circular, with twisted spires around its circumference like the tines of a crown, and must've pre-dated the surrounding grey stone-block buildings by several centuries. These new additions looked to have been built as extensions to the shadowy cathedral in the centre and resembled military dorms. Light from their windows illuminated the plateau, throwing pools of light on the unblemished snow.

Hami had taken them to the summit on foot. Not a long journey from where they'd camped the night before, but a steep gradient and thin air had made it a tough one.

Only Louis, Narok and Indomit remained back at camp, their fall-back position. A shallow cave where they could shelter from the wind and Louis could recover from his days of hard travel.

Leiss had joined Sammy so he could fulfil his obligation to Borzin by returning her home, even though he'd already done that once. The fact that she didn't want to go was just a technicality and hadn't stopped him coming. Neither did it stop Eva joining him, along with Calven who insisted on coming to accompany Eva.

They waited, huddled together on the slopes above the base, while Hami worked out a strategy.

Sammy was fairly confident the portal would be in the shadowy cathedral in the centre. What kind of strategy did they need? Other than to sneak in and destroy everything?

After a period of silence, Hami led them down the side of the mountain and across the snow to the closest building.

Inside the dimly lit structure, beds were lined up in rows, and candles on the bedside tables had burned down their wicks leaving deformed lumps of wax.

The other buildings were similarly empty.

"Where is everyone?" Mehrak whispered.

"Probably in that evil building in the centre," Sammy said. She refrained from adding 'duh' at the end.

"Come on." Hami led them further into the base to a square, bordered by empty stables. He stopped in the middle and gestured to the ground.

Hoof prints and wagon tracks led out of the stables and away between the buildings.

"They've left," Hami said.

"Ramaask's dead," Mehrak said. "No reason for them to stick around. Makes our job of destroying the portal easier."

"They wouldn't know Ramaask's dead. How would the message reach them here? We've only just got here and we took a shortcut across the Kuchak Sea."

Hami turned his attention to the ground, to something in the snow. He followed a set of tracks several paces, scanned the ground, then continued across the square to one of the stables. He slid the door open.

Tied up against the back wall were two greenbuck. They raised their heads when he entered, then went back to eating the bag of feed at their feet.

"The magi Aegis sent are here," Hami said. "They'll know the demon is past the column and will have been instructed to shut the portal down."

"Good," Sammy said.

Hami opened his mouth to respond, then stopped. He turned his head. Waited.

"What is it?" Eva asked.

Hami gave no answer but ushered everyone into the darkness of the stables. The greenbucks edged away, but otherwise seemed unconcerned and returned to eating their food. Hami pulled the stable door most of the way back across, but left a gap to see out of.

"What are we hiding from?" Leiss asked as everyone gathered by the opening.

"Quiet," Hami whispered.

A group of seven horsemen entered the square between the stables. All were dressed in furs, bar a man at the front who wore a hooded black cloak that billowed with smoke.

He raised a gloved hand and the others stopped.

The man in black leapt forward over the top of his horse's head and seemed to float to the ground on a blanket of smoke that trailed out behind him.

He knelt down, placed a hand to the ground and remained that way for many moments.

Then he turned to the stable where Sammy and the others hid and lifted the cloak back from his head.

It was a person unlike any Sammy had seen before. A man forged of molten rock. Glowing orange fissures split the blackened crust of his head and his face was dark and featureless, inset with burning yellow eyes that roved across the stables devouring everything in their gaze.

Sammy held her breath and concentrated on a stirrup dangling close by. She pictured it in her head. Closing off her brain and thinking of nothing else.

"She's been through here," the magma man said. "I want her found undamaged. If she's brought before me in any other condition, I will incinerate every last one of you." He strode purposefully towards the stable Sammy and the others hid in.

Hami silently guided everyone backwards through the dark, into the horse stall furthest from the entrance. They made it inside just as the door crashed and an orange glow filled the stables.

They couldn't see the magma man, but the greenbucks whinnied, reared up and pulled at their reins.

Even hidden in the stall furthest from the door, Sammy could feel the heat coming off him. She thought of the stirrup. Iron and leather. Cold iron, atoms moving slowly.

Silence.

"The magi are here," the man said at last. "Find them and bring me Azertash." Then the orange glow dimmed, followed by receding footsteps.

Hami held everyone back until it grew quiet. "It can't be Azertash," he whispered, almost to himself.

"I only know one Azertash," Mehrak said. "Azim Azertash. The General. And he died a hundred years ago."

"Sammy and I are going after the burning man," Hami said, leading Sammy out of the stall. "The rest of you, see if you can find Gisouie, but don't get caught."

"Wait," Mehrak called after them, straining to keep his voice low. "Shouldn't we stick together?"

"We're too big as a group. I need to find out what's going on here and Sammy has powers that are useful to me."

"You'd better not be scheming to send her away through the portal," Mehrak said.

Hami opened a door in the back wall. "I'm not," he said and stepped out.

–FIFTY-FOUR–
Tracking the Magma Man

Sammy and Hami crept around a second stable block and past an empty kitchen hall before they joined the trail of the magma man.

How did you know which way he was heading? Sammy communicated.

I was following the sound of his footsteps. Magi can magnify sound. It's not that powerful, but it can give you an edge.

Why hadn't Hami taught her how to do that yet? Sammy listened and zoned in on the area up ahead. With a little concentration, she managed to increase the sound of snow crunching underfoot accompanied by the hiss of it melting. She refocused her hearing, aiming higher, and was able to pick up the ragged inhalations of the man's breathing.

Now she could add enhanced hearing to her list of superhero skills. Not one of the best abilities, but certainly a useful addition to her repertoire.

Tracking magma man turned out to be super easy. Not only did he leave wide, melted footsteps, but he trailed a substantial amount of smoke in his wake too.

They ducked out of sight when he stopped to speak to a guy in furs—Sammy utilised her enhanced hearing to discover he was asking after Azertash—then he was off again, working his way through the compound towards the black cathedral at its centre.

When magma man entered the building closest to the cathedral, they followed the trail to the door and stopped outside.

Hami opened the door a crack and they both peered inside. A single long hallway ran the length of the interior with multiple rooms lined up on either side.

Magma man took a left at the end of the corridor and disappeared.

Hami led the way in and along the hallway. The left-hand turn took them to where the building joined the dark cathedral. Grey stone was cemented to black, framing grand double doors in the centre.

On the other side of the doors, a high vaulted hallway curved away to the right and left. A wide, doughnut-shaped space that could only be the hollow centre of the loop that formed the crown shape. It was a vast space and lacking in furniture or decoration. Only columns of black stone holding the ceiling distant above their heads.

Sammy followed Hami across the hall feeling conspicuous in the wide open space. They moved slowly, trying to keep their footsteps from echoing on the stone, moving towards a door on the opposite side, a door that presumably led to the inner circle.

Either side of the doorway were stone steps leading up and around the outside of the curved walls.

He went through that door in the middle, Hami communicated. *Let's find a vantage point.* And he led Sammy up one of the curved staircases and along the tunnel at the top.

They slowed as they neared the end.

The area inside the crown was a colosseum of sorts. Seating consisted of increasingly large stone rings stepping up from the flat central area, up to Sammy's tunnel and past, all the way to the ceiling, like terraces at a football ground.

It's an amphitheatre, Hami said. *This place will have been built when Perseopia was in its infancy, maybe even before it was sealed from the Mother World. The veil between worlds is thin here. But I can sense other strange forces that I don't recognise. Some sort of convergence of power. There's clearly a reason why the portal was built here.*

Sammy's skin prickled. She could feel it too. A deep permeating chill but unlike the type you get from cold.

In the centre of the amphitheatre, a circular metal plate had five curved prongs reaching up around its circumference giving the impression of a grasping claw. Inside the claw, blue wisps of light streaked around a central core of expanding and contracting air. Cables trailed from the plate across the room to a large steam-powered machine. It was covered in levers, oscillating pistons, whirring cogs and hissing tubes. Two women were shovelling coal into a boiler at one end. A third was at a control panel on the side. And three men were at a trestle table nearby making notes in books and mixing colourful chemicals in weird-shaped bottles.

Above the claw, in the centre of the room, hung a doughnut-shaped gantry with three radial walkways leading out from it. Each stretching to the top terrace of the amphitheatre near the ceiling.

Magma man had stopped behind the woman working at the machine's control panel. She had a slight frame and black hair tied up in a bun, and continued to tweak dials and scratch notes onto a piece of parchment apparently unaware of the man looming behind her.

Sammy focused her hearing on him and increased the volume.

"Why is the portal powered up?" magma man asked.

The woman flinched. She began trembling as she turned to face him. "The General told us to keep it powered up. For when Ramaask arrives."

"Ramaask is dead."

The revelation appeared to catch the woman off guard and at first she had no response. "I ... I was not told," she stammered. "Please don't punish me, Lord Mantis."

Hami froze. Sammy had been watching the exchange on the floor of the colosseum, but she felt his tension as he seized up.

Who is it? Sammy asked. *The name sounds familiar.*

The sorcerer that brought Ramaask into Perseopia. The one that died when the Sultan's Palace blew up.

How can he be here if he's dead?

Quiet. They're saying something.

"He's said nothing?" Mantis asked.

"Only that the portal should be operational for Ramaask's arrival."

Mantis tore a golden ball of light out of the air. He held the burning mass in his hand as black smoke curled around it and floated up towards the ceiling.

Hami half-rose from the floor, lowering his staff, poised to leap.

"Stop!" the woman screamed. She threw herself between Mantis and the machine.

Mantis made no move. He watched her calmly as the orb continued to burn in his hand.

"I'm sorry." The woman dropped to her knees. "I should not have screamed, my Lord, but the portal has to reach equilibrium before we power it down, otherwise we risk setting off a chain reaction that could destroy half the mountain."

The orb vanished from Mantis's hand and the smoke dispersed. "How long to shut down?" he asked.

Hami lowered himself back into a crouch.

"I can't be sure, it's not an exact science. The sequence changes every time we run the machine. A few hours maybe. Sorry, that's the best answer I can give. I would speed up the process if I were able. We have to finish powering it up, equalise the pressure and energy flow, then we can ease it off and begin shutdown."

"Begin now."

"The General has threatened to kill us if we do that."

"Where is he now?"

"In his quarters."

"Start it up. Run it. Shut it down. Whatever you need to do, but make sure it's shut down as soon as possible. I will talk with the General. No harm will come to you. I'll see to it." Then Mantis left the hall, passing under Sammy and Hami.

Hami pulled Sammy back from the edge of the tunnel.

"The portal will soon be powered up. This may be your only chance to use it if Mantis convinces the General to close it down."

"Mehrak was right about you. You split us up so you could send me back unchallenged."

"Does that matter? You have the opportunity to escape the Ahriman. You've seen what it can do."

"You're asking me to jump into that pulsating blue thing in the centre of the claw?"

"I'd suggest waiting for the portal to fully power up first, but yes. Why not? Home is just on the other side."

"Home? Or the Mother World? It's not the same thing. The portal might not be configured to take me to the same time and location I came from. The Mother World is huge and history was … long. What if I land in the middle of an ocean? Or a desert? What if I get taken to a time when dinosaurs were roaming the earth?"

Hami led her back down the tunnel to the hall they'd entered from. "That didn't happen last time you left Perseopia by portal, did it? You got taken back to the exact moment you left." He watched Mantis walk back the way they'd come.

"I was using portal pearls," Sammy whispered. "I arrived using one and I returned using another that was identical. That portal thing is different."

Hami turned to her and put his hands on her shoulders. "I have to go after Mantis. Ramaask said this portal will take him to the Mother World. This is your chance to get out of the problems created by your arrival."

"You're the one that took me to the fire temple."

"I didn't tell you to go looking for the Temple of Paths or to cross the seal."

"Maybe if you'd been honest with me from the beginning I'd have done what you asked me."

Hami took a deep breath and glanced back over his shoulder. Mantis passed through the doorway on the opposite side of the hall and was gone.

"You know what? You're right. You aren't responsible for this mess. I am. You don't need to get involved. Perseopia is not your problem."

He had a point. Sammy needed none of this. Perseopia was going down the toilet. Maybe she should bail while she had the chance.

"Are you going or not?" Hami asked.

Sammy shook her head. "We promised Mehrak."

"He'll understand."

"I'm not going until I see him."

Hami scowled. "Keep up then. We need to catch Mantis."

They picked up the sorcerer's trail in the snow and caught up with him on the outskirts of the snow base. A lone building sat apart from the others, not far from the plateau edge. They watched Mantis enter, then took a wide detour around to the side.

So he doesn't see our footprints when he comes back out, Hami explained.

They crept up to the building, crouching under the windows on the dark, far side of the building. Sammy shivered and pulled her hood up over her head, tightening it around her face. Away from the shelter of the other buildings, a harsh wind cut through her, bringing the misery of bone-deep cold. Using the portal to take her to a world blessed with central heating was getting more attractive by the moment, but she wasn't going home, even for central heating. And besides, Eggie had a stove. That was good enough.

Hami pointed to his ears and Sammy homed in on the conversation taking place on the other side of the wall.

"I have their lightning staffs here." A man's voice. One Sammy hadn't heard before. A big voice that could only belong to a big man.

"And where might the owners of those staffs be?" It was Mantis talking now.

"Hanging from the walls of the castle."

Hami sighed quietly, but the news didn't seem to surprise him.

"You killed them?" Mantis asked.

"They're magi. What would you have me do with them? They were sneaking around my portal."

"Ramaask's portal."

"Ramaask is dead. We're free men."

"Then why is the portal still running?"

"Because, now that Ramaask has no need of it, I mean to have the golden poniard for myself."

Hami gripped Sammy's arm, his face became pale even in the shadows.

"To do what with?"

"To rule, Mantis. What else? Ramaask is gone, who will stop us taking over Perseopia?"

"The Ahriman is closing in on this location as we speak. He covets the same object you do."

"Even the Ahriman will fall before the one who carries the poniard."

"And the magi?"

"Like the two that came here tonight? I can kill most magi without the poniard. With it, I can kill them all."

"The two that came here were middle tier magi. How would you fair against a grand master?"

"And when am I likely to run into one of them?"

"Sooner than you may think."

"I've heard enough excuses, Achaemen. Tell me where the poniard lies, then step aside so that I may retrieve it."

"I can't let you do that."

"So you'd put yourself in my way?"

"You aren't going through that portal."

Hami pulled Sammy towards him just before the side of the building exploded outward, ejecting the two men. They barrelled through the rubble and rolled to a stop in the snow.

Sammy was geared up to run but Hami held her down, keeping her in the shadows.

The big man was up first. A skin-coloured hulk. Big head, hands, chest. A giant dressed in furs. He stood over Mantis, arms and legs as thick as tree trunks. His head was like a block of stone, solid, grim and ancient as if it had weathered centuries of hardship and pain, like it belonged jutting out of the earth on Easter Island.

He brought a huge fist down on Mantis. The sorcerer barely raised his hand in time and the fist collided with an invisible barrier and rebounded. Mantis pulsed a second shockwave that sent the General flying backwards towards the building, landing close to where Sammy crouched in the dark.

Hami held her still. Panic made her want to get up and run, but Hami placed a hand on her shoulder, letting her know not to move.

Mantis ripped a fireball from the air and held it aloft. "I wish there was another way, Azertash. It always saddened me to know I'd be the one to kill you, but you left me no choice."

As Mantis raised the burning orb, a stone block came flying towards him, clipping his shoulder. The fireball went out as Mantis staggered backwards and the General dived on him.

We should go, Sammy transmitted to Hami.

Not yet, he replied, but he was poised. Ready. *They'll see us.*

The General swung a fist at Mantis. It only glanced off his head, but he went down. The sorcerer managed another shockwave that sent the General back a little way, but not far enough.

Mantis rolled to the side and tried to get to his feet, but he was all over the place. He staggered, fell to one knee.

The General came at him again. He unsheathed a giant broadsword from his belt, stepped over Mantis, raised it up and brought it down.

The blade stopped short of Mantis's neck.

Hami was standing now, his arm outstretched.

What are you doing? Sammy screamed in his head.

The General turned towards them then. "More magi?" There was confusion on his big face, then a colossal force knocked him backwards across the snow towards the mountain's edge. Mantis stood and turned towards Hami, his yellow eyes burning in his blackened and cracked face. He nodded once, then leapt towards the General, streaming a comet tail of smoke behind him.

Mantis landed beside the General, tore a fireball from the air and pounded it into the General's skull.

Azertash shrieked as a second fireball slammed into his face.

The explosions came thick and fast. Fireball after fireball accompanied by bloodcurdling screams.

Hami held his arm out to the hole in the building. A lightning staff leapt to his hand, he tossed it to Sammy, then he bundled her away around the building.

"Why did you help him?" Sammy shouted as they ran.

"Because the poniard must be protected at all costs. And as corrupted and twisted as Mantis has become, he knows that too. No one can be allowed to possess it. It's too powerful."

Too powerful in the wrong hands? Or too powerful for someone like Sammy? "Will Mantis be heading to the portal next to shut it down?"

"I believe so. Which means we need to find Mehrak … so you can say goodbye."

–FIFTY-FIVE–
Unwelcome Introductions

They ran through the compound, glancing in through the windows as they went. They found Mehrak and the others in the long hall leading to the black castle.

Sammy ran towards them. Then slowed.

The group that had formerly consisted of three Marzban and Mehrak had expanded. The scientist from the portal chamber was there, her colleagues too, and others. A combination of men and women, some plainly dressed in aprons, some in furs.

One of the women stood close to Mehrak. Too close.

She was heavier than Sammy, curvy with bigger breasts, but sexy with it. She toyed with a plait of hair draped over her shoulder, twirling it around a finger.

Mehrak stiffened when he saw Sammy. He smiled, but it was strained, nervous. "Sammy," he said. He took a deep breath. "This is Gisouie. Gisouie, this is Sammy."

Sammy stopped, leant on her staff to maintain balance.

"Is this young girl Sammy?" Gisouie linked her arm in Mehrak's. She smiled. "Thank you for helping my husband find me," she said. She didn't sound particularly thankful.

Sammy's throat became dry. She didn't trust herself to talk. She looked at Mehrak, then back to Gisouie.

"And this is my aunty, Kimia," Mehrak said. He removed himself from Gisouie to approach the scientist that had been working on the portal, the one Mantis had threatened.

"Aunty?" Sammy croaked. It was the only word she could manage.

"We haven't got time for introductions," Hami said.

"But my aunt worked on the portal," Mehrak said. "She knows how to shut it down without killing everyone on the mountain."

"That's great, because Mantis is on his way here and we need to do it now."

"Mantis?" Mehrak shot a glance at his aunt.

His aunt nodded. "*The* Mantis."

"There's no time to explain," Hami said. "The General is after the golden poniard. The Ahriman too. Perhaps even Mantis. I don't know, but the portal must be shut down. Now."

"Mantis knows where the poniard is," Mehrak said. "My grandfather studied him. There's information in one of his journals—"

"Mehrak!"

"The journal has the coordinates to Mantis's base. It's in Eggie …"

"We don't have time for this!" Hami barked. "We can track him down later. Right now we have work to do." He began to usher the crowd towards the end of the corridor.

Sammy watched Gisouie sidle up to Mehrak, and hated her for it, even though she'd done nothing wrong. Sammy was the one that had encroached on the relationship. She was the outsider. In their lives and in the realm. In fact, the damage she'd done to Mehrak's relationship was probably the least of her crimes against Perseopia. It was time to leave, to remove herself from this place. From Gisouie *and* Mehrak.

Her thoughts crystallised then. The portal was her way out.

Hami wanted her on the other side of it. Mehrak might've wanted her to stay, but she wasn't bedding down in Eggie's kitchen while Mehrak slept upstairs with his wife. Sammy had overstayed her welcome.

"I wanted to say goodbye before I go," she said to Mehrak.

Mehrak stopped. "What?" He moved away from Gisouie. "But you're coming to live in Eggie." He came closer, lowered his voice. "With me. You'd decided. We'd decided …"

Sammy couldn't look at him. It would make the decision too hard. She was going to stay strong, but her eyes were filling.

"Sammy, please."

She blinked the tears away.

Gisouie watched them both. Frowned. Then her eyes widened, and the realisation came. Realisation, then anger. Her jaw set.

"If Sammy's made up her mind," she said. "Then perhaps she should go back to where she belongs."

Mehrak glanced over his shoulder at her, then back to Sammy. "You don't want that, Sammy. You want to come and stay in Golden Egg Cottage to continue our adventure." Mehrak held out his hand to Gisouie. "You'll love Sammy. She's funny and clever …"

"… and pretty."

Mehrak fell silent.

"There's plenty of room in the kitchen," Gisouie said. "I assume I'll be returning to the bedroom?" She stepped up to Mehrak and put her arms around him. Sammy watched her large breasts squeezing up against him. Jealousy raged inside her. All the time they'd spent together. The closeness that had formed between them.

Mehrak's eyes were wide. He mouthed the word 'no' but Sammy couldn't bear it any longer. Her head and limbs no longer seemed connected. She'd overloaded her ability to cry or to mourn. She watched Mehrak and Gisouie together, somehow detached from herself. Sammy was an almost-homewrecker. Two years ago she'd forced herself on Mehrak, not the other way around. He didn't love or need her. Hami didn't either. Or her mother. Only the magi wanted her and that was to exploit her powers. Hami was right. She should go home. Or wherever the portal took her. It didn't matter as long as it took her away from here. There would be as much chance of someone caring for her wherever she landed as there would be anywhere else. Maybe she'd go looking for the poniard. The poniard was the ultimate weapon. And it was on the other side of the portal. She could find it for herself, gain its power and return to Perseopia to kill the Ahriman and rule everyone. She'd show Mehrak how he needed her. How they all needed her. And she'd punish those that stood in her way.

"Thank you for helping me with the General," announced a voice behind Sammy. "But it won't save you."

Mantis stood in the hall behind them, a group of armed men in furs on either side of him. He looked to be in bad shape. He was hunched to one side favouring one leg over the other, and he held his left shoulder where the General had wounded him.

Keep behind me, Hami communicated to Sammy. *Keep your hood up so they can't see your hair. Ramaask may have told him to look out for the girl with golden hair.*

"We want the same thing you do," Hami called back.

"I very much doubt that," Mantis said. "You want to send the girl through the portal. I don't. Now where is she?" He moved forward, casting his gaze over their group.

Sammy turned away, slunk further behind Hami into the crowd. Her heart was beating hard, adrenaline making her flighty. She'd lost Mehrak, her life was as good as over, but there were worse things than death, and she had no desire to find out what Mantis was capable of. It was her he wanted. She needed to remove herself from the group.

Mantis moved closer. Then two men burst into the room behind him. "The army of the dark lord is here!" one of them shouted. "They've reached the base."

That was Sammy's cue to run. And she took it.

———

Mehrak reached for her, his heart stalling. "Wait!" he yelled, but too late. She'd already disappeared around the bend of the corridor. Gisouie put her hand over his and lowered it.

"Stop that magus before he gets to the portal!" Mantis shouted.

Three men split from his group and exited through a side door. The rest charged.

Hami fired his lightning staff into the advancing men. They scattered, hitting the walls and falling to the floor.

His second shot was for Mantis. The screaming torrent of lightning hit the sorcerer's outstretched hand and vanished into his palm. Mantis stood his ground as dancing arcs of electricity ran up his arm and dissipated.

"I am familiar with magi practices," he said. "You'll have to do better than that to best me."

It was a standoff. The small number of Mantis's men that had survived Hami's lightning blast shakily got to their feet, then remained where they stood, unsure whether to try their luck rushing him a second time.

Leiss pushed his way forward to stand beside Hami.

"Get everyone out of here," Hami spoke under his breath. "And get that portal shut down."

Mehrak glimpsed a flash of staff light, but obscured by Leiss's large frame. The big Marzban twirled Mehrak on the spot and bundled him along with everyone else in the direction Sammy had gone.

Mehrak held on to Gisouie while the group got moved around the bend in the corridor and through the large double doors into the black castle.

There was a cry ahead. And the people in front of him stopped.

Mehrak shouldered his way through the crowd to get to the front.

On the far side of the hall, Sammy's body hit a column and collapsed to the floor.

Standing over her was a giant of a man. Not a large man. A literal giant.

The General. It could be none other.

He was panting, hunched over. His face was battered and bloody. Gore had soaked through his jerkin to his belt. Yet despite his injuries, the man had no trouble lifting a broadsword the length of a man in a single hand.

He raised the weapon over Sammy's neck, pausing to make eye contact with Mehrak and his newly arrived audience.

He smiled, a crescent of white in the dripping carnage covering his face. Then he swung down.

–FIFTY-SIX–
The Dark Army Arrives

A smoking fireball hit Hami in the chest knocking him to the floor. Air rushed from his lungs and he couldn't draw breath. Mantis descended on him in a blanket of smoke, enclosing his throat in his hands.

Hami's skin burned as his throat was constricted. He opened his mouth, but could force no sound out. Spots formed before his eyes.

"Where is the girl?" The sorcerer enunciated his words slowly, yet they had an indistinct dreamlike quality to them. "I know she's here. You will bring her to me."

Hami lit his staff orb, pulsing a shockwave of energy.

They separated. Mantis knocked back, Hami sliding away along the floor. He slowly gained his feet, propping himself on his staff.

Mantis stood his ground. The small number of his men that weren't unconscious had retreated back to a safe distance.

Hami tensed in anticipation of Mantis's next move, but none came.

A tremor in the ground vibrated the corridor doors in their frames. Candles on the walls guttered, a few went out.

"The Ahriman's host is here," Mantis said, matter of fact. "Soon everyone on this base will be dead, including Sammy. Tell me where she is."

He'd left off 'before it's too late' but Hami understood the implication. Something in the way the sorcerer had spoken Sammy's name made Hami want to help him. A softness in his tone akin to genuine concern. And he'd known her name. How?

Hami held his tongue. He was not so easily manipulated. If he could buy Sammy a little more time, it might allow her to escape. If not into the portal, then at least to a safe distance.

A distant scream behind Mantis. The men in furs shuffled nervously. A few glanced back to the outside door, then to Hami, concern clouding their faces.

"No response?" Mantis's yellow eyes burned fierce. "Then you leave me no choice."

He snatched a burning orb from the air and drew back his arm, then the door behind him shattered off its hinges and the grey-faced dead of the Ahriman's army shambled into the building.

–FIFTY-SEVEN–
FATALITY

Mehrak screamed out as the General's sword came down. He couldn't watch Sammy die, but he couldn't look away. He faltered, unprepared to witness her head separated from her body. Yet as the sword neared its mark, she flew backwards as if pulled by an invisible rope.

The sword missed the top of her head and crushed a flagstone beneath it.

Before Mehrak could fully process what had happened, Leiss, Eva and Calven set off running towards her. Mehrak hesitated, unsure whether to go after them or remain with Gisouie.

Sammy staggered to her feet as the men in furs that Mantis had dispatched to intercept her piled into the room through the portal chamber door. The General pulled his sword free from the stone and swung it at them as they came close. They clearly hadn't expected him to be there and seemed unsure whether to fight him or run. One hesitated longer than the others and lost his head. The headless body remained upright a moment, seemingly as indecisive as its owner, before launching blood into the air and collapsing in a heap.

The other men ran.

Azertash turned his attention back to Sammy and that was the incentive Mehrak needed to spur him into action. He shrugged off Gisouie and sprinted for his companion.

"Oi!" Leiss shouted as he ran in, waving his sword above his head. The General ignored the diversion and thrust his sword at Sammy.

She moved in a blur and was at the General's side before he'd finished lunging. Her staff flew from the ground to her hand, ignited, and she swung it into his face. The explosion at the point of impact knocked the big man backwards. He lashed out as he went down, missing Sammy by a hair's breadth as she calmly ducked beneath the blade.

The three Marzban arrived and descended on the General before he was able to get up.

"Leave him to us, Mehrak," Calven shouted at him as he caught up. "Just shut down that portal."

Kimia came in at a sprint, trailing her colleagues behind her. "This way," she called.

Behind her, Gisouie was on her way across the hall, heading towards them.

"But Sammy …" he began to say. He wasn't going to leave her again.

Kimia touched his arm. "You can't fight the General, Mehrak, but you can help me shut down the portal … if you want to stop your friend from leaving." She spoke the last part under her breath.

Mehrak nodded. He took Gisouie's hand when she reached him and led her after his aunt and the other scientists, past the fight and into the portal chamber.

———

Sammy dropped to her knees as the three Marzban took over from her. Their swords hacked and slashed at the General, shredding his clothes. Violent and repeated contact was made, yet the big man wasn't going down and no blood was spilling.

She watched the fight play out in slow motion as if the fight were taking place under water. It was a thing of beauty, a ballet of thrusts and countermoves, twists and parries.

She glimpsed Mehrak in the background.

He was leaving her. Following his aunt and the other scientists into the portal chamber, holding hands with his *wife*. The word lodged in her throat. Hopelessness welled up inside and the last vestiges of energy deserted her. Her back ached from where she'd hit the column and she found herself unable to go on. She would remain where she knelt and pray for a quick death.

The General regained his feet. A powerful kick to Leiss's chest launched him backwards, tumbling him along the floor.

Eva was next. She was swatted away by a brutal backhand. She collapsed, limp and unmoving.

"Eva!" Calven screamed. He thrust his sword into the General's belly, bending the giant over at the waist.

For a moment there was silence. All eyes were on Azertash.

Then he began laughing.

Calven withdrew the sword clean.

The General raised himself to his full height. A sadistic grin cracked his bloody face and he thrust out his sword. The blade speared Calven through the chest, exiting out of his back.

Azertash raised both Calven and sword together, holding them aloft one-handed. He watched the Marzban spasm and fall still, then he upended the blade and let Calven's corpse slide off onto the floor where he kicked it away into the shadows.

Leiss was back on his feet again, but he was in no state to fight. His sword was lowered in his right hand, his left arm clutched his chest, and he was struggling to breathe.

The General turned on him.

That was too much for Sammy. Her inaction had cost Calven his life. All because she'd been pining for Mehrak. Heartache and misery threatened to consume her and she found herself slipping into a chasm of despair.

But she couldn't allow another death. There would be no more. She stood, lit the staff and unleashed a column of burning fury into the General.

He roared as he was flung backwards.

She hit him again. And again, sending him back towards the portal chamber. The General dodged the next shot and launched himself at her, swinging his sword down in a wide arc. Sammy caught the blade against the staff orb, igniting it as she did so and detonating an explosion between them.

The General hit the staircase on the outside of the amphitheatre, Sammy was thrown backwards in a wide arc. She latched onto the molecules in her clothes to turn her body and completed a backflip to land in a crouch. She was getting good. A surge of hope bolstered her. Then her eyes fell on Calven's body and threatened to undo everything. She turned away from it. She couldn't get distracted. Her job wasn't done yet.

She regained her feet in time to see the General crest the stairs and dive down the tunnel Hami had taken her along when they'd followed Mantis.

He was heading for the portal.

———

Hami's lightning bolts did nothing to slow Mantis's advance. Each one that he sent in the sorcerer's direction got sucked into the man's outstretched hand and absorbed.

Mantis had incinerated a great number of the Ahriman's troops as they entered the hall behind him, yet they continued to force their way through the narrow doorway, clambering over the burning remains of their comrades.

Mantis pulled another fireball from the air with his spare hand and held it aloft. This one was for Hami. And that gave him a target. He aimed the beam high, hitting the smoking ball before Mantis could release it.

The explosion floored the sorcerer. He was only down a moment, but that was enough for the grey-faced men and women of the Ahriman's army to reach him and descend on his prone body.

Hami didn't wait to see what happened next.

A gargled scream chased him along the corridor and continued into the black cathedral as he ran after Sammy.

Sammy took the stairs two at a time. She heard Hami call out behind her, from the other end of the hall, but she kept going.

The General is heading to the portal, she communicated as she dashed into the tunnel.

There was a brief pause, where she assumed he was processing what she'd told him and coming to terms with the fact that the General was still alive. And heading for the portal.

We've got to stop him, he responded. *At any cost. See if you can slow him down until I get there.*

Sammy emerged from the tunnel, squinting into the blue light of the portal. The gentle, swirling wisps that had danced between the metal prongs the last time she'd been there had multiplied to become an expanding and contracting maelstrom of blue and turquoise plasma.

Mehrak and his aunt were below, working on the machine that fed the portal. Mehrak was turning a wheel on the side releasing steam. His aunt was alternatively pouring liquids from two separate test tubes into a funnel while calling out instructions.

Wifey wasn't doing anything. She spotted Sammy then. Their eyes locked and she narrowed hers.

Sammy didn't have time to analyse what that meant, as Azertash had reached the gantry above the portal. She ran for the top terraces taking two stairs at a time.

The General was already halfway down the walkway when she reached the ceiling.

He paused, dark ooze dripping off his chin. The blue portal light had turned his blood mask black while its swirling patterns danced in his eyes.

He hefted his sword back.

Sammy lit her staff as the General threw.

She side-stepped as the blade spiralled past her. It was a clumsy throw, but its purpose didn't require accuracy. It only needed to buy its owner time.

Sammy shot at the General, but too late. The lightning bolt sailed over his head as he dropped through the hole where the walkways met.

Sammy reached the doughnut-shaped opening over the portal as the General's body dispersed into millions of individual glowing blue particles and disappeared.

Hami stumbled into the amphitheatre at ground level, his chest pumping, his eyes wild. "Where's the General?" he shouted, barely audible over the portal machinery. "Where's Sammy?"

I'm up here, she communicated. *The General's already gone through the portal. I'm going after him.*

Hami looked up. Saw her. *It's too dangerous. Let me go.*

Mehrak spotted her then. "Sammy!" he called out. "What are you doing up there?"

I know the Mother World, she spoke to Hami. *I understand its workings. It's where I'm from … and where I belong.* She didn't believe any of it, but at least it sounded heroic. And it was what Hami wanted to hear. It would give him peace.

"Sammy?" Mehrak called again. "What are you doing?"

"Stop the portal!" Mantis shouted as he entered the amphitheatre. He shoved his way past Hami and reached out towards Sammy.

Say goodbye to everyone for me. Sammy pulled back her hood. She smiled and held up a hand to Mehrak.

"Sammy!" Mantis screamed. He tore a burning orb of flame from the air.

And she jumped.

–FIFTY-EIGHT–
Escape

Watching Sammy drop into the light was the longest moment of Mehrak's life. Infinitely slower and more painful than the last time she'd left him.

He never saw her disappear. Mantis's fireball hit the machinery beside him and the world around him became one of light and noise.

He came round facing the portal, momentarily captivated by the shrinking blue vortex. It sputtered, sparked, died, then ignited into a burning orange fireball.

"Evacuate the base!" Kimia's voice. Arms under his lifted him to his feet and another hand took his. Gisouie. She pulled him along, coaxing him into a jog.

Sammy? His brain was slow. They were running in the wrong direction. They should be going after her. He looked back at the portal-turned-fireball. There was no going after her now.

Mantis was on his knees by the burning portal. He howled as if in agony and did nothing to stop them fleeing.

They left him where he remained, bundling into Hami and shoving him back out through the doors.

They found Leiss in the hall kneeling over Eva, stroking her hair back from her face. She was unmoving, but had no wounds that Mehrak could see.

Calven hadn't been so fortunate. He lay in a pool of his own blood, his eyes wide and skin pale. Mehrak turned away, not wanting to believe the fate of the gentle human being that kept him company while Hami was off teaching Sammy the ways of the magi. The companion that had helped him clear dishes after supper and talked at length about his nieces and the games he'd play with them when he got home.

A crash rang out across the hall. Mehrak wiped the tears from his eyes. The grey-faced army of the dead streamed in through the doorway on the far side.

"There's another way!" Kimia yelled. "Follow us!"

The scientists broke into a sprint, leading the way around the curved wall of the portal chamber. Hami helped lift Eva over Leiss's shoulder. Mehrak collected Eva's sword, took Gisouie's hand and ran after them.

They left Calven's body. It seemed a despicable act to leave him to whatever dark forces would be making a puppet of his flesh, but they couldn't carry him. They only had one Leiss and his hands were full with Eva. The only consolation was that when the portal blew, he'd be cremated in an explosion worthy of a man with a heart as big as his.

A narrow door further round the hall led to an adjoining utility room and then out into the snow.

Grey men, women and crabmen were everywhere.

Hami blazed a trail through, dropping them with snaps of light from his staff. Leiss transferred Eva to his left shoulder, unsheathed his sword with his right hand and waded in one-armed.

Mehrak held out Eva's sword and swung it loosely in an arc back and forth to keep the dead at bay.

Crabmen and humans alike were ice-covered and walked stiffly, and most wandered directly in front of Hami's staff or Leiss's sword. Death had evidently stripped them of their self-preservation and none wore more than what they'd have been wearing when they'd begun marching. No furs, layers, nothing.

Black smoke rushed in along the ground, between the buildings and over their feet as they ran.

Hami shot a dark crabman that rose up stiffly from the crowd. Its carapace cracked, its frozen limbs fractured, and it dropped, lost beneath the horde of dead bodies that moved towards them.

"Put me down," Eva groaned. She wriggled off Leiss's shoulder, landed on her feet, then dropped to her knees.

"Eva!" Leiss tried to pick her up again.

"I'm fine," she said, as she staggered to her feet. "Where's my sword?"

Mehrak tossed it to her. Thankful he hadn't had to use it properly. The army may have been dead already but he still didn't want to stab anyone.

They reached the outskirts of the complex and began climbing the ridge that Mehrak hoped Louis was still safely tucked behind. The grey people had fallen behind. Too slow to keep up, but persistent enough to keep dragging their stiff bodies onward.

Then one grey-faced dead man burst through the shambling bodies and came at them. Calven. And he was screaming like an animal.

He launched himself at Eva, thrusting his sword at her stomach. Eva batted him away and kicked him backwards.

Leiss lunged in, putting himself between them. He swung his sword across Calven, opening a gash across his chest. But Calven didn't stop, didn't flinch, as he kept coming. Leiss hacked at the guy's arms and legs, until enough tendons had been severed to halt Calven's progress. The guard slumped down in a heap, twitching and squealing.

Leiss brought down his sword one last time, silencing Calven by severing his head.

Eva stared at him, tears in her eyes. Then she turned and stumbled after Kimia and the scientists.

"Eva?" Leiss called after her, but she didn't turn around. "Wait!"

Hami remained behind, blasting back the fastest of the dead as they staggered up the slope after them.

Mehrak glanced back at the snow base. The entire complex was shrouded in smoke. Thousands of men, women, crabmen, even some karkadann, horses and silverskins, crowded in around the black castle in the centre. And in the smoke, a shape, an indistinct monster that dwarfed both Louis and Eggie together, moved up to the castle. Two great arms emerged. Each took hold of a castle spire, and with a rending crunch pulled both down.

Black smoke obscured the damage from view. The remaining spires remained above smoke level as the beast moved forward, wading into the building.

The explosion was immense.

The entire mountain shook beneath them as the skies lit up. Mehrak slipped on the unstable surface and sliding snow. He held on to Gisouie and she helped drag him up the slope.

"Keep going!" Hami shouted, as fragments of stone hit the mountain around them, burying themselves deep in the snow.

Their climbing became frantic, they stumbled, tripped, scrambled on all fours. Hands going numb in the snow.

They moved higher, eventually out of the radius of falling rubble. Panic levels receded and the remaining climb to the summit slowed.

Mehrak paused to catch his breath at the top. He took one last look at the place he'd lost Sammy.

The base was in ruins. The castle in the centre had been replaced by a growing mushroom cloud. The surrounding buildings were flattened. And nothing on the plateau stirred. No Ahriman, no dead. The bodies that had comprised his army remained, but unmoving. Ants against the scorched mountaintop beneath them.

Had the demon been destroyed? Nothing living could've survived that explosion.

And none of his aunt's equipment would be salvageable. There would be no going after Sammy now. If he'd been quicker, he could've run for the portal and dived in after her. Maybe. Or perhaps if he'd only said the right thing, she might've stayed.

She'd gone because of Gisouie. If they hadn't rescued her, then Sammy would still be with him. And now he'd never see her again, unless she re-used the Midnight Emerald Dial, which he already knew she wouldn't.

The fluctuation when she'd entered the realm had indicated three people. Two instances of her arriving. The third was the boy.

Sammy was gone. This time for good.

–FIFTY-NINE–
After Sammy

The mushrooms appeared high in the fog, their wide canopies reaching out over their heads as they drew near.

The man hadn't come this close to the Fungi Forest for many years, and even then it had been in the company of a Marzban envoy.

The forest was still. Imagined danger lurked in the vegetation, stalking closer, preparing to pounce. He shivered and pulled his furs tightly about him as he eased his horse to a stop.

The boy climbed down from the cart and came around to the front where the man was sitting. "Thank you," he said simply, then turned to leave.

"Wait."

The boy turned back to face him. Icy blue eyes locked on his. There was something wrong about this yellow-haired child. A bold fearlessness uncommon in someone so young, and disconcerting to be in the presence of when made the focus of his gaze.

"Are you sure your father told you to meet him here?" the man asked. "At the edge of the Moat? There could be anything hiding out there in those 'shrooms."

"This is where I am to meet him."

"What does he do? Is he a Marzban?"

"I paid you well," the boy said. His eyes never broke contact. "You have fulfilled your end of the bargain. You may leave."

The man looked away first, ashamed he'd been stared down by a child. He wanted nothing more than to leave the freaky boy out here to whatever fate befell him, but what kind of man would he be if he did that?

"I'll wait until he arrives."

"Your presence here is no longer necessary."

"I insist." It was the man's turn to assert himself this time. He was expecting a protest, yet that wasn't what he got.

The boy grinned, teeth clenched behind a wicked smile. He extended the index finger on his right hand. His eyes flashed and he bared more teeth as he raised his arm, pointing first at the man's foot, then tracing a line up his body. A burning sensation followed the focus of the boy's finger until it reached the man's chest. He was getting hot, sweating. He fumbled with the clasp at the top of his furs as his clothing caught light, and he went up in flames.

———

Back at the rendezvous point, Gisouie ran for Louis and fell on his head, wrapping her arms around him.

Mehrak hung back, imagining she was Sammy, watching the woman he'd traded his best friend for. Gisouie noticed him then, smiled, and came over to put her arms around him. He sighed as he inhaled her familiar scent. He'd missed it. Missed her even, and the comfort of her presence in his life. A knot tightened in his chest. He still cared for the woman a great deal, loved her even, but there was no spark. Gisouie deserved better than that. The guilt gnawed at him, yet he still couldn't summon feelings of excitement when he looked at her. But should there be? Wasn't desire something that faded with the passing of time? Thinking back, he wasn't sure if there ever had been any. Perhaps it was only her company he'd enjoyed.

The hug was brief, as was Gisouie's way. She looked up at him.

Even though they'd been apart, she still possessed that uncanny ability to know what was on his mind. "She's gone to a better place," she said smiling, but there was no warmth in her eyes.

Baxter arrived early for his meeting with Aegis at the magi embassy, and was promptly taken to the grand master's suite.

The room was utilitarian, lacking in any material possessions or decoration. It seemed almost deliberately stripped of embellishment. Like a magus. A thing of pure function and purpose.

Aegis sat slumped forward at the desk with his head in his hands. He looked up when Baxter knocked on the door frame. His eyes were bloodshot and his forehead was lined with worry.

"Hami is back on the network," the Grand Master said.

Baxter nodded solemnly, but excitement prickled his skin. "And?" he asked, keeping his voice even and measured.

"The portal was destroyed. The resulting explosion took the demon and much of the mountain with it."

"So we've rid ourselves of the portal and the demon?"

Aegis shrugged. "Hami returned to the site afterwards. He found no sign of the demon, and the reanimated corpses that had been following in its wake have not reawakened."

"But that's excellent news, is it not? Both Ramaask and the demon vanquished?"

"We lost the girl. She left Perseopia through the portal before it was destroyed."

"Is that a problem now that the demon has gone?"

"I think it could be. Do you recall me telling you about the three rifts that appeared in the fabric of our realm? Two of them we know to have been caused by Sammy."

"Do we know the identity of the third person yet?"

"Only that it's a boy."

"Have we found him?"

"No. And that is what concerns me. He was discovered by a Marzban out in the Fungi Forest close to where Sammy arrived. The guard took the boy into his home, was going to adopt him as his own."

"*Was* going to adopt the boy?"

"Until he was burnt to death by Ramaask's servant, the lesser demon that betrayed him to release the Ahriman. The one that burns everything it touches."

"And now the boy is missing?"

"We found the burned remains of a wagon on the edge of the Moat. We think the boy's skipped town, possibly with this other demon."

Neither of them spoke for a time.

It was the Grand Master that broke the silence. "Legend tells of two children returning to Perseopia. One good, one evil. One lives, one dies. No one knows which is which."

"The chosen children." Baxter frowned.

"You think me a senile old man, Baxter? Lending credence to the myth?"

Baxter smiled. "You may be many things, but senile is not a word I would use to describe you."

"I never believed in them. The chosen children. Part of me still doesn't. But these two have been brought to Perseopia, to this specific time, for a reason. Something significant is happening. And Ramaask's demon has the boy."

Baxter waited for Aegis to go on, but the Grand Master lapsed into silence. When it seemed like he had nothing further to say, Baxter dipped his head and turned to leave.

"I don't believe the Ahriman has truly gone," Aegis said. "I think it's still here somewhere, forced to remain in Perseopia because the portal's gone. And now that we've lost the girl, we no longer have the means to stop it."

–EPILOGUE–

They travelled through the night and didn't make camp until the early hours of the following morning. Gisouie took herself upstairs and fell asleep sprawled out across the bed. Mehrak left her where she lay, put on a thick coat and crept downstairs. His aunt was at the stove heating water for a cup of tea. Her scientist buddies were sat around the table. Mehrak nodded on his way past, then continued down to the back door hatch.

He slipped out quietly, trying to minimise the crunch of snow underfoot. Louis didn't flinch. Hard days of walking had taken their toll on the poor fellow, and he wouldn't be waking any time soon. Mehrak crept away up the slope to where the Marzban had made camp.

With Sammy gone, his life seemed directionless. He had no plan for what to do next and no desire to make one either. Where would he go? And what would he do when he got there?

All he knew was that he'd part ways with Hami when they reached the bottom of the mountain. There was nothing keeping them together anymore. It had only ever been Sammy.

Hami had barely spoken since the destruction of the base. He would be dwelling on what came next for him, too. He'd have to either submit himself to the magi for his actions, or go on the run. Mehrak felt sorry for the guy. He'd tried to do what he believed was right. Admittedly, his decisions had been clouded by personal loss and smog sickness, but he'd been doing it for those he cared about.

What would the magi do with him once they caught him? Mehrak could at least make a new life for himself, even though there seemed little point in carrying on his search for the *Rule Book* without Sammy. Gisouie had never been as bothered with the pursuit as he had. Only in as much as her desire to leave Dungalor. Besides, Perseopia had become too dark and treacherous now. Maybe it always had been and he'd been foolish to make the journey. Travelling the realm had killed his grandfather. It had almost killed him several times, too.

Hami sat alone by the glowing boulder he'd heated for the Marzban camp. He stared unblinking into the light, his eyes bloodshot.

Mehrak sat opposite. He held his hands out to the stone to warm them. Neither spoke to the other. Mehrak assumed Hami was feeling equally as broken and redundant as he was.

A little way off by a second heated stone, Leiss was trying to talk to Eva. They were arguing in low voices, imagining they were being discreet but the volume was rising and it wasn't hard to make out what they were saying.

"Can you leave me alone, please?" Eva asked.

"He'd become one of them. What else could I do? He was trying to kill you!"

"I saw the way you took him apart, Leiss. There was no hesitation."

"That thing wasn't him. You know it wasn't."

"You hated him because you thought he was together with your wife when she left you. But he wasn't. He had a boyfriend."

"They … wait. He had a boyfriend?"

"Your wife didn't cheat on you, Leiss. She stayed at Calven's because he had a spare room. She left because she couldn't put up with your mother any longer."

Leiss moved back away from her. "You knew this and never told me?"

"Calven didn't want anyone knowing he was gay. He'd been beaten up in the past because of it. A couple of times pretty badly. He asked me to keep it a secret."

"But you let me think the worst about him. You let me hate him. Why would you do that?"

"Just go away," Eva said.

The big Marzban clenched his jaw, rose slowly, and trudged over to his tent and crawled inside.

After a time, Gisouie emerged from the cottage dressed in the fur coat Sammy had worn when they'd crossed the Moat to Honton Keep. It had always been Gisouie's, passed down by her mother, but the only person Mehrak could see in it now was Sammy.

"Are you missing your friend?" Gisouie asked.

Mehrak looked up at her. Had there been a smugness in her voice then? It almost sounded like there had. He wasn't going to lie to her. "Yes, I suppose I am," he said and turned away.

"Why don't you come up to bed?"

A tear traced a line down his cheek. He was going to have to face Gisouie to answer. She'd learn that he'd fallen for Sammy and she'd be devastated. His world was falling to pieces.

Then a voice called out from the darkness further up the slope. "You've ruined everything."

Achaemen Mantis staggered into the light and fell over.

Hami was on his feet and lighting his staff as Mantis rolled over onto his back. Smoke unfurled from the sorcerer's body as he lay there wheezing.

Hami approached cautiously.

"You could've stopped her," Mantis groaned. "The General would never have found the poniard by himself."

"It's your fault." Hami closed in, lowering his lightning staff towards Mantis's head. "Everything. Ramaask. The Ahriman. Sammy leaving. You caused all of this."

"You don't know anything."

"I'm going to do what my brothers should've done 150 years ago." The orb at the end of his staff grew bright.

"Do it then!" Mantis shouted. He made no move to protect himself.

Narok stumbled out of the tent nearest them. "What's going on?"

Further across camp, Leiss emerged from his tent.

Mantis remained, arms outstretched, legs splayed.

Hami aimed the orb at the sorcerer's head.

"Stay your weapon!" A distant voice down the slope.

Hami froze.

Two men entered the camp leading horses. A grey-haired magus with bandages over his eyes and, trailing him, a dishevelled but brawny man with a vacant stare. Behind them, the karkadann carrying Rougetta and Sasan followed.

"Behnam?" Hami whispered. There were tears in his eyes. He took a step towards the man. Stopped. Levelled his staff back at Mantis.

"He's not our enemy," Behnam said. "He might be the only person left that can help."

––––––––––

Absolute darkness.

A chill was setting in to Sammy's jaw and temple where her cheek rested on cold stone. She forced herself up onto her knees, cradled her head gingerly as the beat of a dull headache pounded inside her skull. She had other aches too. An elbow, a wrist, a thigh. She must've hit the floor hard after exiting the portal.

She'd really done it this time. In a fit of jealousy, she'd left Mehrak behind and leapt into the portal. There was no going back from here. Panic rose in her chest, threatened to surge up out of her throat. She took a breath. Held it. She reached out with her mental feelers. No immediate threats.

Sammy searched the floor around her. Hands running over smooth flagstones, down rough mortar seams, and closing around the shaft of a smooth piece of wood.

She gripped the lightning staff, her anxiety temporarily abating. She was no longer defenceless.

Her motives thus far hadn't been heroic, but she could still be the hero, if not a champion. The General was here in the Mother World and he was heading for the poniard. She would find him and claim the prize for herself.

Sammy turned up the volume on her hearing.

Distant footsteps. Movement in the dark.

Sammy ignited the staff.

Book 3 in *The Vara Volumes* is out now!
Find out what happens next in:

QUEST
FOR
THE
GOLDEN
PONIARD

For all things Perseopian or to receive updates
about John Kerry's forthcoming books:

Subscribe at eateom.com
Or like and follow us on:
facebook.com/EatEoM
X @EatEoM
Instagram @VaraVolumes